Pratt à Manger

David Nobbs was born in Kent. After university, he entered the army, then tried his hand at journalism and advertising before becoming a writer. A distinguished novelist and comedy writer, he lives near Harrogate with his wife Susan.

Praise for David Nobbs

'Nobbs's hilarious satire on celebrity culture is fuelled by an inexhaustible supply of jokes, while its sense of human frailty creates moments of true pathos' *Mail on Sunday*

'He perfectly encapsulates the British sense of humour in all its many guises. Nobbs has a matchless ear for the rich absurdities of human life . . . His love of finding "comedy in the little things of life" is positively inspiring' *Daily Telegraph*

'He got where he is today by being very funny over a very long period of time' *Observer*

'A bold novel … told with humour and courage' *Daily Mail*

'A highly readable and strangely affecting comedy of embarrassment, resentment, grief and love' *Sunday Times*

'An extraordinarily rich and satisfying novel . . . I
Jonathan C

'A funny and moving exploration o
are'

'A delicious entertainment, as comic *uardian*

'The most wonderful book I have read for a long, long time' Miles Kingston

'A rich and loveable book' *Sunday Times*

'One of the most noisily funny books I have ever read' Michael Palin

'Genius got him where he is today . . . breezy, funny and often touching account of his life . . . Like all the best comic writers, he spins a healthy line in self-deprecation. . . . This book is more than just a collection of memories of life in television' *Daily Mail*

'Very funny sketches of provincial newspaper life' Sue Townsend

'*I Didn't Get Where I am Today* is anecdotal, angry, heartfelt and laugh-out-loud funny' *Time Out*

'Nobbs is undoubtedly one of our finest [novelists] . . . a warm, charitable autobiography' *Independent*

'A marvellously comic novel' *Sunday Times*

'A more delightfully understated memoir you couldn't wish to find' *Mail on Sunday*

'The funniest character ever to emerge from the world of the commuter' *Daily Express*

'Wry, gentle and funny autobiography' *The Times*

'Playwright, comedy scriptwriter, and author of some of the finest humorous novels of recent years, David Nobbs has extended his range yet again, showing he can be just as funny writing about real events … Read all his novels you can lay your hands on, then read this book for a rare glimpse at the roots of comic inspiration' *Sunday Express*

'Cleverly, deftly written and wonderfully funny' *Financial Times*

'Like all the best comic novels, mixes sadness with laughter to great effect' *Independent*

'Another fascinating gawp at ordinary suburban life through the wrong end of a telescope' *Big Issue*

'Richly funny, and rich in many other ways. Buy it' *Mail on Sunday*

'Nobbs tells it with tenderness and humour' *Image*

'A funny, touching and reflective study of life and love that not only reinforces his status as one of Britain's finest comic novelists, but also lays claim for him to be considered as one of our shrewdest and most compassionate writers . . . a wonderful novel, mature in its handling of life's triumphs and tragedies, warm-hearted and witty in its insight into the nature of love' *Yorkshire Post*

'*I Didn't Get Where I Am Today* is full of rich anecdotes about exactly what has got him to where he is today, as one of Britain's most celebrated comic novelists and scriptwriters' *Sheffield Telegraph*

'In the hands of such a professional, a book like this could not be anything but entertaining, and it is always enjoyable to read about well-known people; their foibles, eccentricities and sometimes feet of clay . . . Nobbs worked during a golden age of British television and played no small part in making it so. His autobiography, funny, insightful and sometimes poignant, does justice to describing that time and the people in it' *Irish Examiner*

'The author of Reginald Perrin deserves a place on the bookshelves of anyone interested in the popular culture of the 20th century and especially in what makes us laugh' *Birmingham Post*

'Nobbs delivers an eloquent, entertaining, and intelligent interpretation of his own experiences' *Norwich Evening News*

'Hugely entertaining' *Nottingham Evening Post*

'Nobbs writes movingly about people he has encountered, his career, and emotional markers in his life. Satisfying anecdotes and wry witticism are injected into accounts of his early years' *Aberdeen Evening Express*

'He has made his reputation creating wonderful images and sharp humour. This book is full of them, capturing all the people he has written for over the years – a veritable Who's Who of the great comics . . . David is a versatile author and telly screenwriter and all this shines through on his joyful journey through life. It's well worth joining him' *Liverpool Echo*

'It's not humour but good humour that explains Nobbs' appeal' *Guardian*

'Celebrated comic writer and legendary creator of Reginald Perrin, the brilliant critique of capitalist absurdity' *Writing Magazine*

Also by David Nobbs

FICTION

The Itinerant Lodger

A Piece of the Sky is Missing

Ostrich Country

The Fall and Rise of Reginald Perrin

The Return of Reginald Perrin

The Better World of Reginald Perrin

Second From Last in the Sack Race

A Bit of a Do

Pratt of the Argus

Fair Do's

The Cucumber Man

The Legacy of Reginald Perrin

Going Gently

Sex and Other Changes

AUTOBIOGRAPHY

I Didn't Get Where I Am Today

David Nobbs

Pratt à Manger

arrow books

Published by Arrow Books 2007

6 8 10 9 7

First published in Great Britain in 2006 by
William Heinemann
Random House, 20 Vauxhall Bridge Road,
London SW1V 2SA

www.randomhouse.co.uk

Addresses for companies within The Random House Group Limited can be found at: www.randomhouse.co.uk/offices.htm

The Random House Group Limited Reg. No. 954009

A CIP catalogue record for this book is available from the British Library

ISBN 9780099469094

Typeset in Ehrhardt by SX Composing DTP, Rayleigh, Essex

The Random House Group Limited supports The Forest Stewardship Council (FSC®), the leading international forest certification organisation. Our books carrying the FSC label are printed on FSC® certified paper. FSC is the only forest certification scheme endorsed by the leading environmental organisations, including Greenpeace. Our paper procurement policy can be found at www.randomhouse.co.uk/environment

Printed and bound in Great Britain by Clays Ltd, St Ives PLC

For Briget, Mark and Max

1 A Quiet Day at the Café Henry

He sensed that she had come into the Café for a purpose, but he had no idea that she would change his life.

'Is it too early for a glass of chardonnay?' she asked.

'It's never too early,' he said.

It was eleven forty-five in the morning, and the Café, in Frith Street in the heart of bustling, sexy, sleazy Soho, was still completely empty.

She was attractive in a rather showy, obvious way. She was wearing tight jeans and a loose, warm leather jacket. He guessed that she was twenty-eight.

'It's quiet,' she said.

'Most unusual,' he said. 'We're usually pretty full at this time.'

On Monday, 13 March, 1995, Tony Blair, the leader of the Opposition, persuaded Labour's National Executive to replace the party's historic commitment to wholesale nationalisation with an acceptance of a mixed economy; eighty police officers in London were asked to wear flashing blue lights to help them to be noticed in the dark; the Bishop of London, pressured by the homosexual group Outrage, denied that he was homosexual but referred to his sexuality as 'a grey area', and Henry Ezra Pratt, who did not refer to his sexuality as 'a grey area', celebrated his sixtieth birthday.

The girl looked round, taking in everything, and again

Henry had the feeling that her reconnaissance was far from casual. What could she want?

He looked round too, wondering how it seemed to her. There was a large mirror on the left-hand wall, making the place seem much bigger than it was. Facing the door was a wall covered in a cheery jumble of picturcs and notices. Against the wall was a cold counter with a splendid array of salads and cakes. To the right was a well-stocked bar, with several tall stools. Behind the bar was a notice stating, 'You are in a no privacy area. If you don't wish to talk to your fellow human beings, please sit at a table.' The tables were wooden and simple, some square, some round, some large, some small. When it was full everything worked, and it was cheery and unpretentious. When it was empty, well . . . he dreaded what she would think.

'Dreaded'? Why should it matter what she thought?

'It's just like Denise described it,' she said.

'Denise?'

'Denise Healey.'

'Ah! I thought it was her!'

The girl looked puzzled. She looked more attractive when she was puzzled, more vulnerable, less assertive.

'Sorry, you thought who was her?'

'Denise Healey.'

'Sorry, I'm still not with you. You thought who was Denise Healey?'

'Denise Healey.'

'You thought Denise Healey was Denise Healey?'

The conversation was not developing as intelligently as he would have wished.

'Exactly. She came in one day,' he explained, 'and I

thought, "That's Denise Healey, the Goddess of the Aga." But we were busy – as we usually are – and she didn't introduce herself and neither did I. Somehow I couldn't. I'm still very shy at heart.'

'That's why you'd be so perfect for us!' she exclaimed.

'It's my turn not to be with you,' he said.

'I'm sorry,' she said. 'I work for Fantasia Television. My name's Nicky.'

'Of course it is,' he said absurdly.

'Have you ever thought of appearing on television?'

'No.'

'Really? Not in your dreams even?'

'Especially not in my dreams.'

'Oh. Well, you'd like to appear on television, wouldn't you?'

'Not really, no.'

'But everybody wants to appear on television.'

'Not me. Sorry.'

'But you'd be so . . . I don't know . . . so "right".'

Her glass of wine looked tempting.

'I think I'll join you,' he said. 'It is my birthday.'

'Is one permitted to ask how old you are?'

'No. One isn't.'

He cursed himself for having mentioned his birthday. He didn't want this young woman to know that he was sixty. He didn't look sixty. People didn't look sixty at sixty these days, unless they were bank managers or tramps. Was it sexual vanity or . . . worse . . . the fact that she wouldn't want him for television if she knew how old he was? Was a little corner of him, deep down, excited by the possibility of celebrity? He shivered. No good could come of that.

She took her coat off, revealing a white blouse that was decidedly scanty for March. He had an uneasy feeling that all her movements were rehearsed.

'Wouldn't you like to be a celebrity and be packed out every day?' asked Nicky from Fantasia Television.

'We usually are packed out,' he protested.

'But not today.'

'It's only ten to twelve,' he said. 'Soon we'll have as many people as we can cope with.'

'Are you frightened of the challenge?' she asked.

'I think it extraordinarily presumptuous of you to assume that my motives are as low as that,' he said. 'No, I'm not frightened. I'm just not interested.'

She leant forward to pick up her glass. He could see the tops of her milky, slightly blotched breasts.

'I'm just not interested,' he repeated.

But the awful thing was that he was, and she knew it.

Her skin was so young. Sometimes he found it hard to resist the touch of young female skin.

He did resist it. He had his pride. He hated gropers. He knew how much women despised middle-aged gropers, even subtle ones who barely touched them, perhaps particularly subtle ones who barely touched them. Sex had destroyed his first two marriages. He'd been so jealous of Hilary's success as a novelist that he'd believed that she was having an affair with her editor. He'd destroyed his second marriage by making drunken love to a married female journalist on a pub snooker table! He wasn't fit to be allowed out alone. It would all be far too dangerous.

'I haven't told you what we'd be interested in you for,'

she said. 'I know you aren't interested, but I may as well tell you. We make *A Question of Salt* for the BBC.'

'*A Question of Salt*?'

'The new culinary quiz show. You must have seen it.'

'No. I don't get to see much television.'

'Well, you must have heard of it.'

'No. Sorry.'

She looked quite shocked.

'It sounds,' he said, 'like a straight pinch from *A Question of Sport*. A pinch of salt, one might say.'

Nicky didn't look as if she might say that. She looked offended.

'I wouldn't describe it as a pinch,' she said. 'It's a natural development, one thing flowing into another. That's what TV does. But you'd be brill. You're everything Denise said you were.'

'Oh. And what exactly did she say I was?'

He'd tried to sound casual, but she smiled, and he knew that she'd recognised the vanity behind his question. Damn!

'She said you were different. Odd.'

'I see.'

'Marvellously odd.'

'Ah.'

'She said, "He's middle-aged, plump, hair greying . . ."'

'Great.'

'"Not good-looking . . ."'

'Terrific.'

'"Which makes it all the more fascinating that he's so attractive to women."'

'I see.'

'And she's right.'

Nicky smiled coquettishly. He wanted to believe that her coquettishness wasn't part of her recruitment drive. He wanted to believe that she wasn't a hard little go-getter. Why should he want to believe this? What was she to him? Nothing. Ridiculous.

'She said you had fabulous muscles.'

'She must have meant mussels with two esses. I haven't any muscles with a C.'

'She did. I realised that eventually, and I felt I'd been stupid.'

Henry didn't comment. He decided to talk about his mussels instead.

'I use cider instead of wine, and *no* cream. I think cream is wrong with mussels. Their texture is creamy, they need something which works against that – but it has to be dry cider, the very best dry cider. You can never cook well with bad alcohol. That's why big drinkers often make bad chefs. They can't bear to waste good booze on food.'

'You see!' said Nicky triumphantly.

'What?'

'She said you talk with wonderful enthusiasm about food. I won't give in till I've got you.'

How Henry wished that he hadn't stolen a quick glance at Nicky's crotch at that moment. If only somebody else would come in. It was twelve now. Where were they all? Ding, the Vietnamese waiter, sauntered in and stood under the blackboard, at a loss what to do. A group of people peered in, saw it was empty, and moved on. People were like sheep.

'Have you decided what you'd like to eat?' he enquired.

'Ah.'

The change of subject threw her. He felt that she hadn't been intending to eat, but that she'd been outmanoeuvred. It would be a bad move, recruitment-wise, if she didn't eat.

'Salads are in the display counter, and the dishes of the day are on the blackboard. We usually do three starters and four mains. It's a very simple operation. I'm not a potential celebrity.'

'I won't have a starter,' she said, 'but those main courses all sound tempting.'

As Nicky considered the blackboard, with its choice of boeuf bourguignon, chicken with mango sauce, hake Lampo and fennel casserole, Henry looked across his empty kingdom and saw himself, in the mirror, looking across his empty kingdom at himself – middle-aged, plump, with greying hair, and not at all attractive to women. Maybe he ought to take himself in hand, lose some weight and dye his hair. Or, more simply, remove the mirror.

'Have you decided what you're going to have?' he asked.

'I think so. I don't eat much red meat. Chicken with mango. Is it free-range?'

'Of course. I deplore battery chickens.'

'You could talk about that. Great. Hake Lampo. I think I had that once in Spain.'

'Now that amazes me.'

'Why?'

'It's my invention. I created it for a great friend of mine called Lampo Davey. I don't see how you could have had it anywhere.'

Nicky blushed. Her cool poise deserted her. Half of Henry was sorry that he'd embarrassed her, because he wasn't cruel. The other half of him was pleased, because he found her blushing attractive.

'Oh dear,' she said. 'You caught me out there – but I just hate seeming ignorant about menus.'

The discovery that she was less secure and confident than she had appeared to be sent a little frisson of desire coursing through Henry's veins.

'I always have at least one dish that is my invention,' he explained, 'and sometimes I call them after friends or people who've been important in my life. It's a way of not forgetting people.'

'That's brilliant,' she said. 'I like that very much. So would the viewers. Fennel casserole!'

'We always have a vegetarian option. I have the greatest respect for vegetarians.'

'I can't conceive what it'll be like.'

'Try it, then. It's got crushed pistachios and pernod to fight with the fennel, and green peppercorns and balsamic vinegar to fight against it.'

'It sounds more like a battlefield than a meal, but I'll try it. Look, you do need publicity. The crowds you speak of aren't here, are they?'

'But honestly, they usually are. We're rushed off our feet all the time. I've never known it like this.'

At last another customer arrived.

'Oh good,' said the new arrival. 'Quiet again.'

' "Again"?' said Nicky.

'It was pretty quiet last Tuesday,' said the man, who had a heavy beard to hide his weak chin.

'Good afternoon, Peter,' said Henry, trying to sound civil.

'My God, I suppose it is,' said the man, whose name was Peter Stackpool, though he was more often known as PS, which had led his wife, after one of their many arguments, to say scornfully, 'You know what you are. You're just a PS tagged on to the end of the great letter of life.'

'Your usual?' asked Henry.

'Please.'

Boring nerd!

'Oh, don't get me wrong,' said PS. 'I like it like this. I don't like it when it's heaving.'

'As it usually is,' said Henry.

'Don't you do the cooking?' asked Nicky. 'I rather thought you did.'

'I have another chef and we share it. Unfortunately Greg's not very good at front of house. No confidence. No conversation. I'm giving him lessons, but he isn't quite ready to face his public yet.'

PS ordered a ham salad and took a glass of sauvignon blanc over to a far table, where he sat in front of a notice which read, 'The Hermits' Ball was a disaster this year. Neither of the hermits could stand crowds, so they both left.'

Nicky was reading another notice, which stated, 'I've just taken my sex test. Failed the written, passed the oral.' Just then Henry deeply regretted that notice.

'You haven't grown up, have you?' said Nicky.

'No. I forgot.'

It was his turn to blush.

'Why are you blushing?' she asked.

'When I was eighteen I said to my army sergeant, "I'm a man." After I'd married Hilary for the second time I felt I'd found maturity. There are times when I think I'm no nearer to it than I was when I was born.'

A third customer entered. It was Lampo Davey.

'Good lord!' he said. 'Where is everybody?'

Henry beamed.

'Lampo!'

'Not he of the hake!' exclaimed Nicky.

Lampo looked at Nicky in puzzlement.

Henry introduced them.

'Lampo, this is Nicky. She's in television.'

'Of course she is,' said Lampo absurdly.

'Lampo, Nicky wants me to appear on TV.'

'Priceless!'

'No, Lampo, it isn't priceless. It's not on.'

'Ah.'

'I was Lampo's fag at school, Nicky,' said Henry. 'I introduced him to the arts correspondent of the newspaper I worked on, and they've lived happily ever after.'

'Happily!' exclaimed Lampo. 'Happily? I live in constant fear.' He turned to Nicky. 'I'm terrified of breaking his knick-knacks, Nicky. Denzil is very attached to his knick-knacks.'

Ding, thrilled to have something to do at last, came in with Nicky's fennel casserole.

'Where are you sit?' he asked.

'Oh, over there, I think.'

Nicky pointed to a table as far away from PS as possible. She knew that he was gazing at her lustfully.

'Very nice to meet you, Nicky,' exaggerated Lampo.

'You too, Lampo,' lied Nicky.

As soon as Nicky had gone to her table, Lampo began to look very serious. He seemed somewhat embarrassed.

'Henry, dear,' he said. 'I've come because I can't come tonight, and I'm devastated.'

'Come tonight?' echoed Henry. 'What to?'

Lampo went pale.

'Oh God,' he said. 'Is the dinner a surprise?'

'Not now.'

'Shit!'

Henry didn't think he'd ever heard Lampo do anything as crude as swear, and he didn't think he'd ever known Lampo to commit a social gaffe.

'We've got an important auction on,' said Lampo. He worked for Christie's, or was it Sotheby's? Henry could never remember. There were streaks of grey in Lampo's hair but even at sixty-two he still looked slim and sleek. Once he had said, 'I was never young', and it was impossible to imagine that he had ever been so. Now it was only just impossible to imagine that one day he would be old.

'I came to bring you this,' he said, getting an elegantly wrapped parcel out of his Harvey Nichols bag. 'A prezzie!'

'Take it back and get Denzil to bring it,' said Henry. 'Otherwise I can't show it to Hilary without revealing that you gave away the surprise.'

'All right,' said Lampo reluctantly, 'but I wanted to see your face as you opened it.'

'Well you could always invite us to dinner and give it to me then.'

'True. You think of everything.'

'I try to.'

'Anyway, I'm glad I came. I always like it here. Though where is everybody?' His voice changed, becoming intimate and intense, 'And . . .'

'And?'

'Look after Denzil tonight. Try to make sure he doesn't drink too much. He's . . . he's beginning to fail. He is very old. Just . . . just look after him. I love him very much, you know.'

'I know, and of course I will. You didn't need to say all that.'

'As I get older, Henry, and time runs out, I'd rather say what I didn't need to say than risk not saying what I needed to say.'

'That's good. May I use that?'

'I'd be flattered.'

'Now . . . are you eating?'

'Please.'

Lampo looked towards the blackboard, and just for a moment he gawped. It was a triple whammy, thought Henry – a swear word, a social gaffe and a gawp – three firsts for Lampo in one day.

'Hake Lampo?'

'I sometimes name my inventions after very special friends.'

'Henry!'

Lampo reached out and kissed Henry full on the lips. Nicky smiled. Peter Stackpool flinched.

'It's hake the way I did it for your birthday.'

'It was delicious. Memorable. Gorgeous. I'll have the fennel casserole.'

'Not your hake, after I called it after you? Not so delicious after all?'

'Denzil thinks he knows how you made it, and makes it himself. He's a magpie. Besides, I feel vegetarian today.'

'Nicky's having the fennel. Ask her how it is.' Henry called out, 'How's the casserole, Nicky?'

'Delicious.'

'Good.'

Lampo ordered the fennel casserole. Henry wrote, 'It's better to say what doesn't need to be said than risk not saying what needed to be said' on a piece of card, and pinned it on the wall just above Nicky. As he did so, he couldn't help getting a really good view of the tops of her breasts.

A few more customers filtered in, but it was still the quietest lunchtime that Henry could remember.

When Nicky came up to pay, he said, 'This really has been the quietest lunchtime I can ever remember.'

'I believe you,' she said.

'No, it's true,' he said.

'I said I believed you,' she said.

Just as Henry was wondering whether or not to charge Nicky, a very unglamorous couple came in, and the man said, 'What would you like, Delilah?' and the woman, who didn't look remotely like a Delilah, said to Henry, 'Have you got such a thing as a glass of white wine? Not too dry, not too sweet?'

'Medium?' suggested Henry.

'Brilliant,' said Delilah.

Henry's eyes met Nicky's, and when Delilah and her partner had moved to a table, she said, 'What a master of your craft!'

He decided, even as he smiled at her gentle mockery, that he didn't want anything personal to enter into their relationship, so in the end he did charge her.

'I imagine you can get it all back on expenses,' he said.

'Maybe not if I have nothing to show for it,' she said, 'but I am going to have something to show for it, aren't I?'

He couldn't understand why he didn't say, 'No, Nicky. You are not. Stop wasting your time.'

But he didn't.

He fetched her leather coat, and tried hard but unsuccessfully to avoid peering down her cleavage as he helped her on with it almost suavely. He also couldn't help admiring her pert, taut backside as she walked out. Then he couldn't help catching sight of PS, who also couldn't help admiring her pert, taut backside, and he thought, 'What a horrible, dirty old man he looks.'

Somehow the Café seemed duller after Nicky had left.

But it seemed more interesting again after PS had left.

When he'd finished his fennel casserole, Lampo came up to the bar for an espresso. You couldn't imagine him with a cappuccino. There was nothing sweet or milky about Lampo, unlike Nicky's breasts. Stop it!

'She's pretty,' said Lampo, as if he could read Henry's mind.

'In a hard, media way, I suppose,' said Henry, trying to persuade himself.

'You on TV, though, that would be priceless.'

'Don't be ridiculous.'

'My little fatty faggy chops, my inelegant Northern hick, a star.'

'Don't be stupid.'

'Fun, though. One in the eye for Tosser.'

Tosser Pilkington-Brick had been Lampo's study mate at Dalton College.

'One in the eye for Davina Foulkes-Effingham.'

'Belinda Boyce-Uppingham. Oh God, did I tell you about her?'

'Often.'

'Oh God.'

Belinda Boyce-Uppingham had been the girl from the big house in the village in which Henry had spent the war. Her great-grandfather had tapped Henry, as if he was a barometer, and said, 'So you're our little town boy, then. Well done.' The memory of his patronising gesture had stayed with Henry for fifty years. It would be nice to get his own back, but no, the old man was long dead, there was no point, what was he thinking of? There were no more ghosts to lay.

Belinda had married a great tree-trunk of a farmer called Robin, who'd wanted a male heir but had got Tessa and Vanessa and Clarissa and Marina and Davina and Petunia, five beautiful girls, no less than three of whom had become frontispieces for *Country Life*, and one plain girl, for life is cruel. It would be rather gratifying for her to see him as a star and wonder what she'd missed by . . . no! Don't even think about it.

'I'm not even thinking about it,' said Henry. 'I want my life to be simple from now on.'

'Oh well,' said Lampo. 'Well, have a good evening. Be very nice to Denzil tonight. I do love him, you know.'

When Lampo had gone, Henry realised that he had a great opportunity to find out once and for all whether

Lampo worked for Sotheby's or Christie's. He rang Sotheby's.

'What time is your auction tonight?' he asked.

'We have no auction tonight.'

That settled it.

So why did he ring Christie's as well? Because of something in Lampo's attitude, something very un-Lampo like in his repetition of how much he loved Denzil.

'What time's your auction tonight?' he asked Christie's.

'We have no auction tonight,' they told him, as he had known they would.

Oh Lampo. Who are you seeing?

Oh Henry. Why did you steal swift glances at Nicky's crotch and backside?

The light began to fade early that afternoon. Was it going to rain, or was the sky filled with pots calling kettles black?

2 And So Say All of Us

He stood at the gate and looked at their house as if he had never seen it before. It was still a surprise to him, every day when he went home, to realise that he, Henry 'Ee By Gum I Am Daft' Pratt, was the owner of a substantial, five-bedroom, Victorian house off Clapham Common in South London.

He swished through a yellow carpet of last year's leaves – they really did need to find a gardener – and entered the house very quietly by the side door, so as not to disturb Hilary. She would be busy on her novel, her fifth, and it wasn't coming on as quickly as she'd hoped.

He walked across the large, rather dark hall, with its large, rather dark paintings of two of the things he liked most in the world – Siena and coq au vin.

He peered round the door of the large, rather dark panelled dining room. The long oval table wasn't laid.

The comfy sitting room, with its unmatching sofas and chairs picked up at auctions, lacked its usual lived-in air. There were no newspapers strewn about. It was suspiciously immaculate.

The kitchen, too, that higgledy-piggledy room, planned by Hilary to resemble a French kitchen but not so formally that it could ever be photographed by *House and Garden*, was disturbingly tidy. Usually there were little bowls of left-overs covered in foil. He would lift the foil and eat a little unplanned afternoon treat – a dessertspoonful of cold ratatouille, perhaps, or a couple of wickedly salted anchovies. Today there was nothing. Not a crumb.

Outside, the South London traffic rumbled and grumbled, but inside the rambling, crumbling house there was total silence and complete good order.

He looked in both ovens. Nothing. He peered in the larder fridge and the food centre. Nothing new. Nothing for a surprise dinner party that was no longer a surprise.

Yet Lampo didn't get things wrong.

Perhaps they were all going out to dinner. A private room at Bartholomew's, across the common, possibly. That must be it.

He wanted to kiss Hilary. He wanted to do more than kiss her. He wanted to prove that one wasn't remotely old at sixty, not these days.

He went to the loo, had a careful pee, aiming at the side of the bowl so that there was no noise. He didn't pull the chain. He didn't want to disturb his beloved's work. All jealousy was long gone.

He washed his hands in the tiniest trickle of water, then stared at himself in the mirror. His old friend Martin Hammond had once said that he looked in the mirror and thought, 'Why am I shaving my father?' Henry could never have thought such a thing. He didn't remember his father well enough. He had only been twelve when his father hanged himself, and only eight when his mother was run over by a bus. He didn't think about them very often, but now, on this milestone of a day, he was suddenly overwhelmed by a sense of loss. It was a strange feeling. He was aware that he was missing the memory of his parents even more than he was missing them. The loss of all those times that other people had with their parents swept over him. 'Oh, Mum,' he mouthed to the mirror. 'Oh, Dad, I wish you could see me now.'

He examined himself again. Martin had always looked old, even as a member of the Paradise Lane Gang, when he'd been four. Henry had never looked old. He didn't look his age now. Did he? Well, not quite, surely?

It couldn't be denied that he looked at least fifty-five, and that was bad enough. It was ridiculous. He felt young and silly still, unformed, immature, developing slowly. He felt twenty-five going on twelve. Sixty! It was just too too absurd.

He went back into the kitchen, made himself a mug of builder's tea, watched a blue tit bravely resisting a great tit's bullying on the bird feeders. The back garden looked sad and sullen as the light faded on that grey afternoon. Spring had not yet touched it.

Why was he so reluctant to entertain the possibility of being on TV? A little fame would be very pleasant, surely? He could handle it, could he not?

No, Henry, he told himself sadly. No, Henry Ezra Pratt, son of a parrot strangler, you couldn't handle it.

How far you have come already, Henry Pratt, from the false paradise of Paradise Lane, with its shared midden and its tin bath taken down off its hook every Saturday. Do you need to go any further? Are you not happy, Henry Pratt, as you are?

He longed to see his darling. He imagined how much her beauty would surprise him when he did see her, even though he saw her every day. He didn't dare disturb her, though, so he did what he sometimes did when he wanted to be with her. He slammed a door, to show that he was home. That gave her the option of ignoring it, if work was too pressing.

She came into the kitchen, smiling broadly, smiling that momentous smile of hers that had at last become as free and trusting as it had been in the early days of their first marriage.

'Happy birthday, darling.'

They kissed. They kissed each other's lips, very gently, then explored each other's mouths very gently with their linked, slurpy tongues. Henry grew slightly embarrassed at the intensity of the feeling, and broke the kiss off.

'I've booked us in at Bartholomew's,' said Hilary.

So it wasn't Bartholomew's.

'Just the two of us. It's the way you said you wanted it.'

That put him in a difficult position. If he said, 'Absolutely. I couldn't bear to share the day with others', she would be crestfallen about her surprise. If he said, 'Absolutely not. What an anti-climax', she'd be pleased about her surprise but hurt that he didn't think her company enough.

Wisely – yes, even he could sometimes be wise – he said nothing.

The merciful darkness hid the soft London rain from them as they washed each other's sexual juices away with pineapple and almond soap, in their en-suite Jacuzzi.

Hilary rinsed his thinning hair with the shower attachment. All thoughts of Nicky were forgotten.

'We haven't ordered a taxi,' he said.

'It's all arranged,' she said.

By this time he genuinely believed that Lampo had been mistaken and they were going to a restaurant and meeting nobody. Then he heard one or two slight noises from downstairs, and he saw that Hilary was beginning to look rather tense.

The moment he got out of the bath, Henry feared that he would begin to sweat and would need another bath. He soaked his flannel beneath the cold tap and squeezed it urgently down his front.

Then he phoned the Café to make sure that Greg was coping and that Michelle, his manageress, was managing.

As Hilary began to put her dress on, he gasped with desire and ran his lips up her thighs, under the dress.

'All that money spent on clothes,' he said, 'and you look best with nothing on at all.'

'I wouldn't be allowed into Bartholomew's like that, unfortunately.'

She smiled, saw there was still some life in his penis, and said, 'M'm. Not bad for sixty.'

He wished he could be sixty every day, if it made him feel as sexy as this.

'My God, you're putting on the full works tonight,' he said, as she got out her ruby and diamond necklaces, her only real extravagance. 'I cannot believe you're doing all this just for little old me.'

That was stupid. There was no point in teasing, since he could never let her know that he was teasing. She gave him a searching look. For a moment he was worried that he might blush.

'Phew, I am hot,' he said, in case his face had gone red, using the words a girl called Mabel Billington had used to him once, when he was still a virgin, more than forty years ago.

'I've laid out your smoking jacket,' she said.

'Isn't that a bit OTT for the two of us?'

Henry! Stop it!

'I love you in it.'

She had laid out his clothes on the bed in the biggest guest bedroom. She made all the decisions in such matters. She was his style guru.

She dried his hair and brushed it.

'You'll be the most handsome man at the party,' she said.

'I thought I was the only man.'

'Precisely.'

They laughed. As they left their bedroom he ran his hand along the inside of the cheeks of her buttocks. She removed it and gave it a little smack.

'Shall we have a quick drink in the sitting room,' she said, 'while we're waiting for the taxi?'

'Great.'

The moment they entered the room, all fourteen guests clapped. Henry hadn't needed to worry about managing to look surprised when he witnessed the surprise that wasn't a surprise. They stood there, all with glasses of champagne in their hands, like . . . like a human autobiography. Henry Pratt, we are your life.

Two charming and very smart waitresses handed Henry and Hilary their glasses of champagne.

'For he's a jolly good fellow,' the fourteen guests yelled.

'For he's a jolly good fellow,' sang his beloved daughter Kate with fervent tunelessness. She was small and slim, but despite this she stood out in that gathering. All the other guests were wearing their party best, but she was in tattered jeans, an old green T-shirt and a frayed denim jacket. Her smile, though, was the broadest and warmest in the room.

'For he's a jolly good fellow,' sang his builder son Jack lustily and lovingly. Beside him, his earth-mother wife Flick, comfortable and comforting, sang equally lustily. They both loved Henry. In fact, they had named their first child after him.

'For he's a jolly good fellow,' sang James and Celia Hargreaves, the parents of his best friend at school. They sang with slight Hampstead embarrassment, letting their hair down bravely, showing the common touch like minor royalty.

'For he's a jolly good fellow,' sang their daughter Diana, Henry's second wife, her body thickened by happiness and Swiss food. Behind her, her dentist husband Gunter opened and closed his immaculately maintained mouth, but no sound emerged. He didn't know the words.

'For he's a jolly good fellow,' sang his step-daughter Camilla, daughter of Diana and her first husband, Nigel (Tosser) Pilkington-Brick. As a child, with her slender neck and long face, she had resembled the horses she loved so much, but in adulthood the equine echo had become faint and rather appealing. She had become a painter of horses, and she was a great deal prettier than Stubbs or Munnings.

'For he's a jolly good fellow,' mouthed her Italian sculptor husband Guiseppe, who was also a great deal prettier than Stubbs or Munnings.

'For he's a jolly good fellow,' sang Nigel (Tosser) Pilkington-Brick, Camilla's father, who had shared a study with Lampo at Dalton College, where Henry had been their fag. Nigel couldn't have opened his mouth wider or with more apparent emotion if he'd been in close-up on *Songs of Praise*. Beside him, his second wife Felicity looked pale and sang palely.

'For he's a jolly good fellow,' trilled Denzil Ackerman in a shrill little voice. His parchment skin was yellow and more cracked than ever. He looked his eighty-five years. He looked gaunt. 'Oh, Lampo, do not destroy this man,' breathed Henry silently.

'For he's a jolly good fellow,' sang Ted Plunkett, his former friend and colleague on the *Thurmarsh Evening Argus*, and his wife Helen, still showing traces of glamour even at sixty-two. Helen sang with fervour and some style, Ted with as little movement of the mouth as was consistent with the minimum of social decorum. Ted's hair was white now, but Helen's was dyed a rich, golden brown. She wasn't going to give her looks up without a fight.

'And so say all of us,' they roared.

'And so say all of us.'

And Henry cried. Tears streamed down his face. The guests all thought it was just the emotion overcoming him, but Hilary knew that it was more than that and gave him one of her looks, love tinged with scepticism. He sometimes had the uneasy feeling that she could read his mind.

'Far too often I haven't been a jolly good fellow,' Henry was thinking. 'I have to be a jolly good fellow all the time from now on.'

It wasn't nice to remember that he had been looking down Nicky's cleavage only that morning, barely seven hours ago.

There could be no question of his ever agreeing to appear on television. It would 'lead to things' as Cousin Hilda, his surrogate mother, might have said.

He pulled a pile of old tissues out of his pocket. Several fluttered to the ground. He blew his nose on the rest of them. Hilary glared at him. He picked up the stray tissues, slipped them into his left-hand trouser pocket, got a clean hankie from his right-hand pocket and blew his nose into that.

As he was picking up the tissues he caught Mrs Hargreaves's eye. She had the same look in her eyes as she had always had on meeting Henry, a look compounded equally of affection, horror and bravery.

One day, before I die, I will be elegant in the presence of Mrs Hargreaves, thought Henry.

'You look as wonderful as ever, Mrs Hargreaves,' he said, and indeed in her mid-eighties she was still a very elegant woman.

'Henry!' she admonished with a smile. 'Don't you think after forty-five years you ought to find it in you to call me Celia?'

'I'm sorry. I just don't see you as a Celia. You're far too beautiful to be a Celia.'

Celia Hargreaves's eyes gleamed, but there was more mockery in them than Henry liked.

'Who would have thought you'd ever turn into such a smooth speaker?' she said, and he sensed her unspoken continuation of 'I think I rather preferred you as you were.'

James Hargreaves was bent and frail. He had shrunk. He looked an ill man. Even doctors end up needing doctors. To Henry he had always represented the epitome of suave masculine sophistication. To feel pity for him seemed to be against the natural order of things.

'You're looking well,' he said.

The retired brain surgeon waved away this irrelevancy as if it was an annoying fly, and said, 'How's your greasy spoon doing?'

'James!' said Celia Hargreaves. 'It is not a greasy spoon. Is it, Henry?'

'Hardly!' said Henry. 'They even want me to go on TV in one of these celebrity chef programmes.'

'Good Lord,' said James Hargreaves unflatteringly.

Maybe I'll have to, thought Henry. I really am fed up with being patronised.

'It's such a shame Paul and Christobel couldn't be here,' said Celia Hargreaves. 'They're in the Seychelles.'

'Why doesn't that surprise me?' said Henry.

James Hargreaves frowned and Henry's eyes met Celia's and he knew that she was laughing inwardly at the memory of past evenings when Henry had been rude and combative. He felt a blush of shame. Oh God, Henry, please, you're sixty, don't blush.

'You and Paul seem to have rather drifted apart,' said Celia.

'Not really. We just have busy lives.' Come off it,

Henry. You know you have. You mock because Paul married a lawyer when he was studying law and a doctor after he'd changed to medicine. You call their home Bedsyde Manor, which infuriates them. You keep up with his parents because they represent an image of beautiful living and . . . be honest . . . because you once had sexual fantasies about Celia and still thirst for her approval.

'I have to be grateful to Paul, though,' he said. 'If I hadn't been friends with him at school I'd never have met you. Or Diana.'

'And we're glad you did, despite everything, aren't we, James?' said Celia Hargreaves.

'What? Oh! Yes! Absolutely! Yes! Definitely!' said James Hargreaves, frail retired brain surgeon, each exclamation mark confirming Henry's belief that the man couldn't stand him.

He saw his ex-wife moving across the room, on her own, towards Denzil. This was his chance of a word out of Gunter's earshot.

'Diana!' he said, intercepting her. It was neatly done, he was so much more accomplished socially now. His only mistake was to take a canapé en route, so that his 'And how's the sexy Mrs Axelburger this evening?' was mouthed through hard-boiled egg and caviar. Even as he said it he realised that Diana didn't look at all sexy any more. She had put on weight. She looked prosperous and Swiss.

'Henry!' admonished Diana, echoing her mother, and brushing crumbs from Henry's canapé off the sleeve of her striking purple outfit. 'You think it's so amusing to mock. "Marrying a Swiss dentist. Surely she could have got something more exciting?" You show up how narrow and prejudiced you really are.'

'Sorry.' His canapé finished, he was now free to kiss her.

'M'mm!' she went, as people do when they want you to believe that they are enjoying the experience of being kissed by you more than they actually are. 'M'mm!'

'Diana? Are you happy? Truly?'

'Happier than I've ever been, Henry. Truly.' She laid an affectionate hand on his sleeve. She had two very expensive rings on her affectionate hand. 'Over the weeks. Over the months. Over the years.'

'Sorry?'

'What I mean is, day in, day out, I'm very happy. There aren't quite the peaks there were with you . . .'

'Ironic, in Switzerland.'

'Henry, I'm trying to answer a serious question very seriously. When will you grow up? At our best, those were the happiest moments I've ever had. But at our worst, Henry, oh my God.'

'Your teeth look well cared for, anyway.'

Diana hit him across the cheek, gently, affectionately, but with just a little irritation.

'I'm paying you a kind of compliment in a funny sort of way,' she said. 'Can you still not cope with that sort of thing?'

'Give me a chance,' he said. 'I'm only sixty.'

'You're looking fine, Denzil,' he said, as he continued his regal tour of the room, his glass replenished, his lies mounting in the face of the relentless ravages of time.

'Nonsense. I'm obscenely old and I look it and I hate it. My face is like crumpled yellowing old paper. I look like an old copy of the *Manchester Guardian*. I disgust me. Lampo is devastated that he can't come, Henry.'

'I'm sure.'

'Oh, but he is. Only something absolutely unavoidable would have kept him away.'

'Ah.'

A brief silence fell between them, as if they had done enough talking for one lifetime.

'Have you found any good biscuit tins lately?' asked Henry.

'Oh my God.'

'What?'

'My little hobby bores you rigid, and you only toss it in when the conversation is seriously flagging. I've never known it to crop up quite so swiftly. I'm becoming a bore. I've lived too long.'

'Nonsense. I'm sorry. I didn't realise it was an unwelcome subject.'

'No, no. No, it really isn't, actually. I found a really sweet little tin in a bric-a-brac shop in Abingdon. It's from the Darjeeling Shortbread Company. It has a picture of a huge Indian in a turban.'

'Fabulous. That's great, Denzil. What a find. Excuse me, I must have a word with my daughter.'

'Kate!'

'Dad.'

'You look . . .'

'What, Dad?'

'Well, lovely, of course, despite . . .'

'Despite what?'

'Well . . . dressing down to hide your loveliness, darling.'

'Sorry, but I had to come straight from the theatre.'

Kate was the artistic director of the Umbrella Theatre in Kilburn.

It hurt Henry that her wonderful smile wasn't being beamed at some lovely young man. It seemed such a waste in a sad world. He couldn't resist asking her about this, as usual, even though he knew that it would irritate her, as usual.

'So, is there still no . . . ?'

'Dad!'

'What?'

'You were going to ask if there's still nobody in my life. Do try to start treating me as an adult. I'm almost thirty-eight.'

'Well, exactly. And . . .'

'And I'll soon be too old to have babies. Dad, accept it. You are never going to hear the pitter-patter of tiny feet.'

She walked away, but came back immediately.

'Sorry, Dad,' she said. 'I don't want to spoil your great day. It's just that I just can't believe . . .'

'What? What can't you just believe?'

'That at sixty you're still so obsessed with sex.'

The hum of conversation grew steadily louder. The champagne seemed inexhaustible. Henry chatted to Ted and Helen. He was amazed that Hilary had invited them. It was thirty-five years since they'd been colleagues on the

Thurmarsh Evening Argus, but Hilary knew that Henry had fancied Helen for most of half a lifetime, and had finally made love to her on a snooker table, dramatically scuppering his political career before it had begun, and all for a moment of pleasure which he'd been too drunk to remember. Were her legs still beautiful at sixty-two, he wondered.

Ted looked at him sourly, Helen looked at him coquettishly, Henry looked at Ted sourly, Helen looked at Ted sourly, Henry tried not to look at Helen at all, but it was impossible. Those pearly grey eyes were magnets. The lips had thinned with age, but retained their pert, blatant invitation.

Hilary joined them.

'I hope you approve of my inviting Ted and Helen,' she said to Henry.

'Of course,' he said. 'I think it's lovely.'

'I wanted to show how much I trust you now,' said Hilary, smiling sweetly at Helen.

Ted scowled. Henry remembered Nicky's cleavage and felt that he'd been punched in the stomach.

Before they went in to dinner, Henry went to the loo, where he telephoned the Café to make sure Greg and Michelle were coping. He knew that Hilary didn't think he trusted them enough, so he spoke very quietly.

He gasped as he entered the dining room. He couldn't believe how it had been transformed while he was upstairs with Hilary. The great table, lit only by candlelight, was beautifully laid. Seventeen napkins had been folded like swans. Seventeen place mats depicted the paintings of

Sisley, to whom Henry had been introduced by Mr and Mrs Hargreaves. Seventeen elegant name tags, illustrated with a small painting of the Café Henry, revealed where people were to sit. The painting was by Camilla.

The guests took their allotted seats, with gasps of pleasure at the brilliance of the scene, as the rain beat impotently on the wide window of the elegant yet cheery room.

'Who's missing?' asked Helen. 'Why is there an empty place?'

Hilary looked rather nervously at Henry across the table.

'It's for Benedict,' she explained. 'For Diana and Nigel's son, who became Henry's son and therefore my son.'

Diana gasped, and Henry had the feeling that in her heaven of cow bells, cuckoo clocks and substantial dental invoices she had almost forgotten that she had a lost son.

'Will you say a few words, darling?' asked Hilary.

This was a great shock to Henry.

'Er . . . well . . . yes. Yes, of course,' he said.

He had absolutely no idea what he was going to say.

'I have absolutely no idea what to say,' he began. He had learnt to rely on honesty when all else seemed to fail. 'I wasn't expecting this. Well, of course I wasn't. I wasn't expecting any of this. I'm completely overwhelmed.

'Well, Helen, Benedict was the victim of . . . of the marital difficulties of Diana and Toss— Nigel. It wouldn't be right to go into that tonight, with Diana and Nigel both here, but Benedict resented me, and he resented his mother for marrying me. He went badly off the rails.'

He avoided looking at Kate, who had run off with her half-brother when she was sixteen. Was that, it occurred to him now, an element in her renunciation of sex?

'He disappeared. We lost all trace of him until last year, when he attacked me and tried to kill me at King's Cross Station. That beautiful boy . . . and he was beautiful, he was so beautiful . . . was drunk, drugged and deranged.

'We don't know if Benedict is alive or dead. There is a great black hole in the middle of our family's galaxy. We've tried to find him, perhaps not hard enough. We lead busy lives. I can't even be sure that he knew who I was when he tried to kill me, though I suspect, from his fury, that he did.

'My dear wife is a very special person and I am sure that her purpose in laying a place for Benedict is to say to him, across the ether, "Dear son, there is still a place for you in this house." Of course there is.

'I once believed in God. I find myself unable to do so now, but I also find myself unable . . . on virtually every issue I think about, actually . . . to be utterly confident that I am right. There's nothing wrong with doubt. Socrates and Jesus had doubts. Kilroy Silk and Jeffrey Archer don't. I think that proves my point. So, I say to you, Lord, if you exist, forgive my doubts and bring Benedict back home.'

His voice cracked. The tears were flowing again. He didn't mind. Stiff upper lips seemed to him as old-fashioned as galoshes and Brown Windsor soup. He looked round the table as he blew his nose. It was difficult to see clearly, but he was certain that Kate and Camilla and Hilary were crying, possibly Diana and Jack as well.

'Right. The emotional bit's over,' he continued. 'Let's all get pissed – but before we do, and before the place setting is removed, having done its symbolic job, may I ask you all to stand and raise a glass to Benedict.'

They all stood, raised their glasses and said, 'To Benedict.' Nigel, Benedict's father, said it loudest of all, but to Henry his expression looked like that of a politician at the funeral of someone he was known to dislike.

There was a brief, stunned silence, and then applause, which began self-consciously and ended fervently.

The meal was delicious but conventional. Hilary hadn't wanted the caterers to outshine Henry. There was smoked salmon, guinea fowl in red wine, cheese and rhubarb fool, with a vegetarian alternative for Kate.

As one of the excellent waitresses provided by the caterers poured him a fourth glass of wine, Henry heard a sniff, a distinct sniff of disapproval. He didn't think anything of it – at the time.

At the end of the feast, James Hargreaves stood up and cleared his throat. There were cries of 'hush' and Hilary banged sharply on the table with a spoon.

'Ladies and gentlemen,' said James Hargreaves when complete silence had finally fallen. 'As the oldest person present . . .'

'After a recount,' interrupted Denzil, who had drunk too much.

'After a recount . . . it falls to me . . . I mean, I welcome the chance . . . to thank that extraordinary lady . . . that extraordinary lady . . .'

There was utter horror on James Hargreaves's face.

'Hilary,' whispered Camilla at his side.

'Precisely,' said James Hargreaves, who knew that Camilla had spoken, but hadn't been able to hear what she'd said. 'Precisely. Just so. Because of course she is an extraordinary woman. A brilliant novelist. I'm not a great reader of fiction, I can't quite see the point of it since it didn't happen, but I once read the first five chapters of one of her books, and they were tremendous. Simply tremendous. So it should be no surprise that she has provided this surprise meal for . . . for . . . for he's a jolly good fellow, and so say all of us.'

This time, James Hargreaves wasn't quite so shocked by the fog that descended on him.

'Some of us have known him for . . . many years, and it's hard to believe he's reached sixty. I don't mean I'm surprised that he's made it, I just mean that he still seems so . . . so . . . so there you are. Terrific. And now, he tells me, that this very lunchtime, a young lady from the television . . . oh Lord, he's shaking his head furiously, I think I've dropped a . . . I . . . er . . . oh dear . . . I don't . . . I don't feel very . . . I wonder if somebody could pass me a . . .'

As he toppled, Camilla tried to break his fall, and they went down together. Camilla hit the ground first and he fell on top of her and trapped her there. There was a shocked silence. Most of the people at the table thought that he had died.

Helen grabbed hold of his pulse.

'He's alive,' she said. 'I think he's just fainted.'

'I'm so terribly sorry,' said Celia Hargreaves. 'So terribly sorry. I'm afraid my dear man has rather lost the plot.'

Guiseppe rushed to Camilla, closely followed by Jack and Flick.

'I'm all right,' she said. 'Just get him off me.'

Jack and Guiseppe lifted James Hargreaves very carefully off Camilla, and laid him gently on the floor.

'Help me up, please,' said Camilla. 'I'm fine.'

'Are you sure?'

'Of course. I ride. I've had worse falls at point-to-points, and, believe me, James Hargreaves is a lot lighter than any horse.'

Jack and Guiseppe helped Camilla carefully to her feet. She walked around very slowly.

'Nothing broken,' she announced.

Quite soon James Hargreaves was revived. Jack and Guiseppe helped him up too, and lowered him solicitously into his seat.

'Sorry,' he said. 'I think I must have passed out. It's rather hot in here, and I've probably eaten and drunk too much. Right. Emergency over. Now shouldn't we have a speech of thanks or something?'

'No need, darling,' said Celia. She went round the table and kissed him gently on the top of his head. He looked up, somewhat mystified, and smiled.

Then Celia hugged Camilla.

'Thank you so much,' she said.

'All in the day's work,' said Camilla.

'So what's all this about the television, Henry?' asked Hilary. 'Why all the hush-hush?'

'It was nothing,' said Henry. 'This girl came into the Café and asked me to go on TV. Some quiz show or something. "A Taste of Pepper" or something.'

'*A Question of Salt*,' said Denzil. 'It's good.' His old, cracked face coloured slightly. 'Well, I'm alone in the flat all day. Oh, you'd be brilliant on it.'

'No, no, it's not me at all,' said Henry.

'Why not?' said Hilary. 'I think you should do it.'

'Think how jealous Colin and Ben and Neil and Ginny and Gordon would be,' said Ted.

'Colleagues on the *Thurmarsh Evening Argus*,' explained Denzil with a shudder.

'I always thought you were a star,' said Helen.

'And all those funny people on the Cucumber Marketing Board that you told such funny stories about,' said Celia Hargreaves.

'Oh Lord, did I?'

'Yes, and they never appreciated you, and they will when they see you on TV. Oh, you must do it.'

'Am I thinking the same thought as you?' asked Hilary, after all the guests had left.

'I think you probably are,' said Henry. 'I'll make it.'

'Make it? Make what?'

'The cocoa. I am sixty, after all, and we can't expect miracles.'

As they sipped their cocoa in their luxurious bed, Hilary said, 'You must do that show, darling. I've realised that I have to do publicity.'

'Yes, but that's to support your publishers.'

'It's to support me. You must.'

Wrong, Hilary. I mustn't.

3 *A Question of Salt*

On 6 June, 1995, Lord Harold Wilson was buried on the Isles of Scilly; the National Lottery operator, Camelot, paid its executive directors £677,000 in salaries and £358,000 in performance related pay; Bosnian Serbs freed one hundred and eight hostages; a Jewish policeman, the only Jew among two hundred in his division, told an industrial tribunal that he had been driven to bulimia by the taunts of his fellow officers; a Church of England report said that living in sin was no longer sinful; and Henry Ezra Pratt took part in his first recording of an edition of *A Question of Salt*.

Why on earth had he agreed to do it? This could have been a nice ordinary cosy evening at the Café Henry. Why was he walking across the foyer of Main Reception at the BBC Television Centre, with a stomach full of large moths and a brick in his throat?

Was it vanity? If it was vanity, why wasn't he more confident? Even Hilary, with her history of withdrawals and depressions, was more confident than him.

'Henry Pratt for *A Question of Salt*,' he said in a nervy, squeaky voice.

The receptionist looked through a list of names and couldn't find him there.

'How do you spell your name?' she asked unpromisingly.

'P R A T T.'

'No. Sorry. I . . . Ah! There you are. Lurking under Jeremy Paxman.'

She laughed. He tried to join in. She handed him a key. He looked at it blankly.

'For your dressing room,' she said, as to an imbecile.

'Ah. I hadn't . . .'

'A researcher from the programme will fetch you and take you.'

His heart leapt. He'd be seeing Nicky again. He didn't want his heart to leap. It was ridiculous that it should leap. He wasn't interested in Nicky.

He smiled at a rather solemn, pompous man with a large nose, small eyes, heavy black eyebrows and a wig. Henry could never understand what possessed men to buy bad wigs. Who could they possibly fool?

Mr Wiggy had a suit carrier, which he was holding level with his head so that it didn't trail on the floor. He looked very uncomfortable. Just as Henry was smiling at him, he transferred the suit carrier to his other hand. He did not return Henry's smile.

Seated at one of the tables in the reception area was another man with a suit carrier, but his was folded easily over his arm. He was wearing expensive jeans and a leather jacket. He looked worldly, confident, cool.

A tall, slim woman entered through the swing doors and went up to the desk. She had long legs, and hair that was pale without quite being blonde. She was wearing an expensive dark green trouser suit. She too had a suit carrier. What was this? Some consumer programme testing different makes of suit carrier?

When Denise Healey entered in all her magnificence, and Henry saw that she too had a suit carrier, the dreadful truth struck him. The people with suit carriers were his fellow contestants. He alone had brought no clothes to change into, having had no idea that he would have a dressing room. He alone was a naïve son of Thurmarsh.

Denise Healey didn't look in his direction and he hadn't the courage to approach her. God, this was all a mistake – and what on earth had possessed him to invite Hilary to witness it?

The researcher wasn't Nicky, but a vapid young man with acne. Henry's relief was enormous, almost as enormous as his disappointment.

'Chefs? Any chefs?' enquired the unprepossessing youth. 'Chefs this way, please.'

The chefs converged on him. The moment Mr Wiggy realised that Henry was one of the chefs, he returned Henry's smile some ten minutes after it had been given.

The spotty young man walked rapidly and vapidly down labyrinthine corridors. Henry with his relatively short legs could just keep up, and he was relieved to note that Mr Wiggy was panting.

Henry found himself beside Denise Healey. It would be the simplest thing to say, 'Hello. You came to my café', but he couldn't. He felt naked without a suit carrier. This was dismal.

He'd never had a dressing room before, with his name on it, 'Mr Henry Pratt'. Just for a moment, as he turned the key, he felt that he was already a celebrity chef. Then he saw how small and empty and bleak the dressing room was, and his brief sense of assurance slipped away.

Another shock awaited him on entering the vast studio with its high ceiling, studded with equipment. What were all those seats for?

'What on earth are all those seats for?' he asked the vapid youngster.

'The studio audience.'

'Ah. I hadn't realised there was one.'

'Ain't you never seen the show?' There was incredulity in the young man's voice.

'No. Sorry. The series hasn't been on air since I was asked to do it, so I haven't been able to.'

'Should have asked for tapes. Should have been sent them. But your wife's coming. Where did you think she was going to sit?'

The young man's voice sounded as acne would sound, if acne had a sound. It irritated Henry, but what irritated him far more was that Nicky hadn't sent him tapes. She had failed him. She was a selfish cow. He had suspected it all along.

He was introduced to the chairman, who was the famous TV quiz programme chairman, Dennis Danvers. Henry had never seen him perform, but he knew of him, of course. Every spat that Dennis Danvers had with every girlfriend was recorded in the tabloids.

'You're in Simon's team,' Dennis Danvers told him.

Henry hid the fact that he hadn't even known that there were teams. Why hadn't he asked for tapes? Why had he been so naïve and unprofessional?

It turned out that Simon was Simon Hampsthwaite, the

self-confessed Bad Boy of British Catering. Henry had never see him perform, but he knew of him, of course. His every tantrum was recorded in the tabloids.

The third member of his team was the tall, slim lady in the dark green trouser suit. Seen at close range she was older than Henry had thought, probably well into her forties. Her face was sagging ever so slightly, and she had a few worry lines, but she had a disturbingly kissable mouth. Her name was Sally Atkinson and she had the only Michelin star in Dorset.

The rival team was captained by Denise Healey. Its other members were the cool smooth man in jeans, whose name was Jean-Paul Gascaud, and by Mr Wiggy, whose name was Bradley Tompkins.

Henry felt much better for a moment when Denise Healey realised who he was and blew him a friendly kiss, but before they could talk they were all shepherded to their seats in the scallop-shaped set.

The floor manager called for 'Silence' and 'Action', and the rehearsal began.

'Welcome to another edition of *A Question of Salt*,' said Dennis Danvers, suddenly all smiles. 'Today we welcome two debutants, two debutants who are making their very first appearance on the show,' he added tautologously. 'Jean-Paul Gascaud of the Moulin Verte in Putney, and Henry Pratt, of the Café Henry in Soho. Our first question is for you, Sally, blah blah blah. Blah blah blah. Correct. Two points. Jean-Paul, a nice easy one from the world of French letters. What French writer blah blah blah?'

Henry was relieved to find that they weren't actually going to be asked questions during the rehearsal.

'And now, a brand new round,' said Dennis Danvers. 'We ask all our contestants to give us the CV, the life story, of a fictional chef invented by them. We've given them advance notice beforehand of this one, so that they can come up with something really good. This should be enormous fun.' He gave them an evil smile. 'What gems have you conjured up for us, Henry Pratt, blah blah blah, blah blah blah?'

Henry shivered. He had thought that the little idea he'd been working on was brilliant. Suddenly it seemed desperately unfunny.

As they drifted away at the end of the perfunctory rehearsal, Henry approached the other debutant.

'Have you ever seen the programme?' he asked.

'Of course not. It's terrible,' said Jean-Paul Gascaud.

'How do you know it's terrible if you've never seen it?'

'I sent for tapes. I could hardly watch. For idiots. About idiots. By idiots.'

Arrogant French bastard, thought Henry.

'I'll tell you how bad it is,' said Jean-Paul Gascaud. 'It's a hit on French television. You will be brilliant. I will be brilliant. It will be, as you English say, a piece of piddle. Excuse me.'

He went off and kissed Denise Healey suavely on both cheeks. Henry found himself walking beside Bradley Tompkins.

'Nervous?' asked Bradley Tompkins sympathetically.

'A bit.'

'It's natural first time. I was very nervous when I began,' said Bradley Tompkins, and he smiled warmly. Henry thought that he might have been wrong to dislike the man on sight. 'I was thrust straight in at the deep end, of course, starring in my own show. You'll remember it: *Bradley on the Boil*.'

'No. I must have missed it. Maybe I was out.'

'Four series of thirteen programmes. Fifty-two programmes in all.'

'Ah.'

'Maybe you go out a lot.'

'No, I . . . well of course, as a chef, I am busy most evenings.'

'They were on at 3.30 in the afternoon.'

'Ah.'

Henry had run out of excuses.

'I bet you've got something really funny worked up for your fictional chef,' said Bradley Tompkins.

'Well, I don't know. It did seem funny. I'm not so sure now.'

'Would you like to run it past me? Would that be a help?'

'Well . . .'

Henry longed to try his routine out on a friendly face. Even in the corridor he felt embarrassed about launching into it, but he forced himself to sound confident.

'It's about a very shy Russian chef called Anonymous Borsch,' he said. 'That's his nick-name, of course, and he was called it because there was an exhibition of the paintings of Hieronymus Bosch in Moscow.'

'That's very good,' said Bradley Tompkins. 'No, that's really clever. Hilarious. That'll go down a storm.'

They had reached the door of Bradley Tompkins's dressing room.

'Are you going to the Green Room for a drink?' Henry asked.

'No. I daren't drink before a show.'

'I daren't not.'

'Actually I have a rather rigid routine on these occasions,' confessed the bewigged chef. 'Shit, then shave, then shower. Usually in that order. Not always, though. Occasionally I shave before I shit, but I always shave and shit before I shower.'

'Thank you for sharing that with me,' said Henry.

'I believe in routine, but I don't believe that one should be too rigid.'

'I'm sure you're never too rigid.'

'Absolutely right. Got it in one.'

And with that utterly meaningless remark, Bradley Tompkins entered his dressing room.

Henry entered his dressing room too and thought, 'I haven't got a razor. I can't shave. I'm scared shitless so I can't shit – and as for a shower, what's the point if I haven't got any clean clothes to put on afterwards? Oh God, I've done this all wrong.' He hung his jacket on the one twisted wire coat-hanger thoughtfully provided for just such a purpose, took off his shirt, folded it neatly on the one elderly armchair, smelt his armpits, grimaced, washed as effectively as was possible without soap or a flannel, knelt down by the radiator to speed up the drying of his top half, tried to think of more hilarious things about Anonymous Borsch, failed, stood up, put his shirt and jacket back on, sighed, rinsed his mouth, sighed again, and left his dressing room.

The first person he saw as he entered the Green Room was Nicky. His heart almost stopped. Nicky in the flesh was smaller than the Nicky he had carried around in his mind, but even more curvaceous and attractive. She was, it seemed to him, unfairly perfect.

She approached him, kissed him demurely on the cheek, said, 'Hello, again,' and moved on. The vapid young man approached him and asked, 'Red or white?'

Even this simple question caused Henry to hesitate for a moment.

'Red, please,' he said at last.

The red wine tasted as acne would taste, if acne had a taste.

In order to avoid having to talk to anybody, he went over to a table covered in things no self-respecting chef would touch – sausage rolls, Scotch eggs, crisps, stale egg sandwiches, eighths of pork pies, and nuggets with their tasteless unidentifiable innards concealed by their breaded exterior. He took the smallest piece of pork pie, and then ate three crisps, one at a time, because it was better than standing awkwardly in the middle of the room, talking to nobody.

To his surprise he found that he had finished his red wine, despite its taste. The spotty youth came over and refilled his glass, and then Hilary entered, escorted from Main Reception by Nicky. Henry was so unbelievably pleased to see her.

They sat in a corner, beside the unappetising snacks. Gradually, other chefs arrived, showered and immaculate in clean clothes. Sally was wearing another expensive, elegant dark green trouser suit.

Henry had no desire to talk to any of them, even Sally, at that moment.

The spotty young man returned.

'Top-up?'

'Please.'

'Should you?' asked Hilary anxiously.

'I need a bit more. Thanks, that's enough. Don't worry, darling, I won't have too much. That really is one lesson I've learnt.'

'I saw Lampo and Denzil in the queue as I came in,' she said, hoping that it might cheer him up, but it had the opposite effect.

'What? How did they get here?'

'They must have applied for tickets.'

'I didn't even know there were tickets. I didn't even know there was a studio audience.'

'Where did you think I was going to sit?'

'I don't know. I didn't think. Oh God, why am I doing this?'

'You'll be fine,' said his third wife, who had also been his first wife. 'You'll be just fine. You're a natural. Just be yourself.'

'That's what everybody says.'

Hilary squeezed his hand.

'I feel as bad as I felt before I did my comic turn in the end of term concert at school.'

'And that was a huge success, wasn't it?'

'I suppose so.'

'Well then.'

'Do you think I'm just a sensation seeker? Do you think I'm self-obsessed? Is that why I'm so self-conscious, do you think? Do you think I ask too many questions?'

They laughed.

Quite soon the vapid young man came over to escort Hilary to the studio audience.

'You'll be fine, darling,' she said, kissing Henry on the lips. 'Just remember. Be yourself. Be funny.'

'Right.'

'But not too funny.'

'What?'

'People don't like people being determinedly facetious.'

'I see.'

'And don't hog the limelight.'

'Chance would be a fine thing.'

'But don't let yourself be steamrollered either.'

'What are you doing to me?'

'Boosting your confidence, darling. Bye. Love you.'

Then she was gone with a last wave and a kiss. He felt so horribly alone. All the other chefs were in a group beside a table covered in drinks. They were chatting so happily, so easily. He so wanted to join them. Almost as much as he wanted not to join them.

Nicky approached.

'She's lovely,' she said.

'I think so.'

'You aren't nervous, are you?'

'Of course I am.'

'Why? You could eat this lot for breakfast. Come over and chat.'

'I don't want to.'

'Henry! I think you should.'

She pulled him to his feet.

'Why didn't you send me any tapes of the show?' he asked.

'Because you're an original. Because I didn't want you to come with preconceived ideas and copy others. I've gone out on a limb over you, Henry. The producer was very doubtful, but I said you'd be an invaluable link between the professionals and the audience.'

'It sounds a rather doubtful compliment.'

'I told him you'd got balls,' she said. 'I hope you have. There's a lot riding on this for me. Don't let me down.'

How could he tell her that he felt like a eunuch on a bad day.

'Nicky! You're making it worse.'

'Come and talk to Denise. She's longing to meet you.'

'That I doubt.'

'She is!'

She pulled Henry across the Green Room like an owner dragging a dog that has found a good spot for a crap. As they got nearer and nearer to the incredibly glamorous Denise, Henry felt that he was growing smaller and smaller.

'Denise. This is Henry Pratt, of the Café Henry. You remember.'

'Yes indeed! Hello. Yes, it's a lovely little place, Henry.'

She took his hand in both her hands and squeezed it. He knew that she didn't mean to be patronising when she called it a lovely little place, but he cringed inwardly none the less.

'Yes, I told Nicky she must have you. As it were.'

Henry tried to stop his eyes meeting Nicky's. He might as well have tried to stop the Niagara Falls.

'You aren't nervous, are you, Henry? Honestly, it's a doddle,' said Denise. 'Have you met the lovely Sally Atkinson?'

'Not properly. Or even improperly.'

'Then you must meet. Sally's a darling.'

Sally Atkinson pumped Henry's hand and smiled from deep in her eyes. Henry noticed how exhausted her pale blue eyes looked.

'Henry?' she said, leading him unobtrusively away from the group, and lowering her voice. 'I saw you talking to Bradley Tompkins in the corridor. A word of warning.'

Why did his heart go straight to his boots?

'What about?' he managed to croak.

'Never let him wheedle out of you what you intend to say on the show.'

Oh God!!

'First time I was on, he asked me if I was any good at jokes. Said he wasn't. He seemed so nice. I found myself telling him an absolute humdinger about a novice monk and some faggots. The bastard only went and told it on the show.'

Henry looked round the room to see if Bradley had come up there after all. He hadn't.

'He's become embittered. He's had a fifth series of *Bradley on the Boil* cancelled.'

'I've never seen it.'

'Don't tell him that.'

'Too late. I already have.'

'He has no sense of humour, that's his trouble. Fifty-two programmes without one laugh. They say they're exploring other formats for him. That's producer-ese for "You're all washed up, mate." He's terrified. He has three posh restaurants in Central London, but no Michelin stars.' She lowered her voice. 'He never will. He can't cook.' She lowered her voice still further. 'He can't fuck either. Michelin star? He wouldn't be worth a detour if you lived next door to him.'

Henry knew that he should congratulate her on *her* Michelin star. He couldn't. He was too upset.

'You've told him something, haven't you?'

Henry nodded miserably.

'I've told him all about my idea for my fictional chef.'

'Oh, you haven't! How can such a bastard be so persuasive?'

'Precisely because he is such a bastard, I should imagine. Do you really think he'll pinch my stuff? I mean, all right, he pinched your joke, but this is a whole routine.'

'I wouldn't put it past him.'

'Do you think I should ask Dennis Danvers to put me on before Bradley?'

'No!' This was too loud. People turned to look. She lowered her voice again. Henry's head was whirling. He couldn't cope with all this. 'Heavens, no. Bradley's only an amateur bastard compared to Dennis. Dennis is poison.' She lowered her voice still further. 'He can't fuck either.'

What *am* I doing here? I'm out of my depth.

'Isn't anybody here remotely nice?' he asked, rather pathetically.

'Heavens, yes. I am. I'm very nice, Henry.' Their eyes met briefly. 'So is Denise. And so is Simon.'

'What? I thought he was a rampaging, shouting, swearing terror?'

'Simon? No! He's a sweetie. A pussycat.' She lowered her voice still further. Henry was beginning to realise that she had an extraordinary talent for lowering her voice. However far down it went, there was always further for it to go. 'He *can* fuck.'

Henry heard a loud and eloquent sniff. He looked round. There was nobody near them. A tremor ran down his spine. He recognised that sniff. It was Cousin Hilda's. It was one of her specials, loaded with disgust and disapproval, and he realised that the sniff he had heard on his birthday had been hers too.

This was ridiculous. One couldn't be haunted by a sniff. A sniff couldn't exist in space.

Or could it?

He didn't like it when the make-up lady smiled at him, and said, 'Oh good. I like a challenge.'

He didn't like the way the warm-up man introduced him to the studio audience: 'And now, a newcomer to the show, Henry Pratt. Let's hope he isn't.'

He didn't like it that the audience laughed.

He smiled at them, though. He smiled relentlessly, and bowed.

None of them liked it when the warm-up man said, 'There's *Only Fools and Horses* in the next studio. I bet you all wish you'd got tickets for that.'

They all trooped to their seats. It was very hot under the lights, but at least he couldn't see the audience. He couldn't see the expression of incredulous scorn with which Lampo would no doubt view the proceedings.

He wished that he could see Hilary, though. Just one smile from her, and he might be all right.

Absolute hush was called for. Suddenly the whole

studio was tense. 'Tension for this rubbish – absurd,' thought Henry, suddenly less tense because everybody else was tense.

'Good evening, and welcome to another edition of *A Question of Sport*. Oh shit!!' said Dennis Danvers.

The audience roared and roared (with the exception of Lampo, who was completely bewildered).

Next time the show began properly, and the applause was all the greater because Dennis Danvers had got it right this time.

At the top of the show Dennis introduced each contestant. When he said, 'We have two men making their debuts. Let's hear a particularly warm welcome for Jean-Paul Gascaud and Henry Pratt,' he spoke the name 'Jean-Paul Gascaud' in a respectful, slightly continental manner, and then descended into a very blunt 'Henry Pratt'. The audience, warmed-up to laugh at Henry's name, did so again. Henry tried to give a spontaneous laugh of delight, as if nobody had ever laughed at his name before. It froze on his face.

The first questions were terribly easy. Henry began to relax. He even thought of a joke that might amuse the studio audience. He would say that Anonymous Borsch had been born in the Russian town of Sodov. Or should it be Pissov? How crude should he be?

'Mr Pratt? Are you with us?'

Dennis Danvers's voice came to him from afar, borne on the wind from the Steppes of Russia. His blood ran cold.

'Sorry,' he said. 'I was miles away.'

This got a loud laugh. Henry was utterly bewildered.

'I was speaking to you, Mr Pratt,' said Dennis Danvers. 'After all, you are, are you not, the only Pratt here?'

By now there was near hysteria in the audience. When it died down, Dennis Danvers asked Henry his question.

'What culinary product is used in the expression, "As keen as . . ."?'

Henry froze. His mind went a complete blank. He could hear the audience laughing, miles away.

'Toffee,' he said.

The audience erupted. Even Dennis Danvers couldn't keep a straight face.

'Henry Pratt, I make a prediction,' said Dennis Danvers. 'The TV audience are going to be as keen as toffee to see you on this show. I'm certain that as you gain confidence you will be giving your answers as bold as pewter. I can offer it to the other side.'

'Mustard,' said Bradley Tompkins with eager, petty pride.

'The scores at the end of that round are, Denise's team eight, Simon's team four,' said Dennis Danvers. 'Never mind, there's a chance here for Simon's team to catch up. We have a completely new round. Each panellist has to give me the CV, the life story, of a fictional chef of his invention. You, the audience, will judge how inventive and amusing their efforts are. Your applause will be measured on the Chipometer. First, to start us off, Bradley Tompkins, what have you for us?'

'I want to talk about the very shy Russian chef, Anonymous Borsch,' said Bradley Tompkins.

Henry's heart sank to his socks. The bastard!

Bradley Tompkins's heart sank to his socks too. His

quip had not brought the gales of laughter that he was anticipating. There had been bemusement, and one or two titters, but only one laugh. Henry recognised it as Lampo's.

'He was born in the small Russian town of Volgograd,' persisted Bradley Tompkins.

Oh good. He'd missed the Sodov gag.

'That wasn't his real name, of course. He was called Anonymous because he was so shy, and Borsch because he made a very famous example of that Russian beetroot soup.' Bradley Tompkins's voice began to falter. He was losing confidence. He was dying on his arse. He was beginning to believe that that bastard Pratt had set him up.

'But of course it was very confusing to be called Anonymous Borsch,' continued Bradley bravely, 'because of the painter.'

He paused.

'What painter would that be, Bradley?' asked Dennis Danvers.

'Well, Hieronymus Bosch, of course.'

'Of course!' Dennis Danvers looked across at the studio audience and repeated, 'Of course!!' The audience laughed. 'What happened to Anonymous Borsch, Bradley?'

'He opened a restaurant. He called it the Anonymous Borsch. Do you know why?'

'None of us know why, Bradley,' said Dennis Danvers. 'We're on the edge of our seats.'

The audience laughed again, perhaps at the difficulty Dennis Danvers was having in not laughing. Mocking

Bradley Tompkins was fine sport for a man who had never missed an easy target in his life.

'He wished to be eponymous as well as anonymous,' said Bradley Tompkins roguishly. This remark was greeted with total silence. Not even Lampo laughed.

'And did Hieronymus ever go to the restaurant of the anonymous, eponymous Borsch?' asked Dennis Danvers. By this time there was laughter at everything he said.

'I don't know,' quipped Bradley Tompkins, his face the colour of borsch.

'Well done, Bradley,' said Dennis Danvers. 'Well up to the standard I'd have expected of you. Now let's put it to the Chipometer.'

The audience's applause was muted.

'Oh dear. One out of ten on the Chipometer. Bad luck,' said Dennis Danvers.

Henry knew that Dennis Danvers would come to him next, and he had nothing whatever to say. 'Funnily enough, my chef is also called Anonymous Borsch' would hardly be a winner.

'Think,' he told himself. 'Don't panic. Think of any food. Quick. Asparagus. No, too elitist. Pasta. Good!'

Dennis Danvers was speaking. '. . . which brings us to Henry Pratt,' he was saying.

Cannelloni. Canaletto. Ah!

'What gem have you got for us, Henry Pratt?'

The sarcasm in Dennis Danvers's voice made Henry angry, and anger gave him strength.

'Luigi Cannelloni, the inventor of pasta, was born in Venice in 1726,' began Henry, with sudden, amazing confidence. There was laughter. Not a lot, but more than

Bradley had got. Henry realised that the audience liked him. The sensitive antennae of Dennis Danvers picked this up too. He would be very careful about mocking Henry in future.

'He was on a Hoseasons' canal holiday there,' continued Henry.

He was surprised to hear himself say this, and even more surprised that it got a decent laugh because of the sheer unexpected banality of it.

'He is very well known for his works of art, almost as well known as Hieronymus Bosch.'

This crack got another decent laugh, but it was cheap and naughty, and he regretted it even as he said it. Later he would suspect that this moment might have sown the seed that in time would grow into a deep hatred of Henry, with all the difficulties that would entail in the years to come.

'He is well known, of course, for his paintings of the Grand Canal. There are two Cannellonis hanging in the town hall of my native Thurmarsh. What is less well known is that he produced pasta models of Venetian landmarks. His Rialto Bridge stuffed with spinach and ricotta was sensational, he really was an expert stuffer, in fact he had six children, one of whom introduced cheese to pasta and was known as Macaroni Tony. Unfortunately he had a weakness – women.' Henry lowered his voice like a newsreader approaching bad news. 'His wife strangled him with five hundred yards of tagliatelle in 1782.'

There was a good round of applause. The Chipometer registered seven out of ten. Bradley Tompkins glowered.

4 Eggs Benedict

It was the strange affair of the pigeon Denzil that gave Henry the idea.

The need to create a special dish for his old colleague and friend came to Henry after a rather difficult dinner at Denzil and Lampo's elegant little mews house in Chelsea, shortly after the recording of *A Question of Salt*.

As they sipped their pre-prandial white wine in the tiny sitting room, choc-a-bloc with bric-a-brac, Henry asked them if they would like to witness the recording of another edition of *A Question of Salt*. They declined politely.

When Lampo went out to get more olives, Denzil said in a low voice, 'I would have liked to, but it's all a bit beneath La Lampo. She only breathes very rarefied air, Henry. She's too precious to live. She looks down on anything to do with television. *So* common.'

When Denzil went to finish off the vegetables, Lampo said, 'I would have loved to come. It's so sublimely awful as almost to be brilliant, but poor old Denzil . . . between you and me and several gateposts . . . has *no* sense of humour, no love of the absurd, no relish for the incongruous.'

It wasn't difficult to deduce that relations between Lampo and Denzil were not at their smoothest. Henry felt sad that he had created a special dish for Lampo, the deceiver, but not for Denzil, the deceived. He longed to confront Lampo over his deceit on the day of his sixtieth birthday, but the moment didn't seem right, and he contented himself with saying, in a low, urgent voice, 'Lampo, don't hurt him, will you?'

Lampo raised his eyebrows.

'Henry feels responsible for your relationship,' said Hilary, 'because he brought you together in Siena.'

'On that memorable day on which he also first met you,' Lampo reminded her. 'It's all so long ago. How banal time is. All it can ever think to do is pass. Pass, pass, pass, second after second, minute after minute, and always at the same rate. *So* tedious.'

'Yours was love at first sight,' said Henry. 'We took a little longer. But no, I suppose I do feel responsible.'

'Ridiculous,' said Lampo. 'How you do overestimate your importancc in the scheme of things.' He looked at his watch. 'He's slower than ever these days.'

'Shouldn't you be helping?' asked Hilary gently. 'Don't you think it's all getting a bit beyond him?'

'He can't bear having me in his kitchen,' said Lampo, 'and when he can't manage it on his own any more, it'll be a dreadful blow. I have to be cruel to be kind. I never lift a finger, much as I might want to. It's a sacrifice I have to make.'

At last Denzil was ready. They had smoked salmon and pork casserole and all the time, as they talked, Henry felt the presence of the shadow of his knowledge of Lampo's duplicity.

The opportunity to speak about it arose while Denzil was clearing away the main course and preparing the dessert. It had seemed wrong to launch into the subject before the meal, but now, well into the evening and mellow with wine, Henry felt that he could avoid it no longer.

'Lampo?' he said in a low voice.

'Oh dear! Ominous change of tone,' said Lampo. 'H.E. Pratt (Orange House) is going into serious mode.'

'Do shut up and listen. Lampo, I know that on the night of my sixtieth you didn't go to an auction.'

Lampo didn't reply. His mouth opened slightly, and his skin looked as if it couldn't decide whether to go white or to blush.

'I phoned Christie's, and there was no auction.'

'Your deep interest in the details of my life flatters me, Henry. I happen to work at Sotheby's.'

'I rang Sotheby's too, Lampo.'

'Oh.'

'There was no auction there either.'

'No.'

Lampo poured a little more Fleurie into their glasses, carefully, immaculately, ascetically. Their glasses had been far from empty, so it was obviously a displacement activity.

'Oh dear,' he said. 'I really am most dreadfully sorry that you've found out. It must have hurt. Your sixtieth too, and I was very, very sorry to miss it. But it was quite unavoidable.'

'I'm not talking about my sixtieth, Lampo. I'm not talking about me.'

'Henry isn't that self-centred, Lampo,' put in Hilary.

There was a loud crash from the kitchen.

'Not as steady as he used to be,' said Lampo. 'Hurry up in there,' he shouted. 'We want our pud.'

'Don't evade the issue, Lampo,' said Henry.

'Oh, I'm not,' said Lampo. 'I'm buying us more time. The more I tell him to hurry, the longer he takes. His desire to infuriate me is what's keeping him alive.'

'Perhaps he senses that something's up,' said Hilary very softly. 'Perhaps he suspects.'

'No,' said Lampo firmly. 'No, I'm very careful.' He lowered his voice still further. 'I will never hurt Denzil. Never. But I have to think of my future . . . after . . . after he goes. I have to . . . prepare the ground. Death is difficult for gays.'

'It's not exactly a doddle for the rest of us.'

'No, but we tend to be lonelier. We have no families.'

'Your choice.'

'Henry! You know perfectly well that choice doesn't come into it.' He lowered his voice even more, and Henry had a sudden, disturbing vision of Sally Atkinson, lowering her voice in the Green Room. God, she's lovely, he thought, to his surprise.

He realised that this was *his* displacement activity. All this was very painful to him, the secrecy, the tension, with poor Denzil slowly, innocently preparing his dessert in their tiny kitchen.

'I . . . er . . . well, you may as well know,' said Lampo, 'I have a friend. A young man. Well, young to me. He's thirty-six.'

'Young to me too.'

'He's . . .'

'I don't think we need to know who or what he is, Lampo, thank you very much.'

Lampo looked hurt. They realised that he wanted to talk about his lover.

'Besides, Denzil may live for years, Lampo.'

'I don't think so. He's failing. I will be very careful, Henry, I promise. He doesn't suspect a thing, and he never will. My opportunities are therefore very limited. Hence the night of your sixtieth, when my friend happened to be on the eve of departing for Kuala Lumpur, and I knew Denzil would be having a happy time and wouldn't check up. Ah!'

Denzil entered with the pudding.

'Something I've never made in my life,' he said. 'Not my usual style at all. Spotted dick.' Hilary looked across the table at Henry. The steamy smell of it transported them back to Cousin Hilda's.

Cousin Hilda sniffed loudly. But was it her, or was it just her sniff? Can a sniff sniff loudly?

Henry shivered. He knew what the sniff meant. It meant, 'Eat it up, there's a good boy. There are people starving in India who'd be glad of some spotted dick.'

Many things happened in the great world outside the Café Henry. President Clinton announced that the United States would re-establish full diplomatic relations with Vietnam; two of Saddam Hussein's sons-in-law were given political asylum in Jordan after fleeing Iraq with their wives; and on the fiftieth anniversary of Japan's surrender Prime Minister Tomiche Murayama apologised for the nation's aggression in World War Two.

In the tiny world of the Café Henry, however, nothing much changed. Food was cooked and served, customers came and went, but this no longer seemed quite enough for Henry. Had he already been corrupted by his very first touch of celebrity? Did *A Question of Salt* seem more real to him than the Café Henry? Had the insidious power of television infected his blood?

Every day he hoped that Nicky would ring and offer him another appearance. Every day he hoped that customers would enter the Café and tell him that they had come because of his irresistible performance in the recording.

And then at last the phone call did come.

'It's Nicky, Henry.'

His heart began to pump furiously. This was ridiculous.

'Well, hello. How are you?'

'*Very* well. How are you?'

'Very very well.' Why did he have to compete and be even more well than her? 'Very busy. Very, very busy.'

He hoped that she could hear the buzz of conversation, the satisfied murmuring of a happy, well-fed crowd, so different from the day of her visit.

'Good. Listen, can you come on the show next Tuesday?'

Yes, yes, yes, cried his heart. So why did he hear his voice saying, 'That's short notice.'

'We've been let down. I immediately thought of you.'

'I see. Well I don't know that I'm thrilled to be second choice, Nicky.'

'Oh God, Henry, you aren't taking offence, are you? I didn't think you were like that.'

He sighed. He knew he was being petty.

'No, I'm not,' he said. 'Not really.'

'You're my discovery,' said Nicky. 'I didn't want to

push for you too hard too soon. I . . . I have a bit of a problem with the producer.'

'You refuse to go to bed with him.'

'How on earth did you guess that? You are clever.'

'I don't think it took much brain power, frankly. Most men would want to go to bed with you.'

'Thank you.' Her voice sounded warm for a moment, then she became brisk and businesslike. 'Anyway, if you come on as a favour, and do well, we'll be halfway to establishing you as a regular.'

He didn't reply. Now that the proposition was actually presented to him, he wasn't sure if he wanted it. He looked round his little domain, and liked what he saw – the happiness of it, the even tenor of it.

'Are you still there?'

'Yes. Yes, I'm still here, Nicky.'

'Wouldn't you want to be a regular?'

Would I? Would I? How can I say that I would positively not want to rise to the challenge? Have I a choice?

'Of course I would.'

He hadn't a choice.

The second recording went well. Henry was relieved not to cross swords with Bradley Tompkins again, but disappointed, unreasonably disappointed, not to come across Sally Atkinson.

A third recording followed a fortnight later. Again, there was no Bradley. Again, there was no Sally. Again, he felt the relief and the aching disappointment.

But still no customers announced that they had come because they had been in the studio audience and had loved his performance. Henry didn't think of himself as a vain man, but he did feel very disappointed. Was it possible that he hadn't been quite the star he had felt himself to be?

If only the transmission of the series would begin. Then he would know.

On Wednesday, 11 October, 1995, Trevor McDonald, the ITN newsreader, was appointed to head a campaign to improve English in schools; rail fares between Exmouth and Paignton were increased by fifty-six per cent because the trains were too full; Duncan Ferguson, the Everton and Scotland footballer, was gaoled for three months for head-butting a player during a match; and Henry Pratt introduced pigeon Denzil on to his menu for the first time.

It was also Greg Pink's first day doing front of house. Tall, gangly, gauche and clumsy, Greg was a cockney lad who had left school at fifteen with an impressive breadth of ignorance over a wide spectrum of life. All he knew about was food. He cooked like an angel.

Greg was dreading doing front of house, and Henry was dreading Greg doing it, but there was no alternative if Henry was going to be able to spend more time in the kitchen. Michelle did front of house in the evenings, but at the moment Greg was his only option at lunchtime.

The main courses were chicken Marengo, pigeon Denzil, plaice *Dieppoise* and cashew nut moussaka. Henry took Greg carefully through them, so that he would be able to describe them to the customers.

He explained that pigeon Denzil had been named as a tribute to an elderly journalist who had been a friend for forty years and was beginning to fail.

'Got you,' said Greg.

'I suggest that you try to make some anodyne remark about the weather to put the customers at their ease,' said Henry.

'Anodyne!' said Greg. 'My mum used to put that on cuts, when I fell over.'

'No, no,' said Henry. 'I'm just using the word to mean harmless, not causing offence, putting the customer at his ease. I'm probably not using it correctly. I just meant, say something safe and harmless.'

'Got you,' said Greg.

Trade was brisk but not overwhelming that morning. Greg served, although he didn't know it and never would, several out-of-work actors; a writer; a deep-sea diver; a nozzle technician; two Belgian auctioneers; a struggling private detective with his lover; an international lacrosse player; a manufacturer of plastic boats with long swans' necks; and four members of a Welsh male-voice choir who drank in unison.

At twenty past one he served an old man who looked really weary. Denzil plonked himself on a bar stool and sighed.

'Morning, sir. It can't make up its mind, can it? Have you made up *your* mind yet?' said Greg.

'I beg your pardon?'

'It was like a link, sir, like what the disc jockeys do. I just meant, "What would you like?", like. That's probably what I should have said. I'm new. Well, I say "new". New to front of 'ouse. Know what I mean? I mean I'm not new here, but I'm new to front of 'ouse, like.'

'I'll . . . er . . . I'll have a glass of dry white wine, please,' said Denzil.

'Got you. Pinot grigio, chardonnay or sauvignon blanc?'

'Er . . . pinot grigio, please.'

'No problem! Coming up! Will you be lunching with us today, sir?'

'Er . . . possibly.'

'Salads in the cold counter, sir. Dishes of the day on the blackboard.'

'Tremendous.'

Denzil wished that he hadn't said 'tremendous'. There was nothing tremendous about the dishes of the day being on the blackboard. He deplored what he called 'the decadent adjectival gigantism of our times'.

All that was forgotten when he saw the words 'pigeon Denzil'.

'Pigeon Denzil?'

'It's pigeon breast, sir, served pink, with black olives and Madeira. It's a dish what he invented for some old geezer what he's sorry for.'

'Is it indeed?'

'We serve it with red cabbage spiked with juniper berries.'

'Do you indeed?'

'You'd love it, sir.'

'Would I indeed? I'd better have it, then, hadn't I?'

'Fantastic.'

Denzil flinched.

'Er . . .' he began, '. . . is our eponymous hero in today?'

'I'm not with you, sir.'

'Henry. The Henry of the Café Henry.'

'Ah. Got you. He's cooking today, sir.'

'Well, will you tell him that an old friend of his is in?'

'No problem, sir.'

'Tell him it's an old geezer what he's sorry for.'

'Got you, sir. No prob— Oh no! You ain't . . . Denzil?'

'I am indeed.'

'When I said an old geezer I meant . . .'

'A word of advice from an old timer, young man. When you're in the shit, shut up. Don't dig a deeper hole, which will only fill up with more shit, since that is the nature of holes.'

'Got you. Chips or mash, sir?'

'Which do you recommend?'

'Oh, mash. It soaks up the juice somethink lovely.'

'Right. Pigeon me, then, with red cabbage and mash.'

' "Pigeon me"?'

'No, not pigeon you. Pigeon me. Pigeon Denzil, which is me. I was . . . trying to lighten the moment with a touch of humour, to ease your evident embarrassment.'

'Oh! With you, sir. Got you. Thank you, sir. Brill.'

'Oh, and . . . could you tell Henry that I'd . . . that if at all possible . . . any time, if he's busy, I'm not going anywhere . . . I'd appreciate a little word . . . in confidence . . . about a subject that's . . . rather intimate.'

'Got you, sir. No problem. Terrific. Tremendous.'

Denzil flinched twice.

It was half past two before Henry had a chance to sit in a corner with Denzil, who was on his fifth glass of pinot grigio.

Denzil had a strange, rather distant smile on his face.

'Why have you got that strange, rather distant smile on your face?' asked Henry.

'Because I don't feel remotely in the mood for laughing today, but you can't not,' said Denzil. 'Your barman!'

'Oh dear.'

'Somebody was saying something about some problem with an ECG and he burst into the conversation and said, "We should never have joined. We're an island." '

'Oh God. He has terrible trouble with acronyms. I just wish I didn't have to expose him to the public.'

'Yes. So do I. He said pigeon Denzil was named after some old geezer you were sorry for.'

'Oh dear. Sorry. I'll have a word.'

'No. Don't. Leave it. I don't want to sound like an embittered old man.'

He raised his glass, rather shakily.

'I'm getting pissed,' he said. 'Lampo hates me getting pissed. He's a control freak. He hates the word "pissed" too. *So* inelegant. I think that secretly he thinks my biscuit tins are slightly common, though he'd never dare say so.'

'Oh dear.'

'He's having an affair.'

'What???'

'There's no need to try to sound so surprised. I can tell that you know. I can tell that you've known what I've come about. You walked towards me with a dread that can only have been born of knowledge.'

'Well I knew you had a problem. You told Greg. And I didn't like the thought of your having a problem. So I dreaded it, yes.'

Henry couldn't bring himself to say that Lampo had confessed. It seemed wiser to wait.

'I imagined that it was your knowledge of Lampo's affair that caused you to be sorry for me. So, if you really didn't know, why *are* you sorry for me?'

'I don't think those were my exact words to Greg, Denzil. I suppose . . . I probably said something like . . . you were a bit old.'

'And failing?'

'No.'

'I am, though.'

'Denzil!'

'Yes. And do you know what really bugs me?'

'No.'

'My biscuit tins. What on earth was the point of spending so much time collecting biscuit tins unless I was immortal? When I'm gone he'll auction the lot at bloody Sotheby's.'

'He's too respectful to do that.'

'Then he'll have to look at the bloody things for ever, and he hates them. What a legacy.'

'Not for ever. He'll die too.'

Denzil brightened for a moment.

'There is that.'

'He might die before you.'

'Only if I poison him.'

'Do you think he knows that you know?'

'No. He'd hate to know that I've said it, but he's not sensitive.'

'Have you come here to ask for my advice?'

'Yes. Sorry.'

'Another wine?'

'I've had too much already, and it'll only make me morbid and him angry. Yes, please, but could I have red? I go acid with too much white.'

Henry ordered a bottle of the house claret.

'So what should I do?' asked Denzil.

'I think you should confront him. Have it out.'

'Oh no. I couldn't do that.'

'Then you should leave him.'

'Hardly practical. It's my house.'

'Well, in that case, throw him out.'

'I couldn't. I couldn't live without him.'

'Well, what do *you* think you should do?'

'I don't think I should do anything. I think we should carry on as before. I think I should turn a blind eye.'

'Well, why don't you do that, then?'

'Thank you. Thank you, Henry. That's good advice. I knew I could count on you.'

They sat in their corner for most of the afternoon. Late drinkers mingled with cake eaters, and Denzil talked affectionately about the man who was cheating on him.

'He's only protecting himself. Only cushioning the blow in advance. He still loves me, don't you think?'

'I'm sure he still loves you.'

'That's what I think. I think he loves me very much. Which is why he just can't face the prospect of my death.'

'He can't handle it.'

'Exactly. You've got to be a bit sorry for him really.'

'He's a pathetic figure. An emotional cripple.'

'Right. Absolutely right.'

*

Next day the choices of main course were beef stifado, lamb with apricots, lemon sole in chablis sauce and eggs Benedict.

'Excuse me, guv,' said Greg, 'but eggs Benedict, it ain't that substantial, not for a main course. I mean it's quite rich, but not substantial.'

'Then we'll have to make it substantial.'

'Couldn't it be a starter?'

'It might not work if it was a starter.'

'I'm not with you.'

They were sitting on stools at the bar counter. It was five past ten and the first customers had not arrived yet.

On the counter was the blackboard, on which Henry had just written 'Eggs Benedict'.

'Do you know what ESP is, Greg?'

'Yeah. I do. It's the starting prices for the Tote.'

'It's extrasensory perception, Greg.'

'You mean like the supernatural, like?'

'Well, sort of, yes. You remember we had hake Lampo on the menu.'

'Yeah.'

'Lampo came in.'

'Christ, he did, yeah.'

'And yesterday we had pigeon Denzil on.'

'And your other mate turned up! Hey! Uncanny. Wow. Not sure I like it.'

'Well, it *is* odd. So I thought, if I put eggs Benedict on, maybe he'll turn up.'

'Who's this Benedict when he's at home?'

'Ah, well, that's the whole point about him. He isn't at home. He's my step-son, by my second wife, Diana, and her first husband, a man called Tosser Pilkington-Brick.'

' "Tosser"?'

'Very much so.'

'Say no more.'

But Henry did say more. He told Greg the whole story of Benedict.

'He may be dead. He may be alive but out of his skull. He may not be. I can't dismiss the thought that, incredible though it seems, maybe some force beyond our comprehension will tell Benedict to come here today. What do you say?'

Henry wished that he hadn't said, 'What do you say?' He knew what Greg would say, and he did.

'Got you,' said Greg.

It was Henry's turn to do front of house. A lot of people came into the Café that day, the majority of them people he would never set eyes on again, including a small party of Swedish therapists over for a conference; an American lawyer and his wife; two cardiologists; a designer of zoos; five shop assistants; a French poet; three publicans; a confectioner from Trondheim; a condom quality controller; a Scottish make-up artist and a Welsh dresser from a production team in nearby Wardour Street; a man called Geoff Little, who formed half of a thoroughly filthy double act called Little and Often; and a German composer with his English wife.

The German composer introduced himself. 'My name is Sigmund Halla and this is my wife Val.' Henry wondered if he'd married her for love or for her name.

The condom quality controller, Geoff Little and Mr and Mrs Halla all ordered the eggs Benedict, but of Benedict himself there was no sign.

He was dead. Henry knew it.

'Can I make a point, guv?' asked Greg next morning.

'Sure. Of course.'

'The eggs Benedict.'

'What about them?'

'Hake Lampo. You created it for your friend. Pigeon Denzil. You created it for your other friend.'

'Your point, exactly?'

'Well, you created them like what you thought they might like, like, know what I mean?'

'Yes, I . . . yes.'

'Eggs Benedict. There wasn't like much thought in it. It was just eggs Benedict. The recipe. Nice, but . . . bog standard. Do you see where I'm coming from?'

Henry frowned. He hated that phrase, but it didn't matter – and he did see where Greg was coming from.

'You need to create a dish that shows your, I don't know, your like love and feeling for Benedict, like you think it's the kind of thing he might like, like.'

'Greg, you're a genius.'

'Thanks, guv.'

'What's duck Benedict?'

'It's a roulade of duck stuffed with lobster in champagne and caviar sauce, served with fried *foie gras*.'

'Thank you. I'll have the wild mushroom risotto, please.'

It was the following Monday morning, and that was typical of the reaction of customers to the first appearance of duck Benedict on the menu. Henry wasn't surprised. It was altogether too much. It was on the menu solely to attract Benedict through forces that we cannot understand.

Trade was brisk again. The Café Henry was visited by two Latvian health and safety officers; a pop record producer; three insurance agents; an obituary compiler; two Cambodian monks; a puppet-maker from Stuttgart; two schizophrenic jewellers, who ordered four glasses of dry white wine; a lesbian schoolmistress and her Madagascan lover; a one-legged librarian; and a Swiss dentist and his wife, but not by Benedict.

Henry's face shone with delighted surprise at the arrival of the Swiss dentist and his wife. He kissed Diana and pumped Gunter's hand.

'We wanted to surprise you,' said Diana.

Henry gave them glasses of wine on the house. They told him that they were in London for a week's holiday. He explained that there were salads in the cold counter and dishes of the day on the blackboard. He felt a frisson of excitement as he waited for Diana's comment.

Suddenly she went very pale.

'Duck Benedict?'

He told them the story. Diana burst into tears and hugged him, and he burst into tears too. Gunter smiled his bewildered dentist's smile, and knew that he could never provide for Diana what Henry had provided, but he also knew that Henry couldn't provide it either now, and that Diana no longer wanted it, so they had a happy lunch –

though neither of them could face the duck Benedict. As trade slackened off after two o'clock Henry managed to snatch ten minutes with them.

'There must be a *bit* of ESP working,' said Diana. 'It may not have brought Benedict . . .'

'So far,' said Gunter.

'So far. But it's brought me. Henry, we must rededicate ourselves to the task of finding my son.'

'If he isn't dead,' said Henry.

'Even if he is,' said Diana.

5 Big Issues

In the middle of the night, in the warm womb of their double bed, in the safety of their love, Henry listened carefully to Hilary's breathing and decided that, like him, she was finding it difficult to sleep.

'Are you awake?' he whispered.

'Yes.'

'I was thinking about Benedict. Wondering if he has a bed to sleep in.'

'I know,' she whispered.

'I'm going to try to find him. Really try. I've been telling myself that I'm not his real father, I'm no longer married to his mother, he isn't my responsibility. It doesn't work.'

'I know.'

Hilary reached over and squeezed his arm, then ran her hand up the inside of his legs.

'I can't remember if you've even met him,' he whispered.

'Only once. At the Hargreaveses' one evening. He was only a baby and so were you that night. You were so rude.'

'Don't.'

She slipped her hand on to his penis and stroked it, but in a friendly way rather than sexily. She didn't expect any response, and she didn't get any.

'This needn't concern you,' whispered Henry. 'It isn't your battle.'

'Of course it concerns me,' she whispered. 'If it's your battle, it's mine.'

He put his hand on the top of her thigh and stroked her soft sweet skin absent-mindedly.

'We're very happy, aren't we?' he whispered.

'Yes,' she breathed.

'Are we as happy as we were first time round?'

'I don't think that's a sensible question to ask,' she whispered.

'I'm sorry, but I'm going to ask it anyway.'

She removed her hand.

'You won't get the answer you want.'

'Oh.'

'I think we're doing very well. I think we really are pretty happy, on the whole, but our past history precludes the possibility of our being perfectly happy.'

It sounded like a sentence from one of her novels.

'Oh. I see.'

Henry removed his hand from her thigh and for a few moments they lay side by side but not touching each other. A night bus roared past, muffled by the double glazing.

'Why have we been whispering?' he whispered. 'We're all alone in the house.'

'I think it's nice whispering,' whispered Hilary. 'It's sexier.'

She put her hand on his penis again and began to stroke it with rather more determination. Don't you dare not to respond, said her insistent touch.

*

He arrived at the Café the next morning well before nine o'clock. He planned the dishes of the day, chalked them on to the blackboard, left notes for the staff, and locked himself in his office. Operation Benedict was under way.

Henry's office, at the back of the Café, was small; his office at the Cucumber Marketing Board had been small. There all similarity ended. That office had been neat, lifeless, dead. His desk had been almost bare. His desk here was cluttered with piles of paper – unpaid bills, paid bills, recipes, memos, invoices, outvoices, guide books. The walls were covered in more recipes, more memos, letters of praise from members of the public, government health warnings. There were further piles of paper on the floor, waiting to be filed. There were papers on the keyboard of his computer. He had to move several letters in order to get to the phone.

He had several phone calls to make. His mood was strange. He had done his fourth recording of *A Question of Salt*. His fictional chef had been a man who opened a chain of fish and chip shops because his headmaster's handwriting was bad and he had thought that his school report said, 'Should do batter'. People seemed to like the absurd silliness of his contributions. He seemed to appeal to an innate childishness in the British character. Already his fifth recording was scheduled for the following Tuesday. Two weeks after that, his first appearance on the show would at last be transmitted to an astonished nation. He was feeling increasingly tense about his new career. Operation Benedict had come at a very suitable time, when it would be a most welcome diversion. He was eager, even excited, but he was also reluctant to begin. In the cold light of morning, the project seemed absurd. However, they had checked with Somerset House, and there was no record of Benedict having died. Surely, under British justice, a man was held to be alive until he was proved dead?

Diana and Gunter were on holiday. Gunter had never even met Benedict. It wasn't fair to involve them.

But Diana had said, 'Henry, we must rededicate ourselves to the task of finding my son.'

He lifted the phone with sudden resolution. He must catch them before they went out.

'Could you put me through to the Axelburgers' room, please?'

He'd had a crush on Diana as a schoolboy. He'd married her in early middle age. He found it very hard to think of her as Frau Axelburger.

'Hello.'

Gunter's guttural voice was a harsh intrusion on memories of sexuality.

'Gunter, it's Henry. I haven't woken you up, I hope. I wanted to catch you before you went on your travels.'

'No. You haven't woken me, Henry. I'm an early riser. I'll put you on to Diana.'

Diana had never been an early riser. Was she now? And was Gunter an early riser in more senses than one?

Why did he think these things?

'Diana, I've been thinking about Benedict all night.'

'All night?'

He recalled the moments that had followed Hilary's

insistent stroking. He recalled the intensity with which he had enjoyed her still lovely body.

'Well, not perhaps quite all night,' he admitted.

'I was thinking of him too, Henry.'

All night. Or had she been enjoying Gunter's still lovely body? Was his body still lovely? Had it ever been? Why did he think such things? Did other people think such things? Did the Duchess of York and Harold Pinter and Gary Lineker think such things? Why did such images come to his mind unbidden?

Because they had once been close and you can't switch memories off. Even as they spoke, he tried to. He looked out at the blackened brick buildings that surrounded the sad little yard behind the Café. Carrier bags eddied in the erratic breezes. There were dirty black wheelie-bins with names on the lids – Café Henry, Club Exotica, Ristorante Perugia. There was the bird shit of decades on the ledges. It was a dark, disgusting place which the sun had never reached. It was the arsehole of a city.

'You said yesterday you wanted to find him. You sounded very determined. Do you still feel like that?'

'Oh yes, Henry.'

'We've checked with Somerset House. There's no record of his death.'

'That's good. Henry, this may sound silly, but I'm sure he hasn't died. A mother knows these things.'

'Well, I feel that too, though not quite as directly, I suppose. Diana, this is a big ask. You're on holiday; Gunter has never even met Benedict; but I was thinking, maybe this evening we could all meet up and hunt for him. Hilary's on for it.'

'I've discussed it with Gunter,' said Diana. 'He's on for it too. He says that in committing himself to me he has committed himself to all my past life, not to someone who only existed from the day we met.'

There was pride in her voice, and her pride moved him. It also made him feel more than slightly uneasy. Swiss dentists were meant to be mocked, in the natural order of things. It wasn't fair that Gunter should prove to be far too decent a human being to mock. It was an outrage against the concept that life is a comedy.

'We can't do tonight, though,' said Diana. 'We have an engagement that can't be broken. Tomorrow?'

'Six o'clock tomorrow, at the Café?'

'Excellent.'

There was no problem over phoning Camilla. She had been very fond of her brother. She would be up for whatever Henry suggested.

He realised, when he heard the answerphone, how much he had looked forward to talking to Camilla or even to Guiseppe. It wasn't fair of them not to be in. It was inconsiderate. However, he kept his irritation out of his message.

He got Jack on his mobile. Jack disliked coming to London, but Henry was sure he would want to take part.

However, Jack said, 'Oh dear. I think you may have to include me out, Dad.'

'Too busy?'

'No. Well, yes, but I don't care about that. No, it's Flick. She's got a girls' night out tomorrow and she's really looking forward to it and we've had a cock-up with our baby-sitter.'

Phoning Kate was slightly more difficult. The theatre never seemed to be able to find her, her mobile never seemed to be switched on, but the greatest problem was that she had run away with Benedict when she was sixteen and the incident hadn't been mentioned by anyone for more than twenty years. He didn't know whether there would come a time, during the search, when they would have to mention it, or whether, if they didn't, the weight of the silence would just grow and grow.

Another answermachine message. Henry watched a puffed-up pigeon attempting unsuccessfully to interest a slim, sleek pigeoness on the ledge opposite. Didn't it realise that October wasn't exactly the height of the breeding season?

Henry felt as frustrated as the pigeon. How could Operation Benedict get off the ground if everybody was out?

It also meant that he'd got round to Benedict's father more quickly than he wanted. He dreaded phoning the man.

He looked up Nigel Pilkington-Brick's work number on his Filofax, couldn't find it, then remembered that he'd filed it under T for Tosser.

'Nigel. Henry here.'

'Henry?'

'Henry Pratt.'

'Ah. Henry. Sorry. It was with you calling me Nigel. You usually . . . don't.

'Sorry.'

'No, no. Water under the bridge, Henry. Now, what can I do for you?'

'Well, this is going to come as a great surprise, Nigel, but . . .'

'Congratulations.'

'What?'

'You've seen the light.'

'What?'

'It's a bit late in the day, but it's never *too* late. I think we should be able to put together quite a nice little package for you.'

'What are you talking about?'

'Well, pensions, of course. Aren't you?'

'No, Toss— Nigel. I'm talking about Benedict.'

'Benedict?'

For a moment Nigel didn't seem to remember who Benedict was.

'Your son,' prompted Henry drily.

'Ah. That Benedict.' He managed to sound as though his was a life over-run by Benedicts. 'Sorry. It's been so long and I am rather . . . in the middle of things. Is there . . . is there any news?'

'Oh, no. Nothing like that.'

'Ah.'

Am I being less than fair, thought Henry, in thinking that his 'Ah' sounded suspiciously like relief?

'Can't it wait, in that case?' said Benedict's father. 'I'm expecting a client in a few minutes. I need time to prepare.'

'It needn't take long,' said Henry.

'Well now that you're on, I suppose we may as well get it out of the way,' said Nigel gracelessly. 'What about Benedict?'

The female pigeon flew off. The male pigeon looked comically deflated.

'I think we should make one last great attempt to find out what happened to him.'

'It's very good of you to care, Henry.'

'Well of course I care.'

'But he hated you. He resented you. He tried to kill you, damn it.'

'I don't resent him for that.'

Henry heard a stifled cry of exasperated incomprehension at the other end of the line.

'He was very, very ill,' Henry continued.

'Exactly. So he's probably dead.'

'Very possibly – but he isn't dead officially, according to Somerset House, and I'd like to find out.'

'And how do you propose to go about that?'

'Well, Diana's in town, with Gunter. We thought we might . . . I don't know . . . traipse the cardboard villages of the homeless, visit hostels . . . I know. Don't say it. It sounds a bit forlorn, but . . . well . . . I don't think I personally would feel very happy about things unless we'd done our best.'

'I wouldn't have thought Gunter'd be on for that. He's Swiss.'

'So?'

'They're a nation of gourmets, Henry. He'll want a good dinner every evening.'

'Have you ever been to Switzerland?'

'Good heavens, no. All those cuckoo clocks. They'd drive me up the wall.'

'Worst place to be if you don't like cuckoo clocks.'

'What?'

'Up the wall. You'd be so close to them.'

'Don't waste my time, Henry.'

'Anyway, we've established that your deep knowledge of Switzerland is untainted by any actual experience. Gunter thinks it's a great idea. He seems to regard Diana's emotional welfare as more important than a good dinner. It seems as though at last she's found herself a good man.'

'That's a bit insulting to me.'

'And to me. I include myself. Be honest, Nigel. We both failed her.'

Nigel didn't reply to that. The male pigeon was peering through the grimy upstairs windows of the Club Exotica. What did he hope to see? Boxes of g-strings? Topless dancers having a topless tea break?

'Diana and Gunter are joining Hilary and me tomorrow night to hunt for him,' said Henry. 'Jack may be able to come, and I've left messages for Camilla and Kate.'

'I see. Well . . . good for you,' said Nigel. 'I really do have to go now, Henry. My client's due. Well . . . thank you for telling me, and . . . good luck.'

'What??'

'Don't you want me to wish you luck?'

'No, I don't. I want you to say you'll come and help.'

'Help? Oh. Ah. Well . . . erm . . . now then . . . tomorrow, you said?'

'Yes.'

'I can't do tomorrow, I'm afraid. We're at the Harmisons', for dinner.'

'Oh well.'

'Well, I can't let the Harmisons down.'

'Heaven forfend.'

'Well I can't.'

'Nobody would want you to. Without your sparkling repartee the party would be an abysmal flop.'

No, Henry. Wrong. No sarcasm.

'Well, that's probably true, actually, as a matter of fact,' said Nigel. 'Well, there we are. Oh, what a shame,' he added unwisely.

'Well, there's always Thursday.'

'Thursday?'

'If we don't find him on Wednesday.'

There was a pause. A long pause.

'I suppose I could do Thursday.'

'I'd very much appreciate it, Nigel. We are both deeply involved in the mess that Benedict's life became. I think we have to take some kind of moral responsibility.'

'I've said I'll come. I'm not too keen on getting a lecture as well. I can't ask Felicity. She's . . . frail. Where shall we all meet?'

'Here. The Café. Six o'clock.'

'Fine.'

There were two messages on the answerphone. Kate would come and so would Jack. He'd squared it with Flick.

His telephone shrilled. It was Camilla. She'd been painting, and had been in the middle of a fetlock. 'I don't answer the phone when I'm in mid-fetlock,' she explained. 'They seem so unimportant, but I have the devil's own job to get them right. They're my Achilles heel, fetlocks.'

Henry told her his plans. When he had finished there was silence.

'Are you still there?' he asked.

'I was crying,' sobbed Camilla. 'Of course I'll come.'

Operation Benedict was fast becoming a reality.

On Wednesday, 18 October, 1995, the Home Secretary, Michael Howard, faced calls for his resignation over the controversial sacking of Derek Lewis, Director General of the Prison Service; Red Rum, winner of three Grand Nationals, was buried at Aintree; it was revealed that a paedophile who had served two prison sentences for sex offences was listed in a national directory of music teachers used by parents seeking tutors for their children; and eight people were summoned to the Café Henry in Frith Street at 1800 hours.

Henry and Hilary were seated at the large round table before five to six. Henry had piles of paper to give out.

He had suggested that they all dress down somewhat, so that they wouldn't look too much like a delegation of do-gooders as they explored the hostels and back alleys and cardboard cities of Central London. He was wearing his old faded gardener's denims, and Hilary was in old jeans and the crumpled, stained, battered leather jacket that she usually reserved for meeting writers less successful than herself.

Kate and Jack entered together, Jack's untidy great body dwarfing her carefully concealed, spare, elegant frame.

'Look at our children, Hilary,' said Henry affectionately. 'I ask them not to look out of place among London's low life, and they come in their working clothes and look perfect.'

It was true. Kate had come straight from the theatre in the torn, frayed, hole-studded jeans that were her everyday garb, while Jack was wearing stout muddy boots, thick muddy jeans and a thick old bomber jacket. The jeans were on the large side and were slipping, the jacket was on the small side and rising, Frith Street hadn't seen a better example of a builder's bum for many moons. Henry was commenting on this as Gunter and Diana arrived, irredeemably scrubbed and clean, despite their best efforts, and Gunter overheard him. After the kissing and shaking of hands were over, and the six of them were happily seated round the table with their glasses of wine, Gunter said, 'So, what is this bum of the builder of which you speak, Henry?'

'Builders' clothes never quite fit their huge frames,' said Henry. 'When they bend down the jeans drop, the shirts rise, you get a vision of the soft, fat flesh of their backsides.'

'I see,' said Gunter. 'This bum of the builder does not happen in Switzerland. Nobody would wish to see such unpleasant things on our construction sites.'

'I'm glad to hear it,' said Henry.

'I put on a play about builders once,' said Kate. 'I was young and naïve and thought that builders would flock to see it. I don't think we had one builder come to the whole run.'

'Terrific of you to take part, Gunter. Terribly game,' said Henry, putting his arm round him affectionately. 'Giving up all those nice holiday dinners.'

'Not at all,' said Gunter, smiling shyly. 'We are in London anyway, and I love Diana. Her son is naturally important to me, therefore. Besides, we had a nice lunch. I prefer lunch. It is better for the digestion. Now Jack here, he has come down specially. He has taken . . .' There was awe in Gunter's voice. '. . . more than one day off work.'

'It's pretty convenient, actually,' said Jack. 'We're almost up to date with our jobs. It's really embarrassing.'

'I don't understand,' said Henry.

'A builder gives an estimate of when he'll start,' explained Jack. 'And when he'll finish. He's always late starting, and he always has to go off to do bits of other jobs, so he's even later finishing. The punters would get worried otherwise. They'd think he wasn't busy. They'd think he wasn't any good.'

'In Switzerland tradespeople start when they say they will and finish when they say they will,' said Gunter.

'It's difficult at first,' said Diana, 'but you get used to it.'

Camilla and Guiseppe arrived full of apologies just after six fifteen. They had tried to look down-market, but had only been partially successful. They looked like two members of the Armani family who had fallen on slightly hard times.

Once they were all there, Henry took command.

'I'm assuming, for the purpose of this operation,' he said, trying hard not to sound like Field Marshal Montgomery, 'that Benedict is in London. If he isn't, I'm afraid that there is nothing we can do. We can't scour the whole world. But I promise you this. If he is in London, we'll find him. And I think he will be. The homeless gravitate towards London. They don't move away. There is no reason for him to be anywhere but London.

'Now, I've divided us into four groups.' His attempt not to sound like Monty was getting less successful by the minute. 'If we descend on hostels en masse we'll look like a delegation of Albanian social workers. I think the pairings are pretty obvious. Me and Hilary, Jack and Kate, Diana and Gunter, Camilla and Guiseppe. I've got photos of Benedict for you all, and I've photocopied and enlarged the *A to Z*, so I'm giving each couple a marked up area which I think you ought to be able to cover. The areas aren't large, I want to be thorough, and I've made lists of hostels and hospitals. I hope it's comprehensive. I have consulted the social services and the charities for the homeless, in fact I've been pretty busy.'

'Bless him,' said Jack affectionately. 'He's the Cucumber Man again.'

'Jack, I'm not doing this for fun. This is serious. Far more serious than cucumbers ever were.'

'I know,' said Jack. 'I went to see him once when he was Chief Controlling Officer (Diseases and Pests, Excluding Berwick-on-Tweed). He showed me his operations room. He had a huge map in the basement, full of different coloured flags for each disease – scab, wilt, cucumber flu, the lot. He looked like Winston Churchill in the War Room.'

'It shows how much you remember,' said Henry, trying to be dignified, trying not to laugh, 'but when I was Chief Controlling Officer it did *not* exclude Berwick-on-Tweed. When I was Assistant Regional Co-ordinator (Northern Counties, Excluding Berwick-on-Tweed) it did exclude Berwick-on-Tweed.'

'As the name suggests,' said Hilary.

'But when I became Chief Controlling Officer I was given Berwick-on-Tweed as well by implication.'

'I'm sure they slept better after that,' said Kate.

'Who?'

'The Berwick-on-Tweeders.'

'OK. Fun over,' said Henry. 'Family laughing at Henry over. Time to be off. We will rendezvous here at 22.30 hours for a late supper. Four hours is enough, and even tramps need their beauty sleep.'

'What do we do if we find him?' asked Jack.

Henry looked stunned.

'Do you know, I hadn't thought of that,' he said. 'Isn't that awful? Somehow I've been thinking of it as a desperate, doomed quest.'

They found that between them they had four mobile phones, so each couple was able to take one. It was agreed that if Ben was found they should all rendezvous at the Café, if he was fit to be taken there, and at the place of discovery, if not.

The mood in the Café had been quite heady. They'd felt a bit like the Knights of King Arthur at their round table. They were having a great family reunion, the wine was good, and they had a common purpose. The idea, the hunt for a lost soul, and, at the same time, the redemption of their own souls, was attractive, even glamorous.

The reality was sadly different, however, right from the outset. The eight of them stood on the pavement outside the Café, reluctant to face the moment.

'Well, here goes,' said Jack bravely, putting an arm round Kate and setting off towards Soho Square.

The other three couples went south towards the

junction with Old Compton Street, where Henry and Hilary turned right while Camilla and Guiseppe turned left and Gunter and Diana continued towards the river.

There was a cool breeze from the north, and it was bringing a few spits of rain. The warmth of the Café and the wine didn't last long, and the vastness of London soon overwhelmed them.

They peered at bundles in doorways and subways. They explored dark alleys that stank of urine. They gently turned over foul-smelling meths-ridden lumps that had once been somebody's baby boy or girl.

They descended into graffiti-ridden subways, silent except for the clattering footsteps of nervous women and the faint sound of distant buskers. Elsewhere, great bundles of dirty blankets and rags lay outside expensive, exclusive shops. Occasionally, a bundle stirred.

Some of the people were awake and begging, begging for money or drink, not interested in a photograph of a young man in his arrogant prime. Others had to be prodded and woken, to stare blindly, resentfully, at this meaningless image from another world. By the end of the first evening, Henry knew the words for 'fuck off' in five new languages.

They showed their photographs of Benedict to wardens in hostels, to drunks, druggies, buskers, policemen, traffic wardens, social workers, charity volunteers, prostitutes, pimps, kerb crawlers and sellers of the *Big Issue*. Their hearts began full of hope, but long before the end their hearts had joined their heads in believing that this was a lost cause. It would be a miracle if anybody recognised modern-day Benedict from these photos.

Henry couldn't believe how many unlovely corners there were in this great city, how many back alleys and back passageways, how many dark arches and sordid access areas. There didn't seem to be such things when you went to Scandinavia or Italy or France or Spain.

Hilary longed to know the unknowable, to trace the tragic paths that had led each of these people to become so lost. Her humanity was appalled at the suffering, but the novelist in her was excited. The humanist in her was appalled by the novelist's excitement.

Kate told Jack that it was time for another great play about homelessness, another *Cathy Come Home*. Jack said that *Cathy Come Home* didn't seem to have achieved anything. Art was just pissing in the wind. Kate was upset, and Jack was mortified at having upset her.

Diana was ashamed of her capital city, in Gunter's presence, and Camilla felt the same way with regard to Guiseppe. Gunter assured Diana that they had beggars in Switzerland too, and Guiseppe tried to comfort Camilla with the uncomfortable words, 'Misery and degradation know no boundaries.'

And then the thing that Henry had hoped might happen did happen, shortly before ten o'clock, on the steps of a hostel for the homeless. A young woman of about thirty, too weary to look attractive, was walking down the steps. As she passed Henry, she looked at him, stopped and said, 'Are you Henry Pratt?'

'Yes,' admitted Henry cautiously. 'I . . . er . . .'

'You won't know me. I was in the studio audience for *A Question of Salt*.'

'Oh!'

'You were fabulous.'

'Oh!!'

'Brilliant.'

'Oh!!!'

'Shall I go in and show the photos?' asked Hilary drily.

'Yes. Yes, darling. Good idea. I . . . I won't be long. I can't . . . I must . . .'

'I know.'

'We're looking for my lost step-son,' said Henry to the young woman. He explained the story briefly, once Hilary had gone.

'Oh, how sad,' she said. 'Might I see a photo? I'm a social worker. You never know.'

He showed her the photo.

'No. Sorry.'

'Ah well.'

'I'm keeping you.'

'No, no. No, no.' He mustn't sound *too* eager. 'No, actually, you're the first person who's . . . er . . . you know. So, you thought I wasn't too awful, then?'

'Not at all!'

'Excellent. Well, thank you. Not that it seems very important compared to all this . . . misery.'

'Oh, I don't know,' said the social worker, who had black bags under her eyes and a black briefcase under her arm. 'We all need cheering up. I . . . er . . . I . . . would you think it awfully silly if I asked you for your autograph?'

'No. No! No, I . . . I'd be glad.'

'Have you any paper?'

'Well, I . . . I have this enlarged map I photocopied from

the *A to Z*. We've just about finished for tonight. I could sign the back of that.'

'That would be fine.'

'Do you have a pen? I wasn't expecting . . .'

'Of course.'

She handed him a pen.

'Shall I . . . shall I put a name?'

'You could put . . . "To Jenny". It's Jenny. Yes, that would be nice.'

'This is stupid,' said Henry. 'I'm shaking. This is my first autograph.'

'Not your last,' said Jenny.

Henry looked round, up at the windows of the grimy hostel, hoping Hilary wasn't watching, and down the dirty, sordid street, hoping somebody was watching, but nobody was.

To Jenny, he wrote, With very best wishes. And thank you. Henry Pratt.

He gave her a quick, shy kiss on her tired, icy cheek.

'Good luck,' she said.

He hoped that in the dark she hadn't seen the momentary blankness in his eyes. Good luck with what? He had forgotten, just for a moment, all about Benedict. He felt a sharp stab of shame, shook his head as if to bring himself back to his senses, and entered the hostel, which smelt of stale cabbage and human wind.

They drew a blank, as Henry expected them to.

'Why do you look so embarrassed?' asked Hilary.

'She asked for my autograph. I signed the back of the map.'

'Oh, Henry.'

She kissed him.

'Either turn your back on your coming fame, or relish it,' she said. 'Don't let your guilt complexes give you the worst of all worlds.'

She kissed him again.

The rain didn't come to much, but the evening grew steadily colder, as evenings do. Four hours seemed a long, long, long, long time. All eight of them, even big, strong, outdoor Jack, were frozen by the time they got back to the Café. The search had brought home to them how awful it must be not to have a roof over one's head. If four hours is a long time, then a night is an eternity. If a night is an eternity, then every night for a week, for a month, for a year . . . it just didn't bear thinking about.

Diana and Gunter were at the bar buying wine when Henry and Hilary entered. Henry rushed up and insisted that the wine was on the house.

'What exactly is "effing knackered" meaning?' enquired Gunter.

'Very, very tired. Why?'

'That's what your barman said I must be.'

'Poor Greg. I'm giving him lessons in conversation. It's early days.'

The others soon arrived. Kate and Jack looked windswept, but Camilla and Guiseppe still looked immaculate.

They formed a weary and subdued little group, at their round table but no longer knights of it. Gradually, though, the Argentinian merlot did its work, and they all found that they were ravenous. The dishes of the day were pork aphelia, duck Benedict, herrings in oatmeal and stuffed marrow.

'That must be the marrow I'm chilled to,' said Kate.

'Duck Benedict?' exclaimed Guiseppe.

'I thought if we did find him he might appreciate it,' explained Henry.

The thought brought them back to the failure of their mission.

'What is it, anyway?' asked Camilla.

'It's duck roulade stuffed with lobster, in a champagne and caviar sauce, with fried *foie gras*. Well, he loved luxury.'

'Silly silly boy,' said Camilla regretfully, lovingly. 'Silly silly silly silly boy.'

Diana leant over and squeezed Camilla's hand.

'What's pork aphelia?' asked Jack, anxious to get off the subject of Benedict.

'It's a dish I had a couple of times in Greek restaurants in the sixties,' said Henry. 'Pieces of pork with coriander seeds – it's delicious, but it seems to have disappeared even from Greek cookbooks. I tried to find it in Greece and nobody had heard of it.'

'It's the Benedict of the food world,' said Kate, and she immediately wished she hadn't. It brought them back to the failure of their mission yet again.

'I don't know if you know this, Gunter,' said Kate, 'but I ran away with Benedict when I was sixteen. I lost my virginity to my half-brother . . . then I realised that he was using me. He did use people, but . . . there were one or two moments during that week that were . . . just lovely.'

She began to cry. Henry put his arm round her and began to cry too.

Soon Michelle, the manageress, sturdy, solid, built, as

she said herself, 'like a brick shithouse', arrived with the first of their food.

Kate had the stuffed marrow, five of them had the pork aphelia, and Henry had the herrings in oatmeal. Jack had herrings in oatmeal as a starter, followed by pork aphelia, with stuffed marrow on the side. None of them had the duck Benedict. They drank five bottles of Argentinian merlot between them.

It's amazing how food can cheer one up. It's amazing how drink can cheer one up. They became chatty and lively. There was laughter. Other customers thought what a great party the funnily dressed people at the big round table were having. It must be a birthday.

And all the time, every moment of the evening, Henry felt, beneath his other emotions, beneath his genuine disappointment at not finding Benedict, beneath his sorrow at all the suffering he had witnessed, an insistent glow that would not go away, and he heard an insistent, unworthy voice that kept repeating, 'Jenny thought you were brilliant. She asked for your autograph. You're going to be all right.'

Towards the end, he became silent. The glow remained, deep down, but on the surface he was nervous. He had something to say, a difficult question to ask, a very short question, just three words, but three of the hardest words he could ever have said, because his question would not be welcome, and it might sound foolish.

He stood up and cleared his throat.

'Same time tomorrow?' he asked.

There was a shocked silence at the round table.

'I'm on for it,' said Jack at last. 'May as well get really behind with work before Christmas.'

'I'll come,' promised Kate. 'The new show's up and running. If I'm at the theatre, there'll be a crisis to sort out. If I'm not there to sort it out, there won't be a crisis.'

'I think it's been a complete waste of time if we don't see it through,' said Camilla.

'It may be warmer tomorrow,' hoped Guiseppe without much confidence.

Diana looked at Gunter nervously.

'We're here till Sunday,' he said. 'Even if it's useless, what are four evenings of our life compared to what he's been through?'

'I think it's appalling not to know for certain what's happened to somebody you loved,' said Hilary. 'Even if, as may well be true, he's dead, I want to know – and I speak as someone who's never known him.'

'You're so right,' agreed Camilla. 'If he is dead, I want a proper . . . a proper recognition of the fact. A proper ending. When I've read about disasters, and people being so distressed because they haven't been able to identify or bury their dead, I've felt that, while it was very sad, it was perhaps a waste of urgent resources once people were known to be dead. I think now it was pitiful of me not to understand it before.'

'You're always too hard on yourself,' commented Guiseppe.

'Well, thank you, all of you,' said Henry. He poured the remains of the merlot – a sip for everybody. 'So we'll see you tomorrow. Oh, and I almost forgot, Camilla. Your father's joining us.'

'What? I don't believe it.'

'I . . . I persuaded him.'

'Well, well done, you. That *is* amazing. I don't feel as pleased as I should, though. You're my father now.'

'I can't tell you how happy I felt when you first said that,' said Henry. 'That was wrong of me. It's flattering, but it's wrong.'

'You're all too hard on yourselves,' said Guiseppe.

Henry had the last word, as usual.

'I hope you've got a satisfactory pension scheme, Gunter,' he said. 'Otherwise it'll be a long night.'

On Thursday, 19 October, 1995, on a go-kart track in London, thirteen-year-old Prince William completed a circuit in 19.66 seconds, narrowly beating his younger brother Harry (19.79) and easily beating their detectives. The newspapers gave the times achieved at the circuit by other famous people. They included Damon Hill (20 seconds), David Coulthard (20.51) and Barry Sheene (20.75).

Not ten miles from the go-karting exploits of the young princes, Henry and Hilary Pratt sat at the same round table as the previous evening, and wondered if the others really would come.

They *did* all turn up, and it *was* a long night, even though Nigel didn't actually mention pensions once. He came in his idea of casual dress – cord trousers, a vicuna sweater and a Crosby overcoat. He looked as if he was modelling clothes for the mature man.

'Nigel,' said Henry – he wouldn't call him Tosser once this evening, in gratitude for his having turned up – 'you can go with Camilla and Guiseppe.'

'So my coming here isn't actually achieving anything,' grumbled Nigel. 'We won't be covering any extra ground because of me.'

'Wouldn't you call having my dad at my side when I search for my lost brother achieving anything?' asked Camilla.

Nigel looked at his beautiful daughter, and Henry saw that he was at a complete loss how to behave with her. He had forgotten how to be a father. He had forgotten how to be human. Being human was a bit more difficult than riding a bicycle. You needed to keep practising at it.

It would have seemed like a nice evening to most people – dry and pleasantly mild. However, when you were out in it for four hours, you knew that it was getting slowly, steadily, remorselessly colder. There was a dank damp windless chill in the meaner streets of London. Henry and Hilary tried to avoid breathing in the fumes from meths-sodden human wrecks, tried to continue to see each person as a tragedy rather than a statistic, tried to respect these ruined souls, tried to be patient, tried not to give up hope.

The areas around King's Cross and Euston stations in the north, and Charing Cross, Waterloo, Cannon Street and Blackfriars in the south were among the districts they explored that night.

Big strong Jack grew tired and was amazed by Kate's stamina. Nigel sighed from time to time, but otherwise remained grimly stoical in his suffering. Gunter was cheery, calm and bright, especially when Diana's resolve faltered.

Many eyes looked at the photos of the beautiful boy that Benedict had been: bloodshot eyes, misty eyes, drunken eyes, deep miserable eyes, paranoid eyes, psychopathic eyes, eyes rimmed with despair, defeated eyes, angry eyes, scornful eyes, nearly sightless eyes. None of them showed any recognition.

Henry was not asked for his autograph, but the glow remained, fainter, cooler, but resilient. 'This is a nightmare, but it will end. Great times are coming for you,' said that faint glow.

By the time they got back to the Café even Jack was shivering deep inside himself. Nigel looked as if he had just trekked to the North Pole.

'Duck Benedict!' he exclaimed.

Henry explained his motives and the nature of the dish.

'He wouldn't be able to eat all that now,' said Nigel. 'His digestive system will be shot to pieces. Assuming he's still alive.'

There was silence round the table. Nobody welcomed these depressing thoughts.

'Face facts, Henry,' said Nigel. 'Stop being a sentimental fool.'

'Henry,' said Guiseppe, 'when I got home last night I thought, "Where's the Henrygraph?"'

The Henrygraph was a sculpture, a rather unflattering caricature of Henry, with a large screen where his large stomach should have been. It was sculpted by Guiseppe, who was a caricaturist as well as a serious sculptor. Henry had made up competitions, and the results had been shown on the screen. It had been a talking point, but Henry had grown tired of it.

'Yes, I'm really sorry, Guiseppe,' he said. 'I . . . I should have told you. I . . . er . . . I decided it was too gimmicky.

I . . . I thought it a bit self-conscious. I don't like the cult of personality. I'm very modest at heart, you know. Too modest for my own good, perhaps.' He recalled the pleasure he'd felt from being asked for his autograph, and felt uneasy. There was a brief silence, which suggested that others might be uneasy as well. 'I am, Hilary!'

'I didn't say anything,' said Hilary.

'You didn't need to. I saw your look.'

'You did your job too well, Guiseppe,' said Hilary. 'Henry didn't like looking at himself. It was too accurate.'

Henry opened his mouth to protest, but he was pre-empted. He was pre-empted by a sniff.

We know you too well, Henry, Hilary and I, said Cousin Hilda's sniff.

Henry tried to hide his horror. To be haunted by a sniff was bad enough, to know what the sniff meant was disconcerting, but to be haunted by a sniff that spoke – that was truly disturbing.

He realised that he must hide his horror. Clearly nobody else had heard anything.

He stood up. His heart was thumping.

'Same time tomorrow?' he asked, without much hope or conviction.

Nigel looked at him aghast.

'You're not going on with this pantomime, are you??' he exclaimed. 'You're fooling yourselves. I'm sorry, but you are. He's dead. I'm sorry, but he is. I can't go, anyway. We have to go to see some of Felicity's farmer relatives.'

The thought of Felicity having relatives who were farmers astounded Henry. The thought of Nigel having to visit them tickled him pink. He hoped they all had their pensions sorted.

He didn't say any of this, of course. What he did say was, 'You're probably right, Nigel, but the more it looks as if he's dead, the more convinced I become that he's alive.'

'I wonder if any of you realise just how stubborn my dear man can be,' said Hilary.

On Friday, 20 October, 1995, the Imperial Cancer Research Fund sacked twenty-nine volunteers, many of them in their seventies, for stealing donated cash and clothes; bureaucrats in Brussels abolished leap years for cows, deciding that milk quotas would henceforward be calculated on the assumption that every year had three hundred and sixty-five days; and Kate and Jack Pratt (known at all his schools as Jack Sprat) showed a photo of Benedict to an old tramp.

The tramp shook his head. The evening had been just as fruitless as the other two, and even colder. They were ready to go back to the Café a few minutes before schedule. They had had enough. They had given up hope.

Then, just as they were about to move on, the tramp made a guttural animal noise and held out his hand for the photo. Kate handed it back to him. He studied it carefully. He was swaying drunkenly. It seemed inevitable that he'd fall over. He burped, and the air was like a garage forecourt – if you set a match to his breath, he would burn to death in seconds – but there was something extraordinary, something deep down that was still functioning, a quality of concentration, a desire to help, which revealed that there was still a human being in there, beneath the hair and dirt and stench.

Then he said something. Well, he slurred something. They couldn't make sense of it. His accent, so far as they could recognise it, suggested that he might be a Geordie. Probably they wouldn't have understood him even if he wasn't slurring. He tried again. He really wanted to communicate. They felt awful that they could barely catch a word he said. He pointed at the picture and nodded, even grinned. They were glad that Gunter wasn't there to see his teeth.

He spoke again. Again, they couldn't quite make out what he was saying.

'Big Ben?' asked Kate, without confidence.

He nodded vigorously. He was pleased, gratified, he still had emotions, he was still a human being.

'Big Ben,' he repeated.

'You saw him near Big Ben?' suggested Kate, speaking slowly and loudly as to a foreigner.

The tramp shook his head irritably, berating them for their stupidity.

'He *is* Big Ben!' exclaimed Jack.

'Of course,' said Kate. 'Of course. How stupid.'

'Well we never called him Ben, did we? You couldn't.'

'He . . . is . . . Big . . . Ben?' asked Kate, pointing at the photo as she did so.

The tramp nodded and said something else. They couldn't understand it. The tramp frowned, and repeated what he'd said. It sounded like 'played skeet'.

'Played skeet?' asked Jack incredulously.

The tramp tried to speak, made a great effort, strained,

swayed drunkenly, burped and farted at the same time, then fell to the ground like a great elm in a gale, except that elms don't shit themselves.

He groaned, stirred, burped again. A foul smell filled the air. They identified the road, and his position on the pavement, and rang 999.

It wasn't their responsibility any more. The authorities would take over. They'd done all they could. Nobody could be expected to do any more. It would be dangerous for them to try to move him. These things should be left to experts. It would be better for the man if he died. He had nothing left to live for.

All that was true, but they both agreed, afterwards, that they had felt really bad about leaving him.

'Played skeet?' said Henry, as he poured wine into their glasses in the Café. He had described the wine to the others as 'a rather exciting syrah from the Cote d'Oc', but the excitement of the wine was completely overshadowed by the excitement generated by Kate and Jack's story.

'Skeet is a form of clay pigeon shooting,' said Camilla, who knew about such things, 'in which targets are hurled from two traps at varying speeds and angles.'

'I find it difficult to believe that our drunken old tramp was telling us that Benedict shot at targets hurled from two traps at varying speeds and angles,' said Kate.

'You wouldn't say "played skeet", anyway, would you?' asked Guiseppe. 'I mean, you wouldn't say, "I think I'll go and play shooting today." '

'Where was this?' asked Henry.

'Off the Edgware Road,' said Jack.

Michelle came over to take their orders. Again, nobody could face the duck Benedict. It remained on the menu out of sheer Yorkshire stubbornness.

Jack asked hopefully if he could have a beer instead of wine. Henry didn't hear him, but he ordered it anyway.

Henry was miles away, thinking.

'Edgware Road,' he said at last. 'I wonder. Could he possibly have been saying "Praed Street", do you think?'

Neither Kate nor Jack had ever heard of Praed Street. You wouldn't have, if you never got trains to Wales or the West Country.

'Praed Street runs from Edgware Road westwards past Paddington Station,' said Henry.

'I suppose it could have been Praed Street,' said Kate. 'He *was* very indistinct.'

It was still a long shot, but, long shot or not, Henry didn't feel it fair that he should give himself and Hilary the honour of covering the Praed Street area that Saturday night. A commander has to make sacrifices. He gave the opportunity of finding Benedict to his mother.

Henry was absolutely convinced that they would find him. Diana and Gunter had no such expectations. Diana's sense that he was still alive had grown steadily weaker during the long evenings of frustration – and even if he was alive, the tramp might not have been saying, 'Praed Street', and even if he had been saying 'Praed Street', the fact that he had seen Benedict there didn't mean that he would necessarily be there that evening.

But Henry's instinct was right. They found him selling *The Big Issue* on Paddington Station. He was very thin, and very pale, and rather yellow, and he looked much older than his thirty-eight years, but he was sober, and he didn't appear to be under the influence of drugs, and he was neat and clean-shaven. He looked at his mother as if he was sure that he'd seen her somewhere before.

6 A Family Party

'I'm your mother,' said Diana.

'Get away.'

'I am, Benedict. That's why I'm out looking for you.'

'I call myself Ben. *Big Issue*! *Big Issue*!'

'Do you really not remember me?'

'I don't remember much. I was out of my mind for about fifteen years, I think. A lot's gone.'

'Well, Ben, I really am your mother and I'd like to give you a kiss. Would that be all right?'

'Spose so.'

They kissed, awkwardly. Behind them, the Swansea train started up, noisily.

'*Big Issue*!' cried Ben.

'I'll have one on the way back,' said a passer-by.

'Cheers, mate,' said Ben. He pointed at Gunter, who was standing awkwardly a little to one side. 'I don't remember him.'

'You wouldn't. You've never met him.'

'He's not my dad, then.'

'No.'

'That's a relief.'

Gunter smiled bravely.

'I'm Gunter,' he said. 'Gunter Axelburger.'

'That's a mouthful.'

'Yes, it is, isn't it? Quite a mouthful, as you say.'

'*Big Issue*!'

At last Ben made a sale. Diana was absurdly pleased for him.

'If he's not my dad,' said Ben, 'what's he doing here?'

'He's my husband.'

'I don't get it.'

It was getting cold on the station forecourt.

'There's a lot to tell, Ben, if you want to hear it,' said Diana. 'We'll take you to a café.'

'I haven't finished selling my *Big Issues*. I've twelve left.'

'I'll buy them,' offered Gunter.

'That's not the point. I like people to read them. I don't like it when people say, "I don't want one, but I'll give you a pound." I'm not a beggar.'

That little surge of pride was the first real sign of Benedicticity, thought Diana.

'I agree, Ben,' she said, 'but there *are* some other members of the family waiting to see you – they've been looking for you too – and I *have* just found my lost son. It's a pretty big moment for me and . . . just this once, for me, will you let Gunter buy them? Please.'

'Well, all right.'

Ben handed his pile of *Big Issue*s to Gunter, Gunter handed Ben a ten-pound note and a two-pound piece, and Diana rang Henry on the mobile.

Henry and Hilary got to the Café first. Henry was all for ordering champagne, but Hilary suggested that it might be wiser to wait till they saw how things went.

All six of them were excited, but they were also, in

varying degrees, apprehensive. It was dawning on them that finding Ben was not the end of the matter. It was only the beginning.

It was a solemn moment when Gunter and Diana led her lost son into the Café.

Henry, who had been confronted by him on King's Cross Station, thought how amazingly well Ben looked. The others all thought how ill he looked.

He stared at them, utterly bemused.

'Benedict!' breathed Camilla.

'He calls himself Ben now, don't you, Ben?' said Diana. She hadn't intended to sound as if she was talking to a half-wit. She wasn't surprised that he frowned.

Camilla went to hug Ben, but he shrank away.

'Who are you?' he said.

Camilla looked across at Diana, who nodded and then shook her head all in one continuous movement.

'He doesn't remember a lot,' said Diana. 'This is your sister Camilla, Ben.'

'She's my sister?'

'Yes.'

'Fucking arseholes!'

'Absolutely,' said Henry meaninglessly. 'Come on, Ben. Sit down.'

They made room for him. Diana and Gunter sat down too. The Café was fairly full, and some of the other customers were looking across at their table and wondering what was going on.

'What would you like to drink, Ben?' asked Henry.

'I'm not allowed alcohol.'

'Oh. Right.'

'One drop could kill me. My liver's shot to buggery.'

'Oh dear. Well, we'll none of us have any alcohol, then,' said Henry.

Seven people valiantly attempted, with varying degrees of success, to hide their horror at this statement. Henry realised, in that moment, that in more moderate degrees they were as addicted to alcohol as Ben had been. And to never be able to drink a drop of it again!

'I don't mind you all drinking,' said Ben. 'It's not difficult for me any more, because I know it will kill me. I don't know who you all are but you seem very nice and I'd like you all to enjoy a drink.'

'No,' said Henry. 'I don't think it would be appropriate tonight. Besides, we do a lovely elderflower cordial. Now, who are we all? Well, you've met your mum and Gunter.'

'Mr and Mrs Mouthful.'

'Yes. Ha! Absolutely.' No. Don't be too eager to please. It's patronising. 'And you've met Camilla.'

'I can't believe she's my sister. Wow! I mean, she's beautiful. Really beautiful.'

'Thanks, Ben.' Camilla blew her nose hastily.

'I'm . . . er . . . I'm Henry,' said Henry. 'I . . . I was married to your mother.'

'You're my father!'

'No.'

'Well where is my father?'

'He's not here.'

Henry nodded to Camilla meaningfully, and she slipped out to phone Nigel.

'She's my sister!' repeated Ben. 'I can't get over it. She's . . . I've forgotten so much. It's . . .'

He began to cry. He blew his nose with a very grubby handkerchief.

'Sorry.'

'Don't worry.'

Henry put his arm round Ben, very diffidently, but he didn't seem to mind. He squeezed Ben affectionately, then withdrew the hand.

'Take your time,' he said.

They were all looking at Ben and half smiling encouragingly. It suddenly struck Henry how odd this was. In their past lives, none of them had got on with him.

But was this Ben? It was Ben's body, much changed, but . . . what was the essence of a person? Did Ben have any Benishness left? If not, was he Ben in any sense but name?

The elderflower cordial arrived. They all raised their glasses to Ben and said, 'Cheers'. Bemused, he raised his glass and said, 'Cheers' too.

'Have I met her?' he said, pointing at Kate.

'Yes,' said Kate, blushing slightly.

'I thought so.' He was pleased with himself.

'I'm your half-sister.'

'What?'

'Your dad and your mum had two children. You and Camilla. Things didn't work out, the way they sometimes don't . . .' There has to be a play in this scenario. No. Get away, greedy thought. '. . . and . . . er . . . your dad and your mum parted and . . . er . . . your mum married Henry . . . and Henry already had two children of his own by Hilary . . . well, I mean, Hilary had two children by Henry, and they were me and Jack there . . .'

'Hi, Ben.'

'Hi, Jack. Hey, that's funny, isn't it? Hi-jack!'

They all laughed a little too much.

'. . . and things didn't work out,' continued Kate, as if the little joke had never happened, 'the way they sometimes don't. Henry and Hilary parted, and Henry married your mum, and things didn't work out . . .'

'. . . the way they sometimes don't?'

'Exactly. The way they always haven't, I suppose, and that's the family history.'

'Right. And who are you?' Ben asked Hilary.

'I'm Henry's wife. I'm Hilary.'

'I thought you parted.'

'We did, but we've married again. This must be difficult for you. It isn't that easy for us.'

'Would it help . . . ?' asked Guiseppe. 'I'm Guiseppe, by the way. I'm Camilla's husband. Would it help if I wrote out a family tree?'

'More like a diseased elm,' said Henry. 'Great idea, though, Guiseppe.'

As Guiseppe began to draw his diagram, Camilla slipped back in.

'No reply,' she said.

'Rather a long "no reply",' said Henry.

Camilla gave him a stern look, and signalled to him to follow her to the bar.

'What's up?' asked Ben, his suspicions easily aroused, as Henry stood.

'Nothing,' said Henry hastily. 'Just ordering more drinks.'

He hurried to the bar, where Camilla unburdened herself

rapidly, in a low voice but not caring if Greg heard or not. She looked shocked and her voice almost broke once or twice. Henry knew that she was on the verge of tears.

'Henry, darling, it was dreadful. One of the most dreadful moments of my whole life. I told him that we'd found Ben alive and well, and there was a silence. It didn't last long, just a second or two, but it was the loudest silence I've ever heard. My dad was horrified at the fact that his son was alive and he would have to deal with him. It was a moment of shattering truth. I had goose-pimples all over. He hid it, of course, with a volley of "terrific"s and "Thank God"s, but I knew, and I should think that even he is sensitive enough to know that I knew.'

Henry touched her arm sympathetically, ordered another round of soft drinks, and returned to their table with the shocked Camilla.

Guiseppe handed Ben the family tree, and he kept it in front of him for the rest of the evening. He checked on it several times.

'We'd better order some food,' said Henry. 'Everybody must be starving. Now, there are four main dishes of the day. Carbonnade of beef, hazelnut rissoles, spicy marlin and . . . er . . . duck Benedict.'

'Duck Benedict!' exclaimed Ben.

'Yes. Yes. Yes, we . . . well, I . . . I . . . er . . . well, we've been hunting for you . . . because . . . because we'd lost you and because . . . because we didn't want to have lost you.'

'You've all been out hunting for me?'

'Yes.'

'Bloody hell.'

'Yes. And . . . er . . . I thought . . . I thought it would be rather nice to create a dish for you . . . specially . . . in case we found you . . . which we have.'

'I don't call myself Benedict any more.'

'I know, but we didn't know that. Maybe . . . Michelle!'

The burly, much-muscled manageress bore down on them like an avalanche.

'Michelle, could you do me a favour? Could you rub "edict" off the blackboard?'

'Sorry, I'm not reading you,' said Michelle.

'Could you rub "edict" off Benedict. That is my edict.'

'What?'

'It was a play on words. Probably a mistake at this moment, but I was attempting to lighten a . . . well, not a heavy atmosphere, exactly. A serious moment. An attempt to leaven a serious moment with humour. A flop.'

'Do shut up, Dad,' said Jack, and Ben checked the family tree to see if Henry was *his* dad and seemed reassured by what he saw.

'Benedict calls himself Ben now, Michelle,' explained Hilary, 'so could you change his name on the board from Benedict to Ben?'

'Duck Ben? It doesn't have a ring to it,' protested Michelle.

'I don't care if it has a sodding ring to it. Just do it,' snapped Henry. 'Please,' he added, but too late.

Michelle gave him a look. I'm Manageress, not a skivvy, said her look, and I'm built like a brick shithouse, and you aren't, so just watch it.

She strode across the Café like a footballer wrongly sent off, and returned a moment later, still bristling, to change duck Benedict to duck Ben on the board.

'So what are you going to have, Ben?' asked Henry. 'Duck Ben?'

'What is it?'

'It's . . . it's roulade of duck stuffed with . . . with lobster in . . .'

It was difficult to continue in the face of Ben's blatant disbelief.

'. . . in champagne and caviar sauce with . . . er . . . pan-fried *foie gras*.'

'Bloody hell. I couldn't eat that poncy muck,' said Ben.

'No . . . well . . . good . . . but, you see, it's the sort of thing you used to like.'

'Is it? Oh my God. Perhaps it's just as well I don't remember anything, eh?'

Henry smiled, but didn't speak.

'No, look, sorry, it was nice of you to create that for me,' said Ben, 'but, thank you, I won't have it. I'll have the beef thing.'

Five of them chose the beef thing, two of them plumped for the marlin thing, Kate settled for the hazelnut thing, and Gunter said, 'Well I'm going to tackle the duck Ben. Somebody has to.'

Michelle came over and took their order. When she had finished, Henry said, 'Michelle, I'm sorry I snapped at you. Nerves are a bit frayed tonight.'

Michelle smiled.

'I know,' she said, 'and I should have taken that into account. I'm going to be docking myself a few decimal points for insensitivity on my self-assessment form tomorrow.'

'What?'

'I assess my performance for the week every Sunday. I want to improve. It won't happen again.'

Henry had a mental picture of Michelle at Sunday breakfast, her huge frame encased in a vast dressing gown, solemnly assessing her performance. He found it hard not to laugh.

Ben went round the table again, reminding himself who everybody was.

Then Henry showed him some photographs of himself in his youth: Benedict with Camilla, Benedict with Nigel and Diana, with Henry and Diana and Kate and John, at Brasenose College and Dalton College.

'Those are me?' he said. 'Christ.' He shook his head in disbelief, whether at what he had been or at what he had become or at both. 'Christ.'

Their food arrived. They were very hungry. Ben suddenly realised that there was alcohol in his dish.

'Don't worry, Ben,' said Henry. 'It's been boiled off. We won't kill you, I promise.'

Ben thought, then nodded, then ate.

'Brilliant,' he said. 'Wicked. Magic.'

Gunter pronounced his duck Ben 'not at all bad, actually rather good'.

Greg pronounced the zabaglione 'zagalobine', but they knew what he meant.

As the crowd began to thin out, Henry's sensitive antennae picked up hints of a kerfuffle in the kitchens.

'Excuse me,' he said, and raced through.

Michelle was standing at the door to the yard, panting and holding a button. Greg entered from the yard, also panting and looking very disappointed.

'What on earth is going on?' asked Henry.

'Ceris was just putting the dishwasher on,' explained Michelle, 'when she heard a noise outside. I went out and I looked over at the waste bit where you park your car and there was a man bending over it and I think he was going to let the air out of your tyres so I rushed at him and grabbed him by the coat, but he managed to get free. This button came off in my hand.'

'Ceris shouted to me and I went out and I chased him, but I lost him,' said Greg. 'I can't believe it. All my life I've wanted to chase somebody and when I get my chance I go and lose the sod.'

Henry went out and checked his tyres. They seemed intact. When he went back in, Michelle handed him the button.

'That's evidence,' she said.

When Henry went back to the table and told them the story, Hilary said, 'You should do something about it.'

'Like what?' said Henry. 'Tell the police? I can just see them saying, "Drop everything! We've got a button off the jacket of a yob who might have let some geezer's tyres down if he hadn't been so rudely interrupted by a restaurant manageress built like a brick shithouse."'

Henry's sarcasm was no doubt justified, but the fact remained, as he realised much later, that if he had been able to identify the owner of the button, a series of unpleasant events might have been avoided in the months and years to come.

'It's Henry Pratt, isn't it?'

A party of four stopped by the table on their way out.

'Yes. Yes, it is.'

'We were in the audience for your show the other night. You were very good.'

'Oh, thank you.'

'Great.'

'Thank you.'

'So we thought, we'll give your café a try.'

'Oh good. Thank you.'

'We're glad we did.'

'Oh good. Thank you.'

Henry was so tired that he could hardly drive home that night. It had been an emotional day, and he still felt a keen mixture of joy and disappointment.

Joy that they had found Benedict.

Disappointment that Benedict was so frail and that so much of his past life had been wiped from his memory.

Joy that the party of four had thought that he'd been great in the recording of *A Question of Salt*.

Disappointment that they hadn't asked for his autograph.

7 Words in Henry's Ear

On Wednesday, 1 November, 1995, John Major revealed that he would vote against measures forcing MPs to declare outside earnings; a study by the Independent Television Commission revealed that the British public had problems with nudity in adverts, especially male nudity – naked bottoms and men 'glimpsed with legs spreading' caused particular offence; Sir Cliff Richard was designated 'too raucous' for Radio Two; a woman in Massachusetts who received silent phone calls every ninety minutes day and night for six months discovered that they weren't from a sex freak but from an abandoned oil tank in Maryland programmed to warn an oil company when its level was low; and Henry and Hilary Pratt gave a supper party to celebrate the transmission of Henry's debut appearance on *A Question of Salt.*

The programme was on at half past six, so they invited their guests for half past five, to give them plenty of leeway in the rush-hour traffic.

Those who had accepted invitations were Kate Pratt, Camilla and Guiseppe Lombardi, Denzil Ackerman and Lampo Davey, Paul and Christobel Hargreaves, Nigel and Felicity Pilkington-Brick, and Ben Pilkington-Brick and his friend, whose name they had not been given.

Those who had not accepted were Jack and Flick Pratt (baby-sitter problems), Diana and Gunter Axelburger

(Gunter's work), and James and Celia Hargreaves (James's deteriorating health).

Henry had been amazed to find how disappointed he was that Mrs Hargreaves, whose beauty had aroused him so much in his younger days, would not be there, so that he could witness her excitement at seeing Paul's clumsy, podgy, clueless school friend transmogrified ('transformed' wasn't good enough for Mrs Hargreaves) into a suave television star.

'A suave television star'? That wasn't how he felt as the great evening was upon him. He felt sick with apprehension. He felt ashamed to have been excited by his participation in this pathetic TV quiz. He dreaded the moment when he would have to sit through the sight of himself failing to answer the question 'What culinary product is used in the expression "as keen as . . ."?' Thank goodness Celia Hargreaves *wouldn't* be there. He didn't want to be cruel, he liked James Hargreaves, but Henry hoped that the man would have a funny turn at a vital moment and prevent Celia from seeing his humiliation.

At twenty-five to six, when nobody had arrived, Henry felt so nervous that he decided to open the first bottle of champagne.

Hilary entered and he poured her a glass. She looked lovely, in a long, very pale mauve evening dress, elegant yet simple.

'My God, you've done yourself up pretty thoroughly,' said Henry. ('You look gorgeous' might have gone down better.)

'It's a great night. Your showbiz launch.'

' "My showbiz launch". It's a piece of crap.'

'Don't drink too much tonight, will you, darling?' pleaded Hilary.

'Darling! Please! Do you mind? I'm sixty. I shall be charming and dignified.'

'Good. It's just that I know how nervous you are. You can't hide it from me.'

By twenty to six Henry was convinced that nobody was coming. He didn't know whether to be pleased or sorry about this.

Kate was the first to arrive. She was wearing a purple dress with a green sweater. Henry couldn't remember when he had last seen her in a dress. She had good legs, too. He knew better than to comment on that, contenting himself with the 'You look gorgeous' that he should have said to Hilary.

She clinked glasses with them both.

'Good luck, Dad,' she said, absurdly, really, since the programme had been recorded and it was too late now. 'This is very exciting.'

'Exciting?' he said. 'It's crap. I wish I hadn't invited anybody. It's worthless. I wish I could do serious media stuff like you.'

'My god, Mum, he's got the bug,' said Kate.

Hilary made a 'you know what he's like' face.

'I've got a writer working on a play idea which is basically about Ben,' said Kate. 'Am I awful? Am I a parasite?'

'It depends whether you're using and abusing him or doing something passionate, worthwhile and with integrity, of which he could approve,' said Hilary, who hadn't been able to bring herself to end sentences with prepositions since she'd become a professional writer.

'He's coming tonight, with a friend,' said Henry.

'Oh, great. How's he doing, do you know?'

'We've seen him a couple of times. I mean it's less than two weeks. You can't expect miracles,' said Hilary.

'He's remembered one or two things,' said Henry. 'Some of it'll come back.'

'We can't force him,' said Hilary. 'We have to leave it all to him.'

It was past a quarter to six. Where were they all?

'Tonight will be his first meeting with his dad,' said Hilary. 'The truth is, with Diana being in Switzerland and Nigel being what he is, he's already starting to think of us as if we were his parents.'

'How ironic,' said Kate. 'Oh, the agony of all that unnecessary hostility. Have you found out what happened to him between King's Cross and now?'

'Not really. We have to be very careful not to seem to be prying,' said Hilary. 'Clearly people did care for him. Probably there was one person in particular. He's bringing a friend tonight. Maybe it was her.'

'I don't think we'll ever really know,' said Henry. 'These people don't boast about what they achieve. Only people who've achieved nothing boast. Obviously he was taken in hand, dried out, introduced to Alcoholics Anonymous, helped off drugs – massive achievements by Good People Anonymous and . . . er . . . the rest is history, as they say. He lives in a squat in Willesden now.'

He looked at his watch. It was five forty-nine. Where were they all? He took a quick refill, only half a glass, no harm in that.

At five fifty-one the doorbell rang. Henry went to the door eagerly, and tried to hide his disappointment when he saw Paul and Christobel Hargreaves standing there. He could have done without them tonight. They were experts in synchronised sarcasm. He'd only invited them out of politeness. Why did he still feel the need to be polite, at sixty?

'Hello!' he said, over-brightly. 'Great to see you.' Then he cut through his own false bonhomie. He was unable to resist asking, 'How are things at Bedsyde Manor?'

They indulged in a quick burst of synchronised frowning. The 'Bedsyde Manor' gag irritated them intensely. He hadn't intended to use it, but their very togetherness, their air of two successful medics joined at the hip, got under his extremely porous skin.

'Ignore him, darling,' said Paul. 'He may go away.'

'Unlikely, darling,' said Christobel, 'since he lives here.'

Paul handed Henry a very good bottle of Gevrey Chambertin – 1986 no less – and Christobel handed Hilary a bunch of spectacular irises that must have cost a fortune in November.

'So,' said Paul, raising his glass. 'Showbiz at last. The culmination of your dreams.'

'What??'

'You used to plaster our study at school with cuttings from *Picturegoer*. You got yourself off, when at last you cottoned on to the idea, on fantasies of Patricia Roc and Petula Clark. Now you're moving into that world.'

'What nonsense.'

Hilary decided that this was as good a moment as any in which to check on things in the kitchen, and Kate scurried off to join her. Paul and Christobel were blessedly unaware that they were emptying the room.

'No, we're actually awfully pleased for you. Mother's terribly excited,' said Paul. 'She always had a soft spot for you, you know.'

'And I for her.'

'God, yes.' Paul turned to Christobel. 'When we were on holiday in Brittany, and he saw Mummy in her bathing costume for the first time he had to bury himself in the sand to hide his erection.'

'You knew??'

'Oh yes.'

'Did she know?'

'I expect so. One didn't discuss such things with one's parents in the fifties.'

'I should hope not. Oh my God.'

In less than forty minutes he would endure total humiliation in front of guests whom he had chosen to invite. Why was he worrying so much about a humiliation more than forty years ago?

Next to arrive were Tosser and Felicity. Nigel had become Tosser again, his Nigelhood banished, perhaps for ever, after his telephone conversation with Camilla on the evening they found Ben.

Tosser was wearing a smart business suit and Felicity looked pretty in pink.

Tosser took Henry aside almost immediately, and said, 'A word in your ear. We may have to leave fairly early. Felicity thinks she may be starting one of her migraines.'

'Oh dear,' said Henry. 'Oh, by the way, Ben's coming.'

He kept his eyes on Tosser's face as he said this. Tosser

barely flinched. Henry sensed that he had been prepared for this.

'Great,' said Tosser. 'Great. Fantastic. Splendid.'

'With his "friend". We've never met her.'

'Terrific. Oh, great. Well, that is good.'

Denzil arrived next. He looked frail and tired, and smaller. Age was consuming him. Henry had a sharp, dismaying fear that Lampo had gone off with his lover again. It took courage to ask, 'Where's Lampo?'

'Parking. Making a mess of it. He'll end up miles away. I can't walk far any more. I told him it was madness to drive – I can't drive now, I'm not steady, my nerve's gone – but he hates spending on taxis, he has a surprisingly mean streak, resents every penny I fork out on my biscuit tins, and he won't use the tube. He says it's because he's frightened of terrorists, but it's actually because his fastidious nose can't stand the smell of the public.'

'Denzil! Please! He *is* my friend. I know things are difficult, but . . .'

'Oh, I love him to bits, Henry. More than ever, damn it.'

When Lampo did arrive, he said, 'I need a word in your ear later, Henry.'

Henry took him straight over to Tosser.

'Well well well,' he said. 'Who'd have thought that forty-four years on from Dalton you two study mates would be turning up to watch your old fag's debut on TV. More champagne, Tosser?'

'For God's sake, Henry. The name is Nigel. Felicity hates Tosser. Things upset her, Henry. She's easily upset. She's not resilient. She's . . . ultra-sensitive. Please be careful.'

Henry poured Tosser some more champagne and gave himself a top-up. Only a small one. No harm in that.

Camilla and Guiseppe arrived next. Within seconds, Guiseppe had fallen into the fashion of the evening.

'A word in your ears,' he said, taking Henry to one side.

'Ear,' said Henry. 'It's ear. You can't whisper into both sides of a man's face.'

'My English is not yet idiomatic, sadly, Henry. It's about Camilla. Take special care of her tonight, will you, there's a good man?'

' "There's a good man"! Not idiomatic! You sound more English every day.'

'Yes, yes, never mind that. It's . . . I have never known Camilla so upset, Henry. That phone call to her father, it has hurt her deeply. To find that you despise your father – and this is the first time they'll have met since it – she's feeling very emotional. People think she is cool. Just painting horses. So detached. Not so. She is hot, Henry. Red hot. Be very loving to her tonight. You are her father now.'

'This is not what I wanted.'

'I'm afraid what you wanted doesn't carve much snow.'

'Cut much ice. Though I like the image of carving snow. Hilary could use that.'

'They won't sit next to each other, will they?'

'Guiseppe! What do you take me for?'

'Sorry.'

The atmosphere in the large sitting room, comfy rather than elegant, was slightly awkward, a little too polite. Nobody was sitting down. Everyone felt that, since they would soon be sitting to watch *A Question of Salt*, it was inappropriate to sit at this stage.

Camilla went straight up to the cluster of well-dressed folk with their glasses of champagne, kissed her father, and said, 'Hello, Dad.' Everyone in the room knew that this was play-acting, that it was her only way of coping. Tosser knew it too. Within seconds they were at opposite ends of the room, and managed, without making it look obvious, not to say another word to each other all evening.

Henry had begun to think that Ben wasn't coming, but at six twenty-two he arrived.

'Sorry,' he said. 'We got lost. This is Darren.'

It was a surprise to Henry to find that Ben's friend was a young man in a T-shirt with a stud in his nose and a tattoo of an anchor on his right arm.

'Darren doesn't do posh,' warned Ben, 'but he's a sweetie.'

The arrival of Ben and Darren into the sitting room created a sudden silence followed by too much conversation.

Ben went straight up to Tosser and said, 'So! You're my elusive dad, Dad. Can't mistake that moon face, seen it in photos.'

'Ah! Ha! Yes. Well . . . well . . . hello, old son.' Tosser took Ben's painfully thin body to his great frame and gave it an awkward hug, so falsely warm that it might have been medically dangerous. Henry almost waited for the noise of Ben's brittle bones being crunched.

'I've got my family tree in my pocket,' said Ben. 'I'm still not quite clear who everybody is.'

'No. No. Quite. Difficult. Problem.'

'This is my friend Darren.'

'Hello, Darren. Jolly good. Yes. Er . . . excuse me, must

go and see if my wife's all right. She's . . . er . . . not very good in crowds.'

Hilary approached Ben, kissed him, shook hands with Darren, gave Ben a glass of nettle cordial and asked Darren, 'Are you allowed to drink?'

'Oh yes,' said Darren so fervently that Ben laughed and Hilary flinched at the prospect.

'Champagne, Darren?' she asked. 'Or would you prefer a beer?'

'Oh champers, please. Any time,' said Darren.

'Good man,' said Hilary, hiding her surprise.

'Yes, he is,' said Ben.

'How are the memories coming on, Ben?' asked Henry while Hilary fetched the champagne.

'Dunno, really,' said Ben in his new, semi-cockney voice so far removed from his old posh tones. 'Dunno. I've been told such a lot in such a small amount of time that I've realised that it's going to be very difficult to know how much I'm actually remembering and how much I'm remembering what I've been told.'

'You'll be all right as long as you're aware of that.'

'Yeah, but, the thing is, if I ever really remember what I was like, I don't think I'm going to find that I've got much in common with myself.'

'Well . . . yes . . . but . . . it's what you are now that matters, isn't it?'

'Is it? Really? To you?'

'Of course. Of course, Ben.'

It was time to get everybody seated, to watch the programme. In fact it was past time and Henry found himself getting very edgy. He noticed that his glass was suddenly empty. He filled it. He'd need some support during the next half hour. One glass in half an hour wouldn't harm him.

The TV was switched on, the sound was adjusted, chairs were moved, the lights were dimmed, people were still getting settled in their seats when the infantile signature tune erupted into the darkened room, and the opening credits rolled.

Oh God, that music! Mrs Hargreaves will hate it, thought Henry.

It was even worse than he had expected. Why on earth had they invited all these people?

His first shock was seeing Sally Atkinson on the screen. His heart almost stopped and he could feel his prick hardening. He gasped. Hilary heard his gasp and, luckily, misunderstood it. She clutched his hand. He might have had some explaining to do if she had grabbed his penis, as she could have done with everyone's eyes on the screen. But it was his hand that his darling wife clutched, and she pressed it lovingly as he stared at Sally's open, weary, sexy face and felt quite, quite dreadful and quite, quite exhilarated.

Then he saw himself. Sixty. Podgy. Greying. Giving a ghastly, stiff, tense smile. His prick shrivelled like a leaking balloon. And then the audience laughed at his name. He'd forgotten that. And there was a dreadful silence in the sitting room.

The first round of questions began. It seemed an age before his question arrived. His body strained and urged Dennis Danvers to get there quickly, to get the dreadful moment over, but it also strained and urged him never to reach it. Quicker, slower, quicker, slower, please!

What did it matter? It was all crap.

It arrived. Dennis Danvers asked him, 'Henry Pratt, a nice easy one to start with.' That was the bit he hadn't heard. 'What culinary product is used in the expression, "As keen as . . ."?'

Then there was a close up of Henry's face, utterly blank, totally unaware that he'd been addressed. His former colleagues on the *Thurmarsh Evening Argus* and the Cucumber Marketing Board would be watching this. He could see them all, pitying him, laughing at him.

'Sorry,' he said on the screen. 'I was miles away.'

He heard the audience laugh. He hadn't realised how deeply his humiliation had amused them. And there was laughter in the room too. He heard Tosser give a kind of subdued laugh that turned into a growl as he realised that it was tactless.

'I was speaking to you, Mr Pratt,' said Dennis Danvers. 'After all, you are, are you not, the only Pratt here?'

He hadn't realised that the audience had been in near hysteria. He sensed that people were near hysteria, politely repressed, in his sitting room off Clapham Common.

Here was the question again.

'What culinary product is used in the expression, "As keen as . . ."?'

He closed his eyes. He couldn't bear to see his blank face again.

The pause seemed to go on for ever. He put his hands over his ears. It was no use.

'Toffee.'

With the great roar from the studio audience, he wasn't

able to be utterly sure that the audience in the room were laughing as well, but he sensed that they were. The bastards! The bitches! His friends!

He had to say something. He couldn't just let this ignominious moment pass in silence.

'It gets better,' he said.

He watched Bradley Tompkins's Anonymous Borsch routine in horror. The man deserved to die a death, but Henry couldn't enjoy it. He actually felt a touch of warmth for the man. After all, he had saved him. But for him it would be Henry dying on his arse there.

His Cannelloni routine was even better than he'd remembered. He'd completely forgotten Macaroni Tony.

He'd also completely forgotten his Lady Windermere gag, which he'd suddenly thought of and dragged in shamelessly.

Dennis Danvers had asked him the searching question, 'How many things do you need to wash when you cook a lentil curry with brown rice?' and he'd thought that, having answered three questions seriously since his Cannelloni routine, it was time to be silly again.

'I don't know,' he had said, 'but I do know who said, "You're an absolute belter, Lady Windermere". It was Lady Windermere's fan.' He could imagine dying a death with a silly joke like that, but on that night, said by him with great solemnity, and in answer to a completely different question, it got a good laugh.

'Incorrect,' Dennis Danvers had said, not quite managing to keep a straight face. 'I can offer it to Denise's team.'

Bradley Tompkins had leapt in, once the school swot, always the school swot.

'Two.'

'Which are?'

'The lentils and the rice.'

'Wrong,' Dennis Danvers had said. 'I can offer it back to Simon's team.'

'You aren't allowed to do that,' Bradley Tompkins had complained.

'I can do what I like,' Dennis Danvers had said. 'I'm the boss. Simon's team, anyone know the answer?'

'Three,' Henry had said. 'The lentils, the rice, *and your hands.*'

'Correct.'

There had been a good round of applause. The camera had cut back to Bradley Tompkins.

Henry shivered as he sat in his sitting room and saw the expression on Bradley Tompkins's face. The burgeoning hatred in his little eyes was there for all the nation to see. Henry felt very uncomfortable. He didn't need that.

Hilary squeezed his hand again. She had sensed his hatred of Bradley's hatred. He took a sip of champagne and his mind began to wander to some of his teachers long ago – the palindromic Mr A. B. Noon B.A, at Brasenose, the hypocritical Mr E. F. Crowther at Thurmarsh Grammar, the hypercritical Droopy L and the absent-minded Foggy F at Dalton, the compassionate Mr Quell at Thurmarsh Grammar, and, before them all, the eccentric Miss Candy at Rowth Bridge, who had thought that he might turn out to be something special.

What would they all have thought if they had seen him tonight?

Oh, Henry.

*

Suddenly the programme was over. Everybody was standing up. His foot had gone to sleep. He had pins and needles. His legs were heavy from the tension, and his head felt light from its release. Nobody could blame him for taking just one more glass of champagne, after that ordeal.

Everyone wanted to talk about it.

'Remarkable,' said Paul.

'Extraordinary,' said Christobel.

Henry smiled inwardly at the careful ambiguity of their adjectives. So Paul. So Christobel.

He preferred Darren's honesty. Darren and Ben came up to him together, just before they sat down to eat.

'Did I used to like you?' Ben asked.

'You couldn't stand me, to be honest.'

'That's what I seemed to think. Things are coming back. It's horrible.'

'Henry, I must give you credit,' said Darren. 'I mean it was crap, utter crap, excuse my French, you know that, I know that, but you played it like that. That stupid Bradley Tompkins took it seriously, the wanker. I mean, let's face it, at the beginning it was so funny because you was so obviously thinking, "What the fuck am I doing here?", excuse my Swedish. You looked about as comfortable as a Jehovah's Witness at a gang bang, but then, you know, suddenly you dragged in that Lady Windermere gag, it wasn't even about the question you was asked, it was corny, yeah, but it was just right. Genius. Just sodding stupid enough. If old Oscar himself had been there he'd have thought, "Yeah! Nice one!" '

'I hardly think so – and he wasn't actually prone to say, "Yeah! Nice one!". Darren, somebody must have . . . really done great things for Ben.'

'Yeah . . . spose so . . . mebbe.'

'You wouldn't know who, would you?'

'Well . . . yeah . . . I spose . . . I spose a bit of it was me. With a bit of help from my friends. I love him, you see. Mad, innit? Keep a bit schtoom about it, eh? Florence Nightingale's not my style.'

'Let's go and eat,' said Hilary. 'It's all very straightforward and simple,' she added.

They started with gravad lax.

Cousin Hilda's sniff sniffed.

'This is what we call simple these days, is it?' said Cousin Hilda's sniff.

'All things are relative,' said Henry.

'What on earth made you say that?' said Camilla.

'Say what?' said Henry.

'"All things are relative." You suddenly said, "All things are relative."'

'Sorry,' said Henry. 'I meant to say it silently. It came out by mistake.'

This was dreadful. He was sweating.

'How do you mean?'

'I mean, I meant just to think it.'

'What a funny thing to suddenly think.'

'I can't help what I think.'

'Are you all right?'

'Just a bit tired. It was a bit of an ordeal.'

'You need another drink.'

As they were finishing their beef casserole – Henry had

expected another sniff to greet its appearance, but there were no more sniffs, although that wasn't much of a relief as, the longer there wasn't another sniff, the more he expected the next one – the question of where Ben and Darren would live cropped up.

'Can you stay in your squat indefinitely?' Kate asked.

'Dunno,' said Darren. 'Mebbe. Who knows? That's squats.'

Henry felt most strongly that he should say, 'You can come and live here.' He longed to say it. He wasn't sure if he longed for them to come and stay, but he longed to say it. He felt most strongly that it needed to be said.

But could he say it without consulting Hilary? He looked across the table at her, so serene and lovely, so matriarchal and yet so unobtrusive, and he gave her a meaningful look, just as she was giving him a meaningful look, and for a moment even these two most loving of partners found that they didn't understand the meaning of each other's meaningful looks – it was impossible, and perhaps undesirable, ever to understand fully what another person was thinking. Then a great burst of love and affection swept over him and he knew that Hilary would be happy with what he said.

'You could come and live here,' he said.

He saw Tosser twitch. He saw Tosser give Felicity a furtive look. He saw her give an answering twitch, and run her hand over her forehead. It wasn't difficult, on this occasion, to put words to their body language. Tosser's twitch was saying, 'We ought to make an offer. Please tell me you couldn't face it', and Felicity's silent reply was 'Of course I couldn't face it. Think how much worse my migraines would be.'

'Thank you,' said Darren to Henry. 'I think that's a fantastic offer. I find it very hard at this moment in time to credit that I have heard such a wonderfully generous offer from people who I would have described, excuse my Portuguese, as members of the middle-class bourgeoisie.'

'Darren's very political,' said Ben proudly.

'I dunno, though, Henry. I really dunno,' said Darren. 'Would it work? Can we think about it?'

'Of course. Of course.'

'I'd hate to do it, and it didn't work out. I'd hate that,' said Darren. 'Anyway, cheers.'

Henry raised his glass and in that moment of emotion took a rather larger sip than he had intended.

One more glass would do no harm. After all, there was cheese still to come.

By the end of the meal he knew that he had drunk too much, and he felt extraordinarily tired. The last thing he needed was Tosser saying, 'A word in your ear.'

He poured Tosser a little digestif, then, on second thoughts, poured one for himself, so that Tosser wouldn't feel uncomfortable. He led Tosser through the hall, past the grandfather clock and the barometer, Cousin Hilda's old barometer which had only come to him a few weeks ago under the will of her old friend, Mrs Langridge. He had once infuriated Cousin Hilda, when he had come home drunk, by tapping the barometer and saying, 'Quarter past stormy. Didn't realise it was as late as that.'

He felt fairly drunk now, but not like that, of course. He was mature now. He could hold his drink.

The study felt cold. The radiator wasn't on. Too late now.

Henry subsided into the leather chair at the side of his large, Georgian desk. Behind him, in pride of place, sat the various editions of Hilary's four published novels – hardback, paperback, audio unabridged, audio abridged and large print.

All round the walls were photographs of scenes from Henry's past life, and against the south wall, opposite the books, sat the Henrygraph, Guiseppe's caricature. Hilary had been right. He didn't want people to see it, in all its wicked accuracy, but he was happy to see it, here, on his own, in private. It would keep him from getting too big-headed, he hoped.

Tosser seemed to have been silent for a very long time. Henry was almost asleep.

'I don't find this easy,' Tosser began at last.

'Clearly. Cheers.'

'Cheers. What is this?'

'Marc de Bourgogne.'

'It's very good. Henry, I don't find this easy. I . . . you offered Ben a home today.'

'Well, yes. I don't think he'll take it, though.'

How big Tosser was. Bigger than ever. He quite dwarfed the Henrygraph.

'I'm not criticising you for offering, Henry.'

'Good.'

'No, it's good of you. I'm not even saying that you're usurping my role as Ben's father.'

'I can only usurp it if you aren't prepared to take it on.'

'I realise that. No criticism will pass my lips.'

'Thank you.'

'I just wanted to explain why I cannot have Ben to stay.'

'You don't need to explain.'

'I do. I need to explain to somebody and you're the only person I can explain to.'

Henry was uncomfortably aware that Tosser was looking in the direction of a photograph of the occasion at Thurmarsh Town Hall when Henry (Liberal), Tosser (Conservative) and Martin Hammond (Labour) had stood beside the Returning Officer (berk) to hear the result of the parliamentary election of 1979, when Henry's actions had resulted in Tosser being elected to a seat he didn't want.

'I cannot have Ben to stay, Henry, much as I might like to.'

'Much as you might like to? You'd hate it.'

'Anyway, it's hypothetical. It's Felicity, Henry. I'm afraid she couldn't take it. She's . . . fragile, Henry. Very fragile.'

'I understand, Tosser.'

'Please do try not to call me that.'

'Sorry.'

'No, you're not. Er . . . there is also the question of Darren. Felicity is rather . . . squeamish. No use pretending she isn't. She can't help it. Studs make her sick. Particularly nose studs. Felicity is ultra-sensitive about noses. We once saw a man with a very deformed, diseased nose in a bar in Rotterdam. She took to her bed for three days.'

'Oh dear. I can't pretend, Tosser, that I was thrilled when Darren came through my door, but actually I think he's great. I think kindness and compassion are rather more important than studs and tattoos.'

'Well, yes, I agree. Of course. But there you are. You're going to think me old-fashioned, Henry, I know you are, but it's a profound shock to me to find that my boy is gay.'

'Good God, Tosser, you fancied me yourself once.'

'I was a child, for God's sake, it was boarding school, you were the only thing with smooth flesh around.'

'And I thought you really cared.'

'Don't be silly, Henry.'

'You've been friends with Lampo for most of your life.'

'He isn't my child, Henry. You don't have a child who's gay. You don't understand.'

'There have been moments when I've wondered if Kate is gay. I still do, actually. It would make no difference at all.'

'I . . . I may not seem to you to be a shining example of a caring father, Henry, but . . . I've come in here to ask you something . . . as an old friend . . . and we must go in a moment, because unfortunately Felicity's migraine is firming up, they go one way or the other, her migraines, and I just want to ask you this one favour before I go. For me, and for my peace of mind, because Felicity does tend to be a little bit . . . obsessive, does take things rather to heart, does . . . well . . . she gets absolutely stricken with guilt, can't sleep, even with sleeping pills . . . I really do think . . . well, she's very . . . she's very resentful sometimes, Henry, and she bottles it up. It honestly wouldn't surprise me if she had a nervous breakdown. I mean that. So, for my peace of mind, because I can have no peace of mind if she hasn't, could you see your way to withdrawing your invitation to Ben and Darren?'

'I can't, Nigel,' said Henry. He couldn't bring himself to refuse the man's request and call him Tosser at the same time. 'I understand why you're asking me, and I sympathise, I really do, but I'm afraid supporting Ben is more important to me than sparing your feelings.'

Anybody would admit that he needed a drink after a conversation like that with Tosser – and the marc de Bourgogne was superb – and really good drink didn't make you drunk.

Tosser and Felicity made their farewells. Paul and Christobel said that they must be going.

Lampo asked to have a word in his ear.

He topped up his glass. Nobody would think it unreasonable to do that before yet another word in his weary, over-used ear.

He trotted across the hall, silently saying 'Here we go again' to Cousin Hilda's barometer, and led Lampo into his study, which was even colder now, because the night was growing colder and because Tosser had recently been in the room.

'When I fagged for you, I little dreamt that you'd both want words in my ear in quick succession in my study on the same evening more than forty years later,' he said, collapsing into the leather chair rather more heavily than he'd intended.

'What did Tosser want?'

'It was confidential.'

'Henry! We're old friends.'

'He doesn't want me to usurp his parental role with Ben.'

'Well, if he doesn't want it somebody has to take it.'

'Exactly. Just what I told him. My very words.'

'I can't forgive myself for being so friendly with somebody so dim. Well, my request is more simple. Will you be doing *A Question of Salt* again?'

'Probably. Why?'

'Could you get me two tickets?'

'You want to go again? Denzil I can understand, but you?'

'Oh, it isn't for Denzil. It's for me and . . . my friend. I don't mind pretending, Henry, that he has very common tastes in some areas.'

'Well, there's nothing like being tactful.'

'Surely I don't need to be tactful with you? Tact can be so patronising.'

'Fair enough, but let me get this straight . . .'

The room began to move: the Henrygraph, the books, the photos, they were going round and round. Why wouldn't they keep still?

'Are you all right?' asked Lampo.

'Fine. Just D I Z Z Y.'

'What?'

'A dizzy spell. That's funny, isn't it? D I . . .'

'I did get it. I only didn't laugh because it wasn't funny.'

'I thought it was.'

'You're drunk and I'm sober. Is it worth going on with this?'

'Yes. Sorry.'

Henry strove very hard to concentrate. He had

something very important to say. He stood up unsteadily, put his hand on the desk for support, and glared at Lampo.

'Let me get this straight,' he said. 'You are asking me, in my house, with your lifelong lover, my friend Denzil, to whom I introduced you to in Siena, actually sitting in my sitting room across the hall at this very moment, you are asking me, sitting there across my desk, separated from Denzil only by the hall, to give you two tickets for you and the youth you're cheating him with unbeknown to him without his knowing?'

'Well, yes, if you put it that way.'

'I do, Lampo. I do.'

'You wait till you're smitten.'

A vision of Sally Atkinson flashed disturbingly across Henry's mind. He swayed, but didn't fall.

'Smitten?'

'Utterly. I wasn't at first, I admit, but . . . well, I should never have started it, of course, but it's too late now.'

Henry sighed.

'Oh, don't worry, Henry,' said Lampo. 'I shan't ever leave Denzil. I couldn't.'

Henry gave a faint smile.

'I know,' he said. 'I do know that, but my answer . . .' He tried to look severe, tried to look as if he was a headmaster in his study. 'My answer, Lampo, is no, no and never. Do what you want with this youth . . .'

'He's thirty-six.'

'Do what you want with him, but don't ever again try ever again to use me in your dirty little deceptions ever again.'

Henry let go of the desk and tried to walk towards the door. His legs wouldn't work. They wouldn't hold him. They were jelly. He was like a drunk in a comic film. He subsided on to the floor.

It took four of them to put him to bed – Lampo, Hilary, Guiseppe and a sniff.

8 Sod's Law

Occasionally, after the transmission of Henry's first appearance in *A Question of Salt*, people stopped him in the street and told him how much they'd enjoyed it. It was awkward if he was in a hurry, but he always stopped to talk. 'I have to respect my public,' he told Hilary, who raised her eyebrows just a little towards heaven, even though she didn't believe that there was anybody there to respond.

'You're my second celeb of the week,' a taxi driver told him one Wednesday. 'I had that Bjorn Borg in the back on Monday.'

Celeb!

'I'm a celeb, Miss Candy,' he told his old teacher silently. 'It's a pity you must have died long, long ago, because I think you'd be proud to see that I *have* amounted to something.'

He felt that he must show the taxi driver that success wasn't spoiling him, that he was still a man of the people, so he decided that he must speak to him.

'Any sign of the Christmas rush starting yet?' he asked.

His remark thudded into the ether with all the subtlety of a steam hammer. Even the taxi driver seemed bored by it, as he replied, without vitality, 'Yeah, well, it won't be long, that's for sure. There'll be Christmas trees in shop windows next week.'

'Ridiculous!' spat Henry confidently. 'Far too early.'

'I like it,' said the taxi driver reprovingly. 'We have enough boring, colourless times in the rest of the year.'

Henry realised that if he wanted to be loved by his public – and what was the point of having a public if they didn't love you? – he might have to be a bit more careful in expressing his opinions, and a bit more subtle in detecting other people's .

He also felt certain that, on Thursday, his taxi driver would be saying to his passengers, 'I had that Henry Pratt in the back yesterday. You know, the chef bloke. I'll tell you what. *No* conversation!'

He would have to pull his socks up, now that he was a celeb.

The Christmas special was his fifth recording of *A Question of Salt*. He felt that it was quite a feather in his cap to be chosen for the special – until he saw Bradley Tompkins there.

It was the first time he'd gone without Hilary. The recording clashed with a Christmas dinner for some leading booksellers, and her publishers wanted her to be there.

There were bound to be such clashes, from time to time. They were lucky not to have had them before.

'You don't need me there now, do you?' she said at their wooden kitchen table, modern but distressed. 'You're a big boy now.'

I do need you there. I don't want to be tempted by Nicky. I don't trust myself, especially if I've had a few drinks.

Then don't have a few drinks.

I don't trust myself not to have a few drinks.

'I'd like you there. Put it that way.'

'I really think I ought to go to this, darling. Sales slipped just a bit last time and I want to emphasise the autobiographical element in this one. I think it might get them behind it more.'

In the taxi to the BBC (not recognised by the driver, slightly to his chagrin) with his change of clothes, all chosen by Hilary, Henry couldn't help hoping that Sally Atkinson would be on the show, couldn't help hoping that Bradley Tompkins wouldn't, kept saying to himself, 'Be sensible. Don't drink too much. You love Hilary. Don't let her down. Don't let Ben down. Don't let them all down. For God's sake, Henry Pratt, don't be a tosser tonight.'

He didn't get any of his wishes. Bradley Tompkins was there. Sally Atkinson wasn't.

After the run-through he showered and changed. He did things properly now. He lingered over them, so that he wouldn't have time to drink too much. He cleaned his teeth extremely thoroughly, so that he could kiss Nicky confidently, even though it wouldn't lead anywhere.

'I am mature,' he told himself as he stood in the lift that would take him to the floor for the Green Room.

'I am mature. I love my wife,' he told himself as he entered the room and strolled insouciantly towards the other chefs. Nicky was among the group. His heart leapt.

He half expected Cousin Hilda's sniff.

Nicky approached him and kissed him on the cheek. There were more blemishes on her skin than he'd remembered, and he'd thought that her breasts were bigger, but that didn't matter, especially as they weren't going to do anything. He was not only mature, he had too much style to force his body on a young woman. The age gap was too great. Her kiss was *extremely* friendly, though.

'Is Hilary coming?' she asked.

'Not this time. She's out to dinner with some booksellers.'

'Ah.'

He wasn't sure what to read into her 'Ah'. He met her eyes. He wouldn't have known what the expression in them meant, had it been important to him, which it wasn't.

'I'll leave you to relax,' she said. 'You're looking very smart. A man with dress sense!'

'Thank you.' He didn't tell her that Hilary had chosen his complete outfit.

She kissed him again.

'Thank you,' she said.

'What for?'

'For being you. You're my protégé, and you're shining on the show. I took a bit of a punt on you, and it's come off. You're a bit special to me, naturally.'

'Oh!'

He wouldn't have known how much she meant by that, had it been important to him, which of course it wasn't.

He only had two drinks before the show. It was all he had time for.

Just after he'd taken his first drink, Bradley Tompkins entered. Determined to be friendly, Henry approached him.

'I thought you didn't come in here before the show,' he said, lightly, pleasantly, careful not to seem in any way challenging.

'What is this – an interrogation?'

'I was just taking an interest. I was just wondering what had happened to the shit, shave and shower routine.'

'I've speeded it up, if you must know. I've decided a drink might help on these occasions.'

Bradley Tompkins moved off, then returned.

'Oh, and if you need it for your records,' he said sarcastically, 'I had the shit before the shave today.'

Fury swept over Henry. He would never, never ever, try to be friendly to the little bewigged bastard again.

Denise Healey drifted over, and said, 'I think I ought to mark your card. Bradley's really getting to dislike you.'

'I'm beginning to realise that.'

'The thing is, he can be pretty vicious. Not a nice man.'

'What do you suggest I do?'

'Just be careful, that's all. Don't provoke him.'

'I won't. Don't you worry.'

'The other thing is, the producer is going to use any of the hostility he can get. If you ever glare at Bradley, or don't laugh at one of his jokes, there'll be a close-up.'

'And vice versa.'

'And vice very versa.'

The programme was all so easy for Henry now. Oh, he was a little nervous, he was bound to be, you had to be if you were to be sharp, but he relished it. The warm-up man described him as an up and coming star, asked how many of them had seen him the previous week. Henry couldn't see how many hands went up, but he got detectably warmer applause than on his previous appearances.

The studio went tense. The opening credits rolled. The hateful signature tune was played on monitors dotted around the studio.

'Good evening, and welcome to another edition of *A Question of Sport*. Oh shit!!' said Dennis Danvers.

The audience, who had no idea that he said this every week, roared and roared. The mistake relaxed them, it got them on Dennis's side, showed them that he was no better than they were. Henry saw why Dennis did it, but . . . dear God . . . how he loathed it.

During the recording, while taking care never to be caught 'miles away', Henry kept telling himself, 'I do not fancy Nicky. I am a happily married man. I will make it clear to her after the show that I do not fancy her.'

Bradley Tompkins's fictional chef was a Greek, called Harry Toffeenose. He put a lot of emphasis on the 'Toffee' and Henry realised to his dismay that it was a deliberate reference back to his moment of shame. He also realised that it was a pun on Aristophanes to an audience who had never heard of him. It was so obscure that Bradley had to explain it to the audience. It was so bad that to have called it a schoolboy pun would have been an insult to schoolboys.

Too late, Henry registered that his incredulity at this pathetic offering had been transmitted to the whole nation in close-up.

Henry's effort was all about Keith Floyd's fictional brother Pink, the singing chef, composer of 'Amazing Grapes' and other hit songs.

The nation was treated to the spectacle of Bradley

reacting to this flight of fancy like Queen Victoria on a bad day.

The show went well. As the final credits rolled, and everybody smiled, Henry was telling himself, beneath the smile, 'I do not fancy Nicky. I am a happily married man. I will be good tonight.'

He would say to Nicky, straightaway, 'I think you're very pretty. I'd ask you out if I was younger and not happily married.'

He entered the Green Room and went straight up to her. Nicky, you're so very . . .

'Hello,' she said, before he had time to speak. 'Brill. You were brill. Come and meet my boyfriend.'

Henry was dismayed. Not dismayed because he hadn't been able to say what he had intended to say. He was mightily relieved not to have made a monumental fool of himself. And not dismayed because she had a boyfriend. Not even dismayed because her boyfriend was young and handsome, with designer stubble, and a designer shirt (Paul Smith) loosely open at the neck, revealing great strands of designer hair on his designer chest.

He was dismayed not by the man's hirsuteness, his evident virility, his extreme laid-back confidence, not even by the fact of the man's existence, but by the fact that he had been so unaware of the man's existence, that he had read more into Nicky's ritual flirtatiousness and pleasant playfulness than she had intended. It was a shock to his pride to think that he had ever had enough false pride to believe that at sixty he could be an object of real sexual desire to young women. He resolved, with fierce determination, never again to dream, even in the privacy of his lavatory, of his body on top of or indeed underneath the body of a lovely young woman, never to touch pretty women unnecessarily with desire masquerading as affection, never to peer down the cleavages of the famous or the obscure, never to give swift, barely detectable glances at the crotches of young women at parties, weddings, funerals, anything. Never to grope, never to hope, never to risk the shame of anybody ever regarding him, even for a moment, as a dirty old man.

He saw Bradley Tompkins watching and smirking as he was introduced to Nicky's boyfriend. Then Bradley approached him, smirk fading, and at last made the accusation that had been festering in his mind.

'You set me up over Anonymous Borsch, didn't you?'

'No! I was naïve. I didn't even realise you were trying to pinch anything off me.'

'I don't believe you. You fed me a load of garbage and I was the naïve one not to realise that.'

'Ignoring the fact that whatever interpretation you put on it, the whole Anonymous Borsch incident only happened because you pinched my material.'

'I was desperate, Henry, and you took advantage.'

'I didn't, Bradley.'

Simon Hampsthwaite came over to them.

'Now then,' he said. 'What are you doing to my team mate, Bradley?'

'Finding out the truth. Fuck off out of it,' said Bradley Tompkins. 'That's the language you understand, isn't it?'

'You should never believe what you read in the papers,' said Simon wearily.

'Thanks, Simon,' said Henry, 'but it'll be all right.'
'Sure?'
'It's better.'
'OK.'
Simon wandered off, back to the other chefs by the table which served as a bar, leaving Henry and Bradley facing each other with all the wary caution of judo experts.
'You knew I was going to use Anonymous Borsch,' said Bradley Tompkins. 'Otherwise why would you have had the Cannelloni routine up your sleeve?'
'I didn't,' said Henry. 'I was going to do Anonymous Borsch. I thought it was funny.'
'You didn't. Nobody could.'
'You did.'
'I have no sense of humour. Everybody knows that.'
'Then why do you do these things?'
'Vanity, Henry. I like being well known – and I was considered good at it until that stupid fictional chef question came on. That won't last long and then I'll be all right again. It's good for business. We all need business. You're not going to tell me you made up all that Cannelloni stuff off the cuff, are you?'
'Honestly. Off the cuff, not up the sleeve.'
'I don't believe you.'
Henry shrugged and walked away. There was no reason why he should feel humiliated, but he did.

On Thursday, 2 May, 1996, Lady Blatch, a Home Office Minister of State, announced that Michael Howard had agreed that the word 'immigrant' should be removed from legislation curbing bogus asylum seekers in an attempt to avoid offending minorities; the Head of the Meteorological Office had to hand back a £2,200 bonus payment because of the weather forecasters' poor performance; at Cardigan Magistrates' Court a brown hen, Gloria, was refused permission to appear as a character witness in the case of a dog said to have harassed chickens, when the magistrates ruled that evidence from farmyard animals was inadmissible – but nobody could stop Gloria laying an egg in the witness waiting room; and Sod's Law, that bane of the catering industry, operated in no uncertain fashion in the Café Henry in Frith Street.

Ask any publican or restaurateur about Sod's Law. You are inexplicably busy when you have a shortage of staff, and seriously quiet when the full complement are on duty. Everyone arrives early when you are late, and late when you want to close early.

Three of the most important men in Henry's life visited the Café on that balmy, sunny, pavement-café spring morning. These men all wanted to speak to Henry, and Henry needed to speak to them all. It was Sod's Law that they all arrived within a few minutes of each other, and that Henry was working in the kitchen that day. These men didn't want to speak to Greg, even to a Greg who believed that, under Henry's patient tuition, he was beginning to master the art of small talk.

'Good afternoon, sir. I see it says men are safer than women with supermarket trolleys, would you believe? What can I get you, sir?' said Greg to the first of the three.

'What red wines have you got by the glass?' asked Bradley Tompkins.

'We've got a Chilean merlot, an Argentinian cabernet

sauvignon, an Australian shiraz and a Spanish tempranillo, sir.'

'I'll try the tempranillo.'

'Very good, sir.'

'Let's hope so.'

'I've seen you on the telly, 'aven't I?'

'Very possibly.'

'Great. It's a good show.'

'Thank you.'

'Pleased to have you with us, sir, on this balmy Mediterranean morning.'

'Thank you. Boss not in?'

'He's cooking today, sir.'

'Oh, how wonderfully hands on. Would you tell him I'm here?'

'Certainly, sir.'

Greg handed Bradley Tompkins his glass of wine and hurried off to the kitchen.

'That cunt off your TV show is here,' he said rather more loudly than Henry would have wished.

'Greg!'

'Sorry. But, honestly, what a . . .'

'Yes, yes. Yes, yes. Damn damn. I'd better have a word with him, I suppose, or he'll complain I'm ignoring him.'

Henry rehearsed a smile, sighed, squared his shoulders, thought of England, and strode into the Café in his full chef's regalia.

'Bradley! How nice of you to visit!'

'Thought I ought to see what all the fuss is about,' growled Bradley Tompkins.

Henry had made four more recordings of *A Question of Salt* since Christmas. He was becoming a regular. He was becoming a favourite. He had been sounded out by Simon Hampsthwaite about replacing him as team captain in 1997 when Simon's contract ended.

Bradley, on the other hand, had made only one further recording. His star was on the wane. No wonder, thought Henry, that he growled. I'd growl, he thought, if I was him.

'It's a shame that I'm in the kitchen today,' he said. 'We could have . . .'

Denzil limped in, his walking stick banging sharply on the floor. He looked older than ever, and he smelt of ointment.

'Denzil!' said Henry.

'I need a shoulder to cry on,' said Denzil.

Oh God!

'Bradley, this is an old friend of mine, Denzil Ackerman,' said Henry. 'We go back a long way. Denzil was a colleague on the *Thurmarsh Evening Argus*.'

'I do so love the provinces,' said Bradley. 'It's a shame I never seem to get to them.'

Greg hurried up to Denzil.

'Good afternoon, sir,' he said. 'I see it says men are safer than women with supermarket trolleys, would you believe?'

'Change the tape,' muttered Bradley.

'What can I get you, sir?' asked Greg to Denzil.

'A glass of red wine, please. Have you a merlot?'

'Greg, this isn't going to work this morning,' said Henry, as Greg poured Denzil's wine. 'You'll have to chef today.'

'Difficult changing halfway through. I need to have a feel for the ingredients. I need to psych myself into it like. Can't just go in and do it stone cold like.'

'I know, I know, but it can't be helped. We have to. I just have to talk to these people.'

'Got you,' said Greg reluctantly.

As Henry was taking off his apron, he heard Denzil say, to Bradley, 'I know you, don't I?'

Good old Denzil. If he could charm Bradley . . . but then, unfortunately, Denzil continued, 'Do you work in the men's department at Peter Jones?'

'You'll have seen Bradley on *A Question of Salt*, Denzil,' said Henry hastily.

'Oh yes! Of course! I remember you now,' said Denzil. 'All that amusing stuff you did about Hieronymus Bouillabaise. Will you go back on the show, do you think?'

'I've been on fourteen times over the years,' said Bradley sniffily.

'Oh,' said Denzil. 'Sorry. Lampo and I don't watch much telly. We prefer Scrabble. Henry, is there any chance of a couple of minutes before you get busy?'

'It's pretty busy already,' said Henry. 'Let's get your orders sorted out first, shall we? The dishes of the day are navarin of lamb, veal escalope marsala, hake Lampo, and the vegetarian dish is rata marseillaise.'

'I've never heard of hake Lampo,' said Bradley.

'No. It's a dish I created specially for a friend called Lampo Davey.'

' "Friend"!' said Denzil. 'Some friend.'

'It's on a bed of crushed garlicky broad beans with a sharp soy and sherry sauce,' said Henry.

'I cook that,' said Denzil.

'Yes, Lampo told me. I created it for him on his birthday, if you remember.'

'I'll never cook it again. The bastard!' said Denzil.

'Oh dear. So, gentlemen, what's it to be?'

'What's the rata marseillaise?' asked Denzil.

'It's a spicy, saffrony vegetable casserole with hard-boiled eggs and couscous.'

'I don't fancy the sound of it.'

Henry frowned at Denzil, trying to get him to be more positive in his attitude to the food in the presence of Bradley. It didn't do any good.

'Is the veal humanely reared?'

'Of course.'

'I'll have the navarin of lamb.'

Henry turned to Bradley and smiled. This was what catering led you into – frowning at people you loved, smiling at people you hated.

'I'll have the hake Lampo,' said Bradley.

Henry handed the orders to a waiter, and said, 'I'm sorry, Bradley, it's so good to see you here, but I think Denzil needs a word with me.'

'Please, Henry, don't even think about it,' said Bradley with a thin-lipped smile. 'I enjoy my own company. I have to. I get so much of it.'

Unbeknown to its owner, who hated this mawkish self-pity, Henry's left arm took it upon itself to give Bradley Tompkins a brief, sympathetic touch. Oh God.

Henry poured himself a large glass of the tempranillo and sat with Denzil in the window, in the glow of the sunny Frith Street morning.

'This'll have to be brief, I'm afraid,' he said. 'So what's up?'

'Lampo has retired.'

'What?'

'Finished with work two weeks ago.'

'Good God! He might have told me.'

'He might have told *me*.'

Henry gawped at him.

'What??'

'Exactly. He's away, Henry. An international conference on forgery, in the Channel Isles. He's always forbidden me to ring him at work, except in emergencies. Our boiler's blown. We've no hot water. I think that's an emergency, and I'm a bit beyond dealing with such things. I phoned. "Hello. This is Denzil Ackerman here, Mr Davey's partner. I wonder if you could give me a contact number in the Channel Isles for him." "I'm afraid not. I don't know it, sir." "Well you must have a number for the conference." "What conference?" "The international conference on forgery." "I think you must be confused, sir. There is no conference, and Mr Davey retired a fortnight ago." I felt such a fool, Henry. Such a dreadful fool. The humiliation! "You must be confused, sir." The smarminess of that voice will haunt me to my grave, or till next Thursday, whichever is the sooner.'

Henry knew that he had to get serving, yet he couldn't snub Denzil.

It was at this moment that he saw the great moon face of Tosser Pilkington-Brick, set in a grim expression as the man strode to the bar in his financial services suit and ghastly Old Daltonian tie.

'Oh God. Sod's Law is alive and well and living in Frith Street,' said Henry.

'What?'

'Never mind. Oh, Denzil, I'm sorry.'

'You know where the bastard is, don't you?'

'No idea.'

'In Siena, with that man of his. In Siena, Henry, seducing him with its beauty, doing what he failed to do with you. In Siena, *our* Siena, sullying the memory of our first meeting.'

'How do you know he is?'

'I got a postcard this morning. How's that for tact? The only postcard in the history of tourism ever to arrive from Italy before the sender gets home. Apologising for having misled me. Says he loves me. Says he loves me, Henry.'

'Well he does.'

'He's a funny way of showing it. If the postcard had come yesterday, I wouldn't have made a fool of myself on the phone.'

'Sod's Law again. Look, Denzil, I usually try to pop home round about three. Hang around and come back with me and we'll have a proper chat. I just have to go now.'

Henry hurried towards the bar.

A middle-aged woman approached him, matronly, on the stout side, beaming and unstoppable.

'It's Henry, isn't it?'

'Yes.' (Do I know you? he thought. If not, it's 'Mr Pratt', if you don't mind. This was a woman made to provoke such a reaction. Her unstoppability was barely tolerable.)

'I knew it was! I said to Anne-Marie, "That's him!" Anne-Marie's my friend.'

'Excellent!' (What's excellent about it? Adjectives should be banned.)

'Only we saw you on the telly on that programme and we like you.'

'Thank you.' (Oh God. I've just realised that I'm going to have to be polite to everyone from now on.)

'We think you're what I call "rib-tickling".'

(Dear God.) 'Thank you!'

'Normally we go to a nice little place in Old Compton Street. Of course you get some odd people in that street nowadays, but not so much in the café, and they do a nice pasta.'

'Excellent.' (Madam, I do not have all day. Can you not see that I am caught on the horns of a triangle whose angles are explosions of human misery and need?)

'But I said to Anne-Marie, "Anne-Marie," I said . . . (Good God, woman. Isn't it bad enough that she has two names without your having to say both names twice?) . . . "We can have a pasta any time. Any day of the week." (Repetition. Get on with it.) "Let's go and see what nice Mr Pratt can tempt us with." (Nothing. Sod off. Is fame worth this?) "We might even catch a glimpse of him." (You have. Now move it.)'

'Lovely! Excuse me, but . . .'

'You wouldn't sign a book for me, would you? I mean, I'm sorry it's not one of yours, but . . .'

'I haven't written any.'

'What? You must have. You're a chef. It's actually by another chef. Robert Carrier. They don't make them like him any more. You don't mind, do you?'

'Of course not, madam!' (Smile and get it over with, be

good-humoured, crack a joke.) 'He always cooked game very well.' He added 'and Henry Pratt' beneath 'Best of luck, Monica, from Robert Carrier'. 'You must try his Carrier Pigeon some time.' (She doesn't get it. She thinks I'm rib-tickling, but she doesn't get it. Thick as a tournedos Rossini.) 'There! Now excuse me. Sorry.'

At last he reached Tosser.

'Tosser! What a privilege.'

He hadn't meant to say 'Tosser'. Not today. It was all the fault of that bloody woman, irritating him.

'Yes,' said Tosser. 'I noticed how you rushed to get to me.'

'I tried! I couldn't help it. I was waylaid.'

'Are they in?'

'I would think so. It's their day off.'

'I know. That's why I'm here. One of my clients employs Darren, would you believe? Ben hasn't spoken to me once, you know. Not once. I want to see him, Henry. I know I've let him down, but I am human and I do want to see him.'

'I understand. Go up, if you want to.'

Ben and Darren had believed that they wouldn't be able to lead their lives in the house off Clapham Common, but the flat on the top floor of the Café had been a different proposition. When Hilary thought of it, neither she nor Henry could believe that it hadn't occurred to them before. Ben and Darren had jumped at the idea, delighted to live in the middle of Soho. They had insisted on paying rent. Ben wasn't selling the *Big Issue* any more: he couldn't cope with much more rain falling on his frail body. He was stacking supermarket shelves. Darren had a job as a courier. He charged round London on a Yamaha.

Tosser went upstairs, and Henry hurried over to Bradley.

'Tosser and I go back even further than Denzil,' he said. 'I fagged for him at school. We were both married to the same woman . . . not at the same time, I hasten to add. His son lives upstairs.'

'You don't have to apologise to me,' said Bradley. 'I know that I come at the bottom of the pecking order. It's natural. Believe me, I'm very happy just to sit here and soak up the atmosphere of your little place, while I'm waiting to be served. I know that freshly cooked food takes time. I'm not complaining about the delay.'

'I'll go and chase it up,' said Henry.

Tosser banged on the door of the flat. There was no reply. He knocked more loudly.

'Let me in. I know you're in there,' he shouted.

There was a shouted reply from quite a long way inside the flat.

'No.'

'I'm your father, damn it.'

'Are you visiting the Café?' shouted Ben. 'What are you having for lunch? I'm having Darren. *Very* tasty. I might have seconds.'

'You're depraved. Let me in.'

'You wouldn't like it. I'm up his bum.'

'Disgusting.'

'Then piss off. You aren't my father. Henry's my father now.'

*

Bradley's food was just about ready. Henry hurried over to him with a basket of bread.

'It's on its way, Bradley.' He put the basket on the table. 'Our bread today is bread flavoured.'

'I beg your pardon?'

'I don't go in for exotic breads. I believe that simple good bread is the perfect accompaniment. If the food is sufficiently flavoured and complex, the bread should be simple. Exotic breads can add confusions of taste, I believe.'

Greg hurried over with Bradley's hake Lampo. Henry was only too aware of Denzil sitting there, waiting for his meal, looking old and broken, but then Tosser entered, very slowly, with a face as grim as a quarry. His sadness drew Henry to him.

'He wouldn't speak to me.'

'I'm sorry. Have a drink.'

'I can't think of drink at a time like this.'

'On the house.'

'I suppose a glass of claret might go down all right. He said that you're his father now.'

'I've done nothing to make him think like that, Nigel.' Henry hadn't the heart to call him Tosser at that moment.

'Oh, I believe you. I've no quarrel with you.'

'Good. I've tried to get him to see you. There you are. Cheers.'

'Cheers. He's stacking supermarket shelves, Henry.'

'He enjoys it. That's all that matters, isn't it? He says it's not nearly as boring as you might imagine.'

'No, but, I mean, the fruit of my loins, stacking supermarket shelves.'

Henry tried not to grimace. He didn't like to think about Tosser's loins.

'I find it humiliating.'

'Nigel, that's silly.'

'What does Diana think?'

'She's just pleased that he's happy for the first time in his life. They've been over to stay twice.'

'Gunter doesn't mind?'

'Not a bit.'

'I find that hard to believe. He's Swiss.'

'I'm sorry, Nigel, but I'm going to have to go. We're getting busy. Will you stay to eat?'

'I couldn't. I wouldn't digest it, with the thought of them doing things up there. He was very rude, Henry. Really very rude.'

'He's very bitter. You can't expect anything else.'

'I suppose not.'

'Why did you come?'

'It was stupid, I know. I . . . I do have a conscience, Henry. I am human. I . . . did love Benedict. Once upon a time. I wanted to see him. I wanted . . . some kind of relationship.'

'I don't think it's possible. You've closed the only relationship that would be meaningful to him. I'm sorry, Nigel, but you can't have it both ways.' Their eyes met. 'Yes, I know. *He* is, but don't even think about that. Have another glass.'

'Better not, Henry. I have to drive. Some of us have to work.'

'What do you think I'm doing? Having lunch?

'Actually, I'm retiring in three weeks. Just time to take out a pension at a very favourable rate.'

'I'll think about it.'

'You do that small thing.'

Tosser walked out, wearily.

Trade remained brisk. Service remained slow. Greg had never quite caught up.

'Will our food be long?' asked matronly Monica loudly as Henry passed her table.

'Hours,' said Henry. 'It's chaos in there. You should have gone for that pasta.'

'*Well!*' said Monica. 'And to think we came here because we liked you! Come on, Anne-Marie.'

Monica stormed out, unstoppably. Anne-Marie, who was hungry, was sucked out in her slipstream. Never ever do that again, Henry. You can't afford to. Things get around. Reputations are destroyed. There are always some pleasures that one has to deny oneself.

As the two women left, in came Geoff Little, who formed half of the decidedly filthy double act of Little and Often, closely followed by Peter Stackpool, who, after much careful thought, said, 'I can't resist the pull of the ham salad today.' What with one thing and another, Henry didn't get a chance to speak to Bradley again until he came out of the Gents and went up to the bar to pay his bill.

'What a show-off!' he said.

Henry assumed that Bradley was referring to a photograph showing Henry's head on the body of Michelangelo's David, which had been mocked-up up in a studio run by one of his regular customers, and which now adorned the Gents.

'A little bit of self-mockery, Bradley. I try not to take

myself too seriously,' said Henry, and immediately wished that he hadn't. Bradley's mouth gave a tiny, tense twitch.

'My bill, please,' he said.

'No, no,' Henry insisted. 'It's on the house. I'm just sorry I couldn't spend more time with you. It's been one of those mornings.'

The phone rang. Henry didn't want to break off his farewell to Bradley, so he asked Fran, the work experience girl, to answer it.

'Well, thank you,' said Bradley Tompkins.

There was a brief silence, into which Henry might have inserted a question such as 'I hope everything was to your satisfaction' or Bradley might have volunteered something like 'It was very good', but neither did. Nevertheless, Henry felt afterwards that everything might have been all right if Fran hadn't held out the phone and said, 'It's for you', adding the unnecessary details 'It's Protein Films. They want you to appear on *Here's One I Made Earlier*.'

Henry took the phone from her.

'Hello,' said a breathless girl who spoke too fast. 'I'm . . .' He couldn't catch her name. 'We're very impressed with what you're doing on *A Question of Salt*. We'd love you to be on the show, if you're interested.'

'Very much so.'

Bradley just stood there, with a strange half-smile, half-smirk on his face.

'You know the format, do you?' said the girl.

'I've seen it. It's a kind of competition between two chefs, isn't it? Each one brings a dish of their own, and there's a vote on which is better.'

'That's right. We just wondered – we always ask this – if there's anybody you wouldn't want to do the show with.'

Henry couldn't stop his neck swivelling, so that he could have a quick, anxious look at Bradley.

'Er . . . that's an awkward one,' he said. 'I . . . I might need to think about that.'

He was almost certain that Bradley realised what he'd just been asked.

'That may not be necessary,' said the girl, 'because we've got a suggestion. We thought we might put you up against Sally Atkinson. We thought the dynamics of that might work rather well.'

'Yes, I . . . yes, I think the . . . er . . . the dynamics of that might work very well. Yes, she'd be fine.'

His heart was thudding. How it thudded! He shook with the intensity of his desire for Sally Atkinson. He knew in that moment that he had never really wanted Nicky, he'd only thought he had.

He was convinced that Bradley could hear the thudding of his heart; Cousin Hilda's sniff certainly could. It came loud and clear.

Bradley Tompkins nodded strangely, turned abruptly and walked briskly to the door. He raised one arm in farewell. He didn't turn round. The effect was contemptuous.

Henry felt as if he was going to pass out. There was an ache in his balls. He had to grab hold of the bar counter for support. He was sweating. Then his funny turn passed off. He poured himself a glass of the tempranillo and joined Denzil for a moment.

'One question,' said Denzil. 'I wouldn't dare ask it if I wasn't getting a bit pissed.'

'What is it, Denzil?'

'Did *you* know Lampo'd retired?'

'No.'

'You weren't invited to his farewell party?'

'That's two questions.'

'It's all one question. Are you my friend or are you in cahoots with him?'

'I'm never quite certain what a cahoot is, and whether there can ever be just one of them, but I'm certainly not in two or more of them, whatever they are. In fact he once asked me for two tickets for one of the shows. I told him what I thought of his treachery, and refused.'

'Thank you, Henry. I'm glad of that. I'm sorry I had to ask. Misery distorts the mind.'

Ben and Darren emerged dozily from their love nest, their bodies heavy from sleep and sex.

Ben admitted – almost shame-facedly, but not quite – what he had said to his father.

Henry sat them with Denzil, who looked put out at no longer having Henry's undivided attention. Henry cracked open another bottle of wine and joined them. Ben and Darren breakfasted at twenty past two on navarin of lamb, Ben eating with careful enjoyment of every mouthful, as if he had to catch up on fifteen years of lost delight. As he ate, he talked about his job stacking supermarket shelves.

'It's not boring at all,' he told Denzil, revealing slightly too much half-chewed lamb as he talked. 'Not at all. I mean, it's fascinating what people buy and what they don't buy. Take apricots. I am here to tell you that I do not work in an apricot-loving area. Take mulligatawny soup. On a Wednesday, I'll be putting out thirty or forty tins. On a Thursday, zilch. Why does nobody buy our mulligatawny soup on a Thursday? Monday, John West tuna goes faster than our brand. Tuesday, a very different story. It's fascinating.'

Henry couldn't remember when he had last seen somebody less fascinated than Denzil, but Darren couldn't take his eyes off Ben, listening adoringly to his every word.

Actually, Henry found it curiously fascinating, this secret world of supermarket preferences, but it disturbed him, he couldn't tie it in with the arrogant golden boy of Ben's youth.

Denzil flinched almost imperceptibly when Darren laid down his knife and fork and placed his hand firmly on Ben's thigh.

'Are you homophobic?' asked Darren, who missed nothing.

'He can't be,' said Henry with a smile. 'He's gay.'

'Dear dear Henry,' said Denzil sadly. 'Dear dear boy. How you do crave simplicity. I am gay, yes, but that doesn't mean I like *other* gays. Thank you for the kind offer of tea with the delectable Hilary. I rather think the time has passed, don't you?'

He picked up his elegant stick, stood up and limped out into the afternoon sunshine with dignity.

Henry invited Darren and Ben instead, but they never had their tea, because, when Henry got to his car, he found that all his tyres had been slashed. He could see Bradley doing it, almost as clearly as if he'd caught him in the act.

It wasn't the act of vandalism itself that upset Henry. That was a nuisance, but no more. The dreadful thing was that the slashes were so deep and vicious: he felt certain that, as Bradley was doing it, the tyres weren't tyres at all. They were Henry's face.

9 *Here's One I Made Earlier*

Before too many years had passed, Henry would be steeped in controversy and catastrophe. The summer of 1996, however, was an unusually peaceful time in his life.

Between 2 May, when his tyres were slashed, and 11 September, when he recorded an edition of *Here's One I Made Earlier* with Sally Atkinson, Henry didn't hear Cousin Hilda's posthumous sniff once. He began to hope that he had shaken it off for good.

The memory of the viciousness of those slashes to his tyres faded. He allowed himself to believe that it had been a one-off incident.

When it had been suggested that he should do the show with Sally, Henry had been taken off guard and had discovered that he could hardly cope with the extraordinary extent of his desire for her.

All that summer he had thought about her, and prepared himself for their meeting. He forced himself to control his emotions. He prepared himself for a day of professional friendship, during which he would let drop no hint of the feelings he might have allowed himself if he hadn't made these preparations.

He was in control of himself.

He tried to concentrate on those world events that fitted his mood. There were disasters, of course. A TWA plane from New York's Kennedy Airport crashed into the

Atlantic, and all two hundred and thirty passengers died. A pipe bomb killed one person and injured a hundred and eleven at the Olympic Games in Atlanta. He told himself how lucky he was and reminded himself every day to feel grateful for his good fortune.

Iceland legalised gay marriages. Henry could just imagine Tosser's indignant reaction – 'That's Reykjavik off the list, Felicity' – but he was happy for the gay men of Iceland. Now they could be gay in the original sense of the word as well. He took Ben and Darren to The Gay Hussar in Greek Street, just round the corner, raised a glass of Tokay, and said, loudly, 'To every gay in Iceland.'

Nelson Mandela attended a state banquet with the Queen as host, and in South Africa F.W. de Klerk apologised for the pain and suffering caused by apartheid. If there had been a South African restaurant in London, Henry would have gone to it and raised a glass of pinotage.

An eight-year-old female gorilla called Biriti Juan rescued a three-year-old boy who fell eighteen feet into a gorilla pit. The gorilla picked him up very gently and carried him to the entrance. Henry put up a notice which stated, 'Gorillas, yes. Guerrillas, no.'

It was a happy summer for Hilary too. At last she had finished her book, and she was pleased with it. It was a story loosely based on the life of her crippled mother Nadezda and her councillor father Howard. It dealt with matters that had affected her and Henry's lives deeply. It featured a newspaper very like the *Thurmarsh Evening Argus*, with journalists not entirely dissimilar to Ted and Helen Plunkett, and Colin Edgeley, and Ginny Fenwick and . . . yes, and Henry too. The fiction writer's art transformed these people so that, when they read the book, if they read the book, they might not even recognise themselves. It was a story about the clash between public and private morality, public and private duty, honour and expediency, love and self-interest, right and wrong. Her publishers loved it. Henry loved it, although he thought the main journalist (the one loosely based on him) unconvincingly moral and caring.

His regular appearances on *A Question of Salt* brought Henry greater and greater recognition. Newspapers rang to ask his opinion about diets and fads and allergies. The Café Henry was constantly full, and, after some soul-searching as to the advisability, it was decided that a modest and very gradual expansion would be a good thing, provided that standards were maintained and it never developed into a franchised chain. A site for a second café was purchased, in South Kensington.

Henry began to think about writing a book.

Occupation of the upstairs flat by Ben and Darren was a great success. Ben continued to enjoy his work, and Darren continued to hurtle round London on his Yamaha, revelling in his speed and skill. On their day off they would sometimes eat in the Café, and Henry would try to sit with them for at least a few minutes. Ben would talk about this other Ben, the Ben he barely remembered, the Ben he was told about. He said that as the weeks and months passed he was beginning to remember and understand his old self. 'I was ambitious. Now I'm not remotely ambitious. The thing I've understood is that there is nothing wrong with ambition, nothing at all, but there is nothing wrong with lack of ambition either.'

Henry turned this into a notice, which pleased Ben enormously. He also created a very silly notice which he showed to anybody unwise enough to comment on Darren's nose stud. It read, 'I intend to open a nose stud and breed noses.' One day Ben thought of a notice that made them all laugh. 'This notice is exactly the right length to fill this gap.' Henry felt proud of him. He often forgot that Ben wasn't his son.

Kate's play about the homeless provided another critical and commercial success for the prestigious Umbrella Theatre.

By midsummer's day Jack's firm were a total of one hundred and twenty-seven days behind at starting jobs and one hundred and sixty-three days behind at finishing them. 'We're a success,' he cried, as he pranced around the garden at one of his barbecues.

Camilla had an exhibition in Mayfair. A painting of the wild horses of the Camargue went for £16,000.

Henry and Hilary went for a delightful long weekend near Lucerne with Diana and Gunter. Over the four days Henry had one steak, two train rides, three portions of rosti, four litres of beer and five fillings. It was the first time he had left the Café in the hands of Greg and Michelle for any length of time. At last his confidence in them was growing.

Nothing went wrong in his absence to dent that confidence, so a few weeks later they went away again, to stay in Copenhagen, where Hilary's younger brother Sam lived with his Danish wife, Greta. Sam had been pretty obnoxious as a boy, but now they all got on well. Henry took Sam to one side, though, and said, 'Don't.' 'Don't what?' asked Sam. 'Do it,' said Henry. 'Do what?' asked Sam. 'Have that affair you're dreaming of.' Sam went white. 'How do you know that?' he said. 'I can read you like an open sandwich,' said Henry.

While Henry was in Copenhagen, giving advice on not having affairs, Sally Atkinson visited the Café.

'Good afternoon, madam. I see that Boris Yeltsin has been re-elected President of Russia, I don't think it's surprising, do you? Speaking of surprises, can I get you something unusual?' said Greg.

'A glass of champagne would be nice,' said Sally. 'Is Henry anywhere about?'

'I'm afraid he's in Denmark.'

When he told Henry of her visit, Greg said, 'Her face fell. You're well in there with that one.'

Henry shook his head and said, 'Those days are behind me, Greg. I will never be naughty again. Hilary is too precious to me. She's a jewel.'

'Got you,' said Greg.

They didn't see or hear from Tosser or Felicity once, and neither did Ben.

Bradley Tompkins was also conspicuous by his absence. Apparently he had a place in the country and spent quite a lot of time there. No wonder he didn't win any Michelin stars, thought Henry. His was a business, not a passion.

Even a visit to Denzil and Lampo for a take-away – Denzil didn't cook any more and Lampo never had – proved less painful than expected.

'Before we eat, we must tell you what happened,' said Lampo. 'I . . . it was very naughty of me. I didn't tell

Denzil I'd retired. I wanted one glorious week with . . . I don't give him a name.'

'I said, "I don't want to know his name," ' said Denzil. ' "I might start picturing him." '

'I had a glorious week. In Siena, actually.'

'Yes, so we heard,' said Henry.

'We . . . we went to that restaurant, actually, in the square, where you two met.'

Hilary gave an enormous, rather strange sigh.

'That was an enormous, rather strange sigh,' said Lampo. 'Do you resent my going there?'

'I have no reason to,' said Hilary. 'Denzil might. Not me. No, I suddenly thought, supposing we'd not met. I wouldn't be here now, with Henry. The enormity of that shocks me. It's very sobering.'

'Very sobering,' said Henry. 'Could we have some more wine?'

'Fill their glasses, Lampo,' said Denzil. 'He's my legs now,' he told them. He tapped nervously on a miniature Yugoslavian biscuit tin, purchased in Dubrovnik. 'Go on, Lampo. Tell them it all.'

'I loved showing him Italy,' said Lampo. 'It was weak of me, but . . . I am human. I fully intended to tell Denzil, on my return, that I was retiring. There would have been no more lies.'

'I accept that,' said Denzil. 'I believe him.'

'He wouldn't speak to me for three days, when I got back,' said Lampo.

'I found it hard to believe that he hadn't had a farewell party,' said Denzil. 'It narked me to have missed it.'

'As if I would,' said Lampo. '*So* banal.'

'I accept that now,' said Denzil.

'I see the person with no name at least once every week,' said Lampo. 'Denzil accepts that, and asks no questions. I'll never stay overnight again. Denzil doesn't like that.'

'It's nerves, not sex,' said Denzil. 'I fear burglars. My biscuit tins . . . I couldn't bear to lose them. There's no sex in our relationship any more. He is repelled by my pale, thin, twisted, tired old body, my old man's breath, my hollow chest, my scrawny pudenda.'

'One should never be surprised that he exaggerates,' said Lampo. 'He was a journalist, after all.'

On Monday, 16 September, 1996, Gerry Adams, President of Sinn Fein, said in his first speech in Stormont that he wanted to 'make friends' with Doctor Ian Paisley, Leader of the Democratic Unionist Party; Frank Dobson, the Health Secretary, confirmed that Viagra would not be available on the National Health Service until further notice; and Henry Ezra Pratt, who didn't wish to make friends with Gerry Adams or Doctor Ian Paisley, and had never needed Viagra, got into a taxi with a box of ingredients and a saucepan full of one he had made earlier.

The format of *Here's One I Made Earlier* was really very simple. Two chefs were invited to create a dish. Each chef was allowed to bring a maximum of three examples of the dish at various stages of the cooking, and one which had to be the finished article. The two chefs talked their way through the cooking process, in turn, three minutes from one, then three from the other, then back to the first, etcetera. At the end the chefs tasted each other's dishes and marked them, the technicians tasted the dishes, a celebrity visitor tasted the dishes, and three members of the public, chosen at random from closely vetted volunteers, tasted the dishes. Everyone who tasted the dishes gave marks, and a winner was declared. The winner took home a substantial prize. The loser took nothing.

Since the beginning of September Henry's peace of mind had gradually burnt away like autumn mist. There was no getting away from the fact that his sense of control was slipping away, and he was becoming more than a little obsessed with Sally Atkinson. The thought of competing with her filled him with excitement, both sexual and professional, and with dread, also both sexual and professional. She had a Michelin star. He wouldn't be able to compete. She aroused him terrifically, and he was a happily married man. He was a tiny raft, being bounced on converging tides and crosswinds, in a most perilous waterway.

If only Hilary could have come, to save him from himself, but she had another of her publishing engagements.

Be good, Henry, he told himself in the taxi. Be grown up. Don't be a berk. Don't cause distress to your family and friends. Don't let your public down.

My public – the thought took his breath away, just as the taxi lurched rather too fast round a steep bend. He only just managed to cling on to the saucepan.

He leant forward very carefully.

'Excuse me,' he said. 'Would you mind driving a bit more slowly? Only I've got the one I've made earlier here and I don't want to spill it.'

'Sorry?'

'I'm appearing on the show *Here's One I Made Earlier* and you have to bring with you the one you made earlier, and I have.'

'I haven't the faintest idea what you're on about, squire.'

Perhaps the thought that he had a public to let down was a bit of an exaggeration. If he did have a public, it had melted away when he needed it. Perhaps that was what publics did. Suddenly he felt very insignificant. Suddenly he felt that he might be imagining that Sally fancied him. He'd reflected once or twice recently how strange it was that, after moments of desperation when he'd been convinced that no woman would ever fancy him, he had begun to believe that almost every woman did.

The excitement of his appearances on *A Question of Salt* had gone to his head. They were nothing. It was nothing. He was nothing. In the great world of the media, he was a speck, a pathetic, deluded speck.

As the taxi pulled up at the obscure studios of Protean Television – it had turned out not to be Protein Television after all – in a very obscure street in Brondesbury, Henry felt a little boy again. He felt desperately uncertain now about his choice of fish stew. He could imagine a communal 'ugh' going up from the viewers. Sally had a Michelin star. She had enjoyed the favours of several chefs. He didn't stand a chance with her, publicly or pubicly. She would eat him for breakfast. As it were.

A cold London autumn morning. A plump, grey-haired man of sixty-one, clutching a saucepan full of cold fish stew. My public! Don't be ridiculous.

He walked up to the young woman on the reception desk. He was very conscious that he carried around with him a strong whiff of fish. Today of all days surely one of the receptionists could have said, 'Mr Pratt! Good to see you' or 'Good morning, Henry. I hope you don't mind my calling you Henry. I feel as if I know you already.' No. The receptionist at Protean Television sniffed and said, 'You must be for the food programme. Name?'

They kissed, politely, professionally, two contenders in a TV game, but then his eyes took over and gazed suddenly at her eyes at the moment when her eyes shot an impulsive look at his. Both held the look for what seemed an eternity, but might only have been a few seconds in real time.

Henry was fascinated by Sally's eyes. They were pale blue, very pale blue, and they were beautiful. However, what touched him most was the weariness in them, and what disturbed him most was their ambiguity. They seemed frank and evasive at the same time.

He turned away before she did. He'd known that he would have to.

'Hilary not with you?' she asked.

'No. No. I . . . I wanted her to come . . .'

Their eyes met again – briefly, this time.

'. . . but she has another engagement. Actually, as it's not a studio audience sort of set up, she might have been a bit of a . . . er . . .'

'. . . spare prick.'

'Exactly. As it were.'

'Yes. Not really very appropriate. Well, to work, then. Good luck. May the best chef win.'

'Oh, I hope not, but I'll not be too upset if you do.'

'What are you cooking?'

'Well, I . . .' Oh God. I feel so ashamed of it. It's fine to knock up a great fish stew for supper, but as the subject of a TV show, what possessed you? '. . . I . . . I thought that with you having a Michelin star and everything . . .'

'Oh God. It's a millstone round my neck, Henry.'

'. . . that I'd go for something really simple. It's my special . . . er . . . fish stew . . . fish casserole, I mean. That's part of the trouble, I don't know what to call it.'

'Prattabaisse.'

'What?'

'Like bouillabaisse, only yours.'

'Sorry. My brain must have seized up. Sally, I just wish I wasn't here.'

'Good God, man, don't you think I do too? I'm a private person. I'm a dedicated, professional chef. Poncing around on TV isn't me, but there aren't enough prosperous gourmets in Dorset to fill my place, and the exposure doesn't half bring the punters in. Anyway, we're here, we've agreed to do it, so it's pointless to moan.'

Henry felt about two foot high. Sally touched him on the shoulder, gently. 'Utterly professional, eh?'

'Absolutely. I . . . I haven't asked you what you're making.'

'Well, I thought I ought to make something a bit challenging, a bit technical, a bit messed about, a bit Michelin star. I mean, this is what today's about, isn't it? The Michelin Star versus the People's Chef.'

'I hadn't looked at it that way.'

'I'm making a guinea fowl and pistachio galantine, with a tarragon and chablis reduction.'

The studio was quite small, and seemed very bare after the big BBC job. It was like working in a barn. You had to make your own glamour.

There were seats for the three chosen members of the public, and there was a paper door through which the mystery celebrity would burst.

The members of the public weren't called for the rehearsal, nor was the mystery celebrity, who was played in the run-through by the stage manager.

Henry discovered, to his horror, that they actually did cook the dishes on the run-through. He should have brought the two that he'd made earlier. Sally had piles of stuff, as she was introducing three different stages, all of which she had to have ready twice.

'You didn't read your bumf, did you?' said the presenter, Dermot Wolfstone, he of the indefatigable smile, soon to become runner-up to Tony Blair in the 'Smiler of the Year' competition.

'No,' admitted Henry sadly, 'I didn't read my bumf.'

This was terrible. Was he to start every new TV project feeling like this?

'It doesn't matter in your case since you aren't really going through any stages as it's all in one,' said Dermot Wolfstone with a smile. 'You'll just have to mime your casserole.'

The run-through was a nightmare to Henry. He lacked all conviction. Sally, on the other hand, was professional, detached and poised.

He felt a real fool, miming preparing his fish, miming chopping an onion and two cloves of garlic, miming frying them, miming the addition of white wine and pernod and a tin of tomatoes and hot paprika and saffron and star anise, miming taking it all off the stove and lifting the lid.

'Wow,' said Dermot Wolfstone with a smile. 'Those aromas! And now, our celebrity guest. Top model, Samantha Hamstring, with her gorgeous long legs and elegant, shapely breasts, and how *does* she keep that stomach of hers so taut and tight?'

Through the paper door – no expense was spared – burst the paunchy, hairy form of the stage manager, so everybody fell about. Henry pretended to find it funny too, and hoped that Sally was only pretending.

'Well,' said Dermot Wolfstone with a smile. 'That honestly really was . . . average.'

There was no Green Room at Protean Television, but Sally had brought a bottle of rioja.

'Fancy a drink in my dressing room?' she asked.

Don't, Henry. Don't be a berk. Think of Hilary. Besides, there will be plenty of time for a drink afterwards, and it would be very unwise to indulge beforehand.

'I honestly don't think I dare,' he said.

He hoped that she would believe that he was talking about the drink.

In his dressing room, which was actually somebody's office, Henry told himself again and again, 'You have a wonderful wife. You have a wonderful family. Don't throw it all away. Don't don't don't.'

Oh God, he wished it was over, his wretched fish stew forgotten, Sally and he parting with a chaste kiss. If he'd never met Hilary and yet had ended up here with Sally this evening – an unlikely scenario – he knew that she would have been the perfect woman for him. But he already had the perfect woman.

He had to accept, as he thought about Sally, that he was feeling sexier by the second. He didn't fancy his chances of persuading himself to part with just a chaste kiss. This made him feel more and more tense.

Only one thing could release him from his tension and desire. He slid off to the loo, hoping nobody was watching. He felt as if he was back at Dalton College again, but even if he met somebody on the way, they wouldn't know why he was going to the loo. Nobody need ever know.

There was no harm in imagining that he was doing it with Sally. Yes, there was!

He would do it with Hilary. He would feel all the better for that. Nobody would ever know, but it was important to him.

He thought about his first meeting with her, in Siena, about the times in Durham, about the reunion after he'd been to Peru, about moments when he had been bursting with love just as now he was bursting with lust.

He conjured up his beloved in all her grave beauty, and gave her a right old seeing to in that unlovely toilet in Brondesbury.

He felt happy.

He felt good.

He felt virtuous.

He felt far too knackered to even contemplate cooking a bloody fish stew.

*

It was only an unimportant little TV show.

Everybody he knew and cared about would see him making a complete fool of himself.

It would be the end of his TV career.

He didn't care about his TV career.

It was rather fun, though.

Sally looked utterly composed.

The programme began. The opening credits and music were played on the sole monitor.

'Good evening, and welcome to another edition of *Here's One I Made Earlier*,' said Dermot Wolfstone with a smile. 'What a battle we have in prospect today. A battle between man and woman. A battle between – dare I say it? – professional and amateur. No insult intended, Henry.'

Henry forced a smile, a poor echo of Dermot's.

'A battle between a posh Michelin starred restaurant and a homely café. Ironically, the posh restaurant is in Dorset and the café is in Soho. It promises to be a *fascinating* contest. Ladies first. Sally Atkinson, of the Dorset Knob restaurant near Bridport, what delight are you making for us today?'

'I had a difficult choice,' said Sally. 'Yes, I have a Michelin star but, as the name of my restaurant suggests, I don't go for pretension. A Dorset knob is a local bread roll, Henry, in case you wondered.'

'Well I did rather, I must admit,' quipped Henry wittily.

'I've decided, though, that I have to make something that shows reasonably advanced professional techniques,' said Sally. 'I've chosen a guinea fowl and pistachio galantine, with a tarragon and chablis reduction.'

'Henry Pratt, of the Café Henry, in Frith Street in the heart of Soho, what have you chosen?'

'Fish stew,' said Henry in an exaggeratedly flat tone, timing it perfectly, relishing the contrast. A miracle had happened. The moment the camera was on him in earnest, all his doubts had fled. 'I wanted to make something that you could easily make at home, with no special techniques required. The term fish stew doesn't sound very promising, but I think my dish is very attractive: an English version of the great fish casseroles of central Italy or France. And of course you can use cheap fish or expensive fish; you can add smoked fish; you can have lots of shellfish or very little shellfish or indeed none at all; it can be an aristocratic dish or a peasant dish. The sauce is the thing that doesn't change, and you must be generous with this sauce, generous with all the ingredients. This should be a rich, sumptuous sauce, not a thin little thing, and every ingredient should play a vital part. And use good wine – always.'

Why oh why had he worried? They were up and running. The contrast between their dishes, and their methods, and the enthusiasm of the two chefs, made this one of the finest editions of the programme. Sally worked with intense fine precision, Henry with largesse and vigour.

'And now it's time to introduce this week's mystery celebrity,' said Dermot Wolfstone with a smile. 'A lady of great beauty and charm, as well as brains and talent. You may not recognise her from her appearance, but many of you will know her for her books. She has written five novels.'

It couldn't be.

'. . . witty, yet serious books that achieve an unusual double – they please the public and the critics.'

It couldn't be.

'Her latest will be out shortly.'

It couldn't be. His beloved didn't leap smiling through paper doors.

She did!

'Yes, it's Hilary Lewthwaite.'

And she leapt smiling through the paper door, as if she did that sort of thing every day.

If she had smiled every day as she smiled that day, she would have run Dermot a good race for second place in the Smiler of the Year competition. She might even have had Tony Blair looking to his laurels.

'Hilary! It's a great pleasure to have you on *Here's One I Made Earlier*,' smiled Dermot.

'Thank you. It's a great pleasure to be here,' smiled Hilary.

'Tell us a bit about your new book, Hilary,' smiled Dermot. 'What's it called?'

'*Simpkins of the* Argus,' smiled Hilary. 'It's about a journalist on a local paper who uncovers a lot of municipal scandal that threatens the life of his wife's crippled mother.'

'Sounds fun,' smiled Dermot Wolfstone. 'Hilary, do you cook?'

'Well, yes to a certain extent, but I let my husband do most of the cooking. He's pretty good.' She smiled.

'Tell our viewers who your husband is, Hilary,' smiled Dermot.

'He's . . . standing just there.'

'Ladies and gentlemen, Henry Pratt's wife, Hilary Lewthwaite.'

Henry smiled and went over to Hilary and kissed her. He felt an absurd temptation to bring the show to a halt by saying, 'I suppose a fuck's out of the question', but he managed to resist it.

'Hilary?' smiled Dermot Wolfstone. 'Do you think your judgement of these two dishes can be unbiased?'

'Absolutely not, Dermot,' smiled Hilary. 'I'll probably bend over backwards to avoid charges of bias – and Sally's dish does sound wonderful.'

Hilary gave Sally five out of five and Henry four out of five. Henry and Sally each gave the other five out of five. The three members of the public voted for Henry by eight votes to seven. It was a tie at seventeen each – the first tie in the series.

When there was a tie, Dermot Wolfstone had the casting voice. 'I give the prize to Sally,' he smiled. 'She's prettier than Henry.'

'Hear hear,' said Henry rather too loudly, smiling.

'Well, thank you, Henry Pratt and Sally Atkinson and our faithful members of the public and of course our mystery celebrity, Hilary Lewthwaite,' said Dermot Wolfstone with his last, best smile.

Everybody was smiling as the final credits rolled, but at least a part of Henry didn't feel like smiling at all.

He felt weak at the thought of what might have happened if he had gone to Sally's dressing room before the show, not knowing that his wife would soon be, or indeed might already be, in the building.

He felt weak at the thought of what might have happened during the rest of the evening, if Hilary hadn't been there. He had been hoping to prove, by walking away from Sally Atkinson, that at last he was a responsible, grown-up family man. That chance had been snatched from him.

Would he have walked away that night? We will never know, and neither will he.

10 *Hooray, It's Henry*

Everyone in the television industry has a talent for something, if you look hard enough. Clive Porfiry was no exception. His talent was for lunch.

Some people said that he gave the best lunches in the business. In fact he often dined out on it. 'My lunches are legends in my own lifetime,' he often said.

He was equally brilliant at eating lunch and at giving it, having a rare combination of two contradictory qualities – greed and generosity. The only thing that he liked as much as eating a wonderful lunch was watching his guests eating wonderful lunches.

The BBC turned a blind eye to his enormous expense account, and he turned a blind eye to the relative smallness of his salary. What did he need a huge salary for? He had few pleasures beyond lunch, and that was paid for.

'I want to take you to lunch,' he told Henry on the phone. 'You're fast becoming a star. You're growing too big for *A Question of Salt*. It's time you had your own series. Do you know Il Mirtillo in Brewer Street? The osso buco is legendary.'

Henry arrived at the gleaming, immaculate little restaurant before his host. The decor was modern and airy, but the walls were dark from the cigarettes of decades. This was not some trendy upstart of a restaurant.

This was a place matured by twenty-two years of giving pleasure. It was therefore ignored by the trendy and the pretentious. He felt at home here from the start.

As he waited for his host, Henry reflected on his wisdom in turning down the offer to replace Simon Hampsthwaite as team captain. It had been an instinctive decision, and, on this occasion, unlike on so many other, his instincts had been correct.

He recognised Clive the moment he stepped through the door. He was a large, shambling man with a shining bald head and a very hairy chest, so that he looked as if he'd been born with a head of hair in the wrong place. He wore an open neck maroon shirt and a beige suit one size too small for him, as befitted a luncher.

Henry had taken the liberty of ordering an aperitif.

'Henry!'

Clive Porfiry clasped Henry's hand gently in his huge hands, as if it was a sick dormouse.

'What's that you're drinking?'

'Punt e mes. I hope you don't mind my starting.'

'Not at all. Splendid idea. I'll have the same.'

Clive Porfiry liked every alcoholic drink that had ever been brewed, distilled, blended or matured anywhere in the world, so he always had the same as his guests, which made his guests feel that they were arbiters of taste. What would he do if his guest chose something non-alcoholic? He didn't know. It had never happened. He chose his guests carefully.

When he had got his double punt e mes, Clive Porfiry raised his glass, clinked it with Henry's, and smiled expansively.

For the next two and a half hours, life will be really quite extraordinarily pleasant, said Clive Porfiry's beaming smile.

They studied their menus in contented silence. The Head Waiter appeared suddenly and silently at their table as if summoned from a bottle by magic.

'Have you decided, gentlemen?' he asked.

'I'm rather tempted by the osso buco you mentioned on the phone, Clive,' said Henry. 'And the linguine alla aragosta sounds irresistible.'

'An excellent choice. I'll have the same.'

Clive Porfiry liked every dish that had ever been roasted, boiled, fried, steamed, grilled, baked or cured by any chef anywhere in the world, so he always had the same as his guests, which made his guests feel like men or women of the world. What would he do if his guest turned out to have a small appetite and a leaning towards salad? He didn't know. It had never happened. He chose his guests carefully. He ordered bottles of white and red wine and said, 'Now. This series of yours. I thought perhaps seven half-hours, and studio-based. I've seen you work so well in studios. Do you have any ideas? Have you had a chance to think?'

'Well, I did have the thought of recording it in my Café, actually,' said Henry diffidently. 'I thought maybe we could close it every Sunday . . . we aren't really a Sunday place . . . invite some guests and . . . er . . . cook and eat a meal.'

'Marvellous idea,' said Clive Porfiry. 'When I said, "studio-based" I meant of course that I didn't see you going "on the road". No, your Café would be perfect. It'll become the studio. Excellent. And doing it on Sundays will mean lots of celebrities will be available.'

'I didn't think of using too many celebrities, actually,' said Henry. 'I was thinking more about people from real life.'

'Real life!' Clive Porfiry looked a little shocked, but luckily the wine arrived and he tasted the white very carefully and forgot his shock.

'Excellent.'

'You see I sort of thought that every programme might have a theme,' said Henry.

'A theme! That's good. No, that *is* good. The controller likes themes.'

'The controller?'

'I can't get this through on my own. I'll have to put it through several layers of management.'

Henry's face fell just as the lobster linguine arrived.

'Oh, don't worry. It'll go through all right.'

Henry's burly host gave a confident, encouraging smile, but then he suddenly looked worried, as if he'd thought of a major snag.

'Is the wine to your liking?' he asked.

'Sensational.'

Clive Porfiry relaxed.

'What sort of themes?' he asked.

'Themes based on people and events in my life. The personal touch. A kind of autobiography in food.'

'An autobiography in food! Brilliant.'

Worry returned to Clive's face. What now? thought Henry.

'Are you enjoying the linguine?' Clive asked anxiously.

'Lovely.'

Relief swept over the corpulent executive.

'There is a mood afoot . . .' he said, through a mouthful of linguine, '. . . yes, it is good, isn't it? . . . there is a mood afoot, in some quarters . . .' he took another mouthful '. . . to recognise that we are failing our core audience of the . . .' another mouthful '. . . mature and elderly. You can fill that gap.'

'I don't want to be a grey icon,' said Henry.

'Heavens, no. But you can be a standard bearer for the mature.'

'I agree with what you say, but I don't want the programme to be . . .' Henry took a mouthful '. . . in any way ageist. The way to combat ageism, as I see it, is to have all ages on, grannies, children, students, the lot, and never . . .' he took a mouthful '. . . refer to their ages.'

'Oh absolutely. We're singing from the same hymn book.'

Apart from moments of concern over whether Henry was enjoying the osso buco and the red wine, the meal proceeded calmly and smoothly until, as they finished their main courses, Clive Porfiry began to look *really* anxious.

'Er . . . do you think we could manage another bottle?' he said.

'Oh, I think so.'

Clive Porfiry gave a deep sigh of relief, and beamed.

'I have a very good feeling about this project,' he said. ' "Project". Can't just call it that. We need a title. I did think . . . see what you think of it . . . "A Pratt Among the Pans". Thirteen episodes of "A Pratt Among the Pans". Sounds good to me.'

Henry tried to hide his horror.

'I'm a bit tired of people making jokes about my name, to be honest,' he said.

'Fair enough. I thought a bit of self-mockery might be appealing, but if that's how you feel, fair enough.'

They ordered Gorgonzola cheese followed by the eponymous whortleberry semi-freddo. Clive Porfiry ordered a half bottle of dessert wine. Only then did he return to the thorny question of the title.

'OK,' he said. 'How about just plain "Pratt and his Pans"?'

'I really would prefer not to use my surname,' said Henry. 'I'd be very happy to use Henry, but not Pratt.'

'"Henry and his Pans",' mused Clive Porfiry. 'Yes. That sounds all right.'

'I'm not sure about the pans, that's the only thing,' said Henry. 'I wonder if they lose a bit of their oomph when we've no longer got the alliteration.'

'Good point. Good point. Probably lose quite a bit of their oomph, actually, and who wants oomphless pans? Henry and his . . . Henry and his . . . Henry and his . . . Ah!'

The Gorgonzola had arrived.

'In an hour or two it'd have begun to go walk-about, but at this moment in time it's sheer perfection,' said Clive Porfiry. 'Henry and his . . . Henry and his . . . I'm damned if I can think of anything in cookery beginning with H.'

'I did think,' began Henry diffidently, 'because it's what we hope people will say, I did think of "Hooray, It's Henry". I mean it has an appealing little alliteration, and there's an echo of Hooray Henries, one of which I am definitely not, so it could seem a bit ironic or even post-ironic.'

'"Hooray, It's Henry".' Clive Porfiry rolled the suggested title round his mouth, as if it was a sip of wine. '"Hooray, It's Henry".' He took a sip of wine, and rolled it round his mouth as if it was a suggested title. 'Do you know I think we may just have got it, between us? "Hooray, It's Henry". I can feel it. I can sense it. I can *hear* it. Twenty-six episodes of *Hooray, It's Henry* – an autobiography in food. Henry, we've cracked it. This merits a large grappa, I think.'

Later, when the series was commissioned and recorded, and proved a success, Clive Porfiry claimed the credit for every suggestion that Henry had made.

Henry didn't protest, for fear that he would never be given another lunch.

Clive Porfiry was *very* good at lunch.

Paul McCartney was knighted; the Queen opened the royal website; Labour won the 1997 General Election with a majority of a hundred and seventy-seven; William Hague succeeded John Major as Leader of the Conservative Party; Tony Blair announced that the Government would no longer supply free university education in Great Britain; Diana, Princess of Wales, and her friend Dodi were killed in a car crash in a Paris highway tunnel; Mother Teresa died; the exchange rate of the Malaysian ringgit reached a twenty-six-year low; the Little Mermaid was decapitated in Copenhagen; President Clinton said, 'I did not have sexual relations with that woman'; and all the time Henry Ezra Pratt was involved in the preparing and making of twenty-six editions of *Hooray, It's Henry*.

It was one of the most prolonged happy times in his life. Let's forget the world's troubles for a few moments and enjoy it with him.

Every Sunday, Henry prepared dishes, cooked dishes, let others cook dishes, discussed the notices which covered the walls of the Café, added new notices and generally had fun with food. Hilary appeared in every show, acting as hostess to their friends, and sometimes helping with the cooking. Her publishers were thrilled. Her sales increased dramatically.

Very few of the guests in the first series were well known. The exceptions were Denise Healey, who after all had been responsible for getting Henry into the business in the first place, Simon Hampsthwaite, who was still his team captain on *A Question of Salt*, and Sally Atkinson. It was a joy to spend a day with Sally under these circumstances, in Hilary's presence, so that there was no possibility of any flirtation. It established, Henry thought, that they were not potential lovers, but real good friends, and good friendship, he told himself, was far more valuable than love affairs.

Why did he not quite believe himself?

Henry's favourite editions of the programme were the ones that involved members of his family. A favourite with viewers was the one he did with Gunter Axelburger about Swiss food. Gunter agreed to appear on one condition – that there were no cheesy jokes about Swiss food being full of holes. The programme gave Henry an idea for a fictional chef for *A Question of Salt* – the sexy Swiss actress-cum-chef Jane Fondue – but it also made some serious points about there being much, much more to Swiss food than fondue, and, above all, it entranced the viewers, who were heartened and inspired by seeing his wife and his ex-wife getting on so well with each other and with him.

Kate featured in an edition on vegetarian food. She brought along members of the staff of the Umbrella Theatre and the cast of her new play, *Simpkins of the* Argus, adapted by her from her mother's novel. Mother and daughter charmed the audience with their shared nervousness over the project, a nervousness born out of great love. Vegetarians responded gratefully in their hundreds to Henry's defence of those who became vegetarians out of their concern for animals and his contempt for those who thought them merely faddy. They responded also to his condemnation of the lack of imagination shown by most restaurateurs in creating vegetarian options. 'If I sat in my office for a day to create vegetarian dishes I'd have several hundred by half past five,' he said.

Luckily nobody ever challenged him to do it.

Another edition featured the staff of the Café Henry. Michelle spoke of the qualities needed to be Manageress of such a café. They included the wisdom of Solomon, the patience of Job and the strength of Giant Haystacks.

Greg spoke of the difficulties he had faced over doing Front of House, and told how Henry had helped him to learn the principles of small talk.

Starring on the programme went to Greg's head

somewhat, and his small talk began to become less and less small.

Starring on the programme brought the burly Manageress seventeen fan letters. Sixteen were from lesbians. 'I've no prejudice against lesbians,' she said, 'but why do people assume I'm lesbian just because I'm built like a brick shithouse?'

She made a date with the seventeenth fan, and, three months later, married him.

Henry, after much soul-searching, decided to invite Bradley Tompkins on to the show. Something in Bradley's personality must have drawn Henry to inverted commas. His email read, 'Dear Bradley. I would be absolutely delighted if you could be a guest on my series, *Hooray, It's Henry*. I know that we have "crossed swords" a bit in the past but I would like to "bury the hatchet". Guests are welcome to participate in the cooking if they want to, and are certainly expected to participate in the eating! I await your reply "with bated breath". The following Sundays would be fine if you can manage any of them . . .'

Bradley replied, 'Hi. Read your email with astonishment. I understand from the publicity, plastered everywhere, that the accent is on your friends. I am not a friend of yours, and have no wish to contribute to the inevitable success of your series in any way. But thank you for asking me. I would like to return the compliment by asking you to appear on my series, but since my *long-running, ground-breaking, serious* cookery programme, *Bradley on the Boil*, was cancelled by a pregnant seventeen-year-old lesbian feminist graduate who decided that I had gone off the boil, I have not had a series.'

Henry found himself wondering how the seventeen-year-old had got pregnant if she was lesbian. 'However, if there ever are plans for a new series, probably called "Oh Bugger, It's Bradley", I will seriously consider you.'

There were other rejections, too, which disappointed Henry, but didn't really upset him.

Tosser declined the invitation to appear with Felicity. 'Food isn't Felicity's forte,' he announced, more alliteratively than usual. 'She's very . . . picky. But thank you for asking us. The gesture is appreciated.'

Another refusal was from Ginny Fenwick, his former colleague on the *Thurmarsh Evening Argus*. She had never realised her two ambitions – to become a war correspondent and to find a good man. Henry knew only too well that she had had her moments, though. Her ardent couplings had caused him many sleepless nights when he'd had a flat directly under hers in Thurmarsh two hundred years ago.

He learnt a lesson from this episode. It's fine to be sorry for people, but you must never let them suspect that you are.

His invitation – disastrously – was for a projected edition on the theme of 'Cooking For One'.

'There is no way I am going to appear as a lonely old spinster for you,' she replied. 'The public might even think I was a sad old virgin. I wish I was a virgin in view of my choice of men to be shagged by, but there you go. I wouldn't be able to resist telling the audience that I've had my moments, so I don't think I'd be very suitable for "before the watershed". Thank you also for inviting me to come and stay with you and Hilary. Again, sorry, no. If you ever want to marry me – ha ha! – I'm yours. Otherwise, fuck off.'

Henry was shocked by the savagery of those last two words, but had she meant them savagely? Had they, perhaps, been an attempt not to sound pathetic or spinsterish (was there such a word?)? Had there been a bit of a glint in those bloodshot eyes, above that unfortunate, squashed nose?

Lampo and Denzil declined the invitation to debate the issue of 'Is there such a thing as gay food?' on the grounds that, while they were in no way ashamed of their sexual predilections, they were a private matter and not to be paraded before the nation.

He was also turned down by his old chum from the Paradise Lane Gang, Martin Hammond, now the Labour Member of Parliament for Thurmarsh. Martin had been resentful of Henry, believing, with some cause, that Henry had caused his defeat as Labour candidate in 1979. Martin had not been blamed by the party, and had got in next time, with a massive majority, but he claimed that the years which he'd lost had been instrumental in denying him the early promotion which would have led eventually to high office. He had seemed to want to be friends again at the time of Henry's marriage to Hilary, but now that he had at last become a junior minister his natural pomposity reasserted itself. His reply came on House of Commons note paper:

My dear Henry,

It was very kind of you to invite me on to your little show, which is no doubt very amusing and will, I feel certain, be much enjoyed by those who have time to watch it.

Regrettably, as I am sure you will appreciate, that rules me out.

Much as I might wish to 'wax nostalgic about racing dog turds in the River Rundle', as you put it, I don't think that it would be helpful except in the context of a serious debate about matters of public health, the inadequacy of recreational facilities for the young, and all sorts of major issues.

Food is not an interest of mine. It is an irritating necessity which can keep me from more pressing matters. Frankly, the design of the digestive system is one of the many things – world poverty, earthquakes and the design of the reproductive system are others – which lead me at times to doubt the existence of an Almighty. The whole process of ingesting roast beef and ejecting turds is not pleasant to reflect upon. Were it the other way round, food might be even less enjoyable, but at least one would have more respect for the processes of the body. I happen to believe that there is an unhealthy obsession with food in our country today. It all comes from the continent and is the direct result of our joining the EU with all those guzzling Belgians etcetera. I believe that there are far too many food programmes on TV. It's what I call public disservice broadcasting.

Turning from the body human to the body politic, I have to say that at this moment in time, with world poverty and starvation such pressing issues, it would not be seemly for me to take up any position that seemed to be in any way friendly to the concept of gastronomy. It might be stimulating for me to attack the whole premise of your show, but I fear that I would do it so well that viewers would desert you in droves. I cannot wish that upon you.

I would not wish to end this letter on an unfriendly and churlish note, so may I say that, given that we have a glut of food programmes, I am at least pleased that some of the benefit is going to you and not to abominations like Bradley Tompkins.

I'm sorry this letter is so brief, but public duty is a hard taskmaster and I have much work to do, even though I have not been considered for high office, perhaps due to my late arrival at the Palace of Westminster.

It only remains, on behalf of Mandy and myself, to wish the very best of health and happiness for you and Hilary.

Your old friend

Martin Hammond M.P.

An edition of the programme that gave Henry particular pleasure was the one with Celia Hargreaves as guest. James very kindly went into a respite care home for the weekend, so that she could do it. Paul and Christobel would have had him to stay, had it not clashed with a snatched week in Barbados.

Mrs Hargreaves was well into her eighties now, but still carried, like a second rainbow, a faded aura of how lovely she had once been. She was as spry and elegant as ever. Under her expert guidance Henry produced the jellied beef consommé and the cold chicken in tarragon cream with which she had delighted him on so many summer occasions. It gave him enormous pleasure to bring a touch of cheer and glamour into her difficult life as a carer, and if an element of that pleasure was the satisfaction of being in control of her, after all the times when he had danced inelegantly to her tune, well, that was only human, wasn't it?

When he did an edition on Italian food, the guests included Camilla and Guiseppe. Guiseppe proved forceful in his condemnation of the 'You wanna black pepper?' school of Italian restaurants in England. There was an amusing discussion on the phallic symbolism of pepper mills – 'those dark satanic mills', as Guiseppe called them – and an impassioned debate on whether restaurants should remain true to the origins of pasta and serve it only as a starter.

Camilla amused everybody with her tale of Guiseppe's scorn when she had fed him that dish which does not exist in Italy except for tourists – spaghetti Bolognese. 'In the world of food, only one instance of two words put together fills me with more horror than spag. bol.,' said Guiseppe. 'What are they?' asked Henry innocently. 'Bradley Tompkins,' said Guiseppe. Henry tried to get this exchange cut out. The director, Sean Cassock, thought Henry's bottle was going. Henry insisted that he didn't want to be a party to gratuitously insulting remarks about Bradley. Sean pointed out that Henry hadn't made the remark, it was just the honest opinion of a guest. Henry insisted. Sean promised that the offending remark would be cut out. It wasn't. Sean said that he had been over-ruled by the BBC's head of food. Henry said, 'I didn't even know there was a head of food.' 'That's how the BBC operates,' said Sean. Later Henry discovered that there wasn't a head of food.

None of the programmes produced a more positive response than the one that featured Ben. Henry told the story of his lost and found step-son whose ruined digestion meant that his diet could no longer be prodigal.

Ben talked about the joy of food, about honesty in food, about simplicity in food, about nourishment in food, about the need for healthy sustenance, about the social pleasure of breaking bread together, about the senselessness of consuming things that took away your self-control and blunted your senses.

He talked, as he helped Henry with a straightforward but tasty, herby, slightly spicy shepherd's pie, about the simple pleasures that he had at last learnt to enjoy – garden birds, the excitement of breathtaking sunsets. He talked with awe about the loveliness of the countryside. He talked about the beauty of dragonflies, and asked, 'Are their lives of no value, just because they are so brief?'

It might all have seemed sentimental and trite, had it not been said by Ben after his particular experiences, and in a tone that was neither trite nor sentimental, and had he not talked openly, with extraordinary frankness and extraordinarily good taste, about the pleasures of homosexual love.

He made an impassioned plea to the young. You only have one body. It's very complex and delicate, and it's the most important possession you'll ever have. Don't abuse it.

'We're getting all emotional,' said Henry at one point. 'There won't be a dry sherry in the house.'

Darren refused to take part, for fear that he'd be praised, but Ben became, for one evening, a star. Then he returned to what he really enjoyed – stacking supermarket shelves.

Hilary was used to occasional fan letters – very occasional, it has to be said – but Henry had been very excited when they had begun to trickle in for him. Gradually, the trickle had become a healthy tinkling stream.

Now, however, with the success of *Hooray, It's Henry*, the stream became a flood. Perhaps this was inevitable, because it was the personal nature of the programme that gave it its edge. The edition with Diana and Hilary produced sack-loads, and the one with Ben brought in even more. Ben revelled in his moment of fame, but was pleased that it was brief.

Henry, however, faced the daunting prospect of one of Europe's greatest envelope mountains. He employed a part-time secretary, Mrs Daventry, mother of three and glad of an occasional escape. She had the perfect personality for the job, since she was as straight as a Roman road and not much sexier, and as a secretary she was brilliant. She sorted the letters into categories and created standard replies in forms loose enough to permit a little individuality here and there.

Some of the letters were easily dealt with. There were requests for signed photographs and for autographs. There was straightforward praise. Some of the writers were even thoughtful enough to say that they didn't expect a reply.

One of Mrs Daventry's categories was 'surname

enquiries'. It was surprising how many Pratts, and how many people who knew Pratts, hoped to claim kinship with Henry for themselves or for the Pratts whom they knew.

'My name is Gwenda Pratt. I am an orphan and cannot trace my parents, though I believe they lived "up North". I am of similar age to you, and wonder if we might be related. I am known throughout Hitchin for my "drop scones", so, who knows, maybe cooking is "in the blood".'

'Do you know if you are related to Thaddeus Pratt, the Victorian railway missionary?'

'I once lodged with a man called Gordon Pratt. He had alopecia and halitosis, and, sadly, was run over by a steamroller in Uttoxeter. If he had lived, he would be ninety-three. I wondered if he was an uncle of yours.'

'Please help an old codger. I have bet my mate Tim that you are related to Larry Pratt, serving a life sentence in the Scrubs for murder. You have very similar features.'

Never once did Henry find himself related to anyone about whom there was an enquiry. Not that he would have admitted it if he had.

Until . . .

Dear Mr Pratt, I am 88 years old, but in the thirties I worked in the Sheffield cutlers, Binks and Madeley (long gone). Among my collugues was a man called Ezra Pratt. I remember him telling me that on the night his son was born he strangled his parrot because it imitated his wife's cries over her labur pains. Mind you, he wus a bit of an odd fish. He had a bright green snap tin and allus ate brawn sandwiches. My wife tells me I'm stupid, no son of Ezra Pratt would ever been famous, but I can't help wundering. Can you enliten me?

Henry's eyes filled with tears, which he tried to hide from Mrs Daventry.

'You're quite right,' he dictated. 'That was my father. A child accepts what he sees as normal, he knows nothing else, but yes, I suppose he was an odd fish. I loved him, though, and I would be very grateful for any anecdotes that might bring him back to life for me.'

He did not receive a reply.

Many of the letters were from women who fancied him. Mrs Daventry always pursed her lips as she handed these over. They ranged from proposals of marriage to naughty suggestions.

'I am a widow and I have double glazing throughout. I would make you very comfortable.'

'Not a day passes but which I dream of you on. Not a meal is cooked but which I cook for you. Please, please, make me the happiest woman in Droitwich.'

'I live very near Junction 42 of the M1, so if you ever fancy a quick blow job on your journeys round Britain, please do not hesitate to call.'

He sent a standard reply to these letters, informing the writers how happily married he was, but just occasionally he couldn't resist a flourish. To the M1 lady, he replied, 'Sadly, I will not be able to take advantage of your most generous offer, as I always use the A1.' Mrs Daventry looked disapproving at this, but he said, 'If we can't have a bit of fun, we may as well be dead.'

He laughed at these letters, and he was flattered by them, but he was also saddened – very saddened. It seemed that there were vast wells of loneliness and frustration out there. Sickness, too. Some of the letters he received were so sick and depraved that they had to be unceremoniously binned.

There were even one or two letters from men who fancied Henry. One of them wrote, 'It is clear from your every appearance that you are gay and fighting it. Wake up. Come out of the closet. It's dark in there.'

And of course there were begging letters. He sent a standard reply to these, stating that he sympathised greatly with their cause, but had his own charitable arrangements in place.

In fact he contributed generously to two causes – help for the homeless, because of his experiences with Ben, and research into Alzheimer's, because of his experiences with his Auntie Doris, who had helped to bring him up after the death of his parents, and over whom the mists had gathered remorselessly.

The success of *Hooray, It's Henry* soon caught the eye of Nigel Clinton.

'Nigel Clinton here, Henry. Hilary's editor.'

'I do remember.'

'I really love your new programme.'

'Thank you.'

'How about a book?'

'Are you serious?'

'Of course. I rang Hilary first She thinks it's a great idea.'

'She would, Nigel. She's very generous.'

'Yes. I wouldn't be dealing with it, we don't do cookery books, but another imprint here at Consolidation House does. I thought I'd check how the land lay first, but if you are receptive, I could set up a meeting with a lovely lady called Carmel Sloane.'

'Terrific.'

'You'll adore Carmel.'

Henry managed not to say 'terrific' a second time. It might well not be terrific. He didn't like being told that he'd adore somebody. It sounded rather like an order. It could be the kiss of death.

Carmel was nervous, edgy, and a great deal older than she claimed. She took him to the Ivy. She had a pale face which had been lifted at least once and not very well. Her smile died at the edges. She had long, straight hair, dyed jet black. She was slim and flat-chested, and she moved her food around on her plate more than she actually ate it, to an extent that got on Henry's nerves, so that he longed to say, 'For God's sake, woman, either eat it or leave it.' She wasn't lovely, and he knew that he wouldn't adore her, but she was far too vulnerable to dislike, and he felt that they would get on well together.

'I want this book to be different,' she said.

'Right.'

'I want it to be more than the series.'

'Right.'

'I take my starting point from your . . . Hello, Melvyn . . . from your own phrase, well, no, I think it was Clive Porfiry's – "an autobiography in food".'

'It was my phrase, actually.'

'Even better. A recipe book primarily, of course . . . Morning, Nick . . . and one with fabulous photos, I think – I have a wonderful photographer lined up. Mohammed is absolutely brilliant – but, threading its way through the recipes . . . Morning, Harold . . . implicit even in the photos, is the story of a life. Your life,' she added unnecessarily. 'A bit of a revolution in cookery books, which is . . . Morning, Sir Tom . . . why I felt we needed to be discreet. I initially thought of the Groucho, but it's crawling with media.'

'Who is this Mohammed?' asked Henry over his tartlet.

'Mohammed El Bashir, simply the best food photographer in the universe.'

'A Muslim? Very little of my food has any Oriental influences.'

'Oh, don't worry, Henry,' said Carmel, toying with her salad, moving bits of avocado round her plate like a listless sheepdog rounding up its flock. 'Mohammed is British. Mohammed is a one-man triumph for integration. He's multi-culturalism in human form. He's ace. He's wicked. He's awesome. He's the incarnation of globalisation.'

'You like him, do you?'

'Like him? Like him, Henry? I should have thought I'd made that pretty obvious. If I told you that his "Yorkshire Pudding at Sunset" won first prize in an England in Spring competition in Hull, perhaps you'll begin to realise what we're talking about.'

'Do you mind if I pour myself another glass?' asked Henry.

'No, no. Of course. So sorry. I don't drink much, so I

forget. No. Help yourself. Order more. Please.' She lowered her voice to bring him the momentous news, which she spoke with awe, as if the Ivy was a cathedral, which in a way it was. 'I've been allowed to spend as much on you as on Minette Walters.'

'I'm impressed. Sunset? A Yorkshire pudding at sunset?'

'Yes. It has a slight crimson tinge, faintly visible in the rich yellows and browns of the pudding, just hinting at what's going on outside in the wider world. That's what you get from Mohammed. The food *and* the wider world.' Carmel Sloane was getting very excited, so excited that for several minutes she didn't even look round the restaurant to see if there was anybody else she knew. 'And that's what your series is giving us. Cookery within the wider world. In your cooking, Henry, I see a deep love of animals and of people, I see a concern for the environment, I see sympathy for the Third World, I see passion about poverty, I see concern over obesity.'

'Not many people can find all that in a fish terrine.'

'Exactly! But you can, and Mohammed can, and that's why it's all so exciting.'

Everything in Henry's life, and in his temperament, led him towards mockery of Carmel Sloane, and many people would later laugh at his disloyal impressions of her, but that day, over that lunch, he actually began to believe that there was something in what she said, that his book would be a cookery book, but also more than a cookery book.

'I've really enjoyed this. Thank you,' he said, and he meant it.

'Oh, so have I,' said Carmel. 'It's been absolutely . . . Goodbye, Melvyn . . . exhilarating. Sometimes my spirits droop at the start of a project. This time they've soared. I'm in a room . . . Goodbye, Nick . . . with lots of talented people, but I can honestly say that I would rather work with you than with . . . Goodbye, Harold . . . any of them. We've got on so well that I haven't really been aware that there's been anybody else in the . . . Goodbye, Sir Tom . . . room. That's a good sign, isn't it?'

This was too much for Henry to take.

'Goodbye, Hans,' he said to a very surprised tourist.

'Who's he?' asked Carmel Sloane.

'I haven't the faintest idea,' said Henry. I just felt like saying "goodbye" to somebody.'

11 A Difficult Relationship

A huge chunk of the Larsen B ice shelf in Antarctica broke off; Pol Pot, leader of the Khmer Rouge in Cambodia, held responsible for the murder of a million civilians, died; so did Frank Sinatra; Amnesty International released its annual report detailing human rights abuses in a hundred and forty-one countries; President Clinton was subpoenaed to testify before a Federal Grand Jury regarding his relationship with Monica Lewinsky; and Henry's food was photographed with enormous thoroughness by Mohammed El Bashir.

Henry knew from the beginning that it was going to be a long process. He chose simple dishes for the first photographic session, beginning with a starter which he had named Prawn Pippins. The recipe consisted of grating an apple, submerging it in lemon juice to retain its colour, shallow frying very fresh, top quality prawns in butter with salt and pepper, letting them cool, removing the shells and leaving the tails for decoration, then draining the grated apple, placing it on the plate as a bed, putting the prawns on the bed of apple in a decorative manner, spooning over the prawn and apple a vinaigrette consisting of one tablespoon of white wine vinegar, one tablespoon of olive oil and one tablespoon of the apple juice produced from the grating process, then sprinkling the dish with chopped dill. The result was pretty, tasty, refreshing and stimulating to the appetite. It was a little gem of a dish, but nevertheless it was in essence a simple starter. Mohammed took three and a quarter hours to film it.

'How come it took so long?' asked Henry, when it was finished at last.

'I just wasn't happy with it. It didn't sit up and say "apple" to me. The problem was to get it as appley as it was prawny.'

'And it's saying "apple" now?'

'Loud and clear.'

A few days later, Mohammed upset Henry considerably. He asked him to add some cayenne pepper to his chicken paprika.

'I don't use cayenne,' protested Henry. 'Any other pepper except hot paprika distracts from the purity of the flavour I'm trying to achieve. Often, in cookery, more means less.'

'This isn't cookery. This is photography. Paprika just isn't paprika-coloured enough. It's too dull, too matt. Photography needs sharpness.'

'But it won't be authentic.'

'I don't want to boast, Henry, boasting's not my line, but my "goulash sur l'herbe à côté de Lac Balaton" won second prize in Budapest. In Budapest, Henry, world capital of goulash. I used cayenne. Nobody complained.'

'I'm just disappointed that you cheated,' said Henry. 'I want my book to be truthful.'

'My dear man! You're living in the past. As we approach the digital age there's no point in photographs being truthful. Anything can be faked. Nobody will be able to trust a photograph ever again.'

Before long, Henry would learn, in the most painful way, just how true that was.

In Chicago, two boys aged seven and eight were charged with the sexual molestation, robbery and killing of an eleven-year-old girl. They wanted her bicycle. The death penalty was abolished in Poland; Geri Halliwell was named cultural ambassador to the United Nations Population Fund; President Clinton called for air strikes against Iraq, citing continued refusal to permit UN arms inspectors to do their work; the warmest year on record ended, and *Hooray, It's Henry* was published.

The book was launched with a modest dinner party at *Le Lièvre Fou*, the most expensive of Bradley Tompkins's three expensive restaurants. Henry thought that this might work as a peace offering. In this, as in so much else, he was wrong.

The restaurant consisted of four smallish rooms, with white walls hung with discreet, tasteful abstract paintings, which looked expensive but had very little to say. Table settings were elaborate, and tables nicely spaced. It had everything, Henry felt, except an identity.

Present at the party were Henry; Hilary; Hilary's editor, Nigel Clinton, balding now and with a slight stoop, a man aged prematurely by an excess of editing; Henry's editor, Carmel Sloane; his house editor, an enthusiastic young woman called Imogen Clutterworth-Baines; Mohammed El Bashir; Mohammed El Bashir's camera; and Carlton Husthwaite, the Managing Director of Impact Books, the imprint that was publishing *Hooray, It's Henry*. Henry had wanted the party to be small. He hadn't wanted to upstage

Hilary in the books department, not because it would upset her, but because she was the real writer.

He knew that he had been wrong about his choice of restaurant before they even sat down. Bradley's eyes were glittering dangerously.

'I wasn't coming in tonight,' he said, 'until I heard you'd booked. I thought, "I can't miss Henry's publication party. What an honour." '

Henry's heart sank. The man meant, *my Bradley on the Boil* books are out of print. Nobody will ever give me a publication party again. It's 'Bugger Bradley' all the way now. I've become the Bognor Regis of cookery.

His heart sank still further when a poncy waiter brought over a poncy basket full of poncy breads.

'Tonight we have raisin and garlic bread, sultana and olive bread and smoky paprika bread,' he smarmed.

Henry recalled vividly the remark he had made to Bradley in the Café. 'Our bread today is bread flavoured.' Bradley would have taken it as mockery.

He couldn't win with Bradley.

The starters passed off reasonably peacefully, although Henry wished that people wouldn't go on and on about how wonderful his book was in Hilary's presence.

Nigel must have caught something of the same feeling, because he began to talk about how brilliant Hilary's new book was. It was a tale of a woman who feels that her life has become impossible.

'It has a brilliantly intriguing title,' said Nigel Clinton, '*Carving Snow*.'

'I've read it,' said Henry. 'It *is* brilliant. Rather puts my little effort in the shade.'

He was going too far. Hilary gave him a look – an affectionate look, but there was definitely dryness there too, gleaming beneath the affection. For the first time it dawned on Henry that there might be limits even to her famed lack of jealousy.

As they waited for their main courses, Carmel said, 'Any thoughts on a follow-up, Henry?'

'Good Lord. Don't rush me,' said Henry.

'It would be wonderful if you could create a diet,' said Carlton Husthwaite.

'Everybody buys diets,' said Imogen Clutterworth-Baines enthusiastically. 'And when they can't stick to them, they buy another one.'

'I do have integrity, you know,' said Henry. 'I haven't got a diet worked out. I don't believe in diets. I believe food should be fun and varied and free of stress and combined with exercise.'

'That's a diet,' said Carlton Husthwaite.

'That's a diet that anyone could stick to, even me,' said Imogen Clutterworth-Baines enthusiastically.

'That has integrity,' said Carmel Sloane. 'Good for you, Henry.'

' "The Pratt Diet",' said Carlton Husthwaite. 'It rolls off the tongue.'

'Just as it'll roll off the presses,' said Hilary. Was there a touch of dryness there too?

Perversely, despite his experience with Carmel in the Ivy – or perhaps *because* of his experience with Carmel in the Ivy – Henry tried a little joke on her.

'We shouldn't have chosen this place,' he said. 'I'm really too proud to go to any restaurant that I can get into.'

'But in that case you'd never eat out,' she said.

'It was a joke,' he explained. 'A modern take on Groucho Marx.'

'I've seen his grave in Highgate Cemetery,' said Imogen Clutterworth-Baines enthusiastically.

'No, that's Karl Marx,' said Henry.

'Was he the dumb one?' asked Imogen Clutterworth-Baines enthusiastically.

'No,' said Henry. 'People said many things about Karl Marx, but nobody said that he was dumb.'

He wondered what they taught in schools these days. And then he thought about how young she was, and how enthusiastic she was, and how ignorant he had been in his youth, and how he had no doubt made many similar faux pas which his elders had been too kind to point out, and he smiled at Imogen Clutterworth-Baines – enthusiastically.

The main courses arrived. The portions were on the meagre side. The presentation was so artistic that it seemed a crime to eat anything, but it all certainly looked tempting.

They all began to eat. There were murmurs of satisfaction. The food was good – but there was no astonishment, no surprise, no real pizzazz.

'Well, Henry?' asked Carlton Husthwaite.

'Good but not great,' said Henry in a low voice. 'Sound enough, but not the flair you'd expect at these prices. No love. No excitement. No intensity.'

'Mine needs salt,' said Carlton Husthwaite. He called a waiter over.

The waiter hurried across the room with tiny steps, and stopped rather too abruptly, as if he was being worked by a man with a remote control that he hadn't quite mastered.

'Sir?'

'We have no salt,' said Carlton Husthwaite.

'No, sir. We don't serve salt, sir.'

'I beg your pardon?'

'We don't provide condiments, sir. All our food is correctly seasoned.'

'Is Mr Tompkins around?'

'Yes, sir.'

'Could you get him, please?'

'Er . . .' said Henry. 'Carlton? A moment?'

Carmel put her hand on Henry's. 'Disagreement with Carlton Husthwaite is not a good career move,' said Carmel's hand. She left it there after it had delivered its message. Henry slid his hand out from under hers as unobtrusively as he could. That might not have been a good career move either.

'Henry? You were saying?' said Carlton Husthwaite.

'I just . . . don't want to make a fuss . . . on my party night.'

'It isn't a fuss,' said Carlton Husthwaite. 'Just a paying customer wishing to enjoy his food. Fetch Mr Tompkins, would you, waiter?'

The waiter hurried off, slightly jerkily. The remote control really did need sorting out.

Bradley Tompkins approached their table like a lorry about to crash into a council house.

'I understand there has been a complaint,' he said incredulously.

'Not at all,' said Carlton Husthwaite. 'Just a request for salt.'

'With respect, sir, we do not serve salt. We do not need to, as all our food is correctly seasoned.'

'I find that a little odd in the case of salt,' said Carlton Husthwaite politely. 'Pepper, perhaps, but each person needs a different amount of salt.'

'With respect, sir, you aren't here for medical reasons,' said Bradley Tompkins. 'You are here to enjoy the flavours we produce, and the balance of seasoning and flavouring is our expertise, which is what you pay for.'

'I thought the customer was always right.'

'With respect, sir, rarely, in my experience.'

'With respect, people who keep saying "with respect" usually have no respect. So will you provide me with salt?'

'No, sir.'

'Henry, what do you say?'

Henry sighed. None of them understood how dangerous it might be to make an even greater enemy of Bradley Tompkins. None of them knew how much he, Henry, hated being hated. None of them, except Hilary, knew how much he wanted to be loved by the whole world. But these were his publishers, his future.

If in doubt, Henry, fall back on the truth.

'The food is good,' said Henry. 'Inventive, original and good. I think we all feel, though, that it lacks . . . that final, elusive, magical intensity which we all strive for all the time but which none of us achieve all the time. In my estimation, Bradley, a little salt would work wonders.'

'Fuck off out of here,' shouted Bradley Tompkins, to the astonishment of the other diners. He grabbed the tablecloth and pulled it towards him. Hilary, Nigel and Imogen practically had to throw themselves out of the way to avoid the carnage. There was a flash and a click which passed unnoticed in the shock and mayhem. The carpet was covered in broken glass and china and red wine and food.

How Henry wished that he wasn't attracted to facetious comments like moths to angora sweaters.

'Your poor carpet, Bradley,' he said. 'All that red wine. I've heard that salt helps.'

'A Question of Salt' was the all too obvious headline. None of the sub-editors could resist it.

'A question of salt fuelled the feud between two of the regular chefs on *A Question of Salt* . . .'

It was Henry's first experience of the down side of press interest in celebrities.

It wasn't to be his last.

Mohammed El Bashir's photograph of the carnage in the restaurant, and of the astonished expressions of the publication party, appeared in every paper, earning him a small fortune.

Henry wrote to him to express his regret and disappointment that he had exploited the situation in such a way.

Mohammed wrote back, saying, 'I am extremely sorry – and surprised – that you are upset, but I can't apologise. It would be hypocritical of me. For a photographer it was just too good an opportunity to miss, and, despite what I said to you last summer, on this occasion the photograph did tell the truth.

'I must say I did not expect you to object. After all, you were the victim, not the villain. You were utterly innocent in the incident, and I believed that my photograph would therefore be most welcome to you.

'I enjoyed working on *Hooray, It's Henry* and will be really disappointed if we cannot continue our collaboration on "The Pratt Diet", which is such a great idea incidentally.'

Henry wrote back. 'Thank you for your honesty. The photo is very embarrassing for me, but you weren't to know that, and I can see that from any neutral viewpoint I am not the villain of the piece.

'I thought the photo was magnificent. It took one second, and one exposure. I find it hard to believe that you needed three hours and fifty-two minutes to photograph my herb and tomato mousse. Perhaps, if we work together again, as I hope we will, we could take just a little less time?'

Three nights after the Mad Night at the Mad Hare, as one newspaper put it, Henry was wakened from a deep, dreamless sleep by a sound that might have been a pistol shot. Hilary was breathing easily at his side. Then the noise came again and he realised that it was the sound of glass being shattered.

Hilary suddenly sat bolt upright, and said, 'What the hell was that?'

'I think someone's broken in,' whispered Henry.

'What do we do?'

'I don't know. Maybe I'd better take a look.'

Naked chef routs burglars.

'Be very careful.'

Tragic stabbing of naked chef.

'I will.'

They were whispering so quietly that they could hardly hear each other, even in the deep silence of the night.

'I'll come too.'
'No.'
'Why?'
'There's no point in both of us getting killed.'
'Oh, Henry. Maybe we should just lie here.'
'That seems so craven.'

He crept out of bed, carefully, silently. His heart was thudding. A car engine was started. It sounded very close.

He tip-toed hurriedly to the window. He heard a car drive off but by the time he'd peered round the corner of the curtains it had gone.

'Maybe that was them.'

He crept towards the door. Behind him, Hilary slipped silently out of bed.

'I'm coming,' she whispered. 'I insist. Should we put the light on?'

'No. We don't want to be a target.'

They crept downstairs, side by side, naked. One of the stairs creaked. They froze.

They listened. Nothing.

They crept gingerly across the hall. Henry collided with a table, and the phone crashed to the ground. They froze again.

Nothing. Utter silence in the dark, dark house. Time passed.

'I don't believe there's anyone there,' whispered Henry very, very quietly.

'Should we put the light on?' whispered Hilary.

Suddenly the silence was shattered by a noise like an alarm going off. It wasn't loud, but they jumped. Their hearts thudded even faster. Then they realised what it was. It was the signal the phone made to warn that it was off the hook. They breathed a synchronised sigh of relief.

The mundane explanation of the startling noise seemed to indicate that there was no longer any danger. Henry switched the light on. The brightness hurt their eyes. Hilary bent down to pick up the phone. Henry, aroused by his fear, placed a soft kiss on her left buttock.

'Henry! Somebody might see.'

They laughed silently, childishly, hysterically, then sobered up. What had the noise been?

They examined the whole house. Nothing. A lifetime's possessions sitting there, snug and secure.

They put on their dressing gowns and went out into the damp sodium chill of London.

Their cars were both parked outside, because their house had been built before the time of garages.

The windscreens of both Hilary's modest Saab and Henry's flashy new red Mercedes sports car – 'there's no point in having money if you don't spend it' – had been shattered, the air had been let out of all eight tyres, and there were deep, angry scratches right along their sides.

'Emotion's an odd thing,' said Henry. 'I feel almost ashamed on his behalf for his lack of imagination.'

'I suppose it *is* Bradley.'

'It has to be, three days after the fracas. It has to be.'

Henry and Hilary debated at some length whether to challenge him. Was it stronger to attack him or to ignore him? Was it *wiser* to attack him or ignore him? Which would provoke him least?

Since they couldn't decide the answer to any of these

questions, Henry decided to ignore them. It was definitely easier.

Once he had made this decision, he felt that his strategy must be to avoid contact with the man at all costs. So, when he was next invited on to *A Question of Salt*, he told Nicky that he would only do it if Bradley Tompkins wasn't on it.

Bradley's face fell as he saw Henry in Main Reception at the BBC.

'They told me you wouldn't be on,' he said.

'They told me *you* wouldn't be,' said Henry.

They marched to the producer.

'Orders from above,' said Sean Cassock.

'It's downright deceit.'

'Harmless. Everyone knows you hate each other's guts.'

'I think we have a case for walking out,' said Henry.

'I agree,' said Bradley.

'There's nothing in your contracts about it,' said Sean, 'and Bradley doesn't get on so many programmes these days. He probably can't afford to walk out. You're in a stronger position, Henry. *Hooray, It's Henry* is very popular. However, that doesn't necessarily carry much weight these days, and with a second series very much under consideration it just might not be a good idea to cause so much disappointment to so many people. The studio audience won't take kindly to either of you when they find out why they didn't have a show to see, and it's bound to get in the papers, however much we try to hush it up.'

'Bastard!' said Henry and Bradley.

'You see, you have more in common than you think. Yes, I am, but I'm only doing my job.'

'The parrot cry of the cowardly throughout the ages,' said Henry.

'Oh come on,' said Sean. 'Look, if you don't want to appear together try to get it written into your contracts. Otherwise, sorry, can't guarantee it. And you don't need to clash. We aren't insisting on it. Shake hands and do your best, eh?'

Shaking hands with Bradley Tompkins was like getting hold of a dead, wet flounder.

The programme went well. They avoided controversy, even laughed at each other's jokes, whether they were funny or not.

The last round was about seasonings. Henry made a joke about Vivaldi's four seasonings. The camera showed Bradley laughing. True, it was a strained, forced laugh, but at least he had tried.

'Incidentally, on the question of seasoning,' Dennis Danvers asked Henry oleaginously, 'do you believe there should always be salt on the table in restaurants or do you go along with those chefs who say that their food is perfectly seasoned and refuse to give any salt?'

'I hoped you wouldn't ask me that,' said Henry.

'That's why I asked it.'

'I . . . I believe there should be salt and pepper on the table. Not necessarily because they're needed, not because I think the public necessarily know any better than the chef how the food should be, but because it's the customer who's paying and to dictate to them is, frankly, in my opinion, arrogant.'

'You cunt,' screamed Bradley Tompkins. There was an appalled intake of breath by the studio audience. Even Dennis Danvers's jaw dropped in astonishment. Bradley Tompkins himself went scarlet with horror at this public revelation of the depth of his hatred.

The camera moved straight on to Henry's face. He smiled. It was the smile of an angel.

'Thank you, Bradley,' he said sweetly. 'I didn't know you thought me capable of giving as much pleasure as that.'

The audience gasped, laughed, applauded. The applause was long and loud, so, naturally, nobody else heard the sniff.

But Henry did.

Bradley Tompkins squirmed in his seat. He ran his hand through his wig in his nervousness, then suddenly remembered that there was a danger of it coming off. He removed his hand abruptly. There was even some laughter at this. His humiliation was total.

'Henry!' said Cousin Hilda's sniff through the last of the laughter and applause. 'I'm not sure I know what you meant by that, but if it's what I suspect, it's mucky. Ee! I'm glad your mother's not alive to turn in her grave at it.'

'Shut up!' hissed Henry. 'I'm on television.'

'What did you say?' Dennis Danvers asked Henry.

'I said, "We can't say that on television,"' improvised Henry hastily. This was awful. What if he started talking to Cousin Hilda's sniff in front of the cameras . . .

'Of course we can't,' said Dennis Danvers. 'We'll have to do a retake.'

Afterwards, in the Green Room, Henry approached Nicky, who was trying to avoid him.

'I asked you not to put me on with Bradley,' he said. 'You said you wouldn't.'

'I'm sorry,' she said. 'Really sorry actually. I was under orders.'

Henry thought of being angry, of asking her if she had a mind of her own, of making facile references to Nazi Germany, but there wasn't any point, because he didn't fancy her any more.

'I understand,' he said.

She was still a very attractive young woman, but she was of a different generation and he couldn't understand how he had ever been excited by her. He felt excited by his lack of excitement. He was no longer in danger of being unfaithful to Hilary. And then a great emptiness swept over him, a sudden feeling of desolation. The room looked so dull. He no longer wanted to talk to anybody in it. He was overwhelmed by a great longing for Sally Atkinson, and realised with amazement that in his shock over meeting Bradley he hadn't even noticed that she wasn't on the show. That seemed like a betrayal, which was ridiculous. Oh Lord, Nicky had been speaking.

'Sorry,' he said. 'I . . . er . . .'

'You were miles away. No, I was just saying, don't worry about the incident with Bradley. He hasn't even dared show his face. You didn't half get the better of him. Game, set and match to you.'

'That's what worries me,' said Henry.

Henry's popularity on television had been assured by his twenty-two appearances on *A Question of Salt*. Now, with *Hooray, It's Henry*, he had become a superstar. Every morning, when he woke up, he had a moment of brief anxiety, when he thought it must all be a dream. Was his show really achieving thirty-eight per cent of the audience share? Was his book really at number three in the Non-Fiction Top Ten, compared to Hilary's fifty-third place in the Fiction charts with *Carving Snow*?

Henry and Hilary did their very first literary lunch together. It was at the Cornucopia Hotel in Throdnall, in the Midlands. Hilary made a thoughtful, witty speech about literature. Henry told jokes about food. Afterwards, the four authors sat at tables and signed their books. There was quite a queue for Henry even before he sat down. Two people were waiting for Hilary. She engaged each of them in conversation, entered into debate about whether they would like a little message and what that message should be. She knew it didn't matter how many books she sold, and she wasn't at all resentful of Henry. Of course he would sell more books than her. He was a television personality. Nevertheless, she really didn't want him to look round and find that there was nobody at all at her table.

'How many books did you sell?' Henry asked her afterwards.

'Seven. How about you?'

'Forty-seven.'

He didn't say it nastily. He certainly didn't gloat. He didn't mention it again. He could have made some explanation, such as, 'Well of course it's only because I've been on the telly so much', which would have irritated her in the extreme.

Nevertheless, she *was* slightly irritated. There had been no reason for him to ask her how many she'd sold.

She felt slightly worried too. It was only a vague feeling, there was nothing to justify it, but she wondered if his success was just beginning to spoil him. Surely not? Surely not her lovely Henry?

Barely a week passed without Henry receiving some kind of suggestion for the commercial exploitation of his popularity.

Hilary warned him against spreading himself too thinly, and, to be fair to him, he did turn down some suggestions.

Not many, though.

He didn't turn down an invitation to visit the Potteries in order to discuss a range of high-quality tableware using his name. The design aimed at the sophisticated simplicity for which he strove. The plates were square, large, elegant, and white, with his initials attractively intertwined in the centre, and with painted miniatures of food items that began with an H and a P – a herring and a prawn on the fish platters, a ham and a parsnip on the meat plates. Henry tried the complete range out before allowing them to be marketed. He still had his integrity.

He didn't turn down an invitation from Asbo Supermarkets to create a Henry Pratt range of foods. In fact, he created two – Pratt's Tyke Treats, loosely based on the recipes of his native Yorkshire, and Henry's Foreign Frolics, even more loosely based on the delights of staple foods from around the world. Again, Henry insisted on trying out every item in the Café, before allowing it to be sold to the public.

There was just time, after the launch of the two ranges,

for Ben to stack them on the shelves of the Streatham Asbo.

'He's my dad,' he said proudly, and all the staff were happy to see his pride, because they all liked him.

'We're more Foreign Frolics than Tykes Treats in Streatham, Dad,' he told Henry (all thoughts of his real dad had long been forgotten). 'But I spose Tyke Treats are more geared to the North. Mind you, we do sell a few Tykes Treats on a Friday. Anyway, the prospects look rosy.'

Sadly, the prospects didn't look so rosy for Ben. He was having to leave the job. His health wasn't up to it: his immune system was shot to pieces, and he had endured bouts of pneumonia and bronchitis, leading his doctor to advise that it was dangerous for him to continue to go out to work.

In the Café, inevitably, more and more fell upon Greg and Michelle. Henry appointed a new chef, a talented and personable young lady called Karen, who looked too frail to withstand the rigours of the kitchen, but wasn't. Henry had less and less time to spend in the Café, whatever he might have wished. In fact this rather pleased him, because his fame had brought a new kind of customer, the celebrity-seeker, the autograph hunter, people who were to humans what twitchers were to birds. This was threatening to disrupt the Bohemian atmosphere on which he prided himself. If he wasn't there so much, it would help to preserve what was left.

Henry would spend even less time in the Café once he had bought his weekend cottage.

From time to time, Henry and Hilary had discussed the possibility of such a thing. They had argued passionately about the social evils caused by weekend homes, the blight on picturesque villages which became ghost communities during the week, the pushing up of house prices in rural areas till the local people couldn't afford to buy, the effect on village shops of people coming up from London with a boot stuffed with goodies from Harvey Nichols and Fortnum and Mason's, and who then bought up the whole stock when they got stranded by snowdrifts.

Joe and Molly Enwright, friends and neighbours of Henry in the Thurmarsh days, had known of a couple, he a theatre director, she a writer, who had two children, he a painter, she an actress. The theatre director and the writer had split up, and the actress had walked out on the painter. The theatre director had homes in London, Herefordshire and Majorca. The writer had homes in Islington and Devon. The painter had homes in Warwickshire and Tuscany, and the actress had homes in Notting Hill and Brittany. Four people, nine homes. And all four of them voted Labour.

Now that they could afford a place in the country, Henry and Hilary wondered if they had been too quick to condemn the practice. The countryside needed new life. The decline of farming as a source of employment had long ago rendered change inevitable. Henry could drink so much in the village pub that he might save it from closure single-handedly. They wouldn't bring groceries to the village. They would support the village store. They wouldn't complain when cockerels crowed at daybreak, and silage or slurry smelt all day. Indeed, they might be able to influence other incomers who were less enlightened in their attitude to country pursuits.

They didn't entirely forsake their principles, though. They wouldn't dream of buying some small place that might suit a young plumber or bus driver. They would buy a house so large that the locals wouldn't have been able to afford it in any case.

They led busy lives and the search for their rural paradise took a long time. The manuscript for *The Pratt Diet* was coming along very slowly. Every house that they saw seemed to have a snag.

The new millennium began. In Uganda, up to five hundred members of the millennium cult, The Movement of the Restoration of the Ten Commandments of God, were killed in a church fire. Police believed it was murder after cult members had demanded their money back when the cult's prophecy that the world would end on the last day of December, 1999 had failed to materialise.

In May, 2000, Ken Livingston was elected Mayor of London, and Henry and Hilary found The Old Manor House in Grayling-under-Witchwood, a pleasantly straggling village in the North Cotswolds, away from the most touristy areas.

The house was a dream, with three gables and mullioned windows, built in honeyed stone, mellow, English, and exquisite. There was a mature mauve wisteria on the front, and a fig tree on a sheltered wall in the garden. It was set back from the village street, and at the rear, apart from one simple cottage in the same honeyed stone, there was open country. Some lambs were having a game, leaping and racing with sheer exultation at the privilege of existence. The place was perfect. Surely there would be no drawbacks here?

'There's only one snag,' said Mr Flitch, of Abercrombie, Abercrombie, Abercrombie, Abercrombie, Abercrombie and Flitch.

A snag! Again! What would it be this time?

'A snag?' said Henry with a heavy heart.

'A very small snag. The lady who lives in that cottage . . .' He pointed to the honeyed stone cottage . . . 'believes that she has a right of way through your land. She thinks that that track . . .' He pointed to a track that ran along the eastern boundary of the garden. '. . . gives her access to the village. There is no gate at the back of your garden but you would be fully entitled to put one up.'

'Does she have any other access to her cottage?'

'Oh yes. Her front door is on the other side, but it's a long, bumpy track to the road. To the shop via that track is one point eight miles. Via your track it's nought point four. You can see why she uses it, but she doesn't need to. The previous occupants chose to turn a blind eye.'

'What's this woman like?' asked Henry.

'Oh, Mrs Scatchard is very quiet. She's middle-aged. These things are subjective, and perhaps I shouldn't say it, but she's no oil painting. I'm amazed she ever married. There's a bit of a mystery, I suppose, in that nobody knows much about her. The village thinks her eccentric, but pleasant. In any case she isn't here very often. I can't see her being a major problem.'

Nor could Henry and Hilary.

They explored the village a couple of times, shopped in

the Post Office cum village store, had a drink in both pubs, warmed to one of them, and decided that they liked the feel of the place. They bought The Old Manor House.

'Lord of the Manor!' said Hilary. 'A far cry from Paradise Lane.'

Henry shook his head slowly, in disbelief, delight and just a little disquiet.

It can take a long time to buy a house. It was September before they actually took possession and October before it was habitable.

Henry and Hilary were very excited about showing the house to their very first visitors, Kate and Camilla. Guiseppe couldn't join them; he had a family crisis in Italy. Darren was working, and Ben wouldn't go anywhere without him.

A little shudder ran through the four of them as the Jaguar turned left at a signpost marked 'Grayling-under-Witchwood 2'. Soon, in the traditional manner of the English countryside, they came upon another turning, with a signpost that read 'Grayling-under-Witchwood 3', but eventually they did reach the village. Now there was total silence in the car.

There was a tiny estate of neat, trim council houses, then a farm, some Georgian houses, a timbered cottage, a brief pastoral interlude, a large Victorian house, a row of modest Edwardian cottages, a large handsome Perpendicular church, and, just beyond the church, on the left, opposite the cricket ground, The Old Manor House. A mellow autumn sun was shining hazily, lighting up the honey in the stone.

'It's gorgeous,' said Camilla.

Kate said nothing at first. She was torn in two. She disliked the principle of buying second homes, but she loved her parents. The love won, as it always did in the end with Kate.

'Yes, it is,' she admitted. 'Gorgeous.'

They'd brought Friday evening's meal with them 'just this once, because we don't know what's available locally yet', and they had a delightful dinner of roasted Mediterranean vegetables, and aubergine and potato curry, looking out on the quiet, gently rolling fields.

'What a peaceful scene,' said Camilla. 'Sheep quietly grazing.'

'I don't want to cast a pall,' said Henry, knowing that he was about to do just that, 'but we saw them as lambs the day we first came here. They were gambolling in that field with all the joys of the privilege of existence. Look at them now. Listless and dull. Why? Because they're thick? No! Because they realise just how tedious the existence they felt so privileged to have is for sheep. "We can do anything," they cried as lambs. "All things are possible." What do their adult grumbles say? "It's bloody grass again for tea." What an existence. Poor things. We really ought to be vegetarian. That meal was lovely tonight.'

While Hilary made coffee, Camilla went upstairs to phone Guiseppe on her mobile. She was very punctilious about using her own phone to make her own phone calls, and it turned out that you could only get a signal on the upper floor at The Old Manor House.

'A woman just drove through your garden at a rate of

knots,' she said on her return. 'Woe betide any birds or small children that might be in the way.'

'What sort of a woman?' asked Henry.

'That's a stupid question, darling,' said Hilary. 'Camilla would hardly have seen her.'

'I wasn't expecting a novelist's description, darling,' said Henry. ' "A woman just drove through our garden, middle-aged, dark, with a slight air of mystery about her, leading Camilla to believe that she might have lived out East, and grown used to her own company, and lived on coconut curry and real turtle soup. Childless, probably, and yet there hung over her a curiously maternal air, as if . . . as if she wished she had been a mother." '

'It's lucky you abandoned your one attempt to write a novel all those years ago,' said Hilary drily.

'No, but the funny thing is, I'd say that's exactly what she did look like,' said Camilla, 'and I'll tell you this. She's no oil painting.'

In the morning, with fluffy clouds appearing in a clear sky like bubbles in a soup that's being reheated, Henry drove out of the gateless exit to his garden, through the field of disillusioned sheep, and into the garden of the stone cottage.

He drove round to the front, parked on the gravel, and got out of his car slowly, curiously reluctant to confront Mrs Scatchard, yet full of curiosity about her. He had agreed with Hilary that they didn't want to fall out with the woman, they didn't want to appear to be pompous berks from London, but on the other hand they had come here to have peace and quiet. They might get some chickens, they might have visitors with small children, their garden must be safe.

Making the classic decision that is actually no decision, they had resolved to play it by ear.

The door swung open, before he had knocked, to reveal a woman who was certainly no oil painting. In fact, Henry's first dreadful thought was that Mrs Scatchard looked like Bradley Tompkins in drag.

His second, far far more dreadful thought, was that it *was* Bradley Tompkins in drag.

The colour drained from Bradley Tompkins's rouged cheeks. His legs began to buckle.

'Oh my God,' he said, as he crashed to the ground beside Henry.

For a moment Henry thought that Bradley Tompkins had suffered a heart attack. His own heart began to race. He was a compassionate man, but he didn't think he would be capable of parting Bradley's over-reddened lips – he had no flair for make-up – and giving him the kiss of life. He felt for the man's (?) pulse. He found it. Relief swept over him.

Bradley Tompkins opened both eyes and shut them again rapidly as he saw that Henry was more than a bad dream. Then he opened one eye.

'I think I should send for an ambulance,' said Henry.

'No!' shrieked Bradley Tompkins. 'No. I'm fine. I just . . . fainted . . . passed out . . . I'm fine. No problem. I can't go to hospital, Henry, dressed like this. Although I suppose it doesn't matter now. The game is up. Unless of course I agree to your demands.'

'My demands?'

'It *is* blackmail, I presume.'

'What are you blathering about? Of course it isn't blackmail. I had no idea you were here. Now how are you going to get up? I don't know if I can lift you.'

Bradley Tompkins managed to turn over on to his stomach, and scrambled to his hands and knees. With Henry's help, he stood up. When Henry let go, he almost over-balanced, but recovered. He moved his legs and arms gingerly, feeling for breakages, but didn't find any.

Henry led him into the hall, which had a marble floor far too grand for its small size. There were glass cases containing stuffed animals. Bradley led the way into a small, dark, stuffy, dusty living room, decorated with sentimental Victorian paintings of babies and doggies. There were two, large, sagging armchairs and an exhausted settee.

Bradley Tompkins collapsed into one of the armchairs.

'Sorry,' he said. 'I'm rather shaken.'

'Have you any brandy?' asked Henry.

Bradley Tompkins pointed to a small drinks cabinet. Henry found the brandy, poured a small glass, and took a sip.

'Thanks,' he said. 'I needed that.'

Bradley gawped.

'I thought you were getting it for me!' he said.

'I was,' said Henry, 'but I've always wanted to do that, and I couldn't resist it.'

He poured another glass, and handed it to Bradley, who was wearing a knee-length tweed skirt and a cream cotton top.

They sat in the large armchairs at either side of the tiny

hearth, in which there was a large bowl of dried flowers. Henry hated dried flowers.

'What did you mean, you had no idea I was here?' asked Bradley.

'Just that. I was as amazed to see you as you were to see me.'

'What are you doing here if not tailing me?'

Henry had to admit that Bradley's wig as a woman was far superior to his wig as a man.

'I came in all innocence, to see Mrs Scatchard,' he said. 'I came to discuss a disputed right of way.'

'Right of way?'

'Through my garden.'

'Oh no!' shrieked Bradley Tompkins. 'You haven't bought The Old Manor House.'

Henry nodded.

'I've often wondered if there's a God,' said Bradley Tompkins. 'Now I know there isn't.'

'How do you think I feel?' said Henry. 'I've spent a small fortune on a rural paradise, and I get you.'

'There's no need to be insulting.'

Henry poured two more brandies. They both needed them.

'Bradley, let me promise you something,' said Henry. 'I have no intention of blackmailing you. I promise you that neither Hilary nor I will ever tell anybody about . . . this.'

'Why should I believe you?'

'No reason. I imagine you're going to be very worried indeed. But for some reason you choose to live this double life . . .'

'Here it comes. The disapproval. The psycho-babble. The curiosity.'

'Curiosity, yes. Of course I'm curious.'

Bradley didn't tell him anything straightaway, but they continued to talk, and they had another brandy, these two men who hated each other, and in an extraordinary way they found it companionable and even rather exciting to be drinking so much so early in the day, so that they had a fourth brandy, and, during the fourth brandy, Bradley opened his heart.

'I don't like Bradley Tompkins,' he said. 'I had a twin, Henry. She was . . . she was what they used to call a spastic. She died when we were six. I hardly remember her. I gave her the life she never had, Henry. I became her twin.'

Henry was astounded. He knew that Bradley wasn't making this up. He didn't know what to say. He wanted Bradley to continue. Well, he knew that Bradley would have to continue. So, there was no need to say anything.

'I don't much like myself,' continued Bradley.

Henry resisted the temptation of saying that he wasn't a bad judge.

'I don't much like myself and neither does anybody else. I suppose I've felt a great deal of guilt that I who was so unworthy of life survived and Grace – that was her name, Grace – who might have been so much more worthy of life – didn't. I felt a growing need to have her around me. So . . . I re-created her. I gave her back some of the life she never had.

'I gave her a husband. I felt she deserved a bit of fun. He had to have died, of course, or where was he? Also, it gave her a different name. I didn't want her to be Miss Tompkins, having to tell everybody I was Bradley's sister. I only mention it when the resemblance is commented on.

'It works, Henry. It works in all sorts of ways. The human imagination is very powerful, and at times I become, I really do believe I do, I become my sister. At other times . . .'

He trailed off. Henry poured a little more brandy. Bradley took a sip, and resumed.

'This is very strange, Henry, and doesn't make much sense to me. I . . . er . . . I'm not much good with women. Never have been.' He gave a deep sigh. 'Humiliating moments, Henry. Moments fate doesn't allow me to forget. Failing to get it up with the gorgeous Sally Atkinson, who made things worse by sympathising. This is quite inappropriate, doesn't make sense at all, but dressed as my sister, being my sister, I find I *can* get it up. I even have a relationship with a . . . a woman, or should I say, "another woman"? I have a true friend, and we have sex, and find just a little peace together. You'll laugh . . .'

'I won't.'

'She's a bisexual bicycle repairer from Bicester.'

I could hardly say it, let alone fuck it, thought Henry.

'Of course I won't laugh. Good for you.'

'I suppose I horrify you like this.'

No, Grace, I actually much prefer you to Bradley.

But Henry didn't say this.

'I fully accept you as you are,' he said. 'I will not interfere with your life one little bit. I can't believe that fate has brought us together like this, but fate always was a mischievous little swine. I will leave you completely alone, Bradley. I won't even make an issue of the right of way.'

'You won't need to. I wouldn't be seen dead in your garden. Are you really telling the truth, Henry? This is just . . . serendipity? Far too nice a word for this ghastly situation.'

'I am, Bradley. Hilary and I will never mention a word of this, even to our friends – and I will let you know, without fail, every time I'm coming to Grayling-under-Witchwood, so that you can avoid me if you wish.'

Henry made the short journey home extremely carefully, because of the brandy, and with a heavy heart.

The two men had talked properly for the first time. They had felt almost at ease with each other, over their brandies, and Bradley Tompkins had every reason to be grateful to Henry for not spilling the beans. However, Henry didn't believe that the man would be grateful for his silence. He had seen him as Mrs Scatchard. He had seen up his legs to his scarlet knickers when he fainted. Bradley had told him that he couldn't get it up. He had told him that he was having a relationship with a bisexual bicycle repairer from Bicester. He would never forgive Henry for knowing these things.

Later, Henry would believe that the events of that particular, never to be forgotten Saturday morning, had tipped Bradley's hatred over into a new, irrational, manic intensity which would stop at nothing and was truly to be feared.

12 A Distinct Risk of Mercury Poisoning

Towards the end of 2001, two jocular remarks upset Henry. One of them was made by his darling daughter Kate. They met in the middle of the afternoon for a late vegetarian lunch at Oat Cuisine in Kingly Street, sometimes said to be the best vegetarian restaurant in Kingly Street.

'You'll be in danger of mercury poisoning soon, if you're not careful,' she said.

'I don't understand.'

Kate took a sip of organic wine and wiped her mouth with her Fair Trade napkin. The tables, walls and floors were made of pine from sustainable forests.

The only pity of it was that the food was so uninspired.

'It's a line from a play we're thinking of putting on,' she said. 'There's a great risk of mercury poisoning if you spend a lot of time at crematoria. The burning releases the mercury from the fillings of the deceased.'

'Your play sounds fun.'

'Well it is a comedy. It's part a modern black comedy and part a tribute to the old British comic tradition.'

'What's it called? "Carry On Up the Crem"?'

Kate blushed.

'Yes,' she said, in a little girlish voice, a disappointed daughter's voice. 'Naff idea?'

'No, not necessarily. It depends how it's treated.'

Henry realised that he was beginning to lay down the law on other people's areas of expertise as well as his own. Dangerous!

'It's pretty good, I think,' she said. 'It's about a crematorium manager who thinks his place is a cut above the rest. He's the Miss Jean Brodie of the mortuary. He calls it the crem de la crem.'

Henry wanted to reply, but a mouthful of nut cutlet just wouldn't go down. Nut cutlets could be so delicious. This one was heavy, too dense.

They didn't understand food, and they ran a restaurant. It was often so.

At last it was gone.

'It sounds as if it could be good,' he said, 'but I do think you have to be careful with comedy about death. But then it's a bit of a touchy subject with me at the moment. I . . .' His voice began to crack. 'I've lost so many dear people this year.'

'Oh God, I didn't mean to upset you,' she said. 'Oh, Dad!'

She reached across and clasped his hands, took them to her lips and kissed them.

'It was a very silly remark. I should have realised,' she said. 'Do you think I may be losing my judgement? Do you think . . . do you think I've been silly to give up sex? Has it made me lose touch with people's emotions?'

'Only you can know that,' said her father. He was feeling very fatherly that afternoon. These snatched moments in their busy lives were so vital, so precious. 'About sex. I don't think there's any disgrace or any harm in not having sex. The Pope's one of the most complete human beings in the world . . .'

'Is he? I don't think he really empathises with women's problems.'

'Well I don't think less of dear Cousin Hilda because she died a virgin.'

Deep in his head Henry flinched, expecting a sniff. There wasn't one. There didn't need to be. Cousin Hilda's sniff was like terrorism. It didn't need to appear very often. Once the fear of it was established, it could do its work with minimal risk.

'But sex isn't all . . . well, it isn't all sex,' he went on. 'It's love and faithfulness and emotion. It can be ugly and possessive and exploitative and chauvinist, but it can also be beautiful. Yes, I do think it's a shame to close your mind to the possibility. I think it profoundly misguided, actually.'

The other remark was made by Bradley Tompkins. Henry had been very successful in avoiding Bradley for many, many months, always giving him advance warning of his visits to Grayling-under-Witchwood, always missing him on his occasional appearances on *A Question of Salt*, so that he was lulled into thinking it unnecessary to have it written into his contract that he wouldn't appear in the same show as the man.

In the first week of December, 2001, they did appear in the same edition. In his CV of a fictional chef, Bradley said – believing it to be an absolute humdinger – 'He'd read English at university and in his last years he fulfilled his ambition to write a book about punctuation. He finished it just before he got cancer of the semi-colon and died from an oblique stroke.'

There was a gasp from the studio audience. The camera went straight to Henry's face. He looked appalled. He saw the red light on, he heard the silence. He had to say something. 'Sorry, Bradley,' he said. 'I've had a bad year with death. I can't see anything funny in it.' There was a round of applause. Henry was sure that Bradley's hatred went up yet another notch.

How many notches can a man's hatred notch before it becomes a threat?

Funerals never come at convenient moments, and for Henry that year they were particularly difficult emotionally.

His fame and fortune were at their height. *Hooray, It's Henry* had reached number one in the paperback charts, and he was busy preparing the second TV series. His manuscript for *The Pratt Diet* was almost ready. Speaking engagements abounded. The Café Henry group continued to expand. Sales of his monogrammed HP crockery and his Asbo foods were excellent. Book signings led to long queues. Money was pouring in. So were offers of marriage.

It was a roller-coaster year of fame and funerals, and he couldn't always separate them. In fact, he took his fame to the funerals. It was inevitable.

The first funeral was in Yorkshire, on a bleak February day, with an easterly wind blowing patchy fog over the Vale of York.

A lady had rung the offices of *A Question of Salt* and asked for Henry's phone number. They refused to give it, on grounds of security, but rang him with her number.

When he heard that a woman called Norma Hutton wanted to speak to him, all sorts of possibilities went through his over-active mind. 'I've seen you on the telly, looking straight at me. You feel the same way about me as I do about you, don't you? We have to meet.' 'Do you remember a certain night in Thurmarsh when you drank too much? I am the mother of your eighteen-year-old son and I can't afford to send him to university.' 'We can offer you 3.9 per cent on balance transfers for twelve months.'

He had to phone her.

'Vale of York Retirement Home.'

'Could I speak to Norma Hutton, please?'

'Speaking.'

'I'm Henry Pratt.'

'How kind of you to ring.'

'Not at all.'

'He said you were a gentleman.'

' "He"?'

'Oh, I'm sorry. I'm not explaining this very well. I'm in a bit of a lather, actually. I'm not used to talking to celebrities. I'm afraid I have bad news, Mr Pratt. Brace yourself.'

He braced himself.

'Er . . . right. I'm braced.'

'What?'

'I . . . er . . . I'm ready for your bad news.'

'Ah. I'm afraid . . . I'm afraid Mr Pettifer passed on yesterday.'

Who the hell was Mr Pettifer?

'Oh dear. I'm so sorry.'

'Yes. Yes, it's very sad.'

Hint, please, woman. Help me.

'Yes, he always spoke very very highly of you. He never missed one of your TV appearances.'

Great, good, fantastic, very gratifying . . . but *who was he*?

'He lived for them. They were the highlights of his life. "I knew him," he used to say. "I've sat as close to him as I am to you now." He'd say that to people who were sitting close to him.'

'Yes. Quite.' Give me a clue, woman!

' "Oh, we had such fun in the old Thurmarsh days," he used to say.'

Thank you. Thurmarsh. Thurmarsh? Ah. Cousin Hilda. Norman Pettifer! One of her gentlemen, of course. Sacked from the cheese counter, moved to general groceries. A weak face positively overflowing with disappointment.

'I remember him well. Yes, we did . . . er . . . have . . . er . . . some jolly moments.'

Jolly moments? At Cousin Hilda's? Dear God!

'He was our very last grocer. It's the end of an era.'

'I beg your pardon?'

'We used to be known as the Yorkshire Retired Grocers' Benevolent Home, but grocers are passé, aren't they? Killed by the supermarkets. We're just general elderly now. It's not the same. Mr Pettifer was our last link with the good old days. His passing is the closing of a book. It would be a tremendous fillip to us all if you could come to the crematorium.'

'Of course I'll come.'

When he told Hilary, she said, 'You give of yourself far too easily.'

'Because it's all I have to give,' he replied. 'Darling, if I ever forget where I come from, I'm lost. I'm not going just because of Norman Pettifer. I'm going for Cousin Hilda and all her gentlemen – Liam O'Reilly, Tony Preece, Neville Chamberlain, and all the ones I've forgotten. I'm going to remember my own life, and I might have time to pop over to Thurmarsh and see a few old friends.'

In the end he decided not to go to see his old friends. He couldn't face it. All that was over. He sat in a cold, desperately empty crematorium chapel and listened to a vicar with no charisma, a poor speaking voice and a tendency to dyslexia, murdering the elegant strength of prayers and psalms and gospels.

There were only five other mourners for the poor forgotten man: Norma Hutton; Sheila Redmond, her friend and formerly her opposite number at what had once been the Yorkshire Retired Drapers' Benevolent Home; Bernard Birstwith, a cousin; and Tommy Crane and Elsie Carter, his friends from the Home.

They were invited back for coffee and sandwiches. Dear God! But he couldn't bring himself to just drive away.

The coffee was served in HP cups. The sandwiches lay meagrely on huge HP plates. Norma Hutton beamed proudly.

'We bought the whole range because of poor Mr Pettifer,' she said. 'It was well over budget – they aren't cheap, are they, Henry? – but Mr Taplow is a wizard with budgets and we saved elsewhere. Swings and roundabouts, as they say. We were so glad we did. Every time he ate, poor Mr Pettifer would regale us with some memory of you.' She clapped her hands. One or two of the more alert residents looked up listlessly. The others continued to stare into space. Dear God, isn't there a better way of ending people's lives than this?

'Boys and girls,' said Norma Hutton. 'This is Henry Pratt. You've seen him on the TV, and now he's here. Isn't that thrilling?'

Henry's whole face seemed to congeal. He had to force his cheeks apart to create a smile. A man laughed hysterically. A woman moaned. Nobody else reacted.

'He read everything about you in the papers – read them aloud, he did – and I think everyone felt that some of the glory rubbed off on them.'

Stop it. Stop it, please.

'Ellen – she's a card, she can be right comical at times, can Ellen – Ellen put HP sauce on her plate and said, "HP sauce on an HP plate – I was always saucy!" How we laughed.'

After the feast, he had to shake hands with every inmate. Goodness knew how many diseases he would pick up – impetigo, psoriasis, ringworm and alopecia at least, to judge from appearances.

'He'd sit there, where Vera's sitting . . .' began Norma Hutton.

'I'm not Vera,' said the woman in the chair that Norma had pointed at.

'Yes, you are, dear.'

'Am I? Oh.'

'He'd sit there and watch you, and he'd say, "To see him now, all suave and sophisticated, you'd never guess that he used to come home drunk and be sick all down the stairs – and on the coal!" ' said Norma Hutton.

'One's sins are never forgotten, Mrs Hutton,' said Henry. 'One's embarrassments gather strength over the years.'

'It's *Miss* Hutton actually,' said Norma.

Henry wasn't surprised.

The death of James Hargreaves didn't surprise Henry either – he'd been in failing health for some years – but there were surprises for him in Hampstead Parish Church, which was packed with relatives, friends and old medical colleagues, some of them very old indeed.

He was surprised that Celia Hargreaves, still a picture of elegance in her early nineties, wore white, contrasting with the conventional black worn by her son Paul and his wife Christobel.

He was surprised to see Belinda Boyce-Uppingham there. He had forgotten that she had been a close friend of Diana. How he had fancied Belinda as a boy and young man. How humiliated he had been by the class divide. Well, he was a star now, and she was a tired, rather gaunt farmer's wife, who had been exhausted by her unsuccessful attempts to give her husband a son and heir. Henry bore her no ill-will, but he felt a little frisson as he anticipated meeting her in his new role as a celebrity chef. Robin towered beside her, looking more like a tree-trunk than ever. Henry would hardly have been surprised to have seen a greater spotted woodpecker trying to nest in him.

He was surprised that Denzil had made it. He looked so desperately frail now, and it wasn't as if he was even close to James or Celia Hargreaves, but style was important to Denzil, and when he couldn't go to other people's funerals, he'd be ready to go to his own.

Henry smiled at Diana and Gunter, at Paul and Christobel, at Lampo.

After the service they walked, in fitful sunshine, through charming streets, and across the main road to an area where charm gave way to distinction.

There were glasses of wine and elegant nibbles in the mellow, slender, four-storey Hampstead house. Henry felt uneasy, re-entering this house where he had made so many *faux pas* in his youth. Diana clearly realised this.

'How does it feel to re-enter this scene of your humiliations, as a successful and world-famous figure?' she asked.

'Hardly world-famous,' he said.

'I think so. We even get you in Switzerland. Dubbed, I'm afraid. I can't watch you. You look like you, and you sound like Adolf Hitler.'

He winced, partly at the thought of his sounding like Hitler and partly at this talk of his fame. It seemed so inappropriate, so crass, so tactless, so invasive on such a sad occasion.

Mrs Hargreaves hurried up to him, kissed him and said, 'Promise you won't forget me.'

'How could I?' said Henry. 'You're my yard-stick.'

'That doesn't sound very elegant,' she said. 'I'm not sure I want to be a yard-stick. What do you mean by it, exactly?'

'Whatever I do, I think, "Would Celia approve?" "Would Celia think I'm making a *faux pas*?" "Will Celia think I'm no longer a Northern hick?" '

'Oh, Henry. We adored that Northern hick.' She grimaced and put her hand to her throat. 'There. *I've* made a *faux pas.* I should have said, "Henry! You were never a Northern hick." '

'I wouldn't want you to lie.' He touched her arm. She was of a generation that didn't show their emotions, but he thought that he ought to help her to do so now. 'How are you really?'

'I'm sad, of course, and when all this is over I daresay I will miss James most dreadfully, but I'm relieved that his struggle is over. His decline has been remorseless and I've hated every second of it. He's been released and I've tried to persuade myself that this means that I've been released too. I'm wearing white to remember our wedding, Henry.'

'You look lovely.'

'Silly boy. I hate black at funerals. They're depressing enough without that. Look at Paul and Christobel, Henry. So conventional.'

'Yes, but a lovely looking couple.'

'You're more my son to me than he is.'

He couldn't hide his shock.

'That's awful.'

'Maybe, but it's how I feel.'

'You can't mean it.'

'But I do. I love Diana dearly, in a way I have never quite managed to love Paul. I'm so delighted she's happy with Gunter. I said to James, "I can't believe I'm happy that she's married a Swiss dentist, but I am." He's so kind, Henry, and I value kindness above all else. But Paul . . . he's fine, a fine son, as they say, but . . . he's like a theory.

A theoretical son. I expect to knock on his face and hear a voice say, "Sorry. He's out today." '

'I don't think you should be saying these things.'

'Perhaps not. You amused James on the TV. He said, "I shouldn't be laughing, but I am." '

Much as he didn't want to discuss his career and his fame that afternoon, Henry couldn't help feeling a little upset by James's remark, 'I shouldn't be laughing.' Why shouldn't he? Was there something not good enough for the James Hargreaveses of this world, something not quite out of the top drawer, about the amusement he gave them?

'I must circulate,' said Celia. 'Promise to come and amuse me frequently.'

'I promise.'

He found himself talking to Paul and Christobel before he'd had time to digest Celia's comments. Conversation was a bit of a struggle. It always was with them, nowadays.

Then Paul astounded him.

'You will keep seeing Mother, won't you?' he said. 'I feel . . . it's strange, but I know that I'd get on better with her if she wasn't my mother, and I wasn't her son. The fact of the relationship throws us into clichéd situations and responses. She's livelier with you. She's always had a soft spot for you, as you for her. I realised that in Brittany.'

Oh, not that again.

Henry looked across the room and met Celia's eyes, and he could have sworn that she knew what they'd been talking about. He began to blush.

'He's blushing!' said Christobel.

'Of course I am,' said Henry. 'It's so embarrassing to be reminded.'

'Sorry,' said Paul complacently.

Henry went in search of more wine and found Lampo.

'How are things, Lampo?' he asked.

'Fine. Really. Really fine. The system really works. I'm not sure Denzil really believes that it does, but it does.'

He was now coming up to Mrs Hargreaves again. She was talking to Hilary and he stopped for a moment.

'I'm making Hilary promise to come and amuse me too,' said Celia Hargreaves. 'To marry Hilary once showed taste. To marry her twice showed taste, persistence and humility.'

Henry laughed, touched Hilary briefly on the bottom, and moved on.

As he steered his full glass back through the lovely 'It's the way he would have wanted it' throng that filled the elegant, well-proportioned rooms of the Georgian town house, Henry saw Belinda Boyce-Uppingham without Robin. It was a moment to be seized, but his route took him past Denzil, and he had to stop.

'So, Denzil, how are things?' he asked, aware that it was becoming his stock question, but unable to think of a better one.

'Fine, Henry. Absolutely fine. The system works perfectly. I'm not sure Lampo really believes it does, but it does.'

Belinda was still without Robin.

'Excuse me, Denzil.'

'Dear boy. Move on. I'm not fun any more.'

'Denzil! It's just that I need to speak to Belinda Boyce-Uppingham. We go back even further than I do with you.'

He approached her determinedly, avoiding all possible further delays by not looking at anybody else.

'Henry! You look wonderful.'

'Well, so do you, Belinda. How's things?'

'Fine. Tessa and Vanessa and Clarissa are married. Marina never will be. She's plain, poor girl. Vanessa can't have children but the others have seven between them. Vanessa's an interior designer, the other two don't work. Tessa's anti-hunt which has shattered Robin. Davina's divorced which has shattered Robin. Petunia's gay which has shattered Robin.'

'He seems easily shattered.'

'He is. People think he's so strong. Like a tree. I'm the strong one, Henry, and even I am swaying in the gale. Davina's the arty one. God knows where she gets it from. She plays in an orchestra. Viola, would you believe? Oh, by the way, we were sorry to hear you and Di had split up.'

'Well, it was painful, but we've landed on our feet. I've married my wonderful first wife again . . .'

'Yes, but poor Di's ended up with some Swiss dentist.'

'He's lovely.'

'Possibly, but he's a dentist.'

'What's wrong with that? They're practically doctors.'

' "Practically". Precisely. That speaks volumes. Would you like to marry somebody who stares into people's mouths all day? Exactly. You wouldn't. Besides, he's Swiss.'

'He's a lovely man, Belinda. Lots of Swiss people are lovely.'

'Ah, well. Robin feels that their farmers get unfair subsidies because the EU thinks they all live on top of an

Alp, so probably we're biased. So, what are you up to these days?'

'I . . . I have a little café in Soho.'

'Really?'

'The Café Henry.'

'Sweet.'

'And I appear on TV.'

'You do??'

'On cookery programmes. You . . . you may have seen me.'

'I'm afraid I don't watch cookery programmes. I'm a very plain cook.'

Belinda said this proudly, as Englishwomen so often do.

'So, what are the programmes?'

'Well, there's a quiz called *A Question of Salt* and a cookery programme called *Here's One I Made Earlier* and now I have my own series called *Hooray, It's Henry.*'

'No, not heard of them. We're probably very out of touch in our rural retreat. Well, good for you.'

She moved on, and Henry realised how vain he had been even to consider that there could be a moment when he wasn't patronised by the Boyce-Uppinghams of this world. That had been decided when he was born, and nothing he could do in his mere life could change it.

He realised, to his horror, that despite his dislike of all the inappropriate references to his fame, he was decidedly miffed that Belinda of all people hadn't heard of it.

The sixteen-year-old great-great-nephew of one of James's old colleagues came up to him and asked him for his autograph.

What should he do?

It was so inappropriate.

It was in such bad taste.

It would give the lad such pleasure.

Sometimes one just has to be unselfish. He signed with pleasure, and he saw Belinda looking across the room with an astonishment that was almost comical. He wondered if, until that moment, she had believed a word he had said.

Despite all his successes, Henry still felt surprised at every new expression of interest in him. He was astounded when Ammonia Productions asked if they could film him for a new series called *A Month in Their Life*.

They didn't propose to film every single minute. No cameras would follow him to the lavatory. No cameras would intrude into his bedroom. They would not film any particular portion of his life every day, but, over a month, they would cover a representative selection of his activities, and he would be bound by his contract to inform them of all these activities and give them access, should they desire it.

He was very doubtful about agreeing to this, flattering though it was. He said that he would have to ask his family and friends.

Greg and Michelle in the Café were all for it. It would be good publicity for the business, and for them.

Kate unashamedly suggested that if he visited the Umbrella Theatre it would help her put bums on seats.

Ben was now helping in the kitchen when he was fit enough, because he was no longer strong enough to hold down a proper job. He felt that it would give him another great platform on which to warn young people of the dangers of drugs.

Everyone, except Hilary, agreed that in the twenty-first century there was no such thing as bad publicity.

Nigel Clinton was very anxious for Hilary to agree. He said that the sales department might take a dim view if she turned down what might be a great opportunity to publicise her books.

In the end, Henry persuaded Ammonia to incorporate in the contract that the final cut of the programme would include scenes of him discussing Hilary's new book with her and a scene at the Umbrella Theatre. They were reluctant, but he was adamant, and in the end they had to agree.

Most of the month went very smoothly. Greg and Michelle in particular played up to the cameras.

The very fact of the filming caused changes to their plans. Jack and Flick brought the family down so that the children could be seen on television. A weekend visit to the Old Manor House was cancelled because Henry didn't want the viewers to be able to identify it. Hilary broke off her work to prepare snacks for Henry more frequently than normal.

But one major problem cropped up during the month. Henry received a rather shattering phone call.

'It's Ginny, Henry.'

For just a moment, a tiny, awful moment, she caught him on the hop.

'Ginny Fenwick, *Thurmarsh Evening Argus*.'

'I realise that, Ginny,' he lied. 'I was just taken by surprise. It's been so long – and, yes, I know it's partly my fault. I should have kept in touch more than I have.'

'Why should you? You escaped. Why should you revisit the zoo?'

'Ginny! I don't feel like that. Surely you know I'm not like that?'

'Henry, there's some news. I thought you ought to know. It's not good, I'm afraid. Helen's dead.'

The shock pierced his heart. He gasped.

'No! She can't be. Not Helen.'

'I know. I think we all feel a bit like that.'

Images of Helen Plunkett, née Cornish, whipped through Henry's mind.

'I didn't even know she was ill.'

Helen at the *Thurmarsh Evening Argus*, exciting even when writing about what women wore next to their skin. Helen, playing games, pressing thighs, teasing pricks.

'I think Ted wanted to keep her to himself towards the end. He'd found it so difficult to do so during the rest of their life.'

'I can understand.'

Helen inviting him back home, getting him all excited, and there was Ted all the time. Games. Bitch. Dead? No!

'When's the funeral?'

The image that he couldn't recall, because he had been too drunk to remember anything, but he'd heard it so often that he almost felt he did remember it. Rather like some of Ben's 'memories', probably.

'Sorry. I was just checking the time. Monday. Thurmarsh Crematorium. Eleven thirty.'

Helen, naked beneath him on the green baize. His biggest ever break, it had seemed at the time. He had told her that she had the most beautiful legs he had ever seen. He couldn't remember them.

'We'll be there.'

Poor Ginny. She only had two ambitions.

'How are things with Hilary?'

To find a good man and to become a war correspondent.

'Fine. Things are great.'

She never fulfilled either of them.

'Good. I'm glad.'

The editorial team at Ammonia Productions grew very excited when they heard about the funeral.

'That's great news. That'll give the programme some real bite,' said one.

'A real focus,' added another

'Absolutely. A real focus,' agreed a third.

'Wait a minute,' Henry told them. 'There's Helen's family to consider. There's her friends. There's my friends. We'll have to ask them.'

'It's in your contract. Sorry.'

'Well, I won't go, then. The contract says you have to be able to go where I go. It doesn't say I have to agree to go where you want me to go.'

He rang Ginny and told her that, devastated though he was not to be able to pay his last respects to Helen, he wasn't going. He told her why.

She rang back and told him that she had spoken to all the relevant people and they were all happy to have the cameras there.

'They lead dull lives, Henry. It'll be an excitement, and Helen would be thrilled. You know that.'

Reluctantly, he agreed.

It was strange to return to Thurmarsh, the town of their birth, the uncompromising, undistinguished town of their childhood, the town which formed them and which held so many memories, good and bad.

Hilary snuggled beside him as the early morning train snaked through the shires.

'Thank you, darling, for something I've never mentioned,' she said. 'Thank you for never mentioning it.'

'What's that?'

But he knew. Amazingly, before she mentioned it, he knew.

'I walked out, after you had suspected me of having an affair with Nigel.'

'I deserved it.'

'I'm not speaking of that, and you know it.' She looked out of the window. They were passing a field with several horses prancing about, made frisky by the train. Behind them was a huge tyre dump. They were approaching a town. 'I left my children.'

'You were ill.'

'I was ill later. My pride in my integrity was so great that when it was offended I walked out and left Kate and Jack. Sometimes I think I must have been a monster.'

'Ridiculous. It's not as if you abandoned them.'

'No. It was actually a remarkable vote of confidence in you, I like to think. I was confident they would be in good hands, even at the moment when you had behaved so badly that I couldn't live with you. What a prig I was.'

'Rubbish.'

The train was going irritatingly slowly. They began to get tense, urging it on with their bodies, willing it on with their minds.

Henry knew that Hilary hadn't finished what she wanted to say, but this time he had no idea what was coming.

'I wouldn't be like that now, if you . . .'

She stopped.

'If I what?'

'Accused me of having an affair.'

'I wouldn't. You wouldn't.'

'I hope not.'

She squeezed his hand and looked away again.

'I wouldn't necessarily leave you now if you had an affair,' she said. 'I don't expect anybody to be perfect any more.'

He could hardly breathe.

'Why do you say that?'

'I was thinking about Helen. You always fancied her.'

'Oh God. I was a fool.'

'It's a hard ask, expecting a man never to be a fool.'

Don't talk like that, Hilary. Please. I need all the help I can get.

'I have no intention of cheating on you,' he said.

'Good.'

She gave him a quick kiss.

Suddenly, after the kiss, they became conscious that a camera had been on them all the time. At last they had grown so used to it that they had forgotten it. At last the editorial team had some real footage, unaffected by their presence. As a result, the footage wasn't high-powered enough, and none of it made the final cut.

They didn't talk much for the rest of the journey, partly because of their awareness of the cameras, and partly because they were busy with their memories.

Henry had been, in popular estimation, very close to being, if not actually being, the worst reporter in the long history of the *Thurmarsh Evening Argus*.

Hilary had suffered her worst moments in the town. It was here, in her teens, that she had been raped. She had taught, briefly, and given birth to two children, and found a way into Cousin Hilda's heart, but she had made no real mark. It was here that she had walked out of her marriage.

'I'm really sorry, Ted,' said Henry as they gathered outside the crematorium on a suitably cloudy, dank morning.

'Me too,' said Hilary.

'Thanks,' said Ted. 'The point is, she's left it too late. Who'll have me now?'

'Nonsense,' said Henry. 'You're still a fine figure of a man.'

He kissed Ginny warmly and squeezed her hand.

'Great to see you again, even in these circumstances,' he said.

She had become distinctly large, and slightly lame.

She hugged him and said, 'Welcome back, and congratulations on everything' loud enough for the Ammonia sound man to capture.

Helen's sister Jill arrived. When she saw the camera, she stopped just out of its range, in order to check her make-up and tidy her hair. She had never been beautiful, but she had been sexy. She was seriously over-weight now. Henry could hardly recognise her. She came up and kissed him enthusiastically. When he had fancied her she had shrunk from him. Now that he didn't fancy her she was all over him, irritatingly tactile. Her husband, Gordon Carstairs, was the man with whom Ginny had kept Henry awake during the long South Yorkshire nights. The years had treated him more kindly than his wife. He still looked craggily sexy.

'Henry!' he said, embracing him. 'Hilary!' He kissed her. 'Chocks away! Rhubarb!'

Hilary raised her eyebrows at Henry, and he shook his head imperceptibly. Gordon had always been enigmatic, but now he was incomprehensible.

They moved into the waiting room, out of the lazy breeze. They wondered how many more were coming.

Colin Edgeley was next to turn up, hair white and straggly, still a gap between his teeth, frail, a ghost of the man called Colin Edgeley, with whom Henry had once drunk.

Terry Skipton, his old news editor, fearsome then, old and harmless now, was wheeled in by his wife Violet, whose moustache had gone entirely white.

'Henry!' said Terry Skipton. 'We have followed your every move with pride.'

'Aye, our kid,' agreed Colin Edgeley hurriedly. 'Fantastic. Great. Always knew you had it in you.'

'Kiss me, Hardy!' said Gordon Carstairs.

Henry didn't think that many of Gordon's gnomic utterances would make it to the final cut.

They filed into the chapel. Apart from the journalists there were a few cousins and nephews and nieces, and the odd neighbour, but it was a sad end for a sparkling woman.

The service began. The undertakers brought in the coffin. The cameras turned. At least, thought Henry, she was in the spotlight at the last.

The vicar was straight out of Central Casting. This was his audition, his performance and his credit. He even introduced himself by name. His thunderous sing-song resounded round the sparsely filled chapel like a fart in a compression chamber. Henry hoped fervently that the man wouldn't make the final cut.

Afterwards, there was a brief reception in a local hotel, a glass of wine and a few sandwiches. The sandwiches, like the function room, were sparsely filled. Hard though Henry tried not to be, he found himself at centre stage. He was the sun, and people were cheered by his glow. 'We are honoured by your presence,' intoned the vicar, who was on orange juice, in case the bishop happened to see the programme.

After the sad reception the journalists went to a sad pub for a sad drink. The camera did not accompany them. The producer felt that he had enough footage of the event.

Without the camera, everything changed. Now the tribute to Henry's success became resentment. Ted scowled. Colin, who never went out any more and so got drunk on a few pints, said, 'I suppose you think you're still my fucking friend because you send a fucking Christmas card every fucking year.'

'New balls! Baghdad!' exclaimed Gordon Carstairs.

'Do you remember Neil Mallet?' Henry asked, desperate for silence not to fall. 'Always going off home to do his laundry.'

'Oh my God!' said Ginny. 'I have to get to the dry cleaners by five.'

Henry gave up after that.

The party soon broke up, by silent consent.

'Those were our best days,' said Ted, as he left rather unsteadily. 'They were our halcyon days. If only we'd known it at the sodding time.'

Henry's eyes met Hilary's, and he knew that they were both thinking the same thing. They still had their rampaging days. They still had their halcyon days.

Later, in a radio interview, Henry gave his opinion of *A Month in Their Life*.

'Everything was affected by the camera,' he said. 'Nothing remained utterly true. To call any non-fiction "reality television" is to admit that we are a society that has lost respect for language and for the rigours of definition and meaning. I think we're in danger, therefore, of removing all meaning from our lives.'

'Pretentious bastard,' muttered Ted to his shaving bowl, in the emptiness of his home, when he heard it.

It was no surprise when Denzil went: he'd been failing for years. Henry couldn't bring himself to write to anybody on the paper to tell them. It was all too far in the past. It was over.

There was a reasonable turn out at Mortlake Crematorium. Quite a few people from Denzil's local – Lampo hated pubs but Denzil popped into one every Saturday morning; one or two of Lampo's former colleagues at Sotheby's; two or three collectors; a biscuit-tin enthusiast; Henry and Hilary and Kate and Camilla and Guiseppe; Mrs Hargreaves; Tosser; two neighbours; and five assorted relatives, two of whom Lampo had never met.

'They think there may be money,' Lampo whispered to Henry in the chapel. 'Little do they know there are only biscuit tins, and he's left them and the house to me.'

There was a small party afterwards at Lampo's. Everybody went except one of the collectors.

'I won't be able to stay, Lampo,' Tosser said to his old schoolmate. 'I'd like to, but . . . Felicity, you know. At the moment she's . . . edgy. She has these edgy times.'

Henry and Hilary invited Mrs Hargreaves out to dinner at a restaurant of her choice near her home on the following Tuesday. She said that none of them were any good, but they could tell that she was thrilled.

The biscuit-tin enthusiast wandered around examining the biscuit tins with such enthusiasm that Lampo asked Henry to keep an eye on him. Henry rather enjoyed doing this. It took his mind off the sadness of the house without Denzil, and it enabled him to try out his untested skills as a private detective. He wandered and talked, watching as he talked, but very discreetly. He felt that he did it to the manner born. The man couldn't possibly suspect that he was under surveillance.

'I'm not going to steal them, you know.'

'Sorry?'

'You're keeping an eye on me, furtively,' said the biscuit-tin man. 'I say "furtively". I've never seen anything so blatant. You make the police look subtle.'

Tosser approached Henry as he was talking to Lampo.

'Well, well,' he said. 'The three of us, eh? The two study mates and their fag, fifty years on. Well, well.' He looked at his watch. 'I shall have to shoot, I'm afraid.'

'Felicity,' said Henry and Lampo in unison.

Tosser nodded, shook hands with them, and left.

Even here, at this low key event, there was no escape for Henry from his fame. One of the collectors approached him and said, 'I have a bone to pick with you.'

'Oh?'

'My daughter's friend was in tears because of you.'

'Sorry?'

'She bought a set of your plates for a friend's wedding.'

'What was wrong with them?'

'She thought HP stood for Harry Potter. She was so disappointed.'

However famous you are, thought Henry, there'll always be somebody more famous than you. He found that reassuring.

Henry and Hilary stayed till everyone else had gone, and then a bit more. They just couldn't find it in themselves to leave.

'How are you?' asked Henry, his banality rescued by his sincerity. 'Really?'

'I can't feel anything except guilt,' said Lampo. 'I just feel so guilty.'

'You stood by him. You stayed with him.'

'He was very hurt. He hid it, but he was very hurt. I can't even feel sad for him. There's too much guilt. And I wouldn't have wanted him to last much longer. He would have gone into a real decline. He was spared that. I'll always be grateful that he was spared that.'

'What about your friend?' asked Hilary. 'Is it too early to ask, or will he move in?'

'Oh, no. No, no. This isn't his kind of place. He'd find

it stifling. I'll sell, and we'll get somewhere else – possibly in the country.'

'May we meet him?'

'Eventually.' Lampo sighed. 'I must warn you he isn't . . . well, let's put it this way: he isn't Denzil. Yes, of course you'll meet him, but not while Denzil's barely cold. Of *course* you'll meet him. You're my closest friends, you know.'

'Thank you.'

'My best friends.'

'Thank you.'

'The most loyal and affectionate of all my friends.'

'Thank you.'

'Damn it, you're my only friends.'

In the vintage Daimler, on the way home, Henry sighed deeply.

Hilary gave him a wry look. He flinched. He knew her wry looks.

'Why the sigh?' she asked.

'Why the wry look?'

'Because I thought I knew what the sigh meant.'

'I thought I knew what the wry look meant.'

'We know each other too well. Yes, I was thinking, you're fed up with all this sadness coming along and interrupting your enjoyment of your success.'

'Well, I am human.'

'I know, and I do love you. Anyway, maybe things will cheer up a bit now.'

Five days later, two aeroplanes flew into the twin towers of the World Trade Center.

*

The modern pine table had been distressed to make it look old. Henry was beginning to look old without help, and this made him distressed.

He was eating his second slice of toast, the one with marmalade, very slowly, while reading a letter.

'I don't believe it,' he said. 'What a year. Another one's gone.'

'Oh my God. Who?'

'Timothy Shitehouse.'

'Should you call him that now he's dead?' asked Hilary.

'Everybody always did. It's a term of affection. All right, then: Timothy Whitehouse. Do you remember him?'

'I remember what he was. Director (Operations) of the Cucumber Marketing Board.'

'Just so. The letter's from John Barrington. I think you'd left me before he came into my life. He succeeded Roland Stagg as Regional Co-ordinator, Northern Counties (Excluding Berwick-on-Tweed).'

'Your boss, in fact.'

'Yes, but I have to give the pompous sod his full title. I disliked him intensely. Being elected Gherkin Man of the Year went to his head.'

He read the letter to her.

My dear Henry,

I am so sorry to bring a cloud into the clear blue sky of your success, which has thrilled us all, but dear old Timothy Shitehouse has gone to join Roland Stagg in the great marketing board in the sky.

We'll be having a bit of a wake, and it would be

wonderful if you could be there. Nobody is likely to forget how much you can drink at parties and you might liven us up a bit.

Dear old Timothy. He wasn't of this world, but I liked him. He died in his sleep; didn't wake up one morning. I think we all want to go like that.

As you probably know, the Cucumber Marketing Board was disbanded two years ago, but it lives on in our annual reunions.

I know that you and I didn't always see eye to eye, Henry, but in my retirement I am much changed. It turns out that having been Gherkin Man of the Year not once, but twice, doesn't cut much ice with the younger generation, with which my family abounds. I am regarded as a harmless old bore. If I was ever a little arrogant – I know people thought I was – I lost that long ago. All in all, I think we could have a jolly little session in the only decent pub in the area.

I know you're very busy, but the Head of Domestic Services (Excluding Berwick-on-Tweed) and I do hope to see you, and please give our very best wishes to Margaret.

Always your friend

John Barrington, FGMY

'Who's Margaret?' asked Hilary.

'You are. Or Diana is. And this from a man who prided himself on his command of detail.'

'What does FGMY stand for?'

'I very much fear it stands for "Former Gherkin Man of the Year".'

'Oh Lord. Are we going?'

'No. I can't face it after Thurmarsh. I've had enough funerals for one year.'

Unfortunately we can't decide when there have been enough funerals, and there was one more to come. This was undoubtedly the saddest of them all.

It's natural for children to lose their parents, but it's desperate when parents lose their children.

Not that Ben was actually their child, but they almost forgot that.

It was particularly sad, particularly cruel of God, if there was one, which they didn't believe, or of Fate, if that was a meaningful word, which they doubted, to take him away from them so soon after they had found him.

Henry and Hilary didn't know how to console each other. To have hunted for him, to have found him, to have nurtured him, to have brought him back into the family, spent patient hours trying – with limited success, it must be said – to fill in the gaps in his memory, and then for him to go – it put the tin lid on a sad year.

The fact was that his body was knackered from abuse. He picked up another dose of pneumonia and died from a mixture of that and liver failure.

Diana and Gunter came over from Switzerland; Jack and Flick came down from Thurmarsh; Camilla and Guiseppe cut short a holiday in Italy; but Henry had an enormous shock when he rang Tosser.

'Thank you for telling me,' Tosser said. 'I hope it goes well.'

'What? Aren't you coming?'

'Why should I? He's your son now.'

'Nigel! This is so important that I promise never to call you Tosser again if you come. You must come.'

'Why?'

'You're Camilla's father. She needs you.'

'She has you.'

'Nigel, this is nonsense. He *was* your son. Fact. You *will* regret it. Fact. You're in danger of excluding yourself from the human race. Nigel . . . if you hadn't retired I'd buy a pension off you, if only you'd come.'

'It's easy to say that.'

'All right. Find some colleague who sells pensions and can give you a cut, and I'll take out a pension with him.'

There was a long pause.

'There'll be no need for that,' said Nigel. 'You're right, of course. I'll come. I . . . I don't know whether Felicity will. She's . . . er . . . up and down, Henry. Up and down.'

In the end Felicity did go, and Henry was pleased. He was also pleased to see Lampo, but shocked by how sad he looked.

There was a contingent from the Streatham Asbo, and Michelle and Greg and the kitchen staff all went, and Kate of course, and Darren in a daze, and even one or two customers who had come to know Ben.

It was a humanist ceremony, with readings and poems that Ben had liked, some of them very spiritual, but none of them specifically religious.

Henry gave the funeral address, and he did so without notes.

'I came to think of Ben as my son,' he said, 'and I came to be very proud of him. We did what we thought was our best for him in an earlier life, but I think now that perhaps we could have done better.

'When we hunted for him, and found him again, we hoped that he would have a long and a full life. He hasn't, but let nobody dare say that it was all a waste of time. In every day of Ben's relatively brief new life he gave pleasure to those around him and, even more important, those around him gave pleasure to him. There was a lot he couldn't do, but what he did he did with enthusiasm and style.

'Nobody could have seen the love between him and Darren and remained homophobic. I must praise our dear friend Darren, who has been magnificent. I know, Darren, I'm embarrassing you. Sorry. I hate tattoos and I don't like nose studs.' He saw Felicity flinch. 'Darren has both, and I wish he didn't, but the point is that we shouldn't let these things influence our judgement of character. Darren, mate, you're one of the good guys, and there'll always be a home for you at the Café Henry.

'I am now hugely successful, something that I never expected. Ben stacked supermarket shelves. That doesn't necessarily make me a better person than him or happier than him.

'We didn't discuss death with Ben. There wasn't any need to. I think he'd known for a long while that he wouldn't live to a ripe old age. I remember something he said when he was on my programme – and what a memorable edition he gave us. He talked about the beauty of dragonflies, and asked, "Are their lives of no value, because they are so brief?" We must all take comfort from the fact that his answer to his own question was clearly so positive.

'The family have decided to give Ben a woodland burial, near The Old Manor House, which he loved. We think this is what he would have wanted.

'I won't say any more about Ben's character. Everyone's character is praised at funerals, which might devalue anything I could say.

'In fact, I won't say anything more, except . . . goodbye, Ben.'

They held a reception at the Café, which was closed for the day.

Henry talked to everybody, and everybody talked to him, and he drank rather too much, as did most of the guests, and in the morning he could only remember three of his conversations – with Darren, with Lampo, and with Felicity.

'I hope you'll stay friends with us, Darren,' he said.

'No. Sorry.'

'What?'

'I can't. Sorry. Can't face it. Can't stay here without Ben.'

'No, but in time . . .'

'No. Sorry. I have to move on. There was this politician, he said, "On your bike." I don't see why people should have to do that because some berk tells them to, but in my case, yes, it suits. I'm off – on me bike.'

'Well, I'm sorry, but . . . take your time.'

'No. I'm going now. Can't stand it here without him. I've got to find a new life. Maybe abroad. I may find somebody and he may even be as good as Ben, who knows? Won't be better, though. Love you, love Hilary, she's fantastic, love the Café, love the food, love the wine list, but . . . time to piss off. On me bike. Bye.'

He walked upstairs, to collect his gear. Henry didn't see him leave. In fact, he never saw him again.

'Thank you for coming, Lampo.'

Lampo shook his head.

'Don't thank me,' he said. 'I came because I can't bear to be alone.'

'Alone?'

'Alone. I put Denzil through all that for nothing, Henry. For nothing.'

'It's over, is it, your . . .'

'It's over. He wanted me for odd moments. Snatched moments. He didn't want me for life. He didn't want me to grow old with him, as Denzil had grown old with me. We had a row. I told him what I thought of him. He got very savage and hit me.'

'Oh, Lampo.'

'What fools we are to let our pricks rule our heads. Oh, Henry. At first, Henry – you'll think this pathetic, what a sad old man – at first I talked to Denzil every day after he died, but I can't talk to him any more. I'm so ashamed. I forgot, in my fury, that I'd given the vindictive little bastard a key to the house. He came and took all Denzil's biscuit tins. Every one.'

'Thank you for coming, Felicity.'

'Well . . . I'm sorry we didn't do more, Henry, but you know what Nigel's like. And then . . . well . . . he seemed so happy here.'

'He was.'

'I bought two of your curd tarts in your Tyke Treats range at the Kingston Asbo, Henry.'

Henry's mouth dropped open at this change of subject. 'And . . . ?'

'They were very dry and crumbly.'

'You're saying this to me now, here, today?'

'Well, I never see you, and I thought you ought to know. I'm not complaining, Henry. I'm marking your card. You have a reputation. They aren't doing your reputation any good whatsoever. I thought you should know.'

'Thank you, Felicity. Thank you very much.'

Was there no escape from the demands of fame?

13 Will Success Spoil Henry Pratt?

Henry and Hilary were having that rarest of luxuries – a quiet evening at home. They didn't have the energy to play Scrabble. They didn't even have the energy to watch television. They lingered, lazily, at the kitchen table, over a bottle of sound red wine.

But Henry couldn't relax entirely. He had to make plans.

'I think we should do something in memory of Ben,' he said.

'We give to the homeless. Why don't we just give more?'

'I'm not sure money is enough. It's too easy. I think we should open a soup kitchen. A mobile soup kitchen. The Ben Pilkington-Brick Soup Kitchen.'

'You're getting to love grand gestures, aren't you?'

'Not grand gestures, no. Action. Symbolism, if you like. Inspiration by example. It's so easy to become selfish.'

The phone shrilled. It sounded particularly obtrusive on so peaceful an evening.

'Damn damn damn!'

'Don't answer it.'

But he did. He always did.

'Henry Pratt?'

'Yes.'

'Oh dear.'

'What?'

'I so hoped you wouldn't be there. We have two hundred people here, Mr Pratt, who have paid good money to hear you talk.'

'Oh shit. I mean . . . I'm sorry . . . who are you?'

'We're raising money for research into Alzheimer's. You've supported us regularly. You've always said it's close to your heart. When we suggested you spoke to us, you jumped at it. You said you'd speak for nothing. We arranged it weeks ago.'

'I'm so sorry. There's no excuse. I forgot.'

Henry didn't think that the second series of *Hooray, It's Henry* was as good as the first. It was no longer an autobiography in food, he had told most of his personal stories, it was more like other programmes. Most of the guests were no longer known to him, they were people who fitted the theme of the week – but the viewing public didn't seem to notice, and the ratings were as good as ever.

Life was now so busy that there was very little time to think about Ben, but Henry and Hilary were both determined that, painful though it was, they must keep his memory alive, in their daily life as well as in grand gestures. It was Hilary's suggestion that, on Sundays, they should turn up at the Café half an hour before the programme began, and have moments of quiet reflection in the top-floor flat, which had lain empty since Darren had roared off.

Sometimes other people who had known Ben joined them – Camilla and Guiseppe obviously, and Diana whenever she was in England, and they talked to and about Ben in ways that gave them great sadness but also much consolation. These moments were now more precious to Henry and Hilary than the programme itself, which had become less of a thrill and more of a routine.

Hilary noticed that Henry was developing a didactic streak. It was born out of enthusiasm, and for that reason seemed to be regarded as endearing – good old Henry, the People's Chef, with another bee in his bonnet – but it worried her. Was he starting to take himself too seriously?

In one edition he spoke passionately about the need to have a space in one's house for eating meals together. It shocked him profoundly that some modern houses had nowhere at all for eating meals. 'I hope you aren't watching this while eating ready-made meals off a tray,' he told his viewers sternly. He moralised about the needs of people to break bread together, as had been done, he said, 'in every society in every age in every part of the world'. Hilary didn't ask him how he knew this. 'Mrs Thatcher said that there was no such thing as society,' he told his viewers. 'You are in danger of proving her right. You must eat together as a family, not necessarily every day, but a few times every week. If you don't, don't grumble if your family becomes dysfunctional. It'll be your fault.'

There were letters for and against Henry in the *Radio Times* and the newspapers. Hilary felt just a little uneasy.

In another edition he told his audience that houses where no proper cooking was done felt and smelt dead. 'It's a joy to enter a house with the smell of fried onions or an honest soup,' he said. 'The whole house develops vitality and joy. Don't be lazy. Cooking is fun. I'd rather you cooked and enjoyed it than watched me do it.'

Hilary *and* the BBC felt just a little uneasy about this. The producer, Laurence Pangbourne, told Henry that 'the powers that be' wanted to warn Henry not to give the viewers hostages to fortune by telling them they shouldn't be watching.

'I think I know what I'm doing,' he said.

In another edition he fulminated against factory farming. 'Nobody has any right to condemn anyone else for cruelty to animals until they give up eating battery chickens,' he roared, almost out of control with what his fans called passion and his detractors called self-righteousness.

A BBC memo congratulated him on his passion and commitment, but warned him not to return to the subject too often. There were mutterings from the powerful farming lobby and the food industry.

'Your craven memo almost encourages me to repeat myself,' he replied, 'but, sadly, I can't. People who repeat themselves are bores. Also, I am only too well aware that people who repeat themselves are bores, which is why you have only almost encouraged me to repeat myself, despite your craven memo.'

Another controversial outburst was about the need for people to be taught how to eat. It was no use chefs creating imaginative dishes if their customers weren't adventurous too. It was a wasted effort for a chef to create subtle masterpieces if people wolfed them down in seven minutes while discussing the sales figures for China and Japan. It was fatuous for a chef to create complex dishes out of disparate ingredients if people put seven different ingredients on their fork at once and pitched them all into their mouths like farmers forking hay.

Hilary ventured a word of warning.

'Darling, I think you should be careful not to insult your audience too much,' she said.

'Darling, I think I know what I'm doing after all these years,' was Henry's reply.

Hilary realised with a shudder that it was becoming difficult to venture any kind of criticism of Henry.

When she accused him of being more irritable than he used to be, he brushed it off as the effect of tiredness.

'Then don't take on so much,' she warned him again.

It made no difference. He accepted every invitation to speak, and remembered most of them. He loved having an audience.

Hooray, It's Henry said the poster at Dalton College.

Henry stood, on the very stage where he had done his act as the headmaster, forty-nine years before, and talked with vast enthusiasm about food. He amused the boys with his tales of his time at Dalton – the bullying, the snobbery. He told them that he had been nick-named Oiky. 'Never look down on people because of their background,' he said. 'Because of their character, possibly; because of their background, no.'

He told them about Lampo Davey, who covered hard-boiled eggs with bottled mayonnaise and bits of anchovies and thought himself sophisticated, and about Tosser Pilkington-Brick, who ate drinking chocolate, in powder form, with a spoon.

*

Hooray, It's Henry said a poster at Thurmarsh Grammar School for boys.

Henry stood in the very assembly hall where, when the headmaster, Mr E. F. Crowther had told the boys that, in the battle to rebuild the nation after the war, there would 'once again be Thurmarshians in the van', thirteen-year-old Henry had whispered 'the bread van'.

He didn't tell this story about the bread van. He didn't tell the boys that here he had been known as Snobby. He suddenly found that he had become tired of telling jokes against himself.

Afterwards, as he walked towards his Porsche, he heard a loud sniff.

Never forget where you came from, it said.

It caught him unprepared, and unsettled him. He came out in goose-pimples; he looked round the badly-lit car park, felt the cool northern breeze, and had a disturbing sensation of having changed so much that he didn't belong here any more.

He drove out of Thurmarsh as fast as he could. He never wanted to see the place again. He was pleased to get to the characterless comfort of his hotel room, double glazed against aeroplanes, traffic, charm and sniffs.

When he got home the next day, exhausted after his drive down the crowded M1, and still shaken by his experience, he wanted to talk to Hilary about these things. Suddenly he realised with a shudder that it was becoming difficult to talk to her about his innermost feelings at all.

On Monday, 1 April, 2002, Prince Charles, upset with the BBC because their newsreader hadn't worn a black tie to announce the death of the Queen Mother, filmed a poignant tribute to his grandmother on ITV; Israeli soldiers in an armoured personnel carrier opened fire on international peace campaigners in the West Bank; the National Union of Teachers threatened a thirty-five hour week if their workload wasn't cut; and, in the Café Henry, a former fag offered jobs to the two men for whom he had fagged all those years ago.

If not all the pleasure he got from this was entirely out of the goodness of his heart, if he felt a certain smug satisfaction at the turn of events, well, only a very rigid moralist would blame him.

Lampo looked smaller, tauter, tighter. Older, which wasn't surprising. Defeated, which was.

'I want to offer you a job, Lampo,' he said, as soon as Lampo was seated on the opposite side of his ever more cluttered desk.

'Is this an April fool?'

'No! I wouldn't do that to you. Besides, it's three minutes past twelve and April fools end at noon.'

'I'm seventy, Henry. You don't get offered jobs in your seventies.'

'Age is nothing to do with it in this organisation,' said Henry. 'It's my business and I can do what I like.'

'What do you want me to do? I can't cook. Denzil did all the cooking.'

He sighed.

'Miss him terribly still?'

'Terribly. More each day. The longer I don't see him, the more I miss him. A day without him is easy, a week difficult, a month distressing, a year almost unbearable. Don't let anyone fob you off with that nonsense of time healing. I even miss his biscuit tins. I even miss his snores. He was never . . . fastidious, and it irritated me. I couldn't care less now. If only, Henry.'

'Mr If Only Missed the Bus.'

'What??'

'One of my teachers, Miss Candy, had a fund of minatory saws.'

'Priceless. I know what you mean, of course. Guilt corrodes. But I can't help it. I go through life and relive the last years quite differently. I can't help it.'

'You need a boyfriend.'

'At my age? Pull the other one.'

'Exactly.'

'I can't even pull this one. I'm a husk, Henry.'

'Nonsense.'

'What is this job, anyway?'

'Manager of the South Kensington Café Henry. It's perfect for you, Lampo. You're so South Ken.'

'I don't know whether that's a compliment or not.'

'Don't sit at home moping. Get out. Meet some nice young man.'

'What nice young man would be interested in me?'

'Meet some nice old man, then. Will you do it?'

Lampo thought long and hard.

'Do you know?' he said at last, sounding very surprised. 'I will.'

'Nigel!' he said, some twenty minutes later. 'Good to see you.'

Tosser looked wary. He always did when Henry called him Nigel.

'I want to offer you a job, Nigel.'

'What sort of job?' said Nigel cautiously.

'I want to expand. Open more Cafés. Go nationwide.'

'Why?'

'I'm a businessman. That's what businessmen do. You know that. Anyway, that's my decision.'

'Where do I come in?'

'I want you to find sites, buildings that might be suitable for conversion. I want you to negotiate on my behalf to buy those sites.'

'I've never done anything like that. I don't know about sites and buildings.'

'It's all about what it will cost and how much we can make out of the site. It's all about money. Food's my area of expertise. Money's yours.'

'Why me?'

'Loyalty, Nigel, and perhaps a belief that you have never been fully stretched, if I may say so, never quite fulfilled your full potential.'

'I see. I'm not sure whether that's a compliment or not.'

'It is and it isn't. You look a bit soft, Nigel, a little puddingy in your retirement, if you don't mind my saying that. You need to get off your arse and face a challenge. It'll be good for you.'

'I don't know. This is so unexpected. I find that . . . you're right. It is retirement. It's the idleness. I've become rather indecisive. I . . . oh dear . . . what shall I say?'

'Of course you'll have to consider Felicity. After all, she's frail, ultra-sensitive, squeamish, edgy, picky, not resilient.'

'What?'

'Just some of the ways you've described her. You must love her very much – and you'll have grown used to being with her all day every day. You may think this will involve too many trips away from home.'

'I'll do it. Damn it, I'll do it, Henry.'

Nigel joined Lampo in the Café, and Henry opened a bottle of his best red wine to celebrate with them. Henry chose the lamb Hilda. He quite expected to hear her sniff at the thought of his eating a dish named after her. He quite expected her to say, 'What is it? Boned shoulder of lamb stuffed with spotted dick?' He hoped that she might express her pleasure at the way he'd kept her memory alive, but ghosts didn't work like that. They didn't appear when you wanted them.

He told Lampo and Tosser about Greg's famed inability to remember acronyms. When Greg brought their food over, Henry asked him, 'Did you ever have TCP when you were a kid?' and he replied, 'Yeah. I had a raincoat made of it. Only left it on a train coming back from watching Spurs, didn't I, and got beaten by me dad. Spurs got beaten as well, by Chelsea, the bastards.'

Henry could see that both Lampo and Tosser were uneasy at his making fun of Greg in this way. This irritated him. What business was it of theirs?

His irritation didn't last long. He felt full of generosity as he discussed their jobs with them and invited them both to spend a weekend later in the month at The Old Manor House.

Lampo was quite frank about it, saying that he couldn't bear the thought of a weekend in an English village.

Wellies brought him out in a rash. Cowpats made him depressed. The thought of a visit to a village pub gave him palpitations. 'You're right, Henry,' he said. 'I'm South Ken through and through. I'm South Kensington Man.'

Tosser said that he would have loved to go, Felicity looked good in green wellies, but unfortunately it clashed with a family do. Henry had no idea whether this was the truth or an excuse. He felt nowadays that he hardly knew Tosser at all.

He went up to the bar to open a second bottle. As he was getting it out of the rack, he heard Greg talking to the double act, Little and Often, who had both come into the Café together for once. He heard Greg say, 'It's rare to see you both here, gentlemen. We often see Little, but we see very little of Often.' If Greg was going to start making jokes . . . and to comedians at that . . . Comedians liked making jokes to people; they did not like people making jokes to them. Their faces were grim. Greg's lack of sense irritated Henry.

He returned to Lampo and Tosser with the second bottle. He felt good. He felt magnanimous. He felt suddenly powerful, the humble fag turned provider to two sad old men.

After Lampo and Tosser had gone, Henry took a walk. He had come to love being in Soho, and wandering round it, popping into the Groucho or the French House for a glass of wine or an anis, visiting the Coach and Horses, where Jeffrey Bernard had so often not felt well. He counted *Fear and Loathing in Fitzrovia* among his favourite books. He read about great Soho characters like the splendidly named Muriel Belcher, who for many years had ruled the Colony Club with a rod of iron.

But now he was beginning to walk as if he himself was one of the Soho greats. Henry Pratt, Bohemian, Sohemian, roving Fitzrovian, is, if not exactly unwell, at least swaying slightly. He began to look scornful as he walked past the shady doormen who manned the shady doors of the shady strip-clubs. 'You are impostors,' his scornful look implied. 'I am part of the real Soho. We have style.'

Perhaps what was wrong with the Ben Pilkington-Brick Mobile Soup Kitchen was that it had too much style. Henry bought a smart cream van, and had stunningly moving pictures of Ben on it. The pictures were of course painted by Ben's sister Camilla. In the back of the van there were gleaming vats of soup – and it wasn't just tomato soup or vegetable soup or chicken soup. He was, as he later admitted, losing his sense of simplicity at this stage of his life. A dirty, smelly old man, who has lost all spirit that isn't methylated, doesn't want, when he is rudely awakened from sleep, to hear a concerned voice say, 'Would you like some soup? It's artichoke and celeriac today.'

'I don't see why, because they're down and out, they should only be offered something basic,' Henry told Hilary.

'Because they can only cope with the basic?' she suggested.

Gradually, without his admitting it, the soups became more appropriate.

The van trundled round Central London, night after night, stopping at various points, where Henry hoped that, in time, small crowds of the homeless would gather. A few did, but not as many as he had expected. He had failed to realise the extent to which time was no longer a factor in their lives. They recognised light and darkness, but didn't necessarily even think of them as day and night. They were just the light bit of their eternity, and the dark bit of their eternity. The concept of an hour was beyond them. They might still know the meaning of the word, but it was of no practical value.

Some of them couldn't drink the soup. Some could drink it, but couldn't keep it down. Some of them burnt themselves. Some, unused to the flavours of real food, described it as 'muck'. Some of them were so shaky with drink that they spilt most of it. Some were so shaky without drink that they spilt most of it. Some of them swore at being woken up. One or two grew violent. Henry was scalded by a mug of soup hurled at him.

The project was just about the first element in Henry's life as a celebrity chef to attract any press criticism. It was criticised as being cosmetic, and done for publicity. Camilla's paintings didn't help in this regard. There were rumblings suggesting that he was not sincere. Since sincerity cannot be measured, allegations of insincerity are hard to counter.

Henry couldn't go on, night after night, delivering soup, while still working by day. Within a fortnight he was utterly exhausted. He needed to find volunteers.

He soon realised that he would have to pay his volunteers. There was danger in the work. There were complications over insurance. There were complications over health and safety. Two London boroughs insisted that his volunteers had protective clothing against possible attack. Henry found himself designing anti-soup masks.

His van was too conspicuous. It attracted drunks who weren't homeless. It became a target for yobbos. Never mind anti-soup masks – soon they would need riot shields.

To carry on with the project for ever was impossible, but unless he carried on for ever it was of no value, so he aborted it and gave increased money to the charities for the homeless, just as Hilary had suggested in the first place.

She didn't say, 'I was right, wasn't I?' She wasn't like that. But her eyes said it. They couldn't help it. They were too truthful.

Henry didn't say, 'You were right, darling.' He wasn't like that. But his eyes said it. They were no good at concealment.

Their silence created one more barrier between them, and the ending of the project brought more criticism and more allegations of insincerity. Everything he did was public property now. 'Henry in the Soup' was just one of many headlines. The criticism was regretful rather than cruel, but it was an intimation of what was to come.

Hilary didn't say anything, but Cousin Hilda did.

Putting on airs. Getting carried away. Having ideas. I don't know, said her sniff.

Henry answered his critics fervently and honestly, saying to them what he couldn't say to Hilary. He admitted his mistakes. He expressed deep sorrow and regret. He said that he had been too eager to build a worthy memorial for Ben, who would not have wanted a memorial at all. Ben's life *was* his memorial. Henry had done it all wrong.

On the whole, the public gave him the benefit of the doubt, and his programmes and books continued to succeed, perhaps all the more so because of the publicity.

The publication of *The Pratt Diet* was a major event in the book world. It was described as 'his latest bestseller' on the jacket, which struck Henry as ridiculous, though he didn't complain, and the boast became a self-fulfilling prophecy, as boasts sadly do in the twenty-first century.

At the back of the book there were detailed suggestions for dietary programmes. Day 8, lunch, 5oz pork fillet with toasted apricots, etcetera etcetera. It was not written with any scientific method whatsoever. It was just Henry's idea of a balanced diet. It was delicious, so people enjoyed it, and the portions were on the small side, so people tended to lose a bit of weight. However, the portions were sufficiently large not to cause any real discomfort.

A lot of the people who bought the book never cooked a single thing from it. They just read the suggestions in bed and slavered at the thought of them. Cooking, in an irritating phrase that was about to run through the language like a virus, was the new sex and, as with sex, people dreamt of it far more than they actually did it.

Mohammed El Bashir's photographs were as good as ever, which wasn't surprising as he still took hours over each one. A photograph of a lemon syllabub won second prize in the soft dessert category at the Strasbourg *Foire de Photographie Gastronomique* – the highest placing ever for a British dessert in France.

When they went to The Old Manor House for a couple of days, Henry took his own book with him and read it from cover to cover. Hilary couldn't believe it and asked him why he should read his own book. She didn't find it easy to ask even this. Each day of success seemed to make him less and less approachable.

'I read it in order to think of all those thousands of other people reading it, and in order to imagine what they think as they read it,' he said. 'I find that exciting. All right?'

Hilary did not think it all right, but she didn't say so. Her silence spoke volumes, however.

'Getting jealous, are we?' said Henry.

Hilary went white. The remark was, in book terms, the equivalent of his having believed she was having an affair. Not as serious as that, but serious enough.

Henry knew that he had gone too far, and said no more on the subject. Hilary didn't deign to reply, and Henry couldn't bring himself to apologise, so because it couldn't be commented on the remark didn't go away. It lay in the middle of the bed – 'Getting jealous, are we?' – separating them, forming an invisible verbal barrier that couldn't be crossed. They didn't touch each other now. They lived together, but apart. They were on different continents in the same bed.

Barely a day passed without a proposition of some sort being put to Henry.

He had laughed when his old priest friend Martin Collinghurst had sent him a postcard from Nicaragua suggesting a TV programme for the Catholic Church, called 'I'm a Celibate – Get Me Out of Here'. Now Paradise Television suggested a far less wittily titled series called

'I'm a Culinary – Get Me Out of Here'. They told him that they were also approaching Jamie Oliver, Delia Smith, Gary Rhodes, Gordon Ramsey, Jean-Paul Novelli, Bradley Tompkins, Sally Atkinson, Denise Healey and Simon Hampsthwaite.

The thought of being in the jungle with Bradley nauseated him – he had taken great pains to avoid the man since his discovery of his double life.

A sojourn in the jungle sharing maggotburgers with Sally Atkinson did tempt him for a moment, but the cameras would be on them all the time, so there would be no point, it would be agony.

He decided not to do it. He could get enough publicity without discomfort. Only those who were celebrity junkies or who desperately needed to revive their flagging careers took part in things like that.

In the event all the other chefs must have decided not to do it as well, since it never happened. Or perhaps the programme makers decided that even in the twenty-first century the swearing might have been excessive.

Henry boasted that he never swore in his kitchen or his restaurant. He didn't need to.

Anaemia Television suggested a series in which he taught the lifers in a high security prison how to cook. Hilary thought he ought to consider that seriously.

'I need it like a hole in the head,' he said.

'Yes, but they might need it.'

'I'm sorry. They're criminals. They're paying for what they've done.'

Hilary thought this reply unworthy of the Henry she knew and loved.

In the case of Thurmarsh United Football Club, it was Cousin Hilda who thought Henry's reply unworthy of the Henry she knew and loved. The club asked him to 'do a Delia' – run a café in the Tommy Marsden Stand on match days and try to wean the crowd off pies and hot dogs.

'What crowd?' he asked loftily.

He half expected the sniff. It rarely came when he expected it, but this time it did.

Forgetting where we're coming from, are we? it said. Forgetting our roots!

'Not at all,' said Henry. 'I have them dyed every month.'

Hilary looked at him in astonishment. He had forgotten that she was in the kitchen.

'What on earth do you mean – you have them dyed every month?' she asked.

He looked at her in horror. What could he say? How could he explain?

Well, he'd have to.

'I hear Cousin Hilda sniffing sometimes,' he said. 'She haunts me, and I know what her sniffs mean. I was . . . replying to her sniff.'

'You need help, Henry. Maybe you ought to see a psychiatrist.'

'No!!'

'Or at least the doctor, Henry.'

'No! I do not need a doctor.'

'You know who you sound like when you grit your teeth,' said Hilary sadly. 'Your Uncle Teddy and your Auntie Doris. The teeth gritters.'

'Please don't mock my relatives, Hilary,' said Henry coldly.

Hilary gave him a sad look, then changed the subject.

'Come on,' she said. 'Let me give you a treat. Let's go to dinner at Bartholomew's.'

He liked that idea. He liked Bartholomew's. The food was fairly good, the atmosphere was very good, and it was just across the common from the house.

They walked over just as the light faded and the headlights of the cars were being switched on. Hilary slipped her hand into his, not very confidently. He stroked hers and she squeezed his. All around them were endless streams of headlights moving round the common as if on a giant roundabout, and, in the middle, Henry and Hilary swished through the grass together, hand in hand. It was as if London was a storm and, just for a moment, they were its still, peaceful eye.

Just for a moment.

'I'm sorry. We're full,' said a man whom they had never seen before at the restaurant.

'For God's sake,' said Henry. 'Surely you can fit *us* in.'

'How can I?' said the man, false regret buttering his voice. 'I've told you. We're full.'

'Don't you know who I am?' exploded Henry angrily.

'It doesn't make any difference who you are, sir,' said the man smoothly. 'We're full.'

'Right. That does it,' said Henry. 'I'm never ever coming here again. Sod you. Come on, Hilary.'

He reached for her hand, but she refused to give it.

'*I* don't,' she said.

'You don't what?' he said, still angry.

'You said, "Don't you know who I am?" Well, *I* don't. Not any more.'

She set off, across the common, away from their home. A cold panic swept over him. He was remembering the dreadful day in Thurmarsh when she had stormed off into the night. It had taken nineteen years to get her back then. It wouldn't take that again. Would it?

He should go after her.

His legs wouldn't move.

He should plead with her.

It was better not to go. He should leave her to cool down. She'd be back. They were different now. They were mature.

He had made a monstrous accusation on that occasion. There was no such thing this time. This was trivial.

Nothing is trivial in human relationships.

His legs wouldn't move.

He flinched just before the sniff came, so he must be developing powers of anticipation.

Now you've done it, said Cousin Hilda's sniff.

'Leave me alone,' said Henry. 'Fucking well leave me alone.'

He stormed home, across the sad grass, fury making him look like a madman.

It was a long, long, lonely evening. The house was so quiet. The air in the house was stale. He opened the side door to get fresh air in, although the air that came in was heavy with fumes and poison.

He made one of the Café's staple meals, prawn Doris, a spicy prawn and leek dish, not quite a curry, simple yet delicious. He sliced the leeks very thinly and cooked them slowly in butter. He cooked the prawns in white wine, with sun-dried tomato paste, fish stock, ginger, cayenne and chilli. Then he thickened the sauce with cream and rice flour, and added the leeks at the last moment.

He laid the kitchen table for two. He listened for her footsteps. There were none.

He ate a portion of the prawn Doris, with a mixture of wild rice and red Camargue rice. He left a portion for Hilary.

It was delicious, subtle and spicy, yet gentle – Auntie Doris would have been so pleased if she could have known that he had called it after her – but tonight he couldn't taste it at all.

When he had finished his meal, he sat at the kitchen table, almost motionless. That night, he was more distressed than the table. He had a glass of red wine in front of him, but he didn't touch it. Getting drunk wouldn't help.

She would come back eventually. If he was drunk it would just make matters worse.

She would never come back. He had blown his marriage for the second time. He had lost this wonderful woman for the second time.

Had a greater fool ever been born?

Eleven o'clock passed. Eleven-fifteen. Half past eleven. A quarter to twelve. Time passed so slowly, and yet so fast.

If Hilary did come back, he would be utterly and totally honest and open in every aspect of life at all times.

Well, no, not quite. He must never tell her that he had used the F word to Cousin Hilda's sniff.

He called out to Cousin Hilda's sniff.

'I'm sorry,' he said. 'Come back and tell me you aren't offended. Please.'

A man in his late sixties sitting at a kitchen table apologising to a dead woman's sniff. Was this madness?

There was only silence. How could there be anything else?

Midnight came and went, and with it all his hopes. He might as well get drunk. He might as well get seriously drunk. He raised his glass to his lips.

No. If he got drunk she would never come. He would never see her again.

This was ridiculous. There could be no connection between his drinking and her returning home.

Nevertheless, he put the glass down without taking even a sip.

And she came. At seven minutes past twelve she came. He almost fainted with relief.

'I was worried,' he said.

'Good,' she said.

And that was all they said. It was grotesque. He had spent the evening longing for her to be there, full of remorse, bursting to open his heart to her, and all he could say was, 'I was worried.'

They undressed in silence. They washed and cleaned their teeth in separate bathrooms, as they usually did, but he feared that they would sleep that night in separate bedrooms.

When he saw that she had got into their bed, his legs almost buckled with relief.

She seemed to have gone straight to sleep, but he was certain that she was feigning this.

He crept in quietly beside her.

In the early hours inhabited by returning drunks and urban foxes, in the silence of their bedroom, Henry sensed that Hilary was awake, and there, in the dark, he apologised for his arrogance, asked her for her help, and promised to be a better human being. He also told her that he knew, deep down, that she wasn't jealous of his success. Now Hilary could hold him close. The barrier had been removed from their bed. It was a pity, she felt, that he couldn't yet say these things with the light on, but she was very grateful that he could say them at all.

He agreed that he needed a rest, and in the morning set about cancelling future engagements so that they could have a whole month off. Now, all the tiredness that he had been refusing to acknowledge swept over him. That night, at supper, he could hardly keep awake.

Hilary leant over and squeezed his hand.

'It's time for something that we haven't had too much of recently,' she said teasingly.

Suddenly he felt very nervous.

'I'll make it,' she said.

He was conscious of a great feeling of shock. Not because she was talking about cocoa, but because he was *relieved* that she was talking about cocoa.

It took a month in the Seychelles to give him the breathing space he needed. They lazed, read, ate, swam, snorkelled, and he came home feeling stronger and better than he had felt for many years. He thought that he was himself again. The new front man at Bartholomew's might not know who he was, but he did.

People say that they feel a new man, but they don't

mean it literally. Henry almost did. Old Henry had become conceited, grumpy and arrogant. New Henry would be mature, compassionate and modest.

He had a feeling that all his troubles were over. Poor Henry. How wrong could he be? They were just about to begin.

14 A Hen is Born

'Henry Pwatt?' the man on the phone enquired.

'Almost,' said Henry foolishly.

'My name is Jonathan Cwomarty. I'm Managing Director of Happy Fields Chickens. I expect you've heard of us.'

'Well, no, actually. Sorry.'

'No, no, not at all. No pwoblem. We're quite a small outfit. No weason why you should have. No pwoblem at all. In fact it's pwecisely because people like you haven't heard of us that we're appwoaching people like you.'

'I'm sorry. I'm not quite with you.'

'No, no, not at all. No pwoblem. No, I haven't exactly explained myself, have I? We're a pwetty chicken fwiendly outfit here. Ecologically sound, as I think our name suggests.'

'In what way?'

'Well . . . Happy Fields. A picture of happy chickens. In the fields. Our chickens are utterly fwee-wange.'

'I see. No, Happy Fields gave me an image of the *fields* being happy, and I'd guess that if fields could speak they'd say they'd be happy without chickens shitting all over them. I certainly would be, if I was a field.'

'Oh. Ha ha. Yes. I see. Yes. Well . . . it's a thought.'

'So, I had an image of empty fields and sheds full of unhappy chickens.'

'Oh dear, oh dear. No, no. No, no. Well, it's a thought. It *is* a thought. Maybe I'll . . . though I don't see how we *can* change our name, to be honest.'

'Of course not. Sorry. It's just me being silly. I have a rather unusual mind, I'm afraid.'

'Exactly! That's it! And we don't. Which is why we want you, Mr Pwatt. All of us. Unanimously. I don't think you'll mind my saying that my wife is tickled pink at the thought. Tickled pink. "He's so . . ." she said. "So . . ." Well, maybe I shouldn't be saying this.'

'Please. I'm not sensitive.'

' "So . . . cuddly".'

'Ah. Like a teddy bear, did she mean?'

'Well . . . I don't know about teddy bears. Pwobably she just finds you . . . er . . .'

'Cuddly.'

'Yes.'

'Which is why she described me as cuddly, no doubt.'

Stop it, Henry.

'Er . . . yes.'

'Shrewd cookie, your wife.'

No! Why are you treating this man like this, Henry? New Henry, post-Seychelles Henry, is responsible and courteous. What is it about this man that is making you be like this? Because he can't say his Rs? That's terrible. Get a grip.

'So, this thought that your wife is tickled pink by, what is it exactly?'

'Ah. *So* sorry. I haven't made myself clear, have I? We would like you to spearhead our advertising campaign.'

'Ah! Before you go any further I have to tell you that while I have been very happy to promote myself – quite ruthlessly, some would say – I have made a decision not to use my name to promote anything else.'

'I know. I know. I've wead about it, and I wespect it, but, Mr Pwatt – or may I call you Henwy?'

'Yes. Do. Please.'

'Thank you. But we are diffewent. Weally diffewent. And we feel that you are extwemely us.'

'Extw . . . extremely you?'

'Yes. Extwemely. I mean, your business is intimate, individual, ecologically wesponsible. Happy. You positively ooze satisfaction.'

'Good God. That sounds dreadful.'

'Oh no. No, no, no. It's your enthusiasm. Your love of food. Your happiness. And we're all about happiness at Happy Fields Chickens. We've heard your comments on your show . . . your excellent show . . .'

'Thank you very much.'

'. . . about battewy chicken farming, which we find as howwendous as you do. Our food philosophies, Mr Pwatt, are identical. We can think of nobody better to foster our business image and at the same time speak out against cwuelty to chickens.'

'Well, thank you.'

'So this would be, as we see it, less the endorsement of a pwoduct and more a mowal cwusade.'

'Well, yes, I can see that.'

'We don't have a vast budget, but with our image we think that your association with us could also benefit you, though not as much of course as it would benefit us.'

'You're very kind.'

Jonathan Cromarty emphasised that as they were such a small outfit the money would not be great, but the adverts would be filmed vewy swiftly and simply in one day in a studio, without the use of weal chickens, as that might cause hardship.

Henry liked the sound of it. He liked the idea of a moral crusade. He insisted on visiting Happy Fields Chickens Limited to inspect it, before lending his name to it, but told Jonathan Cromarty that, if the place satisfied his criteria on animal welfare, he would do it.

He visited on a fine day in late spring and was charmed by the place. A long drive led to a cheery, seventeenth-century, brick farmhouse with smiling windows and two picturesque gables. At the entrance to the farmyard, a discreet, modest sign proclaimed 'Happy Fields Chickens. Please drive slowly. Beware chickens.' Above the sign was a delightfully amusing picture of an alarmed chicken trying to get out of the way of a car.

Jonathan Cromarty emerged from the front door, smiling broadly, holding out an expansive hand of welcome. He was thin and extremely tall – about six foot five – and he towered over Henry.

'It's an honour to have you here,' he said. 'My wife is so disappointed.'

'I beg your pardon?'

'Not to be able to be here. Alas . . . family.'

'Quite. So she'll never know if I'm cuddly in the flesh.'

'What?'

'You said she thought I was cuddly.'

‘Ah. Yes. Sorry. Ha ha. Yes. No. Quite. So . . . let me show you wound.’

The happy fields were drenched with ecstatic dew, and studded with jolly apple trees amongst which large numbers of cheerful chickens clucked and fed. A gaggle of gladsome guinea fowl ran away from them, their heads bent, their little legs scurrying in awkward small steps, like diminutive nuns who were late for matins. The sheds where the birds spent the night were spacious and clean. There was a smell of healthy rot and warm straw.

Perversely, Henry felt rather depressed. Even in these ideal circumstances, it wasn’t much of a life, being a chicken.

Jonathan Cromarty led him into a pleasant farmhouse kitchen, its table cheerfully over-run with newspapers and magazines. He offered him a coffee, then had some trouble finding the jar.

‘Sowwy. What a give-away. My wife always does the honours. I’m no host,’ he said. ‘My wife makes wonderful coffee. Such a shame.’

Over Jonathan Cromarty’s rather less than wonderful coffee, Henry agreed to do the adverts. A date was fixed. Jonathan Cromarty handed him a contract.

‘I’m not twying to wush you,’ he said. ‘No need to sign it now. Better get your agent to have a look at it.’

‘I don’t have an agent,’ said Henry.

He flicked through the contract. Everything seemed in order. The fee was as agreed. He liked the place. A man who was so kind to his chickens wasn’t going to cheat him. He signed.

The filming was done in a small studio in Limehouse.

Henry hadn't realised how dotted London was with small studios.

He also hadn't realised that he would have to wear a yellow chicken costume.

'You didn't mention anything about dressing as a chicken,' he said. 'I'm sure there wasn't anything in the contract about it.'

'There wasn't anything excluding it either,' said Jonathan Cromarty. 'There's a clause stating that you agwee to accept editowial decisions within weason. If you think this is unweasonable, fair enough, but I had you down as a man with a sense of fun, a man who doesn't take himself too sewiously, a man who put animal welfare above his own dignity.'

'Well, that's true, of course.'

'I actually think Henwietta will be a huge success.'

'Henwietta?'

'Henwietta the Happy Hen. That's you.'

'Oh.'

'I mean fwankly my scwipts won't work vewy well without the costume,' said Jonathan Cromarty.

'You wrote the scripts?'

'Tom Stoppard wasn't available. Ha ha. No, we're a family business, keep it in the family. And I have to admit I've always wanted to be a witer. I mean, if you do wefuse, we'll have wasted Paul's day. Paul's our diwector.' Paul was a young man who looked about twenty. 'And we'll have wasted Vince's day. He's our camewaman.' Vince was aged about fifty, and had a straggly beard with egg stains on it. 'But, if we have to, so be it. I want you to be happy.'

Henry knew that he had to agree. Vince and Paul were listening. He couldn't stand on his dignity and waste their day. He was New Henry now. New Henry couldn't stand on his dignity. He didn't have any dignity to stand on. He had to agree, but he wasn't going to make it too easy.

'I think I'd better look at the scripts,' he said.

'Of course,' said Jonathan Cromarty. 'I only wote them. You have to say them, so you outwank me.'

Henry decided, before he began looking at the scripts, that he would read them without a flicker of amusement. There was something about Jonathan Cromarty that encouraged him to do this.

There were five scripts for five different adverts. The first was quite straightforward. 'Hi, I'm Henrietta the Happy Hen. Why am I happy? Because I live at Happy Fields. How happy I am in the happy fields of Happy Fields. It's a clucking good life for a hen. That's why I lay such gorgeous eggs.'

In the second advert, Henrietta laid an egg. This required just a bit of acting from Henry. 'Oh, isn't it egg-citing. I think I'm going to lay an egg. O'ooh! O'ooh! Aaaargh! That was painful. It's such a big egg. An egg-strordinarily big egg. That's because I'm fed so well at Happy Fields. That's why all our eggs taste so clucking good.' The script required Henry to bend down and pick up a huge egg. 'Oh, what a whopper.'

In the third advert, a stern voice spoke to Henrietta out of vision. 'Henrietta Hen, aged one, of Hut Three, Happy Fields, England, you are up before the beak because you told the manager of your farm to cluck off. How do you plead?' 'Not guilty,' said Henrietta. 'I'd been dreaming.

I'd dreamt I was in a great big shed with thousands of other chickens all in the dark with our beaks cut off and unable to move and the smell was horrible and I thought I was still there when I said, 'Cluck off.' Oh, please, Mr Beak, let me go back to Happy Fields, where we are not like those chickens, our sad sad battery brothers.'

The fourth advert required Henry to attempt an American accent. 'Hi-dee yokes, I mean folks. Here on the range life is clucking good because this is the free-range range. Hey, you guys, do you have a range in your kitchen? If you do, get our chickens, because, like me, they're free range, and we're fed on corn, and I don't mean no BBC sitcoms, so we taste clucking good.'

The fifth and final advert required Henry to make mechanical movements and clucking noises which gradually slowed down and stopped – quite a challenge to his acting ability. A man rushed in with two huge batteries. 'What are those?' asked Henrietta. 'Your new batteries.' 'Where are you going to put them?' 'Up your . . .' 'No! I don't need batteries. There are no battery chickens at Happy Fields.'

Henry put the scripts down very slowly. He could have wished that it had not been quite so easy for him to read them without showing a flicker of amusement. He looked Jonathan Cromarty full in the face.

'Well Tom Stoppard it isn't,' he said.

'No, no. Quite. Ha! But . . . will you do it?'

What could he say? What could he do? He'd agreed. He'd signed the contract. He would have to go through with it, and if the scripts lacked the cutting edge of a Waugh or a Wodehouse, at least their heart was in the right place. What did it matter if he made a complete arse of himself in a good cause? It was all just a bit of fun, wasn't it? New Henry didn't mind being mocked.

He did feel, though, that he must insist on one or two changes, so as not to look like a complete wimp in front of these people – and there was one thing to which he genuinely objected.

'I don't swear,' he said, 'and I won't say "cluck off". I'll accept "clucking", that's comparatively harmless, but "cluck off" is too blatant.'

'Fair enough. It's the main gag in the piece, and nothing else will have the same wing to it, but never mind. Your second point?' said Jonathan Cromarty with bad grace.

'I don't think an American chicken would make a crack about BBC sitcoms. It wouldn't have heard of the BBC. Could we say TV sitcoms?'

'It's only a bit of nonsense and if we're being pedantically logical I have to say I don't think a chicken would have heard of TV at all, but if it makes you happy, that's the main point,' said Jonathan Cromarty with more bad grace.

It was a long day. Jonathan Cromarty, stung by Henry's criticisms, didn't always agree with his interpretations.

'Watch your motivation,' he would say. 'Focus on the motivation.'

Henry focused on the motivation for nine long, hot hours.

15 Unhappy Fields

Although he had accepted that he would seem ridiculous, and although he had decided that in the strength of his belief he would not mind seeming ridiculous, Henry felt terrible during the days that followed the first transmissions of his chicken ads.

He imagined that *everybody* was laughing at him.

He imagined the scorn of his former colleagues on the *Thurmarsh Evening Argus* and the Cucumber Marketing Board. He imagined them phoning each other: 'Did you see Henry? What was he playing at?'

He imagined Sally Atkinson thinking, 'My God, and I almost fancied him.'

He imagined all sorts of people whom he admired – Helen Mirren, Steve Davis, Michael Vaughan, Harold Pinter, Paula Radcliffe, David Hockney – saying, 'Good God. What a wanker.'

He imagined Lampo Davey and Tosser Pilkington-Brick saying, 'Once a silly little fatty-faggy-chops, always a silly little fatty-faggy-chops. We must have been out of our minds to take jobs under him.'

He imagined Celia Hargreaves watching with open mouth, her astonishment leading her into the first really graceless expression she had ever shown.

He imagined – and this was the worst image of all – Bradley Tompkins jumping up and down with glee, or, if he was being Mrs Scatchard at the time, lying back and kicking his legs with childlike delight, quite happy to reveal his scarlet knickers to his bisexual bicycle repairer from Bicester.

Nobody made any direct comment to him about the quality of the adverts. He fancied, though, several times, that he heard clucking noises from behind him on the pavement, and his local postmistress, while handing him his pension, said, 'What a clucking nice day,' and looked as if she thought herself recklessly bold.

'What an eggs-hilarating morning,' commented the local traffic warden, full of good humour on a day of thirty-seven bookings. 'It's egg-citing just to be alive.'

Henry returned to a silent house. Hilary was doing a book signing in Guildford.

'Cluck off, the lot of you,' he shouted in the emptiness of the kitchen.

He didn't dare go to the Café for three days, which wasn't unusual, due to all the pressure of his other work.

He didn't even dare show his face at the supermarket.

It seemed that at last he had freed himself from Cousin Hilda's sniff. Perversely, during those three days, he found that he was missing it. He would have liked it to have come back once at least, so that he could reassure himself that it hadn't been too offended by his swearing.

On Wednesday, 28 August, 2002, Jaguar announced a four-day week due to slow sales of the new 'Baby Jag' X-type; Tory leader Ian Duncan Smith announced that he would go on the Countryside March with his family, stating, 'This is all about freedom'; it was revealed that

British commandos, sent secretly to Afghanistan by Tony Blair, were threatened with being shot by local forces because the Foreign Office had failed to get clearance for their arrival; and Henry Pratt decided that he was being absolutely pathetic.

He'd had ongoing reservations about his fame, but on the whole he had revelled in it. How could he let himself be defeated so easily by his first real setback? He would go to work at the Café Henry as if it was an absolutely normal day.

Usually, he liked mornings in the Café, when the atmosphere was quiet and warm, there was a smell of good coffee, and he still had time to talk to the customers. That day, however, he simply didn't seem able to get out of the house. He wasn't aware that he was inventing excuses for delay, he felt that he was hurrying, but he was fooling himself.

By the time he left it was already eleven forty-three. It was a pleasant summer's day, and suddenly he felt that he had been worrying over nothing. The ads weren't that bad, and probably very few people had seen them. When his friends watched ITV, most of them recorded the programmes so that they could fast-forward through the adverts. No, there was no problem.

He no longer drove to work. Even before the congestion charge he had decided that it was socially irresponsible to add to London's congestion. He soon found a taxi.

'Clucking good morning,' said the taxi driver.

Henry's good mood dissolved in an instant.

The driver was fast, even reckless.

'Not scaring you, am I, guv?' he asked. 'Hope you aren't . . . chicken!!'

He roared with laughter at his wit.

'Please don't lay no eggs in my cab,' he said. 'I'm not licensed for it.'

He roared again.

It seemed to take hours to get to Frith Street, despite the driver's recklessness.

'I'm sorry you've been cooped up so long,' said the taxi driver on arrival. He was having a wonderful time.

It was a test of post-Seychelles Henry's tolerance. He was very aware of it, and he passed with flying colours, smiling at the driver and tipping him generously.

'Thank you very much. Cheep cheep at the price,' said the taxi driver.

Henry almost asked for the tip back.

As he entered the Café, Greg was in full flow.

'Good morning, sir. I see the West Coast main line is to be closed for forty miles for repairs. Forty miles!' he was saying. 'And how about the underwater cameras the Carmarthen Fishermen's Federation has installed, eh? Anglers can check on their website for reports on the number, size *and swimming direction* of the fish. Poor old fish, eh? Don't stand a chance. Nice turbot today, sir, in *beurre blanc* sauce, or what else can I get you?'

'I thought you'd never ask,' said the customer.

I must talk to Greg about his links, thought Henry.

As he was serving the customer with his drinks, Greg said 'Hello, stranger' to Henry.

Leave it out, Greg, thought Henry, but he didn't say so. He smiled benevolently.

Another customer came in and greeted Greg warmly.

'Morning, Greg.'

Henry realised with a sinking heart that, in his absence, his beloved establishment had become the Café Greg.

He went into the kitchen, and chatted to the chef, Karen. All was peace. All was calm. There were no temperaments on show, no eruptions.

It was a well-oiled machine, and there was nothing for him to do. This should have pleased him, and it did to an extent, but it also made him uneasy. He felt like a spare prick in his own genitalia.

None of the staff mentioned the adverts. Not once. It was inconceivable that none of them had seen them. Clearly an instruction had gone out, from Michelle probably (who was now larger than ever, and very happily married to the one non-lesbian who had written to her after her TV appearance, so that Greg now referred to her as 'ecstatic of Edmonton'), 'Don't mention the adverts, whatever you do.'

How humiliating.

But none of the customers mentioned them either. Henry was convinced that customers and staff had conferred, had decided that the adverts were so awful that the subject must be avoided at all costs.

It was terrible. It would have been better if somebody had said, 'Henry, what on earth were you doing agreeing to that crap?' and he'd have said, 'Well, it's in a good cause and who cares?' and they could all have had a laugh about it.

Henry realised that he had become the sort of restaurant proprietor that he despised – all smiles and no product. Good morning, sir. Good morning, madam. Lovely day. Is everything all right? Excellent. How was

Minorca? Oh good. Just occasionally get a chance to serve a customer, from time to time manage to carry a plate so as not to look too idle.

Some of the regular customers had cottoned on to Greg's hopelessness with acronyms, and deliberately made fun of him, fun of which he was totally oblivious. Just as Peter Stackpool entered, Henry heard a loss adjustor say, 'What do you think of PVC, Greg?' and Greg's reply of 'I dunno. I haven't never been on French trains. Can't afford it on my pay.'

This was Henry's chance to serve somebody and look busy.

'Peter!' he said. 'What's it to be today? Let me guess. I know. Ham salad.'

'Do you know,' said Peter Stackpool roguishly, 'I think I've been a bit of a stick in the mud. I think that today . . .' Henry could see him plucking up his courage. 'I think that today . . .' He spoke with just a touch of devil may care brio. '. . . I just might go for the *beef* salad.'

This little incident filled Henry with a sense of the joyous absurdity of life. What did it matter if he had made himself look ridiculous? It had been in a good cause. That was what mattered. He felt happy, and at ease with the world. He wanted to laugh out loud at what Peter Stackpool believed to be his courage, but the phone rang and he answered it instead.

'Good afternoon,' he enthused. 'What can I do for you this lovely day?'

'Henry Pratt?'

'Yes.'

'Fergus Horncastle, *Daily Smear*.'

'What can I do for you, Mr Horncastle?' He handed the chitty ordering PS's salad to a passing waitress.

'Your adverts for Happy Fields chickens, Mr Pratt . . .'

The man was enjoying himself. Why was he enjoying himself?

'What about them?'

'We have it on good authority that the chickens at Happy Fields are battery hens kept in conditions of extreme cruelty.'

'What???'

'As an ex-journalist yourself you'll be able to imagine the headlines. "Top Chef's Goose is Cooked", "Not So Clucking Happy After All, says Henrietta", "Henry the Hypocrite in Henhouse Horror", "Free Range Henry Faces Battery of Criticism".'

Henry's head began to swim. What was all this? Why did he believe immediately that it was true?

Because, he now had to admit to himself, something about Jonathan Cromarty had been nagging him.

The fact that he hadn't known where the coffee was had been nagging him. He could see the man now, searching for it.

It hadn't been his kitchen!

He looked round the Café, amazed that lunch was still proceeding so happily, so normally.

'Are you still there, Henry?'

What makes you think you can call me Henry?

'Yes. I'm still here, Magnus.'

'Fergus. We have photographs, Henry.'

'There must be two chicken farms called "Happy Fields".'

'We've thought of that. We've made exhaustive checks. We can find no trace of another one.'

'How have you found out about this?'

'A phone call.'

'Who from?'

'Anonymous. We rang 1471. The caller didn't wish to leave his number.'

'I bet he didn't. My "Happy Fields" is in Sussex, near Battle.'

'Ours is in Kent, near Tunbridge Wells.'

'I'm going down there,' said Henry. 'Hold the front page.'

'Real journalism isn't like the films, Henry,' said Fergus Horncastle.

It was late afternoon by the time Henry approached the farm in Sussex. He felt very nervous.

He had been duped. He knew he had. Jonathan Cromarty had been a fraud. There *was* no wife who found Henry cuddly. He felt disappointed about that. How vain he had allowed himself to become. New Henry couldn't shed all this vanity straightaway. He would have to work at it.

The road dipped into a valley, shimmering silently in the heat.

He knew he'd been fooled, yet he still hoped that everything would be the same on this sultry afternoon as it had been on that fresh early summer morning, before the sun's breath had become stale.

It was the same. The lane fringed by smart white fencing. The orchards. The fields.

Only the name board at the entrance to the farmyard

was different. 'Martin Wildblood Farms – Organic is our Middle Name.'

He parked in the yard and walked to the front door with crunching steps and a thudding heart.

He half expected the door to be opened by Jonathan Cromarty, or the man who called himself Jonathan Cromarty.

Nobody opened the door.

He went round the side, where the immaculate frontage gave way to chaos – old bits of rusted metal, dogs' bones, a chewed tennis ball, frayed shirts on a line, an empty fuel drum on its side.

He knocked at the kitchen door and it opened immediately.

It wasn't Jonathan Cromarty. It was a woman, a farmer's wife, middle-aged, chunky, cheeks chapped by the wind.

'Yes?' she said suspiciously.

'My name's Henry Pratt.'

'Oh?'

It meant nothing to her. He felt a stab of irritation. What was the point of being well-known if nobody had heard of you?

He fought off the irritation. New Henry didn't think such things. New Henry was modest. New Henry found it refreshing to be unknown. New Henry knew that it was good for him to be brought down to size.

Absurdly, though, he wanted this very real woman to find him cuddly, as the invented farmer's wife had. He was certain that this woman was not married to Jonathan Cromarty. They didn't go together.

He told her his story. Her mouth dropped open. She rang her husband's mobile. He came immediately. *His* mouth dropped open. Henry took them to the board with the name of their farm. He told them what the board had said on his previous visit. They stared at the board as if it might provide an answer to the mystery.

'It said "Happy Fields Chickens"?'

'Yes.'

'I don't understand it.'

They went back to the kitchen. Martin's wife, whose name was Marie, offered Henry a coffee. She found the jar without difficulty. Martin found the date of Henry's visit in his diary without difficulty too.

'We were in Majorca,' he said.

Marie smiled briefly at the memory, then realised that holidays in Majorca didn't fit easily with their hard-working image.

'Just for a week,' she said. 'Our first holiday for five years.'

'I don't doubt it,' said Henry. 'I know how hard farmers work.'

She softened. Henry felt sure she was beginning to find him cuddly.

'We left our man in charge,' said Martin.

'We only have one man now,' said Marie.

'There were eighteen at harvest time in that old photo above the settle,' said Martin. He sighed. 'I'd have trusted Colin with my right arm.'

'I wonder how much they paid him,' said Marie.

'Can I speak to him?' asked Henry.

'He's in Madeira. Three weeks. We have to give him proper holidays.'

'What was the man like?' asked Martin.

'Very thin,' said Henry. 'Very tall. Six five, I'd say.'

'Don't know anyone like that.'

'He called himself Jonathan Cromarty. He couldn't say his Rs.'

'Like Jonathan Ross,' said Martin. 'We watched him the other day. I fell asleep. Well, I work hard. You enjoyed him, didn't you, Marie?'

'You've got it, Martin,' said Marie.

'What?'

'He was phoney. Ross and Cromarty used to be a county in Scotland. We were on holiday there once. Must be twenty years ago,' she added hurriedly. 'As I say, we can't find time for many holidays.'

'I'm not with you,' said Martin. 'What are you on about?'

'He was imitating Jonathan Ross and calling himself Jonathan Cromarty.' Marie tried not to sound as if she was talking to idiots.

Henry felt as if he'd been kicked in the stomach.

'Good God!' he said. 'Bloody hell! Jonathan Cromarty! Couldn't say R! They must think I'm really stupid if they thought I'd fall for something as obvious as that.'

'But you did fall for it,' said Marie gently, as to one she found cuddly.

'Well, I know,' said Henry. 'Because I had absolutely no reason to be suspicious. I don't go through life expecting that everything that happens is going to turn out to be a complete con. No, I'm not so upset at falling for it. What I *am* upset about is that they *knew* I'd fall for it.'

*

He drove a couple of miles, then stopped to phone Fergus on his mobile. He explained what had happened. 'I was duped,' he said.

Fergus sounded disappointed.

'OK,' he said. 'I suppose we have to accept that.'

'Well, don't sound so disappointed.'

'Of course I'm disappointed. What we'd really like to do is expose you as a complete and utter cynical, hypocritical, greedy fraud.'

'But I'm not.'

'I know. I've accepted that. It's just a shame, that's all. You can't expect me to be pleased.'

'I know who's done it, of course.'

'What???'

'Forget I said that.'

'No chance, mate. I don't forget things. Come on. Who do you think's doing it?'

'In the words of my granny, "I'm saying nowt."'

'Bradley Tompkins?'

'I'm saying nowt.'

'Thank you, Henry. I find that very revealing.'

'Oh shit. You are a bastard, aren't you?'

'Just doing my job, mate.'

Stealthily, under cover of the heat haze, dark clouds slid into position, ready for a storm.

'You shit-hole!' said Henry with petty fury. 'You sewer in human form.'

'Thank you,' said Fergus Horncastle smoothly. 'Your comments are noted and they endear you to us most warmly – or should that be us to you? We don't do grammar at the *Smear*. Clever tactics, Henry, I don't think. Goodbye.'

Henry switched his mobile off with shaking fingers. Then he realised that he hadn't even asked the question that he'd rung up about, so he had to phone again.

'You're ringing to apologise! Good move!'

'Well, no, actually . . . well, I mean, yes, yes I do apologise, but no, what I wanted was to know exactly where your "Happy Fields" farm is, the one you have photos of.'

After Fergus told him, Henry looked at his map, worked out his route, and was on his way just as the storm broke fiercely. The temperature dropped twelve degrees. The rain bounced off the roads and streamed muddily off the fields. Carefully tended grapes were washed off their vines. Cows cowered. Sheep tried to find shelter under the hedges. Dogs barked in panic. Cats shivered.

It ended as abruptly as it had begun. Soon there was sunshine again, and the world was steaming. The steam rose off the roads, off the fields, off the sodden sheep, off the frightened pheasants and the squashed rabbits in the lane.

A young man in a red MG Sports drove through a puddle deliberately, soaking two elderly ladies waiting for the only bus of the day. His girlfriend laughed.

Fergus would have laughed, thought Henry.

The steaming countryside was beautiful and it smelt succulently of drying grass and drying tarmac.

Then another smell assailed Henry's nostrils most unpleasantly. It was a fishy, mealy, stale, hot, sulphurous stench, drifting on a sluggish wind.

It was the smell of the farm.

The lane went under the dark arch of an abandoned

railway, took an immediate sharp curve to the left, and there it was.

The owners of the real Happy Fields lived in an ugly squat stone bungalow, with no soft edges. It was surrounded and dwarfed by three large sheds. There was a concrete bay big enough to load enormous lorries. In the dull, sterile field behind the barns there stood a vast pylon. It throbbed like an angry monster. The wires that led to the next vast pylon, on the edge of a decrepit wood, hummed ominously, as if the energy trapped within them was grumbling with suppressed fury because it couldn't escape to pollute the world.

The owners of Happy Fields had ugly squat bodies and ugly stone faces with no soft edges. They were bungalows in human form. On a square table in the square kitchen there was a meal that could not be described as square. It was mean and pitiful.

Henry didn't like the owners of Happy Fields Limited. The man in him was offended by the ugliness of the woman. The chef in him was offended by the ugliness of their tea. The human being in him was offended by the ugliness of their lives. No, he didn't like Mr and Mrs Brown, but he did believe them when they said that they had never heard of Jonathan Cromarty, or Martin Wildblood Farms, and had been completely mystified when they'd seen the adverts.

He didn't ask them for a list of all the people they could think of who might have known of the existence of Happy Fields. It might have saved him a lot of bother if he had.

16 For and Against

'Clucking fowl play,' screamed the *Daily Smear*.

'Hen Advert Row' said the billboards rather more lamely.

The *Daily Smear* quoted Henry's comment that he knew who had done it, and his refusal to deny that he suspected Bradley Tompkins.

They quoted Bradley's impassioned expression of complete ignorance about the incident.

Later editions of other newspapers picked up the story. TV blunders were always good copy, so were chickens, and controversy over adverts was an old favourite at thin times for news. Several of the papers quoted Bradley's furious denials, which included the phrase, 'I have nothing whatever against Henry Pratt', which was unfortunate, as people didn't believe it and, therefore, didn't believe any of his denial.

In any case, a denial is usually more damaging than an admission.

All the chicken jokes came out again. 'Henrietta of the free-range eggs was shell-shocked today . . .', 'The yoke's on Henry, and he doesn't see the funny side . . .', 'Henry may see himself as hard-boiled, but . . .', '"Cock-a-Doodle Don't", cries harassed Henry.'

He found it even more difficult to leave the house, especially as there were photographers lurking night and day.

He'd sometimes thought that it must be rather nice to be so famous that you were plagued by paparazzi.

No longer.

Hilary tried to persuade him to continue to behave as if everything was normal, but he couldn't.

'I can't,' he said. 'My courage has gone. I'm a useless person, aren't I?'

'Not at everything,' said Hilary.

But that afternoon, in the master bedroom, with the curtains open lest the paparazzi guessed what they were up to, Henry found that he was no longer up to what the paparazzi might have guessed he was up to.

'It's the worry and tension,' said Hilary. 'Plus all those bloody photographers.'

'It's my age,' he said.

'Don't think I don't sympathise, darling,' said Hilary, 'but I really do draw the line at self-pity.'

The phone rang endlessly. He didn't answer it. The emails poured in. He didn't read them.

The nation was laughing at him. He was certain of it. Not with him. At him. Their love of the People's Chef was very skin deep. He began to feel very resentful of his public. Hilary left him to his despair, and worked at her book. It went quite well. Sometimes, when things weren't good around one, the need to blot them out produced an inspiring intensity.

Henry began to miss her and made one of his very best fish stews for her. They washed it down with a bottle of white wine from the Greek island of Santorini – his latest discovery.

'How has it gone today?' he asked.

She hesitated. She didn't like to be too enthusiastic when he was down. He could be so prickly then.

But her hesitation didn't work any better.

'I see,' he said. 'Went well but you don't like to admit it or I'll get grumpy. Well, I won't. I promise. I love you.'

'Do you really?'

'Well of course I do.'

'You haven't said it recently.'

'It sounds silly after so many years.'

'It never sounds silly. And I love you too. And it's gone really rather well, actually.'

'Great. No, it is. I'm delighted. No, I am. It's clucking marvellous. Oh shit. I'd actually forgotten for a moment.'

Next morning, Henry trawled through his phone calls. A lot of them were from the press. He ignored those.

One was from Lampo. He said, 'Priceless!'

He was amazed to get one from Tosser. 'It's Nigel here, Henry. Just to say it's all bollocks. Lie low for a while. It'll blow over.' That was surprisingly nice of him.

The one that he valued most was from Sally Atkinson. 'It's Sally here, Henry. Not many people know how private you are. I do, so I know this won't be an easy time for you, so I thought I'd let you know that I'm thinking of you. Take care, darling – oh, and love to Hilary too.'

He went weak at the knees. He played it four times before wiping it. He knew that she could be a bit actressy, but he felt that her 'darling' was meant in a different, more personal way – and the reference to Hilary, of course, was an afterthought.

It's painful to have to report that after listening to Sally's message, and before listening to the others, he went upstairs, to the loo furthest from the study in which Hilary was working so intensely, and there he succeeded in what he had failed with the previous afternoon in bed.

'I thought I ought to warn you that Fraser Goldthorpe of the *Smear* has been on to us about *The Pratt Diet*,' said Imogen Clutterworth-Baines on the phone, and, for the first time in Henry's experience, she didn't speak enthusiastically.

'In what context?'

'They're questioning whether it's all a con. They're questioning whether it's a diet at all.'

'I see.'

'I don't think it's serious, do you?'

'Yes, I do, actually.'

'Oh. Well, I think you'll have to talk to him.'

He didn't like to interrupt Hilary when she was working, but he needed to. He had a sense that his whole career was beginning to unravel.

'Sorry to interrupt, darling,' he said, 'but I need help. I need strength.'

She got up from her desk immediately. She looked worried.

'Only you can give it,' he said. 'You're my rock.'

Her face softened. She looked pleased, despite her worry. He was beginning to be able to say nice things to her in daylight. She went over to him, held him, hugged him. They were close again.

'What's happened?'

'All my life I've been expecting that one day I'll be found out. Now I have.'

'I don't want to be unkind, darling, but you've been found out before. Mr Redrobe found you out on the *Argus*. The Liberals found you out in Thurmarsh. The only reason the Cucumber Marketing Board didn't find you out was because they'd known right from the start.'

'Yes, but this is different. I'm famous now. I'm not funny little Henry Pratt any more.'

'Yes you are.'

'I see. Terrific.'

'I'm not mocking. You're famous and you're rich and you're loved and it's wonderful, but you're also still a funny little man and that is part of why you're rich and loved.'

'I see. I thought I'd rather transcended all that. I thought that was the whole point.'

'Oh, Henry.'

'I thought maybe I'd got to a point where people would stop saying "Oh, Henry".'

'Oh, Henry. That isn't in life's gift, I'm afraid. It's what you are. It's why you can ride this storm, provided you acknowledge it and face it. You faced the press after your fiasco with Helen on the green baize. You can face this.'

'I just thought I'd given up having to face things.'

'Yes, I know, and so did I.'

He nodded glumly.

'I'll go and ring the *Smear*,' he said.

He went to the door, stopped, turned, looked at the modest, serious room, with its computer and printer, its prints of Old Thurmarsh (as if Hilary needed help with not forgetting her roots?) and its piles of notes all over every available space: notes about characters, notes about plot, chapter headings, things that she needed to go back and insert, lists, dates, ages, all the entrails of her complex, subtle new book. He felt so proud of her, so thrilled by the seriousness of her work, so contemptuous of the unimportant nature of his, that he went back and kissed her and ran his tongue into and around her glorious mouth.

How he wished that he hadn't done what he'd done, less than an hour ago, in the more spacious of the two upstairs lavatories, with Sally Atkinson.

'Henry Pratt. I believe you've been trying to get hold of me.'

'Got it in one, old boy,' said Fraser Goldthorpe fruitily. He was a journalist of the old school, hard-drinking, hard-living. 'I'm our books editor, Henry, and . . .'

'Books editor!' said Henry. 'You don't do books on the *Smear*. You're the racing correspondent.'

'Racing correspondent as well. Sadly we don't cover books as much as *I* would like, and one has to earn a crust. My wife, who is so addicted to cookery books that she never has any time to prepare meals, says your book isn't a diet at all. It's a con.'

'You're out to get me, aren't you?'

'Not particularly. Nothing personal. Rather like you, actually. However, the powers that be believe you to be ripe for character assassination. They just love to destroy TV stars. Couldn't do it before. People liked you too much. Now the seeds of doubt have been sown, and we can begin to cut you down to size. Just doing our job. Just filling our readers' sad, empty, vengeful lives.'

'The dictionary's first definition of a diet is "the food

and drink habitually consumed by a person or animal",' said Henry. 'The word doesn't necessarily mean a regime designed for weight loss.'

Fraser Goldthorpe treated Henry's arguments as if they were horses, describing them as 'lame' and 'non-starters'. In the next day's paper, he savaged Henry's book as a con. 'If you really want to spend £16.99,' he said, 'you'd do better to back Random Dancer in the 3.30 at Redcar.'

The question of whether *The Pratt Diet* was a con was taken up by other newspapers. Henry was asked to appear on the popular TV magazine show, *Food for Thought*. He was taken to the BBC in a limousine with darkened windows and rushed into the building with his raincoat hiding his face, like a mass murderer entering a court-house. He was interviewed by Candy Beasley, sometimes known as Candid Candy and sometimes as Beastly Beasley. Her hair was jet-black, her eyes were dark and deep, her smile was supercilious, and she spat accusations like an angry cat. Off stage she was charming and delightful, but being beastly was her career. Henry thought that he would have liked her more if she was nasty through and through.

His publicist at Consolidation House had been confident that Henry could handle Beastly Beasley, but her confidence was misplaced. He was nervous. He knew that the next five minutes could be extremely important for his career.

'People are saying that *The Pratt Diet*, your number one best seller . . .' began Candy Beasley after the introductions.

'Thank you,' interrupted Henry unwisely.

'Oh, it wasn't a compliment,' said Candy Beasley.

'Ah!' said Henry. 'You mean that popularity is proof of mediocrity. I have more faith in the British public than that.'

Candy Beasley ignored him.

'People are saying that *The Pratt Diet* is in fact not a diet at all,' she said.

'Are they? One or two people in the media may be. I don't think the general public are.'

'I've read your book . . .'

'I'm amazed.'

No, Henry. Wrong!

'. . . and I couldn't detect any scientific basis or any specific nutritional theory behind it.'

'Ah. Well. There's a reason for that. There isn't any.'

'Ah.'

Be decisive, Henry. Be strong.

'I've never claimed that there was,' he said. 'I am presenting a concept of eating varied food, in modest quantities, and eating it without worry, without guilt; so that even if one doesn't lose weight – and I make no specific claims about losing weight – one will be healthier and happier than if one . . . er . . . didn't eat the food in my book.'

He was painfully aware that, after a confident start, his little speech had ended very lamely.

'So the question is,' said Candy Beasley, 'when is a diet not a diet?'

'When it's the legislative assembly of Japan.'

Oh God!

'It wasn't a riddle, Mr Pratt.'

'Sorry. I can never resist being silly.'

'So it would appear,' said Candy Beasley icily. 'I believe that there are serious issues of credibility here, Mr Pratt. Serious issues about one's responsibility to one's public. I don't think one should be silly about that.'

'I'm sorry.'

He was on the back foot now. He had to be more assertive.

'A diet only means what people eat,' he said. 'Many diets are conceived as aids to slimming, but diet could be for putting on weight. We talk about varied diets, an interesting diet . . .'

'That's perfectly true but in book terms, Mr Pratt, in book terms, a book with the title *The Pratt Diet* would be assumed to have a basis in controlled, well thought out dietary considerations. People will have a right to expect, if they follow your diet, that they will lose weight.'

'I'm not really very interested in what people have a right to expect,' said Henry. 'I believe . . .'

'The People's Chef, who has such faith in the British people, isn't really interested in what the public has a right to expect,' interrupted Candy Beasley. 'How very fascinating. Henry Pratt, thank you so much for talking to us tonight.'

It was over almost before it had begun. He had had no time. His shock and anger were very evident as the interview ended.

'And now,' said Candy Beasley, 'a man who eats nothing but limpets, and has survived to be ninety-three.'

*

Next morning, when he woke up, he couldn't believe how badly he had done. He couldn't believe that he had been silly enough to mention the legislative assembly of Japan. He couldn't believe that suddenly the whole world didn't love him.

Some people did, though and thank God that included Hilary.

In fact people took sides. There were letters in the *Radio Times.* There were discussions on chat shows. There were telephone votes about whether *The Pratt Diet* was a good thing, and whether Henry was a good thing. He had become public property.

If any conclusion could be drawn, it was that he had been seriously damaged, but not destroyed.

His publishers were cautious about the long term, and said that they would 'put the idea for your next book on ice, just till the controversy dies down'.

The BBC were less equivocal. They cancelled a proposed third series of *Hooray, It's Henry.* A spokesperson put her personal spoke in and said, 'This decision has absolutely nothing to do with the current controversy. It was felt that the series should go out on a high and that it would be difficult without repetition to maintain the standards of the first two series. We have continued faith in Henry Pratt as a TV cookery personality and will be exploring different formats for possible future shows.'

Henry had a strong fear that this was executive-ese for 'Goodbye'.

Among the newspaper headlines on Friday, 11 October,

2002, were 'Poll Countdown for Tory "Quiet Man"'; 'Archer Faces Loss of Prison Pay over Diaries'; 'Major Evades Questions of Affair' and 'Book Chain Withdraws *Pratt Diet*'.

Henry always enjoyed his occasional weekends in his country retreat, but he had never looked forward to one quite as keenly as to this one. The peace and quiet would mend his tormented soul.

His spirits rose the moment he stepped into the Land Rover. Well, he was at least in part a countryman now, so he needed a four by four: he couldn't afford, with all his commitments, to be cut off, even though this was unlikely, since the only land he ever had to rove over were the twenty-eight yards of gravel from the garage to the road, and in any case it had hardly snowed, in Grayling-Under-Witchwood, for more than a decade.

It wasn't perhaps surprising that, with all the controversy, he should forget, for the first time, to warn Bradley Tompkins that he was visiting The Old Manor House.

He decided that here in the country, where people were friendly but respected your privacy, he wouldn't hide away from the public as he had recently done in London. On his first evening there, he would go to the pub.

There were two pubs in the village, one at each end. The Crown was an example of Henry's *bête noir* – the Gastropub. An ugly word and, in his opinion, an ugly concept. Every table was laid ready for meals. There were no stools at the bar. He didn't regard it as a pub at all. The food wasn't bad, but it was over-priced and uninspired. They employed migrant workers because they were cheap. When the Polish barman put angostura bitters instead of tabasco into his Bloody Mary, Henry said, 'It's not your fault, Piotr, but I am going now and never coming back.'

The Coach and Horses, on the other hand, was a fine example of that declining species, the Village Pub, where people from different walks of life could meet and talk and laugh and listen and learn. Young and old, rich and poor, men and women, believers and atheists, Manchester United and Tottenham Hotspur supporters, Conservatives and Socialists, artists and plumbers could mingle and realise that what they had in common was more important than what separated them. It was a great tradition, envied by the world, and like other traditions envied by the world it was slowly, agonisingly dying in a fragmented land.

Regulars gravitated, in the Coach and Horses, to a rather windy bar opposite the main entrance. This was known for miles around as Rodney's Back Passage. Rodney Merganser, the landlord, was a character. He didn't like cyclists, people who ordered tap water, or people who ate baguettes. He smiled at least twice every year, and if you were in trouble he would always help you.

The moment Henry entered The Coach, as it was known locally, he knew that it was the pub for him. There was a large sign in the porch – 'No Norwegians or Hockey Players'. When Henry asked Rodney about this, he said that it was completely arbitrary. He hoped to be arrested and become a martyr to the absurdities of political correctness.

He was going on about things as Henry entered that evening.

'I believe,' he was saying, 'that there should be

establishments for men only, for women only, for whoever you like only. Personally I would like there to be a bar for golfers only, where they could bore themselves into mass graves with tales of their iron shots.'

Lovely, prejudiced man. Henry's heart warmed to him.

There was a good crowd in. Bomber Walsh – Henry had a theory that every good pub had a customer called Bomber – was arguing passionately about the uselessness of wasps with Tina Benson, who stood and drank pints while her husband Ewan was at home cooking the supper. Michael Ewart, the world's least likely tax inspector, was drinking large glasses of the Spanish red, very quickly, and laughing, very loudly, at almost anything anybody said. The Merricks had brought their Slovenian *au pair*, who was very pretty. It promised to be a vintage Friday evening.

And then in he/she came. Mrs Scatchard in a grey green sweater that emphasised her artificial breasts, and a long velvety dress that looked as if it had been made out of abandoned curtains.

It was the first time Henry had seen him/her in there. His heart sank.

If Mrs Scatchard's heart sank, he/she concealed it well.

'Mr Pratt! My neighbour!'

'Hello, Mrs Scatchard. What are you having?'

'A pink gin, if I may. One of my little peculiarities.'

Oh God. It was going to be a farce. Why did farce pursue him like a lovesick stalker?

He wasn't going to be able to confront Bradley. He had promised that he wouldn't reveal his double identity, and damn it, there could be honour even among chefs.

He handed Mrs Scatchard her pink gin and heard himself say, 'So, what are your other little peculiarities?'

'Ah. That would be telling. Bottoms up.'

'Bottoms up.'

'To continued good neighbourliness.'

'To continued good neighbourliness.'

'You've been in the news a lot recently, haven't you?'

'Yes, I . . . I have . . . haven't I?'

'Difficult for you?'

'Pretty much so.'

'Somebody got it in for you, do you think?'

'Looks like it.'

'I thought you thought you knew who it was.'

'I think I do.'

'My brother?'

'I . . . er . . . I don't want to be specific.'

'Afraid he'll sue?'

'Possibly.'

'How could he ever find out what you're saying in an out of the way place like this?'

'Well, how indeed? Unless you told him.'

'I wouldn't betray a confidence.'

They stood on the edge of the Friday crowd, unnoticed. Henry was popular enough, but nobody quite knew what to say to him under the present circumstances, and nobody ever knew quite what to say to Mrs Scatchard. The general view was that she was harmless but strange.

'Well, come on, then, Henry,' said Mrs Scatchard, eyes glittering. 'Spill the beans. Let a simple rustic into the secrets of the world of metropolitan intrigue.'

'Well, let me put it this way,' said Henry. He would have to be careful. It didn't look as if anyone was listening, but you never knew. Oh God, how this was spoiling the glorious simplicity of his planned evening. 'I think somebody is very jealous of me. Your brother might be such a person. He hasn't been very nice to me.'

'Have you been very nice to him?'

'Well, no, I suppose I haven't.'

'He's always struck me . . . I don't see him very often, you know, we aren't close, considering we're twins, so it isn't always easy to know . . . same again?'

'Please. Thank you.'

Why on earth did I accept, Henry asked himself as Mrs Scatchard edged his/her way uneasily to the bar.

When he/she returned, he/she said, 'Where was I?'

'About to tell me how your brother strikes you.'

'Ah yes,' said Bradley Tompkins. 'He strikes me . . . seen mainly from a distance . . . as all mouth and no trousers. Might dream of doing such a thing. Wouldn't actually have the bottle to go through with it. All sauce and no steak. Could be wrong.'

'Well, yes . . . yes.'

'Have to be very sure, wouldn't you, before you went around openly accusing him?'

'Oh absolutely. Yes. Absolutely. Oh yes. Cheers.'

17 An Unwelcome Gift

Slowly, gently, firmly, exquisitely, truly, madly, deeply he entered Sally Atkinson.

There was a sudden loud crash of something hitting the window. He sat up with a start. Where was he? Where was Sally?

He realised, with a sharp intense stab of relief and regret, that he'd been dreaming.

He thought he was in The Old Manor House, and reached for the bedside light, but he was in the Clapham house, and the light was above his head, so he knocked his glass of water all over the sheet. One moment, glorious sex. The next moment, wet sheets, but not for the right reason. He swore.

Hilary switched on the light.

'What was that noise?' she said.

How lovely she looked, even when she was awakening from a deep sleep. How could he even have thought of dreaming of sex with Sally?

'A bird flying into the window?'

'At half past three in the morning?'

'An owl?'

He padded across the carpet, and pulled back the curtains. A smashed egg was still slithering slowly towards the sill.

Hilary came and stood beside him. He ran his hand gently over her buttocks.

'Kids?'

'I'll take a look.'

He hurried into a pair of jeans, both legs in one leg for a moment, and Miss Candy flashed through his mind, saying, 'Mr Hurry was late for his wedding.' He grabbed the previous day's shirt from the laundry bag hanging on the door, put on a pair of outdoor shoes, and hurried along the corridor, down the wide stairs, into the spacious entrance hall with its two large dark paintings – one of Siena, the other of coq au vin.

There was an envelope on the floor. He ricked his back slightly as he picked it up.

'To Whom It Might Concern'.

He ripped it open.

My Dear Henry,
Life is too short for enmity, so I have left you a little present. Well, quite a large present, actually. I didn't want to wake you in the middle of the night, so I've left it in the porch. A lot of thought went into it, and I hope you'll agree that it is most appropriate.
With very best wishes
Bradley.

He began to unlock the front door.

He could smell it. The warm, sweet, stifling, curiously nourishing smell of horse shit.

He thought better of opening the front door, and locked it hurriedly. He switched on the outside light, and went out by the side door. As he rounded the corner of the house, he gasped. There was a huge mountain of the stuff.

It covered the front door completely and reached up almost to the landing. It covered most of the windows of the sitting room and dining room. Hundreds of horses must have evacuated their bowels for Bradley Tompkins. The smell, which might have been vaguely reassuring in the country, was sickening here off Clapham Common.

He just stood and stared. He was barely aware of a click and a flash as a paparazzo took a picture.

Hilary came out and joined him. She was shivering. She looked horrified. Homes are wombs for women. They feel outrages against them more keenly, more emotionally, than men.

'Oh God,' she said. 'How very predictable.'

'Bradley *is* predictable. That's one of the many things he can't stand about himself.'

Hilary made a *cafetière* of good, strong coffee, and they sat at the kitchen table with the Yellow Pages in front of them. There were several pages of 'Waste Disposal Services'. No one firm struck the eye. There was no 'Manure Mountain Removal Company'. They wrote down the phone numbers of the likelier sounding companies, but in the event it was Tuesday before anyone could do the job.

'It's terrifying to be hated so much,' said Henry. 'It's humiliating. It's awful.'

The story was a gift to the national press at a quiet time for news.

'Foal Faeces Fuel Food Feud' was merely the most alliteratively ambitious of the headlines.

The bottom half of the front page of the *Daily Smear* showed a picture of the People's Chef, standing beside the great pile of manure, mouth open in shock and disbelief. The top half of the page was covered by just two words, two words containing a total of six letters, two words in vast, black, bold type, just two words from the great rich language of Shakespeare and Keats and Dickens and Trollope and P. G. Wodehouse.

OH SHIT!

Henry's fury knew no bounds. He was happy to give a press conference accusing Bradley. He waved the letter and read it to the massed journalists called to a press conference beside the offending pile.

'I've been to three party political conferences,' commented one journalist, 'and, even so, this is the biggest amount of shit I've ever seen in one place.'

Even in his fury, Henry didn't reveal Bradley's double identity, but he couldn't resist saying, 'Beware of freaks bearing gifts.' When asked what he meant by 'freaks', he said, 'Don't you think a man who hates another as much as this is a freak?'

When he was asked why he thought Bradley hated him, he ascribed it to jealousy. 'I do what I do better than him.'

Next day Bradley told the press that he was entirely innocent, the letter was a forgery, he would sue Henry 'for every penny he's got', and sue any newspaper which had been unwise enough to do more than quote Henry, for the grievous damage done to the reputation of an innocent, honest man.

The day after that, Henry received a cold, brief, businesslike letter from Bradley's solicitor.

That night he didn't sleep. Could Bradley possibly be innocent? He had made bad mistakes before. Had he now made his worst and most costly mistake of all?

It had to be Bradley. Who else hated him that much?

It had to be Bradley. The man had signed the letter.

It could be a forgery.

He was ruined.

It had to be Bradley. There was nobody else.

The clock struck four. Half the bloody night still to go.

On Thursday, 20 March, 2003, twelve marines became the first British casualties in the war against Iraq; hundreds of thousands took to the streets around the world to protest about the war; a magician announced that he intended to spend two days encased in a six-foot chunk of mature Cheddar cheese in a shopping centre in Weston-Super-Mare equipped only with a mobile phone and a jar of pickle 'in case I have to eat my way out'; and a surprising visitor entered the Café Henry in Frith Street.

It was a busy morning. Henry's recent controversies had stimulated a surge in visits by celebrity spotters, but there was a difference now. Some of them still gawped in admiration at a sighting of the great man, but others looked at him as if he was a traffic accident.

One of the customers, a shy, awkward young man, used sympathy as a device to get into conversation with Henry, in order to get the chance to talk about himself. This was not a clever move. Henry didn't want sympathy from strangers. He wasn't used to it.

'I have my problems too,' said the awkward, shy young man.

'Oh?' said Henry very cautiously.

'I'm a writer . . .'

'Oh bad luck,' said Henry sympathetically.

'. . . and I've had this fantastic sitcom idea and the BBC have turned it down flat. How can they not see it's funny, with some of the things they put on? I'll tell you my idea and you'll see how incredible it is.'

Henry looked round for some urgent task that he could do. He couldn't see one.

He braced himself.

'It's a remake of *Dad's Army*, but gay.'

Henry tried to stop his mouth dropping open, but it was too strong for him.

'People think there weren't any gays in the good old days. There were. There always have been. Look at the dandies.'

'Well, you have a point, but wouldn't it be stretching credibility to have every man in the unit gay?'

'No! That's the whole point. They're attracted because of discrimination elsewhere – and I have a great catchphrase. "They love it up them." In the first episode . . .'

'You're right,' said Henry. 'It is incredible.'

'Thank you. In the first episode . . .'

'You must excuse me,' said Henry. 'I'm needed in the kitchen.'

He made his escape. He was too tired, after another sleepless night, to cope with that sort of thing. God, he was tired.

Not all the customers knew of the horse shit affair. Several were foreigners. The Café Henry was on all the tourist lists. That lunchtime there were two big cheeses from the Gruyère Chamber of Commerce, with their big wives; three Greek musicians; two men of French letters; a New Zealand archivist on her way to the British Museum; and the editor of a French underground magazine called *Metro* with his journalist friend and lover, the editor of a gay German magazine called *Mein Kamp*.

But most people did know of the incident, and there was a communal gasp, followed by an eerie silence, when the surprising visitor strode in at nine minutes to two.

Only Greg, with his huge insensitivity and his rare talent for being oblivious, was unaffected by the atmosphere.

'Good afternoon, sir,' he said. 'What about the school-children, eh? Thousands of them have streamed out of school to join the protests. Is it just an excuse or do they really care? And what about that cheddar mountain and that magician, eh? We have reasons here to be careful about big mountains. What is worse, eh, cheddar or horse . . . Shit, it's you!'

'Yes, it's me,' said Bradley Tompkins, 'and if you've finished the one o'clock news bulletin I wonder if I could speak to Mr Pratt?'

'Of course, sir. No problem. He's in the kitchen.'

'Straightaway, please.'

'Got you.'

Henry hurried out of the kitchen, where he had been busy pretending to be busy.

'Bradley! What can I get you?'

'I'll have a glass of red wine, please, Henry.'

Bradley Tompkins held out his hand. Henry thought

about refusing to shake it, then relented. His heart was like a steam hammer.

'Here's a list of the ones we do by the glass, Bradley, but of course I'll open anything specially for you.'

How polite they were about the nuances of their trade!

'No, no,' said Bradley. 'No, these are fine. I'll . . . er . . . have a glass of the tempranillo, I think, if I may.'

'Jolly good.' Henry winced. He never said, 'Jolly good', a Northern lad like him. It was nerves.

Henry also took a glass of the tempranillo, and they settled themselves at the only vacant table, beside the salad counter. Conversation had returned to normal in the Café, and so they could be totally private in the middle of the hubbub.

'Have you got the letter?' asked Bradley.

'Your letter?'

'No. *The* letter. I didn't write it. You're being duped. I'm being framed. We're both being made to look ridiculous. Cheers.'

'Cheers.'

They clinked glasses, to the astonishment of nearby tables, and drank.

'Mmm,' said Henry. 'Do you taste hyacinths?'

'Hyacinths! No. More a faint . . . just the faintest . . . suggestion of . . . raspberry.'

'Really??'

'I didn't come to see you after your original comments in the *Smear*,' said Bradley in a low voice, 'but I was pretty miffed, I can tell you.'

'I didn't actually accuse you. I just said, "I know who did it." Big mistake. I back-tracked hurriedly.'

'Because you don't?'

'Don't what?'

'Don't know who did it.'

'Don't I?'

'No, Henry. You don't. I did none of it. Why do you assume that I did? How could you be so conceited? Mmm. This *is* delicious. Very well balanced. Lovely soft tannins.'

'Another?'

'Why not?'

Henry made 'two more of the same' gestures to the new girl. She didn't understand. Thick as a fish kettle. He signalled to her to come to the table. She didn't like it.

'Two more of the same, please, and I'm sorry to have offended you, but owning the sodding place does give me some privileges.'

She reddened and walked off as slowly as she dared. He smiled at Bradley.

'Can't get the staff.'

'I know how you feel.'

'What do you mean, Bradley – "How could you be so conceited?"?'

'To think I hate you enough to do these things.'

'You do hate me.'

'Well, are you surprised?' Bradley began to look less friendly. 'I'm a real pro, worked at it all my life. You're an amateur. This is a café. Oh, it's nice enough, but you shouldn't be a star. Of course I resented you – but why should I waste time and energy on you? You aren't worth it.'

The new girl brought their glasses of wine, as slowly as she dared.

'It's from a new bottle. Do you want to taste it, sir?'

'Did somebody ask you to say that?'

'No, sir, but I thought it might not be like the other one. It might be corked.'

Far less thick than a fish kettle. Henry was irrationally pleased.

'She understands, Bradley,' said Henry. 'Hundreds of restaurants don't understand that. She does. Well done.'

He gave the girl a radiant smile, and she blushed again. She wasn't unattractive. He wondered what she would say if he took her into his office and . . .

Henry!

It was the tension. The tension of all this. Down, boy.

He gestured to Bradley that he should taste it. Bradley shook his head politely. The girl poured Henry a sipful. He swirled it round his glass and sniffed it, then tasted it thoughtfully.

'Yes. Fine. Thanks.' He raised his glass to Bradley. 'Cheers.'

'Cheers. Why should I go to such lengths? I have a life of my own.'

'Two lives of your own,' said Henry softly.

'Well, yes, quite. Thank you, incidentally, for not saying a word about that.'

'A promise is a promise.'

Henry was surprised at the turn the conversation was taking. Bradley seemed almost friendly. Now, however, he returned to the attack.

'I repeat, Henry. Why should I go to such lengths?'

'To destroy my reputation.'

'Which it hasn't – well, not entirely and only

temporarily – because it was soon revealed that you'd been duped rather than dishonest. If I had done it, I'd have been a bit more thorough than that. And even if it did destroy your reputation – you don't think this new bottle *is* corked, do you? – why should I care enough to go round fixing farm notices and gathering vast mountains of horrid, steaming horse shit? I'm fastidious, Henry.'

'Maybe you've become blinded by hatred, Bradley. Besides – no, I don't think so. I think it tastes a bit sharp when it's first opened. Give it five minutes. If we still don't like it, we'll change it.'

'This is what I mean. You're conceited in your estimation of how important you are in my life. "Blinded by hatred"! You must think I think of you an awful lot. I suppose you think I can't sleep at night because I think of you, seething with envy, loathing your success, envying your orgasms while I pull my flaccid cock without response. I need to see the letter, Henry, and take a copy, so that I can prove it isn't my handwriting.'

'Fair enough.'

'My lawyers have sent you a letter, Henry. I'm very serious about this. If I don't get a total and handsome apology I *will* sue you for every penny I can get. You're destroying my reputation. I will destroy you. You're right. It isn't corked. It just needed air. It's going to be delicious.'

'Good. It certainly sells well.'

'It deserves to.'

Henry took an olive, chewed it, sighed deeply.

'This is terrible.'

'The olive?'

'No, no. Not the olive. Well, I mean, it isn't actually very good, but no, I meant . . . you and me . . . sitting here . . . I suddenly find . . . this is really dreadful, Bradley . . . I mean, we've never actually talked at all, have we? Not properly . . .'

'What are you getting at?'

'I'm . . . I'm actually rather enjoying sitting here chatting to you. I'm finding . . .'

Bradley gave a faint smile. There was the suspicion of a gleam in his beady little eyes, sardonic, perhaps, but no longer hostile.

'. . . that you like me?'

'Well, no. Not as bad as that. But . . . that I want to like you. That's almost as bad. Damn it, Bradley, I'm beginning to want to believe you. I'm beginning to think that maybe . . . but if not you, who? Who else hates me?'

'Only one enemy, Henry? That sounds most unlikely. Haven't you investigated at all?'

'No. I had a closed mind. Bradley, I won't go public yet, I . . . I just don't feel certain enough to do that, but I'll promise you this . . . I'll investigate. I'll investigate thoroughly. I haven't investigated at all. I should have. If I'm wrong, Bradley, you'll get the most handsome apology a man could ask for. Oh God. Oh shit, if you'll pardon the expression, it *isn't* you, is it?'

'No, Henry. It isn't.'

'Oh dear. When this comes out . . .' Henry shook his head gloomily. 'Already I feel as if I'm a sinking ship.'

'You mean rats are leaving you?'

'Yes. Another one today. Production of my monogrammed tableware is being discontinued. Oh, they didn't say, "We think you're on a slippery slope and we're abandoning you before it's too late." They said, "Unfortunately, the rise and rise of Harry Potter means that it is no longer viable to base a design on the letters HP. The range has done very well and we are hopeful that we will be able to work together again some time in the future."'

'Welcome,' said Bradley Tompkins, 'to the wonderful world of obscurity.'

'Are we on for a third glass?' asked Henry.

'Sounds rather a nice proposition to me.'

When their new glasses arrived, Bradley raised his to Henry, with a wry expression on his face.

'There's good news and bad news,' he said. 'The good news is, we will appear on television again. The bad news is, the programme will be called *Where Are They Now?*'

18 On the Trail

Two days later, after the Saturday evening rush in the Café had ended, Henry and Hilary drove along increasingly deserted roads to Grayling-Under-Witchwood, to spend all of Sunday and most of Monday in a time warp, steeped in idleness. It was to be the calm before the storm.

Late on the Sunday afternoon the calm was rudely broken.

They'd just finished a game of Scrabble. They often had a game of Scrabble on Sunday afternoon, in the elegant sitting room of The Old Manor House. Henry had beaten Hilary by three hundred and sixty-eight points to three hundred and forty-seven.

The phone had a pleasant ring to it. It was gentle and mellow. It didn't sound like a harbinger of bad news.

Henry answered it. Hilary, listening to just one end of the conversation, found it distinctly unnerving.

'Hello . . . Hello, Jack.'

He sounded pleased. No worries so far.

'No, we don't bother with the papers when we're here . . . What??? . . . Naked??'

Hilary began to feel slightly worried.

'Urinating??'

Hilary began to feel rather more worried.

'Good God! . . . It said what?? . . . Bloody hell!'

There was a long pause while Henry listened, grim-faced. Hilary wasn't enjoying it one bit.

'I see. Well, they're certainly going to town, aren't they? It's Open Season for Shooting at Henry Pratt. I'm flavour of the month for not being flavour of the month . . . Jack, I didn't! . . . I didn't . . . It's a set up. You can do anything digitally these days. You can't trust any photos any more. Mohammed told me. He didn't know how prophetic he was being. It probably isn't even my penis.'

What? What is all this? Get off the phone. Tell me.

'Well of course I'm upset . . . No, not with you, Jack . . . No, of course you had to tell us.'

Us? I haven't heard a thing yet.

'No, of course you haven't spoilt my Sunday. Well, you have, but you had to . . . Don't apologise. How are things? . . . A hundred and forty-eight days behind schedule. That's terrific . . .'

Never mind the small talk. Not now. Get off the phone.

'Kids OK? . . . Great. Flick OK? . . . Great. Look, I'll have to go, Jack. Hilary's bursting to know what this is about.'

Bursting isn't the word I'd choose. Terrified, more like.

'Bye. I love you too.'

I? What about *me*?

'Oh, and Hilary's making frantic signs. She sends her love too . . . Bye . . . Yes. Bye . . . Bye.'

At last he put the phone down. He gave Hilary an intense look.

'Jack says there's a photo of me in the *Sunday Grime*,' he said. 'I'm standing on a restaurant table. I'm stark bollock naked. I'm peeing into a wine bottle. There are people round the table, laughing, men *and* women, and

I'm holding up a board which says "Cock au vin". That's cock with a k.'

'Henry!'

'I didn't do it. It's a fake.'

'Are you sure? Absolutely sure? When you were drunk once?'

'I don't get drunk like that.'

'You did the night you were on the snooker table with Helen.'

'That was a one-off. And it was years ago. I don't do things like that any more. All right, I drink too much sometimes, but I do it in a civilised way, and I can hold it. I've never stood on a table naked. I've never peed into a wine bottle. I've never held up a board which says "Cock au vin" with a k. I haven't.'

'All right, darling. I believe you.'

'Are you sure you do, absolutely and totally? You see, this is what they rely on. That mud sticks. There's no smoke without a fire. I can hear them all saying it. Fickle bastards. It says "Is this the kind of behaviour we want from the People's Chef – the holier than thou chef who never swears?" '

'Somebody's really gunning for you.'

'I know. Oh God. There's also a photo of that photo in the Gents at the Café, with my head and the body of Michelangelo's David. Bradley could have done that.'

'The cock au vin, though. The thought for that could have come from the painting in our hall.'

'Bloody hell. So it looks as if it's someone who's been to our house.'

'Almost everyone's been to our house.'

'But not Bradley.'

'No, not Bradley.'

'Oh God. I want it to be Bradley.'

'This probably isn't the time to mention it,' said Hilary, 'but I do hate that painting. I mean, who else would have a picture of a portion of coq au vin in his hall?'

'Exactly. That's why I like it,' said Henry.

They sat in silence for a few moments.

'This can't go on,' said Hilary. 'You've got to stop it or it'll get worse. You've got to get off your arse and do a bit of detection.'

'I will. As soon as we get home. I'll start with the two farms. They have to be at the heart of it.'

On Tuesday, 22 April, 2003, thousands of commuters returning to London after the Easter break found chaos because 'a fresh breeze' had delayed signal repairs, and Paddington Station had remained closed; Cherie Blair defended the invasion of Iraq as acceptable under international law during a speech in Perth, Western Australia; and Henry went into the Sussex countryside with his beloved daughter, Kate.

As they drove to Martin Wildblood Farms, Organic is Their Middle Name, the conversation inevitably got round to Kate's love life, or the lack of it.

'So?' asked Henry, after they had at last left the shabby, congested streets of South London behind and were travelling through the rich, rolling countryside of East Sussex, studded with magnolias and camellias and the pink and white blossoms of cherry and apple trees at this most beautiful time of the year.

'No,' replied Kate.

That was the beauty of their relationship. They understood each other so well.

'But not because I've ruled it out,' she added. 'I did think about what you'd said.'

'So?' he asked again, but with a completely different meaning. Again Kate understood.

'I just haven't met the right person. I haven't met anyone good enough for me.'

Henry winced and smiled at the same time.

'I've shocked you.'

'A bit. I'd be more comfortable with me saying it, as befits a proud parent with a marvellous daughter. It did perhaps sound a trifle arrogant coming from you.'

He turned off the main road on to the side road that would lead to the farm. His spirits usually soared when he left main roads. Today, though, he felt only a sharp increase in tension.

'I didn't mean it in an arrogant way,' said Kate. 'I just meant that there isn't a vast gap in my life, I'm not lonely or pathetic, I don't feel unfulfilled, so I wouldn't want to share my life with anybody who wasn't pretty special.'

'What about actors? You must meet plenty of them.'

'Actors tend to be specially pretty rather than pretty special.'

They wound through a long, unpretentious village, pretty houses among plainer ones, council houses at both ends.

'But, yes, Dad,' said Kate, 'I would like to give and receive love. I remember sex with a nostalgic glow. Only . . . don't hold your breath. Your daughter is fussy.'

Henry turned into the drive leading to the farm.

'Is this the place?' said Kate. 'It's lovely.'

When they got out of the car, Henry went up to Kate and kissed her on both cheeks.

'Very continental,' he said, 'and talking about continental, I see the point of what you say, but I just wouldn't want you to be left on the shelf.'

Kate gave him a dry, exasperated look, and he felt obliged to explain like a second-rate comic.

'Continental shelf? Get it?'

'Oh, I got it,' she said. 'Good old Dad with his jokes – but I just have a fear that it was a warning dressed up as a joke. It's a disastrously chauvinist expression – "on the shelf". Missed the great experience of a man's love. I certainly don't feel like that.'

Henry didn't reply. He didn't feel the need to. They had reached the front door of the mellow old farmhouse. There was nothing more to be said. He had made his point, Kate had seen through him, and he had been reassured – to a certain extent, at least. At times he almost wished that he didn't love Kate so much. Caring deeply was hard work.

At the last moment he remembered that Marie and Martin didn't use the front door. They went round the side.

Marie broke into a smile when she saw who it was. So she did find him cuddly!

'This is my daughter, Kate,' he said, trying to hide his pride, knowing that it would irritate Kate if he showed her off as if she was a prized possession.

'Lovely,' said Marie.

Henry explained that he wanted to make further enquiries. Marie made them mugs of steaming coffee, and fetched their man, Colin, who had returned from Madeira. His face was tanned. His manner was apologetic.

'I'm so sorry,' he said. 'All it was was, a man rang, and said he wanted to play a practical joke on a chum, and would I just make myself scarce for a couple of hours on Saturday morning. Two hundred quid. A hundred an hour for doing sod all. I didn't think there was any harm in it.'

'Of course not. Did you ever see this person?'

'No. Just heard his voice. He left the money as arranged, and I thought no more about it.'

'Was there anything you can usefully say about his voice? Can you describe it?'

'I *have* thought of one thing,' said Colin, 'because I've been thinking about it quite a lot. I've sort of tried to play the voice back, in my mind, and one thing struck me, though in a way it tells you nothing. The person who phoned me – I don't think they were using their own voice. I can hear it now. It was careful, it wasn't natural, and it was rather odd: high-pitched.'

'So he must have thought you'd recognise his real voice,' said Kate. 'That narrows it down.'

'I hadn't thought of that,' said Colin. 'That's clever of you. It never crossed my mind.'

Nor mine, admitted Henry to himself wryly. Black mark, Sherlock Pratt. Well done, Kate Watson.

'I'm in the theatre,' said Kate. 'We do improvisations a lot. When you start you think you'll never be able to think of anything, but in the end you find yourself thinking of far more things than you ever thought you could think of.'

The two men laughed.

'I know,' said Kate. 'I thought it sounded ridiculous as I was saying it.'

'It's great, though,' said Henry. 'A great thought. You said the voice was high-pitched, Colin. Could it have been a woman?'

'I wondered about that,' said Colin. 'I think I was a bit stupid not to suspect the voice at the time, but you don't, do you? You don't answer the phone thinking, "I wonder if this person is using their real voice", do you? I think now . . .'

He paused.

'Yes?'

'I think now . . . I could be wrong . . . but I think it could have been somebody pretending to be the opposite sex to what they were.'

'Mrs Scatchard and . . .' Kate saw Henry's urgent warning look and stopped without mentioning Bradley's name. She blushed slightly as she realised her carelessness.

'Possibly,' said Henry. 'Or possibly not. Do you think, Colin, that it sounded more like a man trying to sound like a woman or a woman trying to sound like a man? Can you say?'

Colin thought long and hard, and it looked as if the process was hurting his brain.

'Could have been either,' he said.

'I know this is going to sound ridiculous, Colin,' said Henry, 'but could you make a list of everyone you know?'

'Everyone I know?'

'Yes. I mean within reason. Everyone who might know

you well enough to feel that they needed to use a false voice.'

'Well I suppose I could. I could rack my brains. Is it important?'

'It could be.'

'I'll have a go tonight.'

'Thank you.'

'Also . . .' Henry paused, narrowed his eyes, looked at Colin severely, lowered his voice and spoke slowly and intensely, in the vain hope that, just for a few moments, he might sound like a great detective. '. . . could you particularly try to remember people who'd have known that Marie and Martin were going to be away?'

'A lot would. They had a big silver wedding party not long before they went. They told everybody. It was no secret. They were that excited about going. They don't get away much.'

Henry thanked Colin warmly, and called out to Marie that they had finished. She came back into the kitchen, and said, 'Was he helpful?'

'Possibly very. Marie, this isn't going to sound very nice, but I have to ask it.'

'Of course. These things are important.'

He explained Colin's feelings about the voice of the person who telephoned.

She nodded gravely. She realised the implications.

'Could you possibly give me a list of everyone who might have known you were going to Majorca at that time?'

'Good Lord. Well, I could try.'

'I'd be grateful, if you would. That . . . er . . . that would include, I suppose, everyone who came to your silver wedding party.'

'But, Mr Pratt, those are our family and our very best friends.'

'Yes, I know. Obviously nice people, and innocent, but just one of them . . . you never know . . . it might mean something. I'll use the information very discreetly, I promise. Please.'

'Well, all right. I'll do it tonight.'

Henry was very quiet on the way home.

'You're very quiet,' said Kate.

'I'm depressed.'

'Waste of time?'

'I fear not.'

'What?'

'A couple of remarks, nothing brilliant, things I knew before, have fallen into place. All too easily. No real detective work needed. Kate, there are people I expect to see on that list, and I don't like it. I don't like it one bit.'

'Who?'

'I'm not telling. I might be wrong. I hope I'm wrong. Except . . .'

'Except what?'

'It has to be somebody.'

They were silent for several miles.

'Kate?'

'Yes?'

'What are you doing the weekend after next?'

'I don't think anything. Why?'

'How would you like to come to Grayling?'

'Has that anything to do with all this?'

'Of course.'

'Well . . . yes . . . I'm intrigued.'

'Good. You made models of people for one of your plays, didn't you, if I remember? Dummies. Puppets. People brought them on to the stage and worked the arms and legs, making extra characters out of them.'

'Yes. Created less out of artistic inspiration than economic necessity.'

'I seem to remember that they were quite realistic.'

'Fairly.'

'Would they pass for real people travelling in a car at thirty miles an hour, if somebody just caught a casual glimpse?'

'I would think so.'

'Will you make some models for me, and bring them with you to Grayling? Realistic, life-size models of real people.'

'What real people?'

'Well . . . you.'

'Me??'

'You. And me?'

'You??'

'Me. Possibly one or two others. Jack, if he's free. He'd be useful.'

'Mum?'

'No, probably not your mum.'

'What is all this?'

'I'm going to lay a trap.'

'Dad!'

'What?'

'Isn't that dangerous?'

'Not very, I wouldn't have thought.'

'Is it wise to take the law into your own hands?'

'I don't think I was ever wise – and do you have any faith in the police?'

'Of course not, but it all seems a bit melodramatic.'

'Like one of your plays.'

'Sorry, Dad, no. It's not at all like one of our plays. It's much sillier.'

On Wednesday, 23 April, 2003, the World Health Organisation warned that the Sars epidemic had made Toronto unsafe to visit; the Headmistress of Harrogate Ladies' College locked herself in a boarding house with forty-three pupils (or, as *The Times* put it, 'with forty-three other pupils', as if the headmistress was a pupil) because they had been in infected parts of the Far East; bird watchers were questioned after a 31-year-old woman was murdered, burnt and dumped at her favourite woodland spot – the Pulborough Brook RSPB nature reserve in West Sussex (which led to Greg being asked, in the Café in Frith Street, what he thought of the RSPB, to which he replied, 'Well, I think it's a good idea. You need to know how many people are coming if you give a party'); and Henry Pratt drove not to West Sussex but to West Kent, accompanied by his very good friend, Lampo Davey.

When he'd asked Lampo if he fancied a day in the Kentish countryside, Lampo had surprised him by saying that he'd love it.

'I thought you hated the country,' Henry had said.

'I hate staying in it. If I can be safely tucked up in Chelsea at bedtime, I'm happy to enjoy its beauties.'

'Of course, don't come if the Café can't spare you,' Henry had said.

'It can,' Lampo had answered drily. 'I've got it running so efficiently that I've rendered myself unnecessary. First big mistake of an inexperienced manager.'

It was a lovely spring morning. The air was fresh, the visibility was sharp, the countryside was bathed in sunshine with the passing shadows of fluffy clouds. The sun shone on mellow oast-houses and lazy rivers, on deep woods and tidy orchards, in a corner miraculously untouched by the motorways and railway lines that marched across East Kent like invading armies.

'Beautiful, isn't it?' said Lampo, 'what's left of it. The best landscape in the world.'

'No better than Tuscany, surely, Lampo?' He imitated the youthful voice of Lampo, laying on the sophistication to discomfort Henry at school a thousand years before: '"The English countryside in summer is a featureless confusion of weeds. Compare it with Tuscany, Pratt."'

'I was full of shit. But how do you remember that? I must have made quite an impression on you.'

'Oh, you did. We didn't have people like you in Thurmarsh.'

They crossed a hump-backed bridge. They passed a duck pond, the ducks arranged on it like blobs of sauce on a plate.

'How are you really, Lampo?' Henry asked. 'Are you . . . well, I suppose you must be . . . missing Denzil as much as ever?'

'More than ever.'

'You're not . . . you haven't . . .?'

'Oh no. My libido has finally bitten the dust, Henry. That's the only good thing about growing old. These days there are youngsters with T-shirts boasting that they're asexual. I wouldn't want to go that far. I get some pleasure from my memories. Oh, but Henry, what a relief it is not to fancy boys any more.'

A rabbit ran across the road in front of them. Lampo didn't spurn the conversational opportunity.

'If only asexuality could become fashionable for rabbits,' he said. 'It'd be so much more painless than myxomatosis.'

They passed a deserted cricket ground, dipped into a village of slate-hung houses, rose through a wood, and dropped slowly towards the only ugly thing they had seen since they left London – Happy Fields Farm.

'Good God,' said Lampo, as he surveyed the bleak bungalow, the low grey sheds, the huge pylons. 'Is this it?'

'There's no need for you to come in with me,' said Henry. 'It would offend your sensibilities.'

'Thank you.'

Henry knocked on the door. There was no bell.

The door opened one and a half inches.

'Yes?' said the farmer's wife, whose name Henry suddenly remembered – Cynthia Brown. She should never have been a Cynthia.

'I called to see you after that advert about Happy Fields on the TV,' said Henry.

'Oh yes. Come in.'

She took ages to unfasten the chain.

'You can't be too careful these days,' said Cynthia Brown. 'There are some funny people about.'

She looked across to Lampo as she said this.

'My friend Lampo Davey,' said Henry.

'You don't have to leave him in the car.'

How could he tell her that Lampo would hate every second he spent in her home?

'I know,' he said, 'and thank you, but he's allergic to bungalows. Gets terrible claustrophobia if there aren't any stairs.'

The bungalow smelt of disuse.

'I was just making a cup of tea,' said Cynthia Brown. 'Would you like one?'

'That would be very nice,' said Henry over-optimistically.

'Howard's out, I'm afraid. He's in Tunbridge Wells, changing his will. He's cutting out a cousin who sent him a saucy birthday card. He was disgusted.'

'Disgusted of Tunbridge Wells.'

'Pardon?'

'Never mind.'

The tea was weak and milky. Henry found that he was closing his eyes every time he took a sip, as if that might help.

He really had only one question to ask, but he dreaded the answer, so he kept putting it off. He explained that he was searching for information on anybody who might have known of the name Happy Fields and used it. Had they had any suspicious callers?

'We don't have callers,' said Cynthia Brown proudly. 'We've made the house what you might call caller-unfriendly. We have each other, you see, and we're happy with that. Well, we get plenty of company from the telly. *Corrie*, *EastEnders*. *Neighbours*. Who needs real neighbours? You probably think we're saddos.'

'Not at all,' said Henry. Having begun to lie, he thought he might as well go the whole hog. 'Nice cup of tea.'

'Thank you.'

He felt an overwhelming urge to escape from the bungalow. He felt a surge of the claustrophobia that he had invented for Lampo. It was the spur that gave him the courage to ask the question. He mentioned a couple of names and asked Cynthia Brown if they meant anything to her.

Her face hardened.

'They're relatives,' she said, as Henry had feared she would.

Then her face softened, as if she'd remembered something nice about them – and indeed she had.

'They never visit us,' she said. 'Never ever.'

Henry had known that he would feel depressed after his visit to Happy Fields, which was why he had needed someone to accompany him, and Lampo had been the perfect choice. He had a talent for not being interested in what was going on around him that amounted at times almost to genius. Henry was glad of it now. 'Mission accomplished,' he said, as he got back in the car, and not a word did Lampo say in reply.

It was too early to tell anyone of his suspicions. He still didn't have any proof. The names that had meant something to Cynthia Brown might not appear on the lists sent by Marie and Colin. There was still hope.

'Lunch,' he said. 'Let's find some nice lunch.'

As Henry drove around the lanes, Lampo let off steam.

'I should have lived abroad,' he said. 'Found some little paradise somewhere. If only the Cretans had been more artistic. Lovely people, but not artistic. I've been cocooned, you see. Chelsea. Sotheby's. Antiques. Cocooned. You know what I hate about the British most. Their hypocrisy. On and on about the cruel French and their *foie gras.* I've seen those geese. Their life is paradise compared to battery chickens, of which we eat millions without giving a shit. Maybe I should go abroad now, while there's still time. Somewhere in the Med. Spend my time looking at all the bronzed and beautiful boys and giving thanks that I'm no longer tormented by desire.'

Lampo sighed as Henry turned into a pub car park.

'Sorry,' said Henry. 'I know you hate pubs, but I'm the driver.'

It was a proper pub, with bar stools and tables for drinkers as well as eaters. The food was simple but good. The beer was good. The wine was good. The landlord was friendly. The young barman was good-looking and had earrings that glinted in the sun.

'Do you have rooms?' asked Lampo. 'I might fancy a day or two in the country.'

The next day, Henry received three unwelcome letters. There was Marie's list, and the two names that he hadn't wanted to see were on it. There was Colin's list, and there were the names again. And there was a letter from Asbo Supermarkets, whose turn it was to let the Good Ship Pratt sail off into the sunset without them:

Dear Mr Pratt,
This is to inform you that, sadly, we decided, at yesterday's marketing meeting, to discontinue both Pratt's Tyke Treats and Henry's Foreign Frolics.

While the appeal of Tyke's Treats was mainly local, we have been very pleased with the success of Foreign Frolics, which has done well for us throughout the country, apart from the one little blip.

We will be ordering no more of your goods when our current contractual arrangements cease. This is a sad moment for us, but change is the lifeblood of the supermarket world.

Henry shuddered at the memory of the blip to which they referred.

He had slipped into the range, without consulting the marketing men, or 'the suits' as he called them, an entirely juvenile and irresponsible private gastronomic joke.

Richard Avec Taches Provençale was, simply, garlicky spotted dick – Henry's final revenge against a dessert that had haunted him almost as much as Cousin Hilda's sniff.

A cluster of complaints had reached the marketing men, and they had not been amused.

What they had never told Henry was that there had been another cluster of complaints when it was withdrawn.

'I hope this trap works,' he said to Hilary, at the breakfast table, 'and works quickly, or I'll have no career left to save.'

19 The Trap

It was National Aubergine Day. As he made that lovely Greek aubergine, lemon and garlic dish cum dip, melitzanasalata, slightly rough in texture as he liked it, Henry told Greg, casually, that he and Hilary were going to Spain for a week. Later he told all his regular customers, and Michelle, and any other members of his staff with whom he spoke both in the Café and on the phone.

To each person he added the information that he had felt it necessary to get house-minders for the Clapham Common property, for security reasons.

He found an excuse for ringing Bradley, and told him too.

He phoned Jack and explained the rough outline of his plans. Jack expressed not a little surprise, but said that of course he would come. He was pleased to have the chance to do something for his Dad. Henry explained that they might have to stay in The Old Manor House for a week. Jack said that it was no problem. If they got even further behind with their work, all well and good.

Henry hadn't told Kate that she might have to stay for a week, but when he did she also said that it would be no problem. She trusted her deputies to run the theatre in her absence. It would be good for them, as she tended to be a bit autocratic. She would bring her pile of unread plays from all the hopeful dramatists who littered our beautiful island.

Stocking up for a week required careful planning. The food was comparatively easy. He bought a week's diet as recommended in the appendix to *The Pratt Diet*, although it has to be admitted that he did increase the quantities in view of Jack's presence and because eating would assume enormous importance in the tedium that was to come. Household goods were more difficult. It would be important to have enough toilet rolls and kitchen rolls and cling film and foil and cleaning materials and torches – no lights would go on at night – and a really good, reliable camera. Nothing, however trivial, must be forgotten. It wouldn't be possible to go to the village shop.

It was lucky that they had an estate car. Even so, it would be a struggle to get all the supplies in, in addition to four people and three life-size dummies.

They picked up Jack at King's Cross Station, and then went to Kentish Town for Kate, who had wrapped the dummies in brown paper, just in case the sight of people loading dummies of themselves into a car aroused unwelcome interest and suspicion.

Hilary drove to The Old Manor House. She drove fast and well. She loved it. It amused the family that behind the wheel she became impatient and ageist – 'silly old sod, shouldn't be on the road' – in complete contrast to her patient and compassionate character in the rest of her life.

On the journey they didn't talk about the days to come. Henry would brief them about that on arrival. They talked of pleasant things. Henry told his two children how proud he was that they were doing so well, even though their achievements were not of the sort that counted for much in a celebrity culture.

Under Kate's leadership – brave, intelligent, tempered with common sense and the need to put bums on seats – the Umbrella Theatre was building a formidable reputation. Three plays had transferred to the West End, and two of them had done well.

Jack was thriving too. They were three and a half months late starting some jobs, and four months late finishing others. Flick had a thankless task, fielding angry, desperate phone calls, but she was brilliant at it – she should have been in the diplomatic corps – and the punters were so thrilled when they finally turned up to do a job and so excited when at last they finished it that they barely queried the bills.

They talked of their delight at Camilla's happiness and success. She had been described in the *Observer* as the best painter of horses since Stubbs. Her painting of the winner of the Cheltenham Gold Cup had been sold to the owner for £60,000. She and Guiseppe were becoming seriously rich. They were in Venice at the moment for the unveiling of an abstract sculpture of Guiseppe's. It was called 'Past Glory' and had been placed in one of Venice's tiniest, loveliest squares. Guiseppe had long outgrown his beginnings as a caricaturist.

The family were always excited on arriving at Grayling-Under-Witchwood, passing the trim council houses with their neat lawns and their swings, seeing the mellow buildings of Grange Farm, the timbered cottages scattered among the stone, the handsome Georgian frontage of Farm Grange, the monumental Victorian vicarage, the handsome Perpendicular church, the exquisite honeyed frontage of the elegant yet modest manor house.

Hilary drove the car round the back, so that they could empty it far from prying eyes. Even so, she reversed it close to the door, so that the unloading could be done as unobtrusively as possible. Henry was taking no risks whatsoever.

It was exciting to stock up the American-style food centre, the two other fridges, the old-fashioned larder and the cupboards.

It was even more exciting to unwrap the dummies. Kate laid them gently on the floor of the landing and removed the paper carefully and neatly.

There they lay, side by side, Henry and his children.

'You're hard on yourself, Kate,' said Henry. 'You're prettier than that.'

'What about me?' complained Jack. 'I don't look like a man you'd allow near your house, let alone build your conservatory.'

They laughed.

Henry looked at his dummy and thought, 'Does Sally really fancy me? Is it possible?'

That evening, Henry held a briefing. He was in his element, satisfying a side of his personality that he had only found very occasional opportunities to express – in his excessively successful campaign against diseases of the cucumber, in his excessively unsuccessful attempt to save the economy of Peru by planting cucumbers all over the Andes, and in his organisation of the successful search for

Benedict. Two successes, one failure. Which would this one be?

There were times, as he briefed them, when his family found it hard not to laugh, but they didn't dare to. There were times when they were awed by the absurdity of the venture, but they didn't dare say so.

Henry explained that they would need to live in almost total silence, giving the impression at all times that the house was empty. All conversations would have to be held in whispers. All the curtains would be drawn throughout. The telephone must not be answered under any circumstances. If there were urgent messages, people would have to phone Hilary in Clapham, and she would have to deal with them. The three in the house would be utterly incommunicado.

'I'm not complaining,' said Kate. 'It's all rather exciting and I'm going to get an awful lot of reading done, but it does seem to be an extraordinarily elaborate and long-winded way of going about things.'

'That's your father for you,' said Hilary.

'Hilary! This may seem mad, but it's not arbitrary or self-indulgent. I know what you're thinking – Field Marshal Pratt and his silly games – but you see, I suspect two people. I don't know which of them it is. How can I go to the police? How can I accuse one, in case it's the other? I want simple, overwhelming proof. I want to catch them red-handed.'

'Supposing they don't rise to the bait?' asked Jack.

'In that case no harm will have been done. I mean it's only for a week. Hostages are cooped up for years with no knowledge of when it will end. Prisoners endure dreadful lives and know only too well how long it will be before it ends. I'm asking you to spend one week at most, possibly far less, without telephones and TV and fresh air. A difficult week, if it turns out to be a whole week, but an adventure. A family adventure.'

'It's all right for you,' said Hilary. 'I won't be here.'

'It's a terrible shame. We'll miss you,' said Henry, 'but there's no other way. You know that. You have to be seen driving away with us.'

'I know, but . . . it's going to be awful . . . wondering what's happening . . . not being able to phone.'

They tried so hard to be normal that evening, eating and drinking, visiting the pub, joking about Rodney's Back Passage. Henry and Hilary discussed their week in Spain with the Cramthornes, who gave them the phone number of friends they would never visit, since they weren't going to Spain. It seemed that pretence now went with Henry every time he went to The Coach.

Charlie Mitten, who had five large furniture vans with the legend, 'Mittens – They Move You With Gloves On', asked if they knew anything about Mrs Scatchard, woman of mystery. Henry was able to say, in all honesty, that they never met socially, except in Rodney's Back Passage.

Freddie Hargreaves opined that it was unlikely that anybody had ever met in Mrs Scatchard's back passage. Jenny Hargreaves, who was a churchwarden, coloured and said, 'For shame, Freddie Hargreaves', but she couldn't help laughing.

Logger Masefield had won the pork in the weekly meat raffle. He asked Henry how he should cook it. Henry suggested inserting a few slivers of garlic, rubbing it well with salt, pouring a generous glass of white wine over it, adding a few sprigs of thyme, leaving it to marinate for a few hours, then putting the meat and the marinade in a baking tin, covering it with greased paper and cooking it in a moderate oven for an hour, adding more liquid if necessary, then coating it with chopped parsley mixed with fine breadcrumbs, lowering the oven and cooking it for a further forty-five minutes.

The general opinion, expressed with much laughter, was that this might be a bit beyond Logger, who became indignant. 'Just because I live in a caravan you think I'm dead ignorant,' he said. 'I'll do that, and I'll invite you to share it, Henry.'

'If only we weren't going to Spain,' said Henry. He wondered if they were mentioning Spain too often.

They had a third drink, Jack thrashed Kate at pool and they left to a chorus of 'Have a good holiday. Give our love to the Spaniards' and 'Arrividerci' and 'That's Italian, you moron.'

'It's odd,' said Rodney Merganser in his Back Passage, after they had gone. 'Usually they're careful to be very discreet about their comings and goings, for fear of burglars overhearing them, but they've practically taken out adverts for this trip.'

Nobody thought any more about it, however.

Before Hilary left, they closed the curtains in every room of the house.

Hilary wandered around outside, pretending to be looking for flowers, but actually keeping watch while Jack and Henry brought the dummies down to the car and

Kate placed them artfully in their seats, Henry in the front beside Hilary, and little Kate and bulky Jack in the back.

'This really is absurd. Is it actually necessary?' asked Jack.

'It's necessary to him,' said Hilary.

'It's the little details that single out the truly brilliant generals,' said Henry with a grin. 'Alexander the Great, Napoleon, Monty, me. No, seriously, why take chances? Somebody sees Hilary driving off alone, the whole thing's blown.'

'Will I really look as if I've got live people in the car?' said Hilary. 'I mean, don't get me wrong, Kate, they're brilliant, but they don't move.'

'People will see a full car flashing by,' said Henry, 'and they won't have time to think, "Good Lord. Three of the four people in that car weren't moving around at all. You don't think they could possibly be life-size dummies of people left behind in the house, do you?" '

Hilary left at about six o'clock on the Sunday evening. She kissed them all inside the house.

'Will you miss me?' she asked Henry.

'Of course I will.'

'Do you still love me?'

'Of course I do.'

'I hope so.'

She went to the door, turned and waved.

'Don't forget not to ring,' said Henry.

'I won't.'

And then she was off, and they couldn't even move a curtain to watch her drive away.

*

The three of them felt very strange when Hilary had gone. Suddenly all the excitement left them, and the realisation of the long, long hours ahead weighed heavily upon them. Jack was about to talk. Henry held his finger to his lips, urgently. Jack nodded.

That evening they talked only in whispers. They cooked with the utmost care, silently. They ate with exaggerated caution, lest a knife scraped against a plate. The phone rang twice but they didn't answer it.

Field Marshal Pratt was a stickler for details, a disciplinarian with an iron fist in an iron glove. His army had time on their hands, and that was always dangerous. They would think his extreme caution more and more absurd, but he was determined to maintain their total discipline at all times.

The question of flushing the toilet was raised in a whisper.

'Only when absolutely necessary,' was Henry's coy whispered reply, 'and with the seat down, and the door shut. It's the one risk that we can't avoid taking. You will be following the Pratt diet. You shouldn't have any problems with wind. Don't laugh, Jack.'

Kate read plays until the light faded. Reading plays depressed her enormously. There were all these hopeful writers longing for their work to be produced. Some of them were hopeless as well as hopeful. Others had talent, but no idea how to discipline it. Some had good ideas, but no technique. Some had good technique, but no ideas. Some of the plays would be fun, but impossible to stage. Some would be easy to stage, but no fun at all. Some would be overly didactic, others would have nothing whatsoever to say. Some needed a cast of thousands. One of them featured a major volcanic eruption, hard to manage at the Umbrella. It had always been so, and it would always be so, but twice in the past, in seven hundred and seventeen plays, Kate had struck gold, and so she took her slush pile very seriously.

Henry, meanwhile, tried to catch up on his mail, since Mrs Daventry was on holiday. The amount had fallen, though not a lot. What had changed was the balance of it. At least forty per cent was now hostile.

'Bradley Tompkins always was an easy target. I'm sad to see you following in the steps of scum like Dennis Danvers.'

'There's no smoke without a fire, and nobody could drop mounds of horse shit in your garden unless you deserved it.'

'I thought you were different from the other celebrities, but you aren't. You're all brushed with the same tar.'

'What a role model. Kids will be standing on tables pissing into wine bottles when they should be at school studying. Photo a fix? Come off it. Face up to yourself.'

'I am Predisent of the Dylsexia Society. We were going to invite you to pseak to us. No longer!'

Some people went to enormous trouble just to put him down. Only two days ago he had received a bulky parcel that had cost a fortune to post. It had been from a woman in Wellingborough, and it had contained a pair of size fourteen boots. 'You're too big for your boots, so these may come in handy,' she had written.

While Henry and Kate toiled, Jack played patience impatiently.

Dusk fell, and the first watch began. Henry and Kate stayed up and waited, sitting in the dark, silently. Jack slept. At three in the morning Henry woke Jack, and he and Jack kept watch while Kate slept.

The realisation that this could go on for days sobered them considerably.

'Come on, keep your spirits up,' whispered their inspiring commander.

But it was hard. In the morning, Jack played patience impatiently. Kate struck no gold. Henry jotted down ideas for his next cookery book, a gastronomic tour of Europe. He wondered idly if . . . His head lolled. The commander was asleep. His foot soldiers both smiled affectionately, and indicated to each other, also affectionately, that they thought that he was just a little mad.

Kate played Jack at backgammon. Henry woke up and dealt with a few more letters.

'I've gone off you, big style. I'm glad now that you never came for that blow job. Consider the offer closed as of today. Incidentally, I've moved. It is easier to come off at junction 39 now.'

'My mum makes better Yorkshire puddings than your Asbo ones, and she's Croatian.'

'My name was Henry Pratt, but recently people have started to make remarks, which was getting on my nerves, so I've changed it by deed poll. Yours sincerely, Jamie Oliver.'

He soon got dispirited, and tried to cheer himself up by making lunch. Then he played Kate at Scrabble, while Jack played patience impatiently. Then Jack played Henry at backgammon, and Kate struck no gold. Then Henry cooked supper. Dusk fell, as it does. They all wondered if there was a glorious sunset.

Jack and Kate stayed up, watching, waiting, in the dark, silently. Henry went to bed, but couldn't sleep. At three in the morning Jack woke Henry, who had fallen into a deep sleep three minutes before Jack woke him, and he and Jack kept watch while Kate slept.

Nothing happened. The troops began to feel, more and more, that this was all a great waste of time, a folly. If their commander shared their thought, he did not show them.

Kate struck no gold, Jack grew terminally bored, Henry cooked. Scrabble was played, backgammon was played, Henry made more notes for his European tour.

The phone rang four times and wasn't answered. Could these calls be the perpetrator of the outrages against Henry, checking up? Henry hoped so.

Claustrophobia began to set in. They longed to answer the phone. They ached to watch television, even *The Fifty Most Amusing Interrupted Orgasms*, which was on that night. They were bursting to listen to the radio. They wanted to rip back the curtains and see if there was still a world out there.

Time passed slowly, agonisingly slowly. Dusk fell, as it does. They all wondered if there was a glorious sunset.

Henry and Kate stayed up, watching, waiting.

Suddenly Henry was awake, horrified that he had fallen asleep on watch. What had woken him? Had he heard a noise? Had there been a car, or had he dreamt it?

He woke Kate very gently, holding his finger to his lips. She nodded, mouthed, 'Sorry. I fell asleep.' He mouthed, 'So did I.' They shared a smile.

There was a noise from the dining room, a scratching, a scraping. Smiles were quickly forgotten.

They tip-toed hurriedly to the dining room and eased the door very slowly, very carefully.

The window was open!

Live chickens began to come in, hurtling through the air, hurled by someone outside the window. They were squawking and flapping and shrieking and shitting.

Kate rushed upstairs and woke Jack.

Henry very carefully, very quietly unlocked the front door. Then he switched the outside light on and rushed out, closely followed by Jack and Kate.

There was a small lorry parked outside the house. Kate clicked her camera. The moon face of the driver was frozen in disbelief and anger, in hostility and horror. He was holding a squawking chicken in each hand.

'Tosser!' said Henry sadly. 'Oh Tosser. I had hoped against hope it was Felicity.'

20 Carry On Up the Crem

The mood in the waiting room at Mortlake Crematorium was sombre. It's difficult to regard a funeral as a celebration of a life when the person being mourned has found so little to celebrate in his own life that he has ended it by his own hand.

Henry felt all sorts of uneasy emotions – sorrow, guilt, shame. He didn't think that anybody, not even Hilary, quite understood why he felt such shame over Nigel's suicide.

It was a great source of comfort to him to have his family around him. Hilary clutched his hand and squeezed it. He wanted to squeeze her hand in response, but he couldn't. He didn't know why he couldn't. He didn't like himself for not squeezing her hand, but then he didn't like himself at all that morning.

Kate came up and kissed him. She had made a great effort to look smart; he had never seen her looking so smart. She was wearing a dark grey suit quite unlike her usual clothes, and she looked beautiful and ethereal.

Jack looked so awkward in an ill-fitting cheap black suit that had never been worn before. Flick was also in black. She was larger than ever now, but the sheer simplicity of her good nature, and her lack of concern for her own appearance, gave her a reassuring attractiveness.

Camilla and Guiseppe had tried to dress down for the

occasion, but looked what they were, a couple of very successful and stylish artists.

Henry kissed Camilla and held her tightly for almost a minute. They spoke no words. There were none to speak. Then Hilary hugged Camilla. All three of them had wet eyes, but they fought against tears. If tears began, where would they end?

Outside, a squirrel, grey as the morning, hopped across the lawns. The air was eerily still. There was just a hint that the sun might break through the murk. Henry hoped it wouldn't. It would be quite wrong if the sun came out that day.

Camilla, of course, was there to mourn for her father. Henry knew that Jack and Kate had only come to support him, they had never really known Toss— Nigel all that well. He was grateful to them for coming, and would have said so, had he trusted himself to speak.

But why was Bradley Tompkins there, immaculate in black? And why did he go up to Henry, avoiding eye contact, and stroke his arm, very gently, before turning away to gaze at the leaden sky over South West London? Perhaps the gesture was in gratitude for the fulsome, even grovelling apology that Henry had felt obliged to make to the assembled hacks at a hurriedly convened press conference.

It was Fergus Horncastle of the *Daily Smear* who had linked the comparatively small story of the suicide of a man who had played one undistinguished game of rugger for England, and had been an obscure Conservative MP for four years, with the much larger story of the craven, even grovelling apology of the People's Chef for his wild allegations against Bradley Tompkins, an apology which seemed in danger of driving the last nail into the coffin of Henry's reputation. Henry never uttered a word on the subject. He had said too much too often, and now, when it was too late, he said too little.

Felicity looked pale and white. Henry had never liked her or understood her and she had never liked or understood him, but they were partners now in guilt, united, in the press's eyes, and therefore in most of the nation's, for their part in causing the tragedy of the fallen sporting hero of Dalton College. The press had dug up, to everyone's astonishment, evidence that Felicity had been having an affair with a Brazilian heart surgeon.

Henry went up to her and kissed her and looked into her eyes and saw nothing, nothing at all, as if she had stayed at home and sent her body to represent her.

He knew what strength a woman's fury could give her, but as he looked at Felicity, he found it hard to believe that he had ever managed to persuade himself that she might have had enough power and enough passion to be the person behind the varied attacks on Henry and his property.

The arrival of Diana, Nigel's first wife and Henry's second, made Henry think about all sorts of things; a great swirl of happy and wretched moments passed by him, and as he gave her a demure social kiss he thought how old she must be, even though she didn't look it, and how old by inference he must be. Then he thought how sturdy and prosperous and Swiss she looked, and he realised that he didn't know what she was thinking, how difficult it was to know what people were thinking. He shook hands with

Gunter, her third husband, and thought, 'She has had three husbands, but what a respectable woman she is.'

The moment Celia Hargreaves entered that sad little room, the atmosphere changed. It was as if the sun had come out. She had presence. She had an indestructible elegance to which her daughter could never aspire. Her skin was crossed by a thousand lines now; she had a limp; she walked with a stick; but all eyes were upon her. It seemed as if perhaps all was not hopelessness and gloom, that life would one day be worth living again.

The eeriness of the morning made Lampo look frail. It had never been possible to imagine him as a small boy, and it had always been difficult to think of him becoming an old man, but that day . . . no, he wasn't quite an old man yet, but Henry could see in him the old man that he would become.

There were other people in the room whom Henry didn't know, but none of them were actually close friends of Toss— Nigel's. There were colleagues from the world of pensions and finance. There was a representative of Dalton College. There was an official mourner from the Conservative Party. There were two representatives of Harlequins Rugby Club.

Among those not present were Nigel's son Benedict, long dead but not forgotten; Martin Hammond, who had shared a bitter electoral battle with Henry and Nigel in Thurmarsh; and Nigel's cleaning lady, Viv, who had found him hanging from a beam at the top of his stairs, and had been a quivering wreck ever since.

It was a great relief to everybody when it was time to move through into the chapel. It wasn't large and it was far from full. Everyone in there must have shared in the feeling that Henry had – an embarrassment at the paltry attendance, to mourn a man who had been a rugby international and a Member of Parliament.

Sometimes one can drive without being conscious of where one is going. One is lost in one's thoughts and frightened to discover that one has negotiated seven miles of road, three roundabouts and two sets of traffic lights perfectly safely without being conscious of doing so. It was the same with the hymns and prayers that morning. Henry wasn't conscious of standing and sitting, of closing his eyes and opening them, of singing the words, almost in tune with everybody else. He was back at The Old Manor House, remembering the moment when he had come face to face with Nigel Pilkington-Brick, his moon face distorted, and a live chicken in each hand. Nigel had dropped the chickens to the ground, where they had picked themselves up and run away. They hadn't been bad judges. It had been a painful scene. Only later had Henry thought about the devastation they would have found on their return from Spain, if they had really been away, piles of dead chickens, blood and shit and feathers everywhere, flies in their hundreds and a disgusting stench.

'Why did you do it?' Henry had asked, before the two chickens had even reached safety.

'Why? Why? You ask why?' Nigel had replied. 'Because I hate you, of course. You've destroyed my life. Oh yes you have. You were my fag. Little Henry. My fucking fag, for God's sake. I was head of bloody house. You were a little oik, for God's sake. You were a Northern hick, and I came from one of the best families in England. To find that counts for nothing. You've had a colourful career. I've sold pensions. I don't have any talent outside sport. I sold sodding pensions for forty years. And you refused to buy one. Laughed at me. Called me Tosser. Tosser this, Tosser that. You smug bastard! Oh yes, boring bloody Tosser and his fucking pensions. Every time you called me Tosser I hated you more. Every time you refused to buy a pension I hated you more. You coveted everything I had. You married my first wife. You made my son love you. You knew I didn't want to become Member of Parliament for that sodding bloody dump Thurmarsh. I was being groomed for higher things. You made sure I won. You made sure there were no higher things. You ruined my political career. You bastard! You didn't do much for my second marriage either, did you? You never liked Felicity. You never helped her. Not a bloody finger did you lift to help us. You made us feel guilty over Ben . . . oh how you rubbed that in . . . and then . . . and then . . . you offered me a job! Me, Head of House, working for my fag. Oh yes, that rubbed it in, didn't it? And haven't you been wonderful? Oh, aren't you wonderful? The people's sodding chef. Fucking hell. Oh and the lovely Hilary, aren't you lucky? Aren't you just so smug? And now you've stolen my daughter. She regards you as her father now. You've had everything off me – my family, my life, and you ask me, "Why have you done this?"!'

Henry would never forget a single word of that diatribe. He could remember exactly how far Nigel was through it when Mrs Scatchard arrived upon the scene in his/her nightdress, so lacking in make-up that Henry had felt that somebody must recognise him as Bradley, though in all the drama nobody did.

At the end of the speech, Nigel had begun to cry. That had been the worst thing of all, to see those great shoulders shaking, and to hear those last tearful broken words – 'You won't tell Lampo, will you?'

Dear God!

Henry forced himself away from that awful night, back to the chapel, and found, to his astonishment, that the service had just come to an end.

A small wake had been arranged by Camilla, in an upstairs room in a pub by the river. They all stood outside the chapel, discussing how to get there, and the sun burst through the mist in all its tactless glory.

Everyone except Felicity went to the wake. She told Henry that she didn't feel up to it, and he had again the strong feeling that she was elsewhere, her body was empty and it had to hurry back to be filled.

The room was too large, really, for the number of people, but it didn't seem to matter. The mourning was over. Tongues were loosened. Everyone was hungry and thirsty.

Celia Hargreaves was helped into a seat, and given a plate of canapés and a glass of wine. She signalled to Henry to sit beside her.

'Dear Henry,' she said. 'What a success you've turned out to be.'

'Success! I don't know about that,' said Henry with a sigh.

'Oh, but you have. I've enjoyed it all so much.'

'Thank you.'

That did make Henry feel better, although he felt ashamed of feeling better.

'Why have you not told the truth about why you sacked Nigel? Why have you allowed the press to vilify you?'

Some of the press had portrayed Henry's decision to sack his old Head of House as the last straw for the fallen hero. Henry had refused to give the real reasons, despite all the speculation. He had taken refuge in phrases such as, 'He just wasn't up to the job any more.'

'Because I'm ashamed,' said Henry. 'Ashamed of my part in his downfall. Ashamed for him, for what he said and did that night. It's to die with him, not to be broadcast.'

'I understand,' said Celia Hargreaves, and Henry felt that perhaps she was the only other person apart from Hilary who did. 'You're a good man, Henry.'

Henry smiled.

'Yes,' he said, 'do you know I think I probably am. I think what I am is a good man, but not good enough.'

Mrs Hargreaves smiled and nodded.

'Poor Henry,' she said. 'That's not a recipe for peace of mind.'

'You knew it was him doing it, didn't you?' said Camilla. 'That's why you didn't want me to be part of the trap.'

'Apart from the fact that you were in Venice. No, I wasn't sure it was him. I thought . . . I even hoped . . . that it might possibly be Felicity.'

'Felicity!!'

'She presents herself as so feeble, but is she really? And

hatred gives enormous strength, Camilla. Enormous. I know, it sounds ridiculous now, but, yes, I hoped it might be her. After all, there are depths to her that we have no knowledge of. We have seen nothing that would entrance a Brazilian heart specialist.'

'How did you come to suspect either of them?'

'Well, I realised with a shock . . . a dreadful shock . . . that it wasn't Bradley. So I started to wonder who else might hate me that much. I began to see that Nigel could. I began to see how it all might be, from his point of view. I began to see the essence of what he said that night, which thankfully you didn't hear.'

'Kate's told me roughly. It was horrible. Simply not true.'

'Oh yes it was. Distorted, very distorted, but a distortion of the truth. In books it's always the least likely person who does things. In life it's usually the most likely. And I remembered being told that there were farmers in Felicity's family. The alliteration stayed with me. I remembered also that Nigel had talked of going to a big family do, which was why he couldn't come to the country one weekend. I didn't know whether it was genuine or just an excuse, but then I learnt that the people at the farm that had the false Happy Fields name board had recently celebrated their silver wedding. I asked them for the list of guests. Nigel and Felicity were on it. They were also known by the ghastly owners of the real Happy Fields in Kent. The wife is Felicity's sister. So different. So I was pretty sure that it must be one of them. Oh I am thankful, Camilla, that you weren't there to see your dad that night.'

'Well, of course it would have been awful, but . . . don't

forget, I haven't regarded him as my dad for a long while. You're my dad now, Henry.'

Henry kissed her warmly on both cheeks.

'You see,' he said. 'Nigel was speaking the truth.'

Henry exchanged a few polite words with Nigel's rugby colleagues, with the man from Conservative Central Office, and with the deputy headmaster of Dalton College, but quite soon they all took their leave, with relief, and to everyone else's relief. Now at last they could stop talking about Nigel. They could talk, less emotionally, about themselves, about each other, about the future. After all, that is how funerals work.

With Jack and Flick, Henry talked about simple things, about Thurmarsh United and Thai red curry, about holidays in Majorca and their children's exam results, about cars and conservatories. Jack and Flick had no hang-ups. Conversation with them was peaceful.

There was something about Kate. Something about the way she was holding herself. Something slightly artificial about her face. Suddenly Henry realised what it was. She was trying not to look inappropriately happy.

He walked over to her, smiling.

'You've found him, haven't you?' he said.

Her astonishment was comical.

' "Him"?'

'The man who's good enough for you.'

She winced.

'You must have sixth sense, Dad.'

'No, just experience. It . . . er . . . it *is* a man, is it?'

She laughed.

'Oh yes. Oh . . . did you fear I was lesbian?'

'No. Well not fear it, no, but I did wonder. I mean, you never know. On the way to the farm you said that you hadn't found the right person, and I did wonder about the use of "person" instead of "man". I hope it goes without saying that I wouldn't have been upset.'

'No, I don't think you would. Yes, I . . . I think I . . . well, actually I pretty well know I have, Dad.'

'So, what is he? An actor?'

'No!' She laughed at the intensity of her reaction. 'No, he's . . . don't laugh at me . . . he's a businessman. And he's . . . this is so embarrassing . . . he's really very well off indeed.'

'Well, nobody's perfect.'

'It's about time we watched *Some Like It Hot* together again.'

Celia Hargreaves made her apologies. 'I'm sorry,' she said, 'but I don't have the stamina for a lot of people any more.'

'Of course,' said Henry. 'I understand.'

'Hilary's invited me to dinner next Tuesday.'

'Fantastic.'

It was his turn to wince.

'Oh dear. Why did you wince? Is the prospect that unattractive?'

'No. No. Good heavens, no. No, I winced because I said, "Fantastic". I've always thought of you as being rather fastidious over language.'

'Oh dear. That doesn't sound much fun. Maybe I am,

though. Anyway, I think "fantastic" is the *mot juste.* I'm in my nineties and in good health, we all enjoy good food, no terrorist has blown any of us up, here we are. I think that *is* fantastic.'

'Good. Well . . . yes. Yes, it is, isn't it?'

'You and Hilary *are* happy, aren't you?'

'Of course we are.'

Lampo's sadness drew Henry towards him.

'I made a big mistake, Henry,' he said. 'I went down to stay in that pub.'

'The young waiter with the earrings?'

'You noticed.'

'I noticed.'

'You notice more than one thinks you notice.'

'Oh, you've noticed that.'

'I . . . er . . . I tried . . .' Lampo shook his head at the memory. 'I forgot how old I am, Henry.'

They went out on to a narrow terrace that overlooked the Thames. A rowing eight was proceeding upstream against the ebbing tide, the cox urging them through their paces. The last of the mist was burning off. They watched the young oarsmen in silence, thinking about those whose lives were largely still in front of them, and wondering whether to envy or pity them.

'Henry? Could I . . . have a word next week?' said Lampo as if from afar, breaking through Henry's thoughts.

'Of course, but . . . why?'

'I think I'm too old to run the Kensington Café.'

'You made a mistake over that young man,' said Henry.

'Well it's not the first mistake we've made over sex, you and I. You know the story of the little boy in the bath, and he looks down at his genitalia, and he says, "Mum, are those my brains?" and she says, "No, not yet." It's time we stopped being ruled by our pricks, Lampo. Don't let sex colour your whole life. You only seem old because you try to be young. Just allow yourself to be your age, and you won't seem old at all. Come and see me by all means, but . . . I warn you, I won't accept your resignation. I need you.'

The cox's exhortations were fading into the distance. Six swans were sailing majestically down the river.

Lampo turned and kissed Henry full on the mouth.

'If only you'd allowed me to do that in Siena,' he said.

' "If Only"!' said Henry. 'Mr If Only missed the tram.'

Henry barely noticed Lampo's departure. He stood watching London's river and thinking so many thoughts all at once that he wouldn't have been able to tell you any of them if you'd asked. He became aware of somebody at his side. He knew, without looking, that it was Bradley Tompkins.

'Difficult day?'

'Yes. Thank you for coming.'

'Well . . . couldn't not. I heard . . . I heard some of what your dead friend said that night. I remembered what an old man once said to me: "Hatred's a bum steer, Bradley." I've always had hatred in me. Never known how to deal with it. I mean, I know that hatred destroys the person who hates more than it damages the person who's hated, but that doesn't help in practice. Mrs Scatchard doesn't hate. That's what I like about her. She's my refuge from hatred. Actually, you know, I haven't really hated you since I realised you were going to keep my secret. I was so grateful. But that night, outside your house, that was a big, big shock to me, Henry. I really felt for you.'

'Really?'

'Really. And I thought, "Not hating him isn't sufficient. I have to do more." I remembered watching one of those Michael Palin and Terry Jones things. On the box. What were they called? *Topping Tales* – that's it. And a marvellous old actor – Richard Vernon – I looked up the name – he said, I mean, I can almost remember the words, he said, "Why can't people be nice? The Butcher of Magdeburg, for instance. Why did he have to go around butchering all those people? Supposing he'd been nice to people. He would have gone down in history not as the Butcher of Magdeburg but as the Nice Man of Magdeburg." I thought that was very wise.'

'And very funny.'

'Funny? No, I didn't . . . but then I have no sense of humour, as you know . . . but I thought, why don't I try to be friendly? Why don't I try to really like Henry?'

'Well . . . that's tremendous, Bradley.'

'So I have tried.'

'Ah.'

'I've tried really hard.'

'Ah.'

'It wasn't easy.'

'No, I suppose it wouldn't be.'

'But I persisted.'

'Good.'

'And I actually found . . . I can't put it into words, I'm not very good with words . . . but I think you're . . . this is going to sound very pathetic and very English . . . I think you're really quite nice . . . on the whole.'

'Thank you, Bradley.'

They drove most of the way home in silence. They were tired. It had been a very emotional event.

'I've invited Mrs Hargreaves to dinner next Tuesday,' said Hilary at last.

'I know. She told me.'

'She squeezed my arm, and said, "You and Henry are happy, aren't you?".'

'She said the same to me.'

'We are, aren't we? Happy.'

'Of course we are.'

21 At Last

On Tuesday, 12 August, 2003, Andrew Gilligan, the BBC reporter who claimed that Downing Street had 'sexed up' a dossier on Iraqi weapons of mass destruction, admitted to Lord Hutton's inquiry that some of his reporting had not been perfect; Lady Diana Mosley died at the age of ninety-three; it was announced that by taking a single pill travellers could avoid Montezuma and his revenge; it was also announced that within three years every person in Britain would be able to see a dentist on the National Health Service; and the window cleaner called at the Pratt home off Clapham Common.

The window cleaner was six foot three and had the unfortunate name of Sid Short. He was heartily sick of the feeble jokes people made about his name, jokes at which he was forced to smile, because 'a businessman can't afford to upset the punters, right?'

He liked Henry and Hilary because they paid with a smile, they treated him as a human being, and – above all – they never made jokes about his name.

He looked in on them as he did the kitchen windows that morning, and what he saw was two busy people utterly absorbed in opening and reading their mail. He stopped cleaning for a moment – he was glad of an excuse – and stood and watched. He wished that he got mail like that. He hardly ever got letters, only bills. He wished that he could write books. He wished that he was a television personality. He wished, suddenly, with all his heart, that he never needed to clean another sodding window. Sid hated Arsenal, Marmite, snobs and the French, but most of all he hated windows. Awkward.

It struck Sid, as he watched, that Henry and Hilary were cocooned in their individual worlds. Those weren't the exact words he would use to Tess that evening. He would say, 'They wasn't taking no sodding notice of each other, know what I mean? I hope they aren't drifting apart.' To which Tess would reply, 'Sid Short! Haven't you got enough worries of your own without worrying about them?' To which he would respond, 'Got to think of something to take my mind off sodding windows, haven't I?'

As soon as she'd finished her breakfast, Hilary stood up and said, 'I'm going to have a bath and get ready.'

'What time's he picking you up?'

'About eleven.'

Henry was no longer jealous of Nigel Clinton, who was now as bald as a politician's ambition. He had been Hilary's editor for all her working life, and he was now her publisher as well. He was retiring within a fortnight, and this would be his very last trip with Hilary. He was driving her to Cheltenham, where she was to give a talk on 'The Seriousness of Comedy'. They would be staying the night in a hotel. Henry had once been dreadfully, disastrously, wrongly suspicious of Hilary and Nigel. He wouldn't make that mistake again. It worried him not one jot that they would be staying in a hotel overnight.

He couldn't go with her to Cheltenham. He was making his thirty-seventh appearance on *A Question of Salt*, now in its tenth year. He had ridden out the storm. His career was picking up again, though whether it would ever reach the old heights again was doubtful.

The clash no longer worried either of them. They were old hands in their respective fields. They were confident. They didn't need support.

In truth, both of them had come to prefer to do these events on their own. Henry liked to show off a bit, make people laugh, tell stories which Hilary knew only too well. He could do without her eyebrows being raised in despair at the commencement of some tale. He could do without her dry, wry resignation at the onset of one of his sillier moments, even though it was a resignation tinged with affection.

Both Henry and Hilary had difficulties when he attended her book events. He was by now so much better known than her. He tried to shun the limelight, but it wasn't in him. One couldn't go so far as to say that Hilary was jealous of him, but it wasn't easy not to feel humiliated at times by the fact that *The Pratt Diet* had sold twenty times more than *Carving Snow*.

Nevertheless, Henry didn't go off to the Café until Nigel had picked Hilary up. He carried her overnight bag to the car. He kissed her affectionately and said, 'Good luck, darling.' It was a pity Sid Short wasn't there to see it.

After a busy lunchtime at the Café, Henry went home, had a bath, changed, picked up the shirt and jacket carefully selected by Hilary, and set off by taxi to the BBC Television Centre.

*

He couldn't really believe it. He'd hoped it would be so, of course; he'd feared it would be so, of course; but when he saw her, his heart almost stopped. She was the best part of ten years older than when they had first met, her face was a little more lined, but he could feel the blood rushing to his prick, and his heart was thudding, and just for a moment he thought that he would pass out.

He hardly noticed Bradley Tompkins at first, but then he realised that the man was smiling at him, and the smile looked genuine – he was a rotten actor anyway, so it must be genuine.

After the brief run-through he went to his dressing room and had a shower, washing himself very thoroughly, cleaning his teeth very thoroughly, using his dental floss very thoroughly. Then he dressed very carefully, and brushed his hair very carefully, even though he would be having it done again in Make-up.

All the other chefs were already in the Green Room when he entered. Unusually, Sally was wearing a skirt, and it was quite short. He just couldn't believe how lovely her legs were. He joined the group, kissed Denise Healey, even though he had kissed her earlier, kissed Sally, even though he had kissed her earlier, gave her a meaningful look, although he would have been hard pressed to say what the look meant, received a meaningful look from her, although he would have been hard pressed to say what *her* look meant, shook hands with Simon Hampsthwaite, even though he had shaken hands with him earlier, and shook hands even more warmly with Bradley Tompkins, even though he had shaken hands with him even more warmly earlier. Whatever happened, he didn't want to go back to enmity with Bradley again. Life was too short.

'May I have a word, Henry?' Bradley asked.

'Absolutely.'

Sally raised an eyebrow as Henry trotted off to a corner quite happily with his red wine and Bradley.

'They've brought that stupid fictional chef round back,' said Bradley.

'I know.'

'I can't think of anything. I'm absolutely panicking. I just wondered if . . . it's asking a lot, I know . . . if you had any . . . I don't know . . . just thoughts . . . anything.'

Henry realised that it no longer mattered to him whether he got audience laughter that night or not. He was beyond all that.

'You can have the one I was going to do,' he said.

'Oh, I couldn't do that.'

'Yes, you can. I want you to.'

'Well, thank you.'

'If you think it's funny, of course.'

'I won't know if it's funny.'

'Well, it isn't another Anonymous Borsch. It's much more acceptable to the punters. It's a chef who specialises in cooking with herbs. Antony Sorrel Thompson. I was going to say that he'd had a long-term relationship with another herb specialist, a very very nice man known to everyone as Sweet Basil.'

'Is that funny?'

'I don't know. I don't think one ever really knows. Humour is always a leap in the dark, Bradley.'

'Oh God. Why do we do it?'

When they went back to join the others, Henry found himself standing next to Sally. He felt a touch on his arm. Could she really feel for him as he did for her? Was it possible?

'Is the lovely Hilary not with you?'

It could be a perfectly innocent enquiry.

'No. Not tonight. She's giving a talk in Cheltenham.'

'You must be very proud of her.'

'Yes, I . . . I must. I mean I am. Are you driving back afterwards?'

'No, no. They've booked me into a hotel.'

'Ah.'

'Well, I don't like night driving.'

'No. Nor do I. Horrible.'

'Absolutely.'

Were they having a meaningful conversation or were they just making social noises? Henry didn't know.

'How long is it since we first met on this?'

'Eight years?'

'Must be – at least.'

'Long time.' Henry wished he hadn't said that. It didn't add much to the sum of their knowledge.

'Yes. We're a bit older.'

Not one of your most intelligent comments either, Sally.

'You don't look it, Sally.'

'Nonsense. You don't. I do.'

'I see it the other way round.'

'I had a Michelin star then.'

'Yes, I'm sorry about that.'

'I'm not. It was a burden. People expected too much.'

'Well, good luck. See you later.'

See you later! Everyone said that. It could be as meaningless as 'There you go.' On the other hand it might not be. He wondered how much of her he would see later. He wondered how much of her he wanted to see later.

Hilary would be just about ready to start. How could you talk about 'The Seriousness of Comedy'? Dear God!

They trooped down to the studio. The warm-up man introduced them. He called Henry 'a controversial figure'.

The applause for Henry was not as warm as it had been in his heyday. He had been involved in too many controversies. Mud sticks.

He wondered if he ought to be feeling nervous. Maybe top executives would be watching him very carefully, to see just how popular he still was, before making a decision on whether to go ahead with a prospective television version of his prospective book about a chef's tour of Europe.

Sally naked beneath him in a bed in Dubrovnik.

Sally naked above him in a bed near Lake Bled.

Sally beside herself beside him in a bed beside Lake Como.

Don't even think about it.

The programme began. Henry didn't feel remotely nervous. That was bad. You had to be nervous in order to perform.

'Good evening and welcome to another edition of *A Question of Sport*. Oh shit!' said Dennis Danvers.

The audience roared. The panellists had to mime being helpless with laughter. Oh God. This was the thirty-seventh time Henry had heard it, and still he had to laugh.

When it came to the round of the fictional chefs, Dennis Danvers said, sarcastically, 'Bradley Tompkins, what is your inspired piece of invention tonight?'

Henry could hardly bear to listen. He didn't mind if he got laughs or not, but if Bradley died a death . . .

He didn't. There was a laugh at Antony Sorrel Thompson. Bradley suddenly gained in confidence. Sweet Basil went down surprisingly well. They cut to Henry for a reaction shot in close-up, as he had known they would. He hoped that his laughter looked unforced. Bradley was off now on a tour of herbs. He mentioned a war-time film called 'Dill Met By Moonlight', and the great herb classic 'Tarragone with the Wind' and the well-known musical 'Rose-Mary Poppins'. Oh do stop, Bradley. Don't overdo it. Have sense.

He did stop.

'That was really very good, Bradley,' admitted Dennis Danvers. 'Henry, we all know what good friends you and Bradley are. Can you top that?'

'We are good friends, yes,' said Henry. 'We weren't once, but now we are. Now my fictional chef . . .'

His mind went blank. He suddenly realised with a shock that he hadn't seen Nicky and he hadn't even expected to see her and he hadn't even given her a thought and he couldn't care less about her. 'Er . . . what did you ask me?'

There was a ripple of uneasy laughter. The audience didn't know whether he was fooling or whether he really had lost the plot.

'Your fictional chef, Henry. Do try not to go to sleep.' Dennis Danvers felt that it was safe now to venture a little light mockery. The People's Chef was no longer untouchable.

Henry dredged up a thought that he had abandoned on the grounds that the studio audience wouldn't know what he was talking about. Well, it would do. It would have to.

'It's not generally known that Rick Stein's mother Gertrude was a literary figure in the Paris of Hemingway and Scott Fitzgerald,' he said, not caring whether the audience had heard of Gertrude Stein or not. 'She gave him sound advice about fish. "Rick, my boy," she said. "A bream is a bream is a bream. Never forget that." "Brill," he said. "That's brill, mum." "No, bream, you silly boy," she said,' said Henry.

He got a lower mark than Bradley for the very first time, and he was glad.

There was no point in trying to fight his desire for Sally Atkinson. He would give in to it gloriously. Oh God. Supposing she hadn't meant anything by her remarks earlier. Supposing something got in the way yet again. Supposing they were doomed never to consummate their . . . their what?

'Henry!'

Dennis Danvers's voice came from a very long way away.

'Sorry. What?'

Again there was a smattering of laughter. Again it was uneasy.

'I asked you a question.'

'So sorry, Denzil. I was miles away.'

'Dennis. It's Dennis.'

'Absolutely. Of course it is, Denzil. What was the question again?'

'Which country is associated with the dish called "red curry"?'

Red. Ah! Reds under the beds. Sally in the beds. Stop it.

'Russia.'

He didn't know how he got through the rest of the programme. He felt sick inside.

He was amazed that his legs took him all the way to the Green Room, where he had to sit down.

Sally hurried over to him. His prick leapt.

'Are you all right?' she asked anxiously.

'Fabulous.'

She was holding a glass of red wine, and her hand was shaking.

'Are you coming to my hotel with me?'

'If I may.'

'If you may! Oh yes, you may, Henry.'

Oh, the relief. It swept over him and took all the strength from his body. He knew that if he stood up his legs would collapse. Besides, if he stood up his erection would be obvious to everyone in the room.

Bradley Tompkins came over and sat beside him.

'Are you all right?'

'Never better. Fabulous.'

He could see Bradley looking at his crotch. Was his erection obvious even when he was sitting down? He saw Bradley look round towards Sally. A half smile stole across Bradley's face.

'Thank you,' he said.

'What for?'

'Antony Sorrel Thompson.'

'It went quite well, didn't it?'

'For me, very well.'

Henry lowered his voice.

'I wasn't going to say this, Bradley, but we haven't seen Mrs Scatchard recently.'

'I've tried to ditch the old girl.'

'Really?'

'She didn't seem necessary any more.'

'Good. That's good.'

'But I can't ditch her, Henry. She's my twin, for God's sake. I've given her life. I can't take it away again. Besides, there's Jackie.'

'Jackie?'

'From Bicester.'

'Ah. Of course. Your tongue twister from Bicester.'

'Well, I must get home,' said Bradley, to Henry's great relief. He didn't want Bradley to see him leaving with Sally. He wasn't utterly sure, yet, if he could trust Bradley completely.

'Well,' he said, as Bradley stood up. 'See you in the Coach and Horses some time.'

'Terrific.'

In the taxi he put his hand up her skirt, and inside her knickers. She contented herself with kissing his ear.

Her hotel room was pleasant if impersonal. The bed was large.

They undressed quickly, urgently, silently. He gasped at her beauty, which seemed to him at that moment to be untouched by age.

'Henry!' she said with admiring surprise at the size of his erection. He bent down and kissed her on the knee, then ran his tongue up the inside of her long, soft, elegant, pale, slender legs. He was on fire. He began to shake. She was shaking too.

His shaking grew worse. He gasped.

He kissed the tops of her legs, at the very edge of her pubic hair. Then he stood up, gasping.

His erection slowly subsided as if demolished by Fred Dibnah.

'Sally!' he said. 'I'm awfully sorry. This isn't going to work.'

'You've not lost your bottle!'

'No!' he almost shouted. 'No. I've found it.'

'What?'

'Oh Sally, Sally, I'm so sorry, I should never . . . I must go. I . . . this is . . . Oh dear. Oh Lord. Oh Sally!'

'It's the lovely Hilary, isn't it?' said Sally drily.

'Yes. No. Well, yes, but . . . no. But you understand, don't you?'

'Oh God! Yes. Yes. Damn it, sod it, fuck it, I understand.'

She tried to smile. He began to get dressed. She sat on the bed. She looked wonderful.

'I would have gone back to her anyway, afterwards, so it's better this way. Isn't it?'

'From my perspective, darling, that is a very moot point.'

It wrung his insides when she said, 'Darling'.

'I'm not being noble or anything,' he said. 'If I was, I wouldn't have started. I'm being selfish. I know that what

I gained from this would be so much less than what I lost. An hour of pleasure . . .'

'As long as that?'

'. . . a lifetime of regret. Oh, Sally, if I wasn't married, if I'd never met Hilary . . .'

'Please! Go!'

'No, but . . . yes. Yes.'

'No! Don't kiss me. Go. Not another bloody word. Please.'

'Right. Yes. Not another word. Sorry.'

'Especially that bloody word.'

He didn't think it could be so far from a bed to a door. It felt like a scene in a dream, when you run and run and get no nearer your destination.

'Henry?'

'What?'

'Your shirt's caught in your zip. It's the right way to remember you, but . . . I thought I ought to tell you.'

'Thank you. Thank you, Sally.'

'One more?' asked Nigel Clinton, in the bleak, over-lit bar of their hotel.

'I shouldn't,' said Hilary.

'Just one more. You deserve it. You were brilliant tonight.'

'Was I? I thought it was a bit heavy.'

'They wanted heavy. They loved it.'

'It wasn't full.'

'It was almost full.'

'It would have been full for Henry.'

'I hoped we could forget Henry tonight, Hilary.'

Their eyes met briefly.

The Hungarian waitress approached their table, smiling. She had been eating out of their hands since they'd praised Lake Balaton.

'Same again, please,' said Nigel Clinton.

He went into the house, checked his answerphone, checked his emails. Nothing from Hilary. Why should there be? He felt a quite astonishing stab of disappointment, though.

He loved her. How he loved her. Why had he not told her recently how much he loved her?

He'd make up for it tonight.

He locked up, and settled himself into the Lamborghini. It wouldn't take long to get to Cheltenham. There wouldn't be much on the roads tonight.

'I've loved you since the first time we met. I've loved your body, your lips, your eyes, your talent, every spare elegant word you've ever written has excited me.'

'Thank you, Nigel.'

He put his hand on her knee.

'I would say, quite sincerely, that I am a happily married man,' he said, 'yet there hasn't been one day, not one single day, when I haven't thought of you.'

'I don't like hearing that,' she said. 'I don't like it one little bit.'

'I know you don't love me.'

'I wouldn't go as far as that, Nigel.'

'What?'

'I never thought of anybody but Henry. It just didn't

occur to me that I could fancy any other man. I knew you were dashing and good-looking. It didn't mean a thing.'

'And now I'm bald and I don't dash. What chance have I got?'

He smiled.

'A pretty good chance, actually, Nigel.'

His smile froze. He was astonished.

'I beg your pardon?'

'Dear dear Nigel. Sadly, I don't think it would matter much to Henry any more. He need never know, but, do you know, even if he ever did know, I don't think his pain would be remotely as great as your joy. Not now, sadly. Love you? Oh yes. It's a love born out of a lifetime working together. It may not be a love that's enough for a lifetime, Nigel, but it's enough for one night if you really want it.'

She stroked his leg very gently.

The Croatian waitress approached them, smiling. She had been eating out of their hands since they'd praised Dubrovnik.

'Same again?'

'No, thank you,' said Nigel. 'I rather think we may be going to bed.'

He was driving too fast. Over ninety. He'd had a few glasses, but he wouldn't be over the limit, not with the amount of time that had elapsed. Besides, he drove better when he'd had a few drinks.

He roared down the dip at High Wycombe, soared up the other side, overtaking everything. There wasn't a great deal on the road. It was well past midnight.

Exultation drove him on. He had been mad to even think of going to bed with Sally. Hilary was wonderful. To lose her again would be dreadfully careless. He shouted it in his Noël Coward voice. 'To lose her again would be dreadfully careless.' He wound down the window and shouted it to the dark beech woods. 'To lose her again would be dreadfully careless,' he shouted, loud enough to shock owls and awaken red kites. He laughed. How mad he had been. How much he loved her.

He wouldn't do the European chef's tour, even if they begged him.

'I am sorry to say that during the interminable delay while you made up your little minds I have decided not to do it.'

He wound the window down again.

'That'll teach them,' he shouted.

The white van was in the middle of the road, and swerving from side to side.

He unbuttoned her trousers and pulled them off gently, then rolled her tights down. He kissed her thigh and gasped. His pleasure hurt.

She ran her hand over his genitals.

'I'm afraid there's not much there at the moment,' he said. 'I'm so terribly nervous, Hilary.'

'Oh don't be, Nigel. It isn't an exam,' she said, 'and there's plenty of time. I'm not going anywhere.'

He braked hard, almost lost control, tried to overtake on the inside of the van. There wasn't room. He was on the hard shoulder, his off-side wheels were on the grass, the car was spinning, he turned the wheel desperately. He heard the crunch of metal, the scream of tyres, the agonised cry of the driver. He heard the alarms of the ambulance and the police cars. He saw, in his mind, Hilary's stricken face.

At that moment her face was not stricken. It was smiling with gentle love.

'Don't worry,' she said. 'Relax. Enjoy this moment, dear, darling Nigel.'

She kissed his lips, gently, lovingly, reassuringly.

He realised that he was still on the road, driving in the right direction, on his own. He looked in his rear-view mirror. The van was there, unharmed. It wasn't just Hilary's stricken face that had been in his mind. All the noises had been in his imagination in that moment of terror.

He longed to pull over on to the hard shoulder and stop, but he didn't dare. The van driver might be awkward about his speed.

He drove on, towards Oxford, towards Witney, towards Cheltenham, towards Hilary.

They lay side by side, fondling each other gently. He felt her stiffen.

'You've stiffened,' he said. 'I should have stiffened, but you have.'

'You were just beginning to,' she said.

'Yes. Yes, I was.'

'Oh, Nigel. Nigel . . . ?'

'I know what you're going to say. Don't say it. Allow me the dignity of saying it myself.'

'Of saying what?'

'Of saying what you were going to say. "Oh, Nigel. This is all wrong. I shouldn't be here in your bed. I still love him. I always have loved him. I always will love him." '

'Oh, Nigel.'

She stepped out of his bed. They both sighed.

Past Burford, on on on. Hilary, here I come. 'Hilary, darling, I don't give a damn about fame and fortune and fast cars any more. I don't care about being loved by the whole world. I only want to be loved by you. I always did, that's the stupid thing. I always did. We'll sell Clapham and all the Cafés and live at The Manor House and I will retire and you will write and we will make love and have Mrs Scatchard and her bisexual bicycle repairer from Bicester to dinner.'

She couldn't get to sleep. She so wished Henry was there.

'Henry, darling, I think you should take the European job if it comes up. I'll come with you and write in the hotels. I can write anywhere. We'll sell The Manor House and just live happily on Clapham Common and travelling around Europe while you do your book. I never much liked the village anyway, and I certainly don't like the thought of being so near to the eerie Mrs Scatchard. Henry, darling, I'll be a proper wife to you from now on.'

*

In the event, perhaps luckily, neither of them said anything much. They just stood hugging each other, and then they both had something warm and lovely, and it wasn't cocoa.